★ WAVE HIGH THE BANNER ★

Wave High the
BANNER

A Novel Based on the Life of
Davy Crockett

★

Dee Brown

Introduction by
Paul Andrew Hutton

UNIVERSITY OF NEW MEXICO PRESS : ALBUQUERQUE

★ *To C. Mitchell* ★

© 1942, 1970 by Dee Brown.
All rights reserved.
First University of New Mexico Press Edition, 1999,
by arrangement with Sterling Lord Literistic.

Introduction © 1999 by Paul Andrew Hutton.
All rights reserved.

Library of Congress Cataloging-in-Publication Data

Brown, Dee Alexander.
Wave high the banner: a novel based on the life of Davy Crockett /
Dee Brown; introduction by Paul Andrew Hutton.
—1st University of New Mexico Press ed.
p.   ed.
ISBN 0-8263-2012-0 (cloth: alk. paper)
ISBN 0-8263-2013-9 (pbk.: alk. paper)
1. Crockett, Davy, 1786–1836—Fiction.
2. Alamo (San Antonio, Tex.)—Siege, 1836—Fiction.
I. Title.
PS3503.R79533W38   1999
813'.54—dc21
99-19825
CIP

★ CONTENTS ★

Note: the text of the novel retains the page numbering of the original edition beginning with the Preface to Part One.

Wave High the Banner

A novel based on the life of
DAVY CROCKETT by
DEE BROWN

The Original Jacket from the 1942 Macrae-Smith Edition.

★ INTRODUCTION ★

Paul Andrew Hutton

The twentieth century was yet full of promise when Dee Alexander Brown was born on February 28, 1908 in the little sawmill town of Alberta, Louisiana. Buffalo Bill and Mark Twain were still alive, Teddy Roosevelt had just triumphantly departed the White House, and the world still moved at the speed of the horse-drawn carriage and steam locomotive. No one could imagine a world war.

The boy got an early taste of the bitter pain the century would bring to so many when his father, Daniel Alexander Brown, a timberman, was killed in 1912. His mother, Lula Cranford Brown, moved her children to the little town of Stephens, Ouachita County, in southwestern Arkansas. Dee was but five. There he spent his formative years, often in the care of his grandmother, Elizabeth Cranford, while his mother worked as a clerk in a local store.

Among his earliest and most important memories was not an event, but a scent: "the singular perfume of printing ink" coming from the press that published the weekly *Stephens News*. It drew him to dare, finally when old enough, to venture into the printing plant. A gruff but kindly printer took the boy in hand and taught him the wonders of old-style typesetting. Now the ink was in his veins as well as his nostrils, and the boy spent every spare hour at the press, soaking in the wonders of the creation of the printed page. It was eventually the *Stephens News* that had the honor of being the first publisher of a Dee Brown composition—a 1918 letter to Santa Claus.

For several years an oil boom infused the area with a frontier boomtown quality. Many Indians worked on the rigs and several of Dee's best friends were their children. "We would go to the western movies together and it was then that I had my first real revelation about Indians," he recalled in a 1971 *Publishers Weekly* interview. "My buddy said to me, 'you know, those aren't real Indians.' I started reading about Indians as soon as I learned to read."

He purchased his first book during a family outing to Hot Springs, Arkansas. It cost twenty-five cents and was a wild concoction of pioneer adventure and bloody Indian warfare laced with gory illustrations. He read it over and over. "Young folk read a great deal more in that time than now," he later noted, "but what they got from it was probably no more uplifting or true to reality than the movies and TV shows they absorb today. An awful lot of bad writing was published in those days when print was King."

In 1924 Mrs. Brown moved with her children to Little Rock, anxious for them to obtain a superior high school education. Little Rock's public library was a tonic to young Brown, and it was there that he discovered Sherwood Anderson and John Dos Passos who, he later wrote, "struck me with the effect of lightening bolts." The works of Faulkner and Conrad also mesmerized the boy, but it was the library 's three-volume account of the expedition of Captains Lewis and Clark that fully captivated him and cemented further a growing fascination with America's frontier past.

The inspired and aspiring young man set out to be a writer. Fortune smiled, and he sold his first story—a two-thousand-word baseball tale—to *Blue Book* magazine for the then-astonishing sum of $100. He was seventeen. He managed to sell two more stories in the next two years, although the rejection slips piled up as well, sobering him considerably on his new calling.

A writer has to eat, and so upon graduation from high school Brown sought employment as a printer. Hired by the Harrison *Daily Times* in Boone County, Arkansas, the young printer soon found himself not only setting type for personal Christmas cards but also hawking them around town. Eventually he was assigned reporting duties, composing his stories on tornadoes of both the natural and human sort directly on the linotype machine.

Dee's sister, Corinne, had by this time graduated from the Arkansas State Teachers College in Conway, and the ever-resourceful Mrs. Brown had rented a large house where she boarded female students. Dee was now invited to move to Conway and help convert the house into a boarding place for male students. This enabled him to afford college, and he enrolled as a history major. He also worked as a writer and editor for the college newspaper and as a student assistant in the library.

During his first day on campus Brown met the man who would, in many ways, set him on his future course. Barely older than his students, Dean McBrien was a history professor from Nebraska and a dedicated disciple of the importance of the history of the American frontier experience. "Before I met him," Brown recalled, "I was interested in the West, but he converted me into a fanatic like himself."

Two of Brown's summers were spent exploring the West in a Model-T Ford with McBrien and another lucky student. They traversed unpaved roads across landscapes little changed from frontier days, often encountering old timers who remembered well the past years of grand adventure. Little Big Horn, Beecher's Island, Fort Phil Kearny, and, most especially, Wounded Knee all captivated Brown. The rude marker at the latter, so different from the grand memorial at Little Big Horn, deeply moved the young student. "That grave remained like the scar of a wound imprinted forever upon me," he declared.

Brown graduated from Arkansas State Teacher's College in 1931 and moved on to George Washington University's library school in Washington, D.C. The nation was in the grips of both the Great Depression and a government refusing to take action, so Brown found it exceedingly difficult to find the employment essential to pay for his education. The fresh college graduate worked dozens of pathetically low-paying and dead-end jobs while taking a few night classes. Eventually he was forced to drop out of school. The expansion of government positions with the New Deal finally rescued him when a minor position in the library of the Food and Drug Administration opened up. This not only allowed him to afford reentry into the library program at George Washington but gave him the minimal necessary resources to pursue matrimony.

Sally Stroud was another Arkansan working for the New Deal. They had known each other back in Conway, and now renewed their friendship in Washington. The relationship quickly blossomed into a lifetime romance for, as Brown put it, Miss Stroud "loved books, wrote poetry, told funny stories, and had lots of sex appeal." They were married in 1934.

Among their best friends during those exhilarating New Deal days in Washington were several members of the Federal Writers Project: editor Jack Conroy, folklorist B. A. Botkin, and novelists John Cheever and Vardis Fisher. They inspired Brown to renew his writing efforts. One of his short stories caught the attention of a literary agent who encouraged him to try his hand as a novelist. Brown found great material for his novel in the growing New Deal bureaucracy, and by 1941 the manuscript was finished. His agent liked the good-natured satire and sold it to the Philadelphia publishing firm of Macrae-Smith. By late November 1941 the novel was copyedited and ready for the printer. December 7, 1941, of course, changed everything.

Edward Shenton, Brown's editor at Macrae-Smith, called him on December 8. He was coming to Washington and wanted to confer with his author. They met at the old Willard Hotel where Shenton explained that after Pearl Harbor it was impossible to publish Brown's satirical novel on the government for it might be considered unpatriotic during this time of national crisis. Shenton offered to publish anything else Brown might have, but preferably a novel considerably more patriotic in tone.

Brown retreated into the ever-so-patriotic frontier past in search of a topic, settling on the life of Davy Crockett. He had long been interested in Crockett, for grandmother Cranford had regaled him as a child with tales of how her father had hunted bears with Crockett along Tennessee's Duck River. The famed hunter-turned-politician appealed to Brown's populist sentiments, and he had often contemplated writing a biography of the frontiersman. He now determined on a historical novel on Crockett and set to work.

There had been a rebirth of interest in Crockett in the 1930s following the success of Constance Rourke's engaging literary biography, *Davy Crockett*, in 1934. Her book had been written in response to the casual dismissal of native-grown American culture by eastern social critics. Crockett, in particular, had been pilloried by Vernon Louis Parrington in *Main Currents in American Thought* in 1930 as "the biggest frog in a very small puddle, first among the Smart Alecks of the canebrakes." Rourke, along with Richard Dorson, who published his study *Davy Crockett: American Comic Legend* in 1939, were concerned with the tall-tale character of the Crockett Almanacs and its influence on American folklore and literary culture. A little Crockett publishing boomlet followed their books.

Charles Scribner's Sons reissued Crockett's autobiography in 1934 in a lavish edition with wonderful illustrations by the famed U.S. Marine Corps artist, John W. Thomason, Jr. Playwright Edwin Justus Mayer, fresh from his Broadway success with *The Firebrand*, published his play *Sunrise in His Pocket or the Last Days of Davy Crockett* with Julian Messner in 1941. Literary historian Walter Blair devoted considerable space to Crockett in his seminal works, *Horse Sense in American Humor* published by the University of Chicago Press in 1942 and *Tall Tale America: A Legendary History of Our Humorous Heroes* published by Coward-McCann in 1944. Irwin Shapiro's children's book, *Yankee Thunder: The Legendary Life of Davy Crockett*, fabulously illustrated by James Daugherty, followed in 1944, again using Crockett as Mayer had done, as a challenge to Fascism and as a clarion call for American unity. This theme was still relevant to novelist-turned-historian John Myers Myers in 1948 when his *The Alamo* was published by E. P. Dutton to great acclaim as the first modern historical overview of the epic battle where Crockett lost his life.

Brown was to be an integral part of this revitalization of the Crockett legend. He worked feverishly to complete the novel, one wary eye on his publisher and the other on his draft board. He had the manuscript finished in an astonishing ninety days. Sally came up with the suitably patriotic title borrowed from an obscure Shelley poem, *Wave High the Banner*. The breathless dust-jacket copywriters at Macrae-Smith exploited the nationalistic potential of Brown's novel, declaring that in the book "Davy Crockett emerges as a symbol for all men fighting for freedom and against tyranny and oppression, a source of inspiration for us today when we are again engaged in a grim struggle to maintain our liberties and way of life."

Macrae-Smith had the book out within three months, and it went through three small printings before being lost amidst the chaos of war. By the time it was published Private Brown was engaged in basic training with the Eightieth Infantry Division. During maneuvers along the very same Duck River where his great-grandfather had hunted with Davy Crockett, he was injured in a truck accident. Placed on limited service, the neophyte soldier was assigned to an intelligence company commanded by Major James Warner Bellah. Brown spent many hours studying battle maps with Major Bellah, eventually discovering that they shared a mutual interest in the frontier Indian wars. Bellah's fascination with Indian tactics led him to commit his troops to various wild enterprises that usually resulted in their capture during maneuvers. "Some of the men disparaged Major Bellah's way of doing things," Brown recalled, "but I thought he had style."

Bellah most certainly had a style that a writer like Brown could readily appreciate. For after the war the major became a writer of prodigious influence upon American popular culture. Bellah's short stories for the *Saturday Evening Post* were the basis of John Ford's classic trilogy of cavalry films—*Fort Apache, She Wore a Yellow Ribbon,* and *Rio Grande.* He also eventually penned the screenplays for Ford's *Sergeant Rutledge* and *The Man Who Shot Liberty Valance.* Bellah's image of the cavalry, while hard-edged, was as unrelentingly heroic as had been the portrayal of the soldiers by that turn-of-the-century master of the military genre, Charles King, who so obviously influenced him. While Brown eventually followed Bellah's lead with intelligent but conventionally heroic cavalry novels such as *Yellowhorse* (1956), *Cavalry Scout* (1957), *Showdown at Little Big Horn* (1964), *The Girl from Fort Wicked* (1964), and *Action at Beecher's Island* (1967), it was his later historical writings, ironically, that forever overturned Bellah's romantic vision of the cavalry.

Brown was not with the interesting Major Bellah for long. The army soon transferred him to the Alabama Polytechnic University in Auburn, then to the University of Pennsylvania in Philadelphia, and finally to the University of Iowa in Iowa City for never-defined and certainly never-realized "specialized training." Brown was eventually liberated from this endless training by a most fortunate transfer to Army Ground Forces Headquarters in Washington, D.C., as a reference librarian. This turned out to be absorbing and important work, disarmingly critical to the overall war effort.

Among his fellow soldiers in the AGFHQ, was another young librarian by the name of Martin F. Schmitt. They soon discovered that they shared a mutual fascination with the Old West. Schmitt, in particular, was a devoted fan of John Neihardt's epic Western poetry, being able to recite stanzas from *The Song of the Indian Wars* and other poems by heart. They got along famously and in their spare time combed the military archives for photographs from the Indian Wars period. Combining their meagre financial resources they had photographs made from old prints and obscure glass plate negatives. By 1945 they had an impressive photographic collection, mostly of American Indians.

A chance meeting with an editor from Macmillan encouraged them to write a narrative around the photographs. Their pictorial history of the Indian Wars, however, proved too expensive an undertaking for both Macmillan and the University of Oklahoma Press. The fledgling historians persevered and finally interested Charles Scribner's Sons in the project. Brown met briefly with legendary Scribner's editor Maxwell Perkins, whose only comment on the project was that there should be more on the Navajos. "We'll make a fine book," Perkins declared, and Scribner's proceeded to do just that. *The Fighting Indians of the West* appeared in 1948, pioneering the then quite rare but now exceedingly popular pictorial history format. Brown and Schmitt published two more pictorial histories with Scribner's: *Trail Driving Days* in 1952 and *The Settlers' West* in 1955. All three proved quite popular, giving encouragement to pictorial histories on a wide range of topics by other publishers.

By this time Sergeant Brown had left the army to accept a post at the Aberdeen Proving Ground in Maryland. In 1948 he happily left behind the anxieties and insanities of the Cold War atmosphere at Aberdeen to take a position as the librarian for the College of Agriculture at the University of Illinois at Urbana. At Illinois he took graduate courses in library science, receiving his master of library science degree in 1951. He was promoted to professor in 1962, a rank he held until his retirement a decade later.

Although busily engaged in the writing of genre Western fiction as a supplement to his slim librarian's salary, Brown never lost his fascination with history. When he came across the letters of two brothers who had participated in Colonel Benjamin Grierson's bold cavalry raid into Mississippi during Ulysses S. Grant's Vicksburg campaign, he realized that he had a marvelous topic for a new history book. General William T. Sherman had pronounced Grierson's raid "the most brilliant expedition of the Civil War," but few had ever heard of it ninety years later. Ben Grierson was an Illinois music teacher who emerged from the war as a national hero. He went on to command the Tenth Cavalry—the famous "buffalo soldiers"—in the Indian Wars. His papers, housed in the Illinois State Historical Library in Springfield, were readily accessible, incredibly rich, and rarely exploited.

Brown soon had *Grierson's Raid* ready for submission to the University of Illinois Press. To his great surprise a professor in the History Department at the University of Illinois attempted to block its publication, questioning Brown's credentials. Only the vigorous advocacy of press editor Don Jackson, who would eventually make Illinois into one of the great university presses and who was a great promoter of the Western history field, secured the press committee's consent for the book's publication in 1954. The incident was Brown's first exposure to a certain class of narrow-minded and turf-conscious academic historian, but it would not be his last. Brown and Jackson were vindicated by the warm reception the book received, the reviewer for the *American Historical Review* commending *Grierson's Raid* as "a minor classic of its kind." It has stood the test of time as the standard work on the topic.

Illinois novelist Harold Sinclair used Brown's book as the basis for his stirring novel, *The Horse Soldiers*, published by Harper in 1956. Brown graciously penned a brief foreword to the novel, describing it as "a first-rate example of art turned upon recorded history so that evocation of past time is made more meaningful to the reader." Brown mused that history might well be eclipsed by the "essential truth" of Sinclair's fictional creations and that "it is more than likely that their richly developed characters and their remarkable adventures will be better remembered than the names of most battles and leaders of the Civil War." His words were prophetic, for the book was purchased by the producing team of John Lee Mahin and Martin Rackin. They readily admitted to turning to Brown's "definitive work on Grierson's raid" in writing their screenplay, although their film, *The Horse Soldiers*, eventually took even more liberties with history than had Sinclair's novel. Released by United Artists in 1959, the John Ford–directed epic starring John Wayne (as Colonel Marlowe, the Grierson character) was a huge box-office hit, helping to kick off the Civil War Centennial.

Brown returned to the Civil War with *The Bold Cavaliers*, the saga of John Hunt Morgan's Confederate raiders, published by J. P. Lippincott in 1959, and *The Galvanized Yankees*, the story of rebel prisoners who served the Union by fighting Indians in the West, published by the University of Illinois Press in 1963. The latter was described by noted Civil War historian Bell Wiley in a *New York Times* review as not only "an accurate, interesting, and sometimes thrilling account" but also as "a fresh and informative study of the Old West in transition from frontier to stable society."

During these years of prodigious output, Brown also often wrote articles for the popular magazines *Civil War Times Illustrated* and *American History Illustrated*. These engaging essays were compiled by editor Stan Banash into *Best of Dee Brown's West* and *Dee Brown's Civil War Anthology* brought out by Clear Light Publishers in 1998. In his foreword to the latter volume Brown admitted that his Civil War writings dealt almost exclusively with what was called the Western Theater of the war. "The reason for this is that I am a westerner and know the terrain and atmosphere of the action far better than in the Eastern Theater," he wrote. "Perhaps I better understand the participants' attitudes, behavior, and manners of thought and speech. After all, several of the survivors were still around while I was a young boy. . . . I felt as if I knew well the men of both sides."

Even in these Civil War forays his heart remained in the West, and so it was no surprise when he returned there for the subject matter of his most successful book of the 1950s, *The Gentle Tamers: Women of the Old Wild West*. Although hardly recognized as such at the time of its publication by Putnam in 1958, *The Gentle Tamers* was a pathbreaking and innovative volume—the first to take seriously the role played by women on the frontier. The book enjoyed considerable success in the United States and was even more popular in Europe, the West German edition remaining on the bestseller list for several months.

The Gentle Tamers proved to be one of Brown's most durable and respected works. Over twenty years later, in a seminal article entitled "The Gentle Tamers Revisited: New Approaches to the History of Women in the American West" and published in the May 1980 issue of the *Pacific Historical Review*, Joan M.

Jensen and Darlis A. Miller acknowledged Brown's important contribution to opening up the rapidly expanding field of Western women's history: "Dee Brown's *The Gentle Tamers*, one of the first books to attempt an overview and analysis of the roles of women in the West . . . elaborated and codified the assumption that the white male 'tamed' the West in its physical aspects and that white women, who followed the men, gently tamed the social conditions (including, of course, white men). By focusing on women as a group, Brown filled a major gap in western historiography, and because he provided a thesis and a framework, his book remains the most widely read book on women in the West."

Brown returned to the Indian Wars for his next two books. The topic had always been a popular one in Western studies—from the pioneering nineteenth-century works of Francis Parkman, J. P. Dunn, and Theodore Roosevelt, through the engaging mid-twentieth-century books of Fairfax Downey and Paul I. Wellman, to the impressive post-war scholarship of Francis Paul Prucha, William H. Leckie, and Robert M. Utley—and standard fare as well for both novelists and Hollywood filmmakers. All of these books viewed the dispossession of the natives as the inevitable if tragic result of the progress of civilization, echoing the characterization of the frontier army set forth by the late-nineteenth-century soldier-turned-novelist Charles King, who wrote: "It is all a memory now, but what a memory, to cherish! A warfare in which the soldier of the United States had no hope of honors if victorious, no hope of mercy if he fell; slow death by hideous torture if taken alive; sheer abuse from press and pulpit, if, as was often inevitable, Indian squaw or child was killed . . . fighting oftentimes against a foe for whom we felt naught but sympathy, yet knew that the response could be but deathless hate. A more thankless task, a more perilous service, a more exacting test of leadership, morale and discipline no army in Christendom has ever been called upon to undertake than that which for eighty years was the lot of the little fighting force of regulars who cleared the way across the continent for the emigrant and settler."

Brown, despite his obvious sympathy for the natives, did not stray too far from this standard interpretive framework in either *Fort Phil Kearny: An American Saga* for Putman in 1962, pronounced by Robert M. Utley as "a genuine contribution to the history of the Indian Wars" and still regarded as the best work on the Bozeman Trail Indian War, or his *Galvanized Yankees* for Illinois the following year. His next book on Indian-white conflict, however, would prove quite different indeed, changing forever the way western history was to be written, and, more importantly, the way the American people were to view their past.

For years, just as he had collected Indian photographs with Martin Schmitt, Brown had also collected Indian speeches. "At first I had no intention of using them in a book," he later wrote, "but collected them simply for what the words express—the human condition, love of the earth and its beings and the sky, devotion to a supreme power, heartbreaks and admonitions—spoken in rhythmic languages, at times lyrical, at times elegiacal."

He finally decided to make use of these speeches in a book on the late-nineteenth-century Indian Wars for younger readers. Brown's literary agent, Peter Matson, loved the idea but insisted that the book should be for readers of all ages. This change of direction added to Brown's writing timetable, and it took over two years to complete the marvelously titled *Bury My Heart at Wounded Knee*.

Brown took the familiar saga of the Indian Wars and, with skill and insight, reversed the point of view. "Americans who have always looked westward when reading about this period," he wrote in the book's brief introduction, "should read this book facing eastward." Keeping this consistent point of view was his greatest challenge. "I would tell myself every night," Brown told an interviewer for the *Wilson Library Bulletin*, "'I'm a very, very old Indian, and I'm remembering the past. And I'm looking toward the Atlantic Ocean.' And I always kept that viewpoint every night. That's all I did."

It was just the right book at just the right time. Published by Holt, Rinehart and Winston in 1970, *Bury My Heart at Wounded Knee: An Indian History of the American West* was an immediate success. It was helped along considerably by Nebraskan Dick Cavett, who had a rather cerebral late-night talk show on ABC. Even if Cavett could never hope to break the grip on late-night ratings held by Johnny Carson's *Tonight Show* his program still reached millions of viewers nightly. Cavett, captivated by the book, often quoted bits from it on his program and then twice invited Brown to appear with him on the show. Cavett's patronage helped push the book even higher on the bestseller lists, where it remained for over a year and sold a million copies. Translated into seventeen languages, it has since sold some seven million copies.

That Brown's book struck a responsive chord in Americans seeking to redefine themselves and their collective past was clearly enunciated by the reviewer for the *New York Times*, Pulitzer Prize–winning novelist N. Scott Momaday. "Having read Mr. Brown," noted Momaday, "one has a better understanding of what it is that nags at the American conscience at times (to our everlasting credit) and of that morality which informs and fuses events so far apart in time and space as the massacres at Wounded Knee and My Lai." Momaday, the nation's most distinguished writer of Indian heritage, found the book "extraordinary on several accounts," not the least of which was that "Mr. Brown's book is a story, a whole narrative of singular integrity and precise continuity; that is what makes the book so hard to put aside, even when one has come to the end."

Momaday's assessment was echoed by many other review-ers. *Life* reviewer Melvin Maddocks praised Brown's "fresh, invaluable contributions." *Newsweek* reviewer Geoffrey Wolff reflected the new sense of awareness of a tortured past that Brown's book had engendered. "No book," Wolff declared, "has saddened me and shamed me as this book has. Because the experience of reading it has made me realize for once and for all that we really don't know who we are, or where we come from, or what we have done, or why." Cecil Eby, in *Book World*, correctly noted that Brown's book "will undoubtedly chart the course of other 'revisionist' historical books dealing with the Old West." Phyllis Pearson, daughter of the long-time chair-man of the Mandan-Hidatsa-Arikara Three Affiliated Tribes, writing in *Montana the Magazine of Western History*, then as now the nation's finest journal of Western history, praised Brown's book as "the first accurate and comprehensive account of how the western United States was taken from the American In-dian." Here was history "told at last from the Indian's per-spective." She urged all Americans to read Brown's narrative, save "those who want to retain a stereotyped image of the American Indian."

The reaction to *Bury My Heart at Wounded Knee*, however, in the two most respected national academic journals was quite different. Professor Lawrence C. Kelly, writing in the *Journal of American History*, accused Brown of using material from his book manuscript of edited documents on the Navajo War with-out proper attribution. Kelly's charges were repeated in the *American Historical Review* by the distinguished scholar, Francis Paul Prucha, who, particularly disturbed by the book's lack of balance, loftily regretted that "this sort of 'Indian history of the American west' gains such popular acceptance." While Brown had indeed made an error in the documentation of his brief Navajo chapter, it was most certainly an error of omis-sion, not commission. This omission was corrected as soon as possible in the book's fourth printing, with the addition of four citations to Kelly's book, *Navajo Roundup*. This was not enough, however, to satisfy Kelly or the academic community.

Prucha's concern for balance, while well taken from an academic perspective, missed Brown's point. Peter Farb, writing in the *New York Review of Books*, saw no problem with this unique point of view, since "whites have for long had the exclusive use of history and that it is now time to present, with sympathy rather than critically, the red side of the story." Farb felt the book to be "an extremely ambitious and readable attempt to write a different kind of history of white conquest of the West: from the point of view of the victims, using their words whenever possible." Far from being historical heresy, Brown's book was an essential historical corrective to an increasingly shopworn and one-sided national narrative.

Brown was stung by this criticism, feeling that Kelly was "making mountains out of molehills," and it forever soured his relationship with the academic community. Brown never joined, nor has he ever been honored by, the Western History Association. This organization, the leading scholarly association of academic and public historians of the American West, has studiously ignored one of the best-known and most- beloved Western historians of the century. The Western Writers of America, however, an organization of novelists, screenwriters, and popular historians, has honored Brown with their Saddleman Award for lifetime achievement. The writers, along with the people, admire his vision, his skill, and his towering achievement.

There is a particular irony in this academic hostility toward Brown, since it was *Bury My Heart at Wounded Knee*, along with Vine Deloria's witty 1969 bestseller, *Custer Died For Your Sins*, that created a massive public interest in Indian history. This eventually translated into the creation of several Indian Studies programs and an enormous explosion of Indian history courses on campuses around the country. Since 1970 Indian history has remained by far the largest and most productive subfield of Western history. At the 1997 Western History Association Conference in St. Paul, a session was held on *Bury My Heart at Wounded Knee*. It proved to be the best attended session at the conference. During it several of the leading younger scholars in the field of Indian history made clear that Brown's book had first inspired them to teach Indian history. This generation of scholars, who came of age in the turbulent sixties and seventies, remain part of Brown's legacy.

Brown remained puzzled yet philosophical over the attitude of the historical community. "I have known for a long time that most professional historians disdain work by non-professionals," he wrote historian Paul Hutton in 1998. "I have never understood this. Professionals from Departments of English usually prefer books that are written by non-professionals rather than those of colleagues. Professional librarians have always welcomed unemployed historians into the library profession, but it does not work the other way. But who cares. When the organization that you head [WHA] was founded, I was invited to join, but I was aware that I would not be welcomed by most of the academic members. I never joined." The loss, of course, has been to the academics.

The academic reaction to Brown's book was, of course, not really about professional ethics or even jealousy over his success, but rather it was about control over the story of the past. That control of the national story is viewed by academic historians as their exclusive domain, and they never relinquish it easily. Despite their hostility, Brown had nevertheless captured the American heart and psyche, changing forever the way the nation related to its own history. *Bury My Heart at Wounded Knee* is arguably the most influential work of Western history published in the twentieth century. Indeed, probably no work save Frederick Jackson Turner's 1893 essay, "The Significance of the Frontier in American History," has so clearly influenced the way the American people view their Western past.

Bury My Heart at Wounded Knee allowed Brown to retire from the University of Illinois, and he and Sally returned at last to Arkansas. Despite the financial security the book had brought him, he was still driven to write. In 1974 Holt, Rinehart and Winston published his *The Westerners*, a biographical approach to the story of the West from Coronado to Teddy Roosevelt, in a lavish edition. A 1977 history of the Western railroads, *Hear that Lonesome Whistle Blow*, exposed the greed and exploitation of both men and resources that marked the rapid expansion of the rails westward. While neither of these books came anywhere near the success of *Bury My Heart at Wounded Knee*, they helped cement Brown's position as the leading popular interpreter of the history of the West. In his introduction to *The Westerners*, Brown clearly expressed his epic vision of the Western story, a vision that touched the hearts of American readers: "The story of the American West has all the elements of the Iliad and Odyssey. It is a heroic world of quests and wars, of journeyings into remote lands, of daring hunts, last stands, and legendary exploits. It is an epic of mighty deeds, of triumphs and failures, of inconsistent heroes and heroines. The West is a tragedy relieved by interludes of comedy. It is a tale of good and evil, a morality play of personified abstractions."

Returning to fiction, as well as to the themes that resonated throughout *Bury My Heart at Wounded Knee*, Brown hit the bestseller lists once more in 1980 with *Creek Mary's Blood*. Brown's national reputation as a historian actually enhanced his credibility as a novelist of historical fiction. "Using fictional characters against a carefully researched historical background," wrote Joseph McClellan in the *Washington Post Book World*, "Brown combines the attractions of both genres. The major incidents of his story are true, but by inventing fictional participants he is able to give events a human dimension lacking in the historical record."

The same powerful themes were evident in Brown's *Killdeer Mountain* for Holt in 1983, but the disjointed narrative structure marked it as the author's most ambitious fictional effort to date. Brown's narrative power, however, sometimes overwhelmed the characters in his novel. "Brown's gift for strong narrative," noted Jonathan Coleman in the *New York Times*, "far outweighs his skill at writing dialogue, which, at times, hurts his novel." Coleman and other literary critics felt that the very narrative strengths that gave Brown such mastery over history, somewhat compromised his power as a novelist in *Killdeer Mountain*. The book, however, still met with some commercial success and critical acclaim. Robert Gish, writing in the *Chicago Tribune*, called it Brown's "most intriguing book to date."

In his eighties Brown kept up a remarkable stream of publications. Popular history like *Wondrous Times on the Frontier* (1991), *The American West* (1994), and, with artist Mort Kunstler, *Images of the Old West* (1996), as well as two more works of fiction—*Conspiracy of Knaves* (1987) and *The Way to Bright Star* (1998)—continued to enthrall a devoted following of readers. Repeated appearances on television documentaries, most notably *The Real West* on A&E and the History Channel, gave these readers the chance to see and hear the man whose written words had so moved them. His impressive persona—a folksy combination of John Wayne and Will Rogers—captivated television viewers. His delightful memoir, *When the Century Was Young*, published by August House in 1993, reflected that same television persona of a wise, witty, compassionate man who is, above all, American in every aspect of his being.

As the century ends Dee Brown still lives and writes in Little Rock, Arkansas. While he moves a bit slower than in the past, the mind and the spirit are as keen as ever. Gentle, unassuming, seemingly unaware, or at least mightily unconcerned, with his fame he continues to follow his calling as a writer and historian. Few writers have ever had such a powerful influence upon their time. Well may it be said, to paraphrase Longfellow, that Dee Brown has indeed left deep footprints in the sands of time.

★ WAVE HIGH THE BANNER ★

☆ ★ ☆ ★ ☆

Oɴ *the morning of March 4, 1801, Thomas Jefferson,
dressed in a red waistcoat, green velveteen breeches, yarn
stockings and a pair of old slippers run down at the heels, left
his rooms in Conrad's Boarding House, and walked across the
muddy square to the north wing of the unfinished capitol.
Immediately the doors of the Senate chamber were thrown
open, and he entered awkwardly, his freckled face more ruddy
than usual. Aaron Burr, the Vice-President, arose and greeted
him stiffly.*

*When Jefferson sat down with Aaron Burr on his right
hand and the Chief Justice, John Marshall, on his left, the
silent Senators in the chamber looked up at three men who
detested one another profoundly. John Marshall's sharp black
eyes were fixed for one second on the large-boned farmer from
his own state of Virginia; then he turned his gaze straight
ahead of him. The imperturbable, immaculate Burr sat rigid,
his lips compressed.*

*Already Jefferson had shifted his weight to one hip, with
one shoulder thrust up grotesquely, a position that made his
clothing appear too small for him. His graying sandy hair was
tousled, his face still red from the excitement.*

*When there was absolute quiet he arose. Shifting his weight
from one leg to another, he began reading his dull inaugural*

address, a state paper which divulged little of his political philosophy.

Thomas Jefferson was now the third President of the United States, a narrow sprawling nation of six million persons scattered along the Eastern seaboard, spreading out in thin lines across the passes of the Alleghanies. Beyond these mountains was a vast rich land, and the new President was certain that ten centuries of time would be spent in filling this territory with farms and towns. Weeks and months must pass before news of Jefferson's inauguration would reach the fringes of settlements to the West, where restless men, ruthless in their attacks on nature and the few Indians who plagued their paths, were driving the outposts deeper and deeper into the wilderness they would conquer in less than one of Jefferson's ten centuries.

And in less than a third of that one century, the sons of these pioneers, gradually awakening to their sovereign powers, influenced by the political philosophy of this man Jefferson, would sweep into power. They would take possession of the government of the United States as boldly as their fathers had conquered the wilderness. In that strange assembly of explorers, backwoodsmen, and farmers who would come to Washington in those days after Jefferson was a man named David Crockett.

This is his story.

PART ONE

★

★ I ★

WHEN David Crockett reached the top of the ridge, he stopped to rest for a minute against a smooth boulder while he looked down into the valley. His father's tavern was there, all right, and except for one or two new clearings in the forest, the valley was physically unchanged.

Yet now that he was here, home at last, the churning discontent in his mind was not set at rest. The idea of coming home had been a single burning force driving him forward through the weeks that he had begged rides from wagoners, and then irked by the slowness of their progress had left them again and again to walk for miles along the endless road that wound like a snake across Virginia. In his imagination, home —the tavern—had been a golden dream, but now that he was here the place was but an ordinary crude building of logs set in a valley no different from a hundred others he had seen along the way.

But he knew there was a difference. There was a difference he could not understand, but he had noted it soon after he left Abingdon, a difference in the feel of things. The people were different, talked about matters that would have seemed unimportant to the people back East. Here everything was new, changing, restless. Already he had felt this restlessness, a discontent gnawing away somewhere inside him. Had he been hungry or thirsty he might have eased the pangs, but this other thing—he knew not what it was, nor what remedy there was for it.

He had thought this mind's plague would disappear when he was home again; instead the thing was accentuated and now as he rubbed his hands across the face of the giant rock, he turned and looked back from where he had come and wondered why he had made this journey.

The creaking and rumbling of a wagon turned his thoughts from himself. It was the wagon he had left an hour ago. For a moment he could hear the driver roaring out a song; then the chill March wind whirled the sound away.

Thinking of the song, David slung his dusty sack over his shoulder and started down the road toward the tavern. He was not one for singing, but he mumbled the words of the song he had just heard:

> Droop not, brother, as we go
> Over the mountains, westward ho,
> Under boughs of mistletoe
> Log huts we'll rear,
> While herds of deer and buffalo
> Furnish the cheer;
> File over the mountains, steady, boys;
> For game afar
> We have our rifles ready, boys,
> Aha!

"Aha, aha, aha," he was laughing now, thinking of old Adam Myer, the wagoner who had taught him the song long ago on the road to Baltimore, and how the team had run away while he was sleeping in an empty flour barrel. Still laughing, David looked at the scar on his finger where it had been almost smashed in two when the wagon turned over at Ellicott's Mill, throwing him out of the barrel. Old Adam was a merry devil, but he liked his liquor too well for driving a fast team.

He stopped in the middle of the road, looking up at the sky where clouds were scudding up in thick gray masses. It would be dark earlier than he had thought. Leaving the road, he cut straight down through the thick forest, and after a few minutes was in the clearing near the tavern.

He was surprised at the number of wagons drawn in a cluster around the small tavern, at the row of horses tethered to the hitching post at one side. He thought that his father certainly must be prospering with all these wagoners stopping for food and lodging.

As he came closer David felt that curious stabbing nostalgia which comes over a person when he returns to a familiar scene, where landscape and buildings surge up out of a dormant remembrance to create dead happenings out of time past.

At either end of the tavern were the two old fire chimneys, chinked and plastered with clay, chimneys that he had watched his father build in an autumn long forgotten. And the grindstone, a rickety old thing now, near the spot where his father had caned him soundly the day before he had run away with the teamsters so many months past.

Thinking of the caning, David stopped short in the gray twilight. How would his father feel toward him now? He was not yet of age. Perhaps if he told his father he was eager to go to school now, was sorry for what he had done—well, the old fellow could do no more than give him another caning.

He walked on, between two wagons, across the ground, bare and beaten hard by the tread of many feet. He could hear loud voices and the rumbling laughter of the wagoners. A light flashed from a crack in the door.

He swallowed hard and then pulled on the latch. Warm tobacco smoke and the good smell of food rolled into his face as he swung himself inside, his feet set firmly on the rough puncheon floor. Flames from the logs in the huge fireplace illuminated the other end of the long room; he was in shadow and apparently none had seen him enter.

For a minute or two, David stood there quietly, watching

the wavering light rise and fall over the familiar tavern room. The wagoners were sitting on the rough benches that ran the length of the wooden dining table. Some of them were smoking their big odorous pipes or drinking liquor out of gourds; the more weary ones rested their heads on the dining table, waiting patiently for food.

Beside the fireplace was his father, grown heavier around the neck and waist; his hair was quite gray. His father was never a man for talk. Always he had kept apart from his guests, sitting silent, while words flew about him unheard or ignored. David smiled, looking at his father, and then went over to the fireplace and sat down on a hickory floor stool. John Crockett did not even glance up from his dreaming. Two or three of the wagoners spoke to David, and he nodded. He looked at all the faces, but he did not know any of the men, and did not care to talk at the moment.

"Here come the fixin's," one of the wagoners suddenly cried out. They all swung around to face the table, their heavy shoes scuffing on the floor. David smelled the food before he saw his sister bringing the huge platter in to the table. When he saw Elizabeth's face glowing pink above the platter, his throat filled up and he felt strange for a moment. She was almost a woman now, and a pretty one, too.

"Find you a place to the table, boy."

David turned back to his father who had spoken to him, and looked straight into his eyes. John Crockett was standing up, and David felt a shock when he knew his father did not recognize him. He told himself that the old fellow was getting fat as a bear around the middle, and perhaps was forgetting things. He felt small and unimportant as he squeezed a place at one end of the table, with a teamster's dirty elbow shoved up against his wooden plate.

Elizabeth had brought in another platter, the old battered pewter one he knew so well, and it was piled high with potatoes and chunks of boiled salt meat. David kept his head down while she walked around behind him. Then he heard his mother's voice. She was just behind him, her arm reaching over to fill his bowl with squirrel broth. Until he smelled the squirrel broth he had not realized how hungry he was. The steam from the bowl billowed up into his face.

" Just corn bread and common doin's tonight, friends," his father said, and David turned, but his father was not even looking at him. None of the wagoners bothered to acknowledge the statement; they were eating noisily, bolting the chunks of salt meat and huge pieces of corn bread which they sopped in their bowls of broth.

David finished his squirrel broth quickly, and then stopped and looked in front of him. Elizabeth was sitting on the opposite side of the table, passing food along to the men.

" Some more broth? " She stared at him and her dark eyes seemed puzzled for a second, and then she turned, calling into the kitchen: " Any more squirrel broth, ma? "

Her mother replied in the affirmative. David sat there, clutching the wooden bowl. All the time he had been away from home he had never once thought of crying, but he knew if all the wagoners had not been there around him now he would have cried like a helpless baby. His mother was coming in from the kitchen, bringing the squirrel broth. If she did not know him, he was determined he would leave the tavern without saying a word and head back for the East. He had never felt so lonely in all his born days.

" Hand me your bowl."

David reached out the wooden bowl and looked at Elizabeth. She was looking at him, too, as she took the bowl from his hand, and then she dropped the bowl and her eyes grew big and round.

" Ma! " she cried. " Ma! It's Davy! It's Davy! It's Davy come back! "

"Sakes alive," he heard his mother shout, and then there was a flutter of skirts, and soft arms were all around his neck. And Elizabeth was hugging him tight and hard. He twisted his head around and out of one eye he could see the big wagoner next to him wiping his greasy mouth and grinning like a 'possum.

All the men had stopped eating; the room was still and quiet. His father had risen to his feet, his mouth open, staring at his son. David looked at him, afraid for a second that his father would denounce him for running away those many months ago. But no, he was smiling and saying, "We thought you dead, for certain, boy."

David could say nothing. He sat straight on the bench, looking at his father, until abashed by the grinning faces of the wagoners. He began dunking his corn bread in the bowl of squirrel broth which Elizabeth had so obligingly filled to the brim.

"You always was partial to squirrel broth, Davy," his mother said.

"You must've knowed I was coming." He tried to laugh, but his voice choked.

"No, son, we never expected to lay eyes on you again. You've been away so long. All our boys have gone away and left us."

David looked at her. "I'm staying here for good, ma. I've had my fill of traveling." He felt warm inside now, felt important. Everybody in this room was looking at him, where a few minutes ago they had scarcely glanced at him. He was somebody, a traveler returned home. He could tell them things. Even most of these wagoners had never been as far east as Baltimore and seen the ships and everything. He sopped his bread with a flourish.

But suddenly a noise at the door distracted the attention of his audience—the laughter of girls and the coarse guffaw of

[16]

a man, a laugh that David instantly recognized. "Ah-hah-hah-hah." Uncle Joe Hawkins!

"Uncle Joseph!" He dropped his bread, turning to face the door and, as it swung open, the draft fluttered the candle on the dining table. Instead of his Uncle Joseph he saw a girl with black eyes that laughed at him as he looked at her, and for no reason at all his face turned crimson. There were other girls in the group, but his eyes came back to her, and as he stood there he assured himself that he must have come back to Tennessee for no other reason than to see this girl.

Now his father was standing between him and the girl, and he saw Joseph Hawkins moving out of the darkness into the tavern, still booming his laugh, ah-hah-hah-hah. Joseph thrust out his big hand and shook John Crockett's shoulder. "Glad to see you, John. How's your health? And Rebecca? Still as peart as ever, hah-hah-hah? And here is Elizabeth. Bless your heart, Elizabeth, you're twicet as purty as you was last Christmas."

"Uncle Joseph," Elizabeth said, "guess who's here?"

"Well, now, it might be anybody, maybe Andy Jackson or maybe President Tom Jefferson. Ah-hah-hah-hah. This tavern is a fine enough place for a President, even a good one like Tom Jefferson."

"It's Davy, Uncle Joseph."

Joseph looked about the room until he saw David grinning at him. Like a huge bear, the man bounded across the room and shook David until the boy's head spun. "Ah-hah-hah-hah. By the eternal, it is Davy. They always said you looked like me, but lad, you've a sight of growin' to do yet. Where've you been, boy?"

David ducked his head. "Traveling."

"I wasn't thinking you'd been sitting still all this time. Where to?"

David was aware that he was again the center of attention.

[17]

He rubbed one foot against a knot that punched up in the flooring. "East. Baltimore, and—places."

"Baltimore, in Maryland. Your ma and me was born in Maryland, but we was never to Baltimore." Joseph Hawkins cocked his head to one side. "I'll wager you never saw any gals in Baltimore as purty as these here with me." He bowed and stepped to one side, and there was the black-eyed girl curtseying to David. "Remember Margaret Elder? Her folks was our neighbors when you two was young-uns. Ain't she a purty gal now?"

David thrust his hands into his pockets, ashamed of his dusty, shabby clothing, and kicked his toe at the knot in the floor. Margaret Elder. He remembered her, all right.

"We've been to a wedding party," she said. Her eyes sparkled as she looked out at David from beneath her gay blue bonnet fastened with a strap around her chin.

"Her sister was wed," Uncle Joseph explained. "I'm taking the gals to home in the morning."

The wagoners had finished their eating and had withdrawn into the shadows at the far end of the room, talking in rumbling undertones, their eyes staring out at the group of girls. Joseph Hawkins' voice still echoed back and forth while he and his young companions waited for Elizabeth to bring more food for them. With his father, David went to the fireplace and sat there, his gaze fixed on Margaret Elder. His father had little to say to him, but Joseph Hawkins shouted question after question across the table, seldom awaiting an answer. Uncle Joseph wanted to know if he had visited Washington City, if he had seen President Tom Jefferson, and if he was going to settle down and get married now that he was back in Tennessee.

"There's some mighty purty gals in these parts, lad. Ah-hah-hah-hah," he shouted, nudging Margaret Elder with his elbow.

David heard scarcely a word for watching the girl. Her blue bonnet shook back and forth when she laughed, but she had never looked at him again. He thought her hands were beautiful, and he could not keep his eyes from the low-cut dress that rose and fell above her breasts with her breathing.

Like a dream the evening passed, and it was time for bed. Even though he had to sleep alongside a dozen snoring wagoners in the upper room, he was glad for even the little privacy of sleep. Alone with his dreams of a pretty face, he squirmed a soft hollow into the crisp corn-shuck mattress.

★ 2 ★

David awoke with the scent of sassafras heavy in the room, with the noise of the wagoners' boots scraping against the ladder as they went below for breakfast. He lay still for a moment looking at the dried sassafras roots hanging from the cross-poles just above his head, wondering if the scent came from the roots or from a boiling kettle of tea down in the kitchen.

Then he heard the voices of the girls, and the laughter of Margaret Elder, louder and bolder than that of the others. Her face had been with him all the night; he could remember every detail, her dark eyes, the way in which curling strands of hair fell out from her blue bonnet, her firm cheeks and slightly tilted nose.

He started dressing hurriedly, but stopped to look with dismay upon his mud-caked moccasins and the shabby leather jacket and leggings he had worn for months without change. Even the wagoners dressed better than he.

After he had combed his tangled hair back with his fingers, he went quietly down the ladder. The March morning was chill; most of the girls were gathered around the blazing fire. Margaret Elder was rolling her curls with a forefinger, and David stopped still, staring at her. She looked at him. " Mornin', Davy."

"Mornin'," he said, the word catching in his throat. She had spoken to him! She remembered his name! He could not suppress his exuberance. He ran out the door, knocked against one of the brawny teamsters who was entering, stumbled, and recovered his balance, leaped over the hitching pole and popped his heels together.

There was spring in the air, the smell of new grass and leaves; the sun was just coming up between the hills to the east. David whistled and leaped back over the hitching pole. The wagoners were busy strapping harness on their teams, and their indifference to his great fortune acted as a check on his excitement.

He went back inside, helping his father set up an extra space of table against the wall. Margaret Elder was pouring pink sassafras tea, while Elizabeth dropped spoonfuls of hominy on the wooden platters set in rows along the table.

Although he felt awkward, David spoke again to Margaret. Her cheeks were red from being near the fire, and he said suddenly: " You're the rosiest-cheeked, purtiest girl I ever saw, and I've been lots of places."

Margaret giggled, and after that David followed her all about the room. They sat next to one another while they ate their hominy and drank the sassafras tea.

" I'm coming to see you," were the last words he said to her, as she waved her blue bonnet at him from Joseph Hawkins' flat wagon. David stood beside his sister for a long time at the tavern door, watching the wagon crawl up the rough winding road that led out of the valley. After it was hidden by the trees he could hear the creaking of the wheels and the ah-hah-hah-hah laugh of Joseph Hawkins. When there was no longer any sound David turned to speak to Elizabeth, but she had gone back inside.

He was alone, with the log tavern emptied of all its beauty, all its gaiety. He hated returning to the fireplace to talk with his father.

For a while he walked around the grounds, and then sat for almost an hour in one of the dilapidated sheds back of the tavern, wondering what his father would have him do around the place. John Crockett had never been much of a farmer, and except for a few rows of vegetables he had never cultivated the rocky ground that rolled back toward the hills. David wondered if anybody could scratch a living from that poor earth.

It was not until after the noon meal that David and his father spoke again with one another. They sat outside the front door on the log stoop. A horseman who had stopped for food was riding away toward the hills. When the sound of the hoofs had died away, John Crockett put his hand on David's knee and said quietly: " Is it good to be home, Davy? "

" It is. I'm glad," said David. The March sun was warm, and the wind blowing in the trees across the road made the tiny leaf buds sparkle like green raindrops. They were silent for a minute, and then his father spoke again. " What do you think of doing now that you are home? "

David made a mark across the hard ground with the toe of one moccasin. " Maybe I'll camp for a spell here, work for you? " He kept his eyes turned to the ground.

John Crockett forced a chuckle. " Work for me? I've no work for you, boy. Tavern work is mostly women's work. Cooking, scrubbing, cleaning. I scarce keep busy myself. There's no work for a boy."

" I had thought to stay with you."

The father pressed his hand hard against the boy's knee. " I'm a poor man, Davy. I owe debts to my neighbors. For food, for whiskey. Abe Wilson supplies the tavern with spirits. I owe him thirty-six dollars, a good sum in times like these." He stopped, his breath coming hard as if he hated the words he had to say. "You'd reckon, from the many folk who stop here, I'd have a plenty. But so many put off the paying, so many are my friends and creditors."

David remembered that his father was never any good at driving bargains. An easy mark, was what Uncle Joseph had called him once.

"And so," John Crockett sighed, "Abe Wilson's due to come tonight. I promised him money last week, but I've got only a few furs the wagoners left. I owe him thirty-six dollars. He needs a boy to help, I heard him say that a week ago. I'll bind you to him for four, or five, or how many months he says. And when the time is up, you'll be free. By law, you're my servant until you're a man. But if you'll work and free me of this debt, I'll lay no more claim to you as father." His voice trailed off. "Without Abe Wilson's whiskey the tavern's business will be ruined."

David drew another line across the hard earth with the toe of a moccasin. "And if I make this bargain, I'll be free to marry, too?"

John Crockett slapped his thigh, and this time his laughter was genuine. "To marry, aye. And who would you be a-marrying, boy?"

David grinned, and looked at his father. "I'll let you know as soon as I've worked out my time over at Abe Wilson's."

Late that night Abe Wilson and his son, Jesse, arrived at the tavern with a barrel of whiskey. David helped Jesse roll the barrel back into the kitchen, and when they came back to the fireplace his father and Abe had gone outside. After a few minutes they returned. John Crockett called David to one side to inform him that Abe Wilson had agreed to count the debt paid provided David would work six months for him.

Six months! A long time to work and receive nothing for it, he was thinking. A long time to wait, six months. But he had promised his father.

The next morning when he looked at the faces of Abe Wilson and the boy, Jesse, David liked less than ever the prospect of living with them for the next six months. Abe was a tall bony man with a scraggly beard and two yellow front teeth which curved out of his mouth most of the time. Jesse was only a few years older than David, but he looked exactly like Abe, except that he had no beard. His protruding teeth gave him the appearance of a vicious young wolf, and David resolved to have as little as possible to do with Jesse. However, when they started on the journey he was told to ride behind on Jesse's horse.

The Wilson cabin was only a few miles away from the tavern. Turning off the Knoxville road near a creek, they followed the stream up into the desolate hill country, and all along the way Jesse jabbed his elbows deliberately into David's stomach. He was glad when the journey was ended, yet as soon as he was inside the unkempt one-room cabin, he wished mightily that he had never come. He had to sleep with Jesse in the loft; the bed was a filthy roll of quilts piled on the rough logs.

In a few days, however, David became accustomed to the habits of Abe and Jesse. He worked willingly from dawn until dark, oftentimes alone in the fields while the father and son lay asleep in the cabin. The Wilsons spent considerable time roving around the countryside after dark, carrying whiskey to various places, and there were often night callers at the cabin. When he was not too weary or sleepy, David would sometimes come down from the bed in the loft, and lie on the dirt floor listening to the talk.

One night a man with one eye completely gone from its socket stopped for whiskey, and after he had swallowed a few drinks he began to tell about his adventures fighting the Creeks and Chickasaws. He said the Spaniards were stirring up the Indians to the south and that there soon would be hell and tarnation breaking loose in the border settlements. When Jesse asked him how he lost his eye the man laughed and said a fellow gouged it out in a fight down in the state of Georgia. He showed Jesse how an eye could be gouged out easily with the thumb, and told him it was a trick that might come in useful to him some day.

After the man left and the boys had gone to bed Jesse suddenly straddled David and started gouging him in the eye with his thumb. David yelled so loud with the pain that old Abe shouted at Jesse and told him he'd beat his breeches off if he didn't stop.

With all the unpleasantness of the place and the petty annoyances of Jesse, time passed much more rapidly than David had expected. As soon as Abe Wilson learned that David knew a good deal about farming, he placed the cornfield under his care. Abe grew nothing but corn; after he had made the grain into liquor he could swap it for anything he might need.

By the middle of summer David found some time for hunting, but, as he had no weapon, he borrowed Abe's rifle without asking for it. When Abe finally discovered this, he told David he wasn't bound to him to waste his time hunting. He put the boy to work chopping down the girdled trees in the cornfield and then splitting them into wood for the winter.

So filled were his days with work, David had never returned to the tavern to see his family. Almost every week Abe and Jesse made the journey with a barrel of whiskey, but there were always so many tasks to be done around the cabin that he was never asked to go along. However, he had never insisted upon going. His mind was more occupied with thoughts and dreams of Margaret Elder than with the members of his

[24]

family, and long ago he had made up his mind to visit her as soon as his six months' service was ended.

On an afternoon in early September, David came in from the field for a drink of water, and found Jesse sitting out in front of the cabin with Abe's rifle across his knees.

Jesse grinned at him, his front teeth sticking out grotesquely. " Want to go huntin' ? " asked Jesse.

David dipped some water out of the spring with a gourd. " Where's Abe? "

" Gone up on the Clinch River. He knows a woman up there."

" When'll he be back? "

" It's a far piece up there. Maybe two or three days."

David drank the water slowly. " He told me not to go hunting any more with his rifle."

" I'll carry the rifle. You just come along."

" When we going? "

" Right now," said Jesse.

They left the cabin and started down the creek toward the Knoxville road. Some of the leaves on the trees had turned yellow, falling in the stream. The leaves rocked and spun along the top of the water, sparkling in the sun. David walked behind Jesse, wondering why he was going toward the road. " Better hunting to the south," said David.

" I'm goin' by to see a little gal I know." Jesse grinned back over his shoulder, showing his teeth.

It was late afternoon when they came to a wide shoal in the creek, a place filled with flat-topped stones, and across the creek David saw two women taking clothing from bushes where it had been hung to dry. One of the women, her arms filled with clothes, was starting up the path away from the creek, but the other had walked down to the edge of the stream, bending over to wash something in the water.

"Come on," Jesse whispered. "Let's scare her. She's my little gal."

Quietly they forded the creek, David's moccasins filling with water. When they were across, the water squished between his toes, making loud noises. Jesse handed him his rifle and whispered to him to stand still.

Before Jesse reached the girl, David recognized her. There was no mistaking the brown curls that swung around the back of her neck. She was Margaret Elder. He watched Jesse tiptoe up behind her, and then run his long hands quickly beneath her arms, squeezing her.

Margaret screamed, breaking loose from Jesse, one bare foot dropping in the shallow water. She slapped his face with the palm of her hand, but Jesse grabbed her by both hands and pulled her close to him on the shore.

"Jesse Wilson, I'll call my sister."

"Holler your head off," said Jesse. "She's too far gone by now to hear."

Before David's eyes the trees and the stream blurred; he could feel his blood thumping in his temples. The weight of the rifle was that of a heavy log. He dropped it suddenly in the sand and was running toward Jesse and Margaret.

When he reached them, Margaret was standing in the water away from Jesse, and David saw her face briefly, her dark eyes wide with fright and recognition. Then he struck Jesse with his shoulder, hurling the boy backward into the sand. Jesse's feet came up instantly, and as David fell toward him, he kicked out with his legs hitting David in the stomach, doubling him up as he sank breathless to the ground.

Gasping for air, David felt Jesse's bony arms encircle his middle; a tearing pain shot through his body, and he flopped over in the sand, his eyes watering so that he could see but dimly. Jesse was choking him now, bouncing up and down on his stomach, yet he managed to twist sideways to relieve the pain.

Like treacherous snakes, Jesse's long wrists slipped under his arms, against his neck, bending his head forward until the world seemed to turn black before his eyes. He could smell the unpleasant odor of Jesse's body, pressing closer and closer against him. One of those greasy hands was over his face now, the thumbnail jabbing unmercifully into the tender flesh of his cheek, slipping nearer and nearer to his eye. Suddenly a picture of the eyeless socket of the old Indian fighter flashed across his mind, and he was terrified. Snatching his arms loose he fought blindly at Jesse's jabbing thumb, rising to his knees, until he was free.

On his feet again, swaying dizzily, his mouth streaked with blood running down from his cheek, he swung out with his fists against Jesse's lanky body. He heard his antagonist grunt, saw him stumble, and then David leaped upon him, his fists pounding furiously. He had Jesse down on the ground, with hands over his face, screaming curses. He was sitting on his enemy, pounding, pounding, pounding. Now he knew he was the victor, yet the bitterness in his heart was intense, and as he pounded the face of Jesse, in his mind was the face of Margaret Elder, and the curses Jesse was shouting in his ears became words that repeated over and over again: " Come on, let's scare her. She's my little gal, she's my little gal, she's my little gal, she's my ——"

David was still beating blindly down with his fists when a powerful hand gripped his shoulder and jerked him to his feet. In a second of surprise his eyes cleared and he was looking into the face of a sturdy old man, a face that was both kindly and stern.

" 'Tis sinful for a man to beat his brother," said the stranger.

David started to speak, but his mouth was filled with blood;

he spat into the water of the creek and watched the red blob float slowly away. " He's not my brother," said David.

" All men are brothers."

" Not Jesse Wilson," David insisted. He saw a trace of a smile appear on the man's broad ruddy face.

" Whose boy can thee be? "

" John Crockett is my father. I'm Davy Crockett."

" John Crockett! A friend of mine. Thee would be the lad he was speaking about. He bound thee to Abraham Wilson."

" Yes, sir. He did." David wiped the blood from his face with the sleeve of his jacket. Jesse had crawled away from them, and was now stumbling up the side of the creek. Margaret Elder was nowhere in sight.

The stranger had removed his flat-topped hat and was stroking the bald front of his wide forehead. " Must thee return to Wilson's place tonight? "

David looked down at the water again. " I don't know, sir."

" In truth, David, the man's house is not a fit place for a good lad. Sure, John Crockett must not know of the reputation it has."

" My six months' service will be done next week."

The man considered for a moment. " I have not told thee my name. John Kennedy, it is, and though in principle I stand against men fighting, I must admit, lad, thee have a fighting heart." He put his hand on David's shoulder. " I hear thee know farming well, too."

" That may be true."

" I need a boy."

David looked into the man's kindly gray eyes. " Would you have me? "

" Let us say thee work for me a week. Should Abraham Wilson demand payment for the last week of service, I'll square the account. And if thee can work only half so well as thee has fought here, I'll give thee hire."

[28]

David shook John Kennedy's hand, and then walked over and picked up Abe Wilson's rifle. He wiped the sand carefully from the barrel.

"I'll return this next week," he said.

John Kennedy's cabin was only a few rods from the Knoxville road, yet when he and David arrived there, night had darkened the surrounding forest, and far off in the hills they could hear wolves howling at the yellow moon in the blue-smoky sky.

"This is the place," John Kennedy said, as he pulled the door back on its leather hinges and motioned David to enter. A single pine knot burning in the fireplace furnished light for the room, simply and crudely furnished, yet so clean that even in the semi-darkness David could see that the puncheon floor was worn smooth from frequent scrubbings.

He was so exhausted from the encounter with Jesse, his mind was in such a turmoil of thinking about Margaret Elder, that he barely spoke when John Kennedy made known to him his niece, Nancy, and his son, William.

Nancy's face, he observed, was very plain, and her clothing even more so, for the Kennedys were Quakers and wore garments so simple that even the frontier folk thought them odd. William was a stolid silent youth, with bristly white hair, and seemed able to sit for hours without moving a muscle.

"William is a good boy," his father said, turning to David. "I trust that thee and he will help one another and become as brothers."

The Kennedy house was larger than most of the cabins in the neighborhood. Originally it had been two long rooms, built end to end, but John Kennedy had constructed ells on each side with a connecting roofed passage at one end so that the building was almost a square. As large as it was, there was nothing pretentious about the house; the beds, the tables, the chairs, everything was of logs, mostly constructed into the sides of the walls.

David slept alone in one of the ell rooms, and the bed was so soft and clean after the floor pallet he had shared with Jesse Wilson that several times during the night he awoke suddenly, trying to remember where he was. But it was not the bed alone which made his sleep uneasy. Over and over again he reconstructed in his mind the scene on the creek's edge. Jesse's assertion that Margaret Elder was his girl still echoed in his ears, and he tried vainly to convince himself that Jesse had been but idly boasting.

But when he remembered the queer expression on Margaret's face while Jesse was touching her, and the fact that she had vanished during the fighting, he was convinced that her feelings toward him were less than casual. And why should he expect her to look upon him with more favor than anyone else? But for Jesse Wilson to speak of her as his girl sickened him, and he was determined that he would forget Margaret Elder forever, and seek another.

His sleep was so fitful during the night that when morning came he overslept, and the sun was high when he sat up suddenly in bed and looked out the window at a fire burning brightly under a cauldron in the yard. Nancy Kennedy was stirring the boiling mixture with a stick, and from the odorous fumes David knew that she was making soap. From the cleanliness of the room and bed, he judged that Nancy could make good use of the soap.

He could see little of her face or figure, as she wore a huge bonnet, and her dress, gathered loosely at the waist with a string, touched the ground. But he thought she looked more attractive than she had appeared to him the night before. And when a sudden gust of wind whirled her skirts almost above her bare knees, he was surprised at the shapeliness of her legs. He almost laughed aloud, thinking of her modesty, and how she would have blushed had she known he was watching when the wind swirled her dress.

In spite of the bruises on his face, he was in good spirits, whistling loudly when he stepped into the other room where he found John Kennedy mending a pair of heavy shoes.

" Good morning, Davy," said the Quaker.

" I slept late," said David apologetically.

" I knew thee would be weary, lad. I did not call thee."

" You ought've rousted me out, sir. But I'll make it up with working the harder."

" Thee must eat first. The table is set."

Out of clean shiny pewter, David ate heartily of corn cakes and honey, and drank a huge mug of milk. Afterwards he went out to the edge of the Kennedy cornfield where he worked all day with William. They were laying a pole fence around a stretch of new-ground on which the trees had been girdled the previous spring.

William was a most taciturn young man; it was with an effort that David got him to talk, and then he said but few words. He did learn that the Kennedys expected to sow wheat on the new-ground and that in a day or so they were planning to capture some wild hogs out of the woods for autumn fattening. Otherwise the day passed in silence.

At the end of the week, John Kennedy drew him aside and showed him a piece of paper which he kept in his huge Bible.

David took the paper and stared at it curiously; it was written in ink, but the scrawls meant nothing to him. He looked at John Kennedy. " I'm sorry, sir. I can't read."

The Quaker was surprised. " No? Thee cannot read? How old be thee? "

[31]

" Sixteen."

" And thee cannot read." He clucked his tongue. " Thee must learn to read." He paused, and then began reading the paper: " I, John Crockett, promise to pay to John Kennedy the amount of forty dollars."

" My father owes you forty dollars? "

" Yes. I wanted thee to know this before I offered thee hire. Thee be a good worker, and I need thee here for the harvest, but this note is long overdue. Unless I can collect it from John Crockett, I'm afraid I cannot pay thee. Perhaps he could advance part of the amount."

David was sick with disappointment. For a moment he thought the Quaker had trapped him into coming to work for him, but when he remembered the man's kindnesses he could not think of him stooping to a trick. He hesitated, trying to determine his course. " But my father has no money."

John Kennedy had slipped the piece of paper back into the Bible, closing the clasp on the huge book. " Would thee like a day or two to think upon the matter? Thee might pay a visit to John Crockett, talk with him, and then decide."

Early the next morning, David took Abe Wilson's rifle and started on the long trail back into the hills. When he reached the Wilson cabin he found both Abe and Jesse sprawling on the ground half asleep. Jesse sat up, glowering at him, but Abe had been drinking and was in a good humor. He took the rifle, saying that he was glad to see David back again. When David told him he was going to work for John Kennedy, Abe was astonished, and offered him two dollars a week to help through the harvest.

" I owe you a week's work," David replied. " John Kennedy said he'd square that."

Abe replied that the account was squared already so far as he was concerned, and gave David a jug of whiskey as a parting gift.

Swiftly the harvest time passed. The days grew shorter, and winter was on the land. It was a year of much snow, and in the evenings the Kennedys and David kept close to the hearth which was always heaped high with oak logs. William and Nancy took turns reading from a book which concerned the adventures of a young man named Christian who was lost in a Slough of Despond. David enjoyed listening to the reading, and became much disturbed over the hero's continued ill luck, fearing that he would never reach his long-sought goal.

Once John Kennedy suggested that Nancy teach David to read, but when he sat next to the girl, he could not fix his mind on the printed symbols. He was such a poor pupil that he begged to be excused from the ordeal.

★ 4 ★

Finally, the spring came again, and early one Monday morning the Kennedys began the plowing. William had already repaired the plows, sharpening and fastening down the iron plates over the wooden frames, and John Kennedy had borrowed his married son's horse so that both David and William might plow at the same time.

They made a game of it, William taking the south side, David the north. Before the week was past, every available foot of the cleared ground was turned back. In the warm spring air the damp loam smelled sweet as flower fragrance. For the sowing, David removed his shoes, moving swiftly ahead of his methodical competitor.

By midsummer, the farm tasks became less arduous; the corn and wheat grew rapidly, almost too rapidly, for the rains had been heavy in the late spring. After a week of weeding the crop in July, John Kennedy told David he might have two or three days to do what he pleased.

"Well, sir," said David, "as you can see for yourself, I need some new clothes mighty bad."

The Quaker laughed. "But Nancy would be glad to make some things for thee."

"I've got my heart set on a store-bought hunting shirt, and well, sir, to tell the truth, I'd like some money if I might have it."

Kennedy pondered for a minute or two. "Thee be a good hard-working lad, Davy, and have long since repaid me the forty-dollar debt of John Crockett. So thee shall have the hunting shirt. Though I have no hard cash this time of the year, my credit is good at a store over in Knoxville."

"Knoxville. I've never been to Knoxville," said David.

"'Tis not much of a town to lay beside the ones in the East, but it's a right good village for Tennessee. Thee can make the journey there and back in four days by catching the wagons right. I give thee leave to go—I'll write a letter giving thee twenty dollars in credit at the store."

Twenty dollars! What a lot of things that would buy! Never in his life had he possessed twenty dollars. He was so eager to be on his way to Knoxville that he awoke before daylight and went off down the road, walking for hours before the wagons began catching up with him.

Before noon the next day he was in Knoxville, a town full of dust swirling up behind the horses and wagons moving rapidly down the long street. For the first time since his return to Tennessee he was in the midst of noisy activity. Excited, he walked back and forth along the street until he found the store where John Kennedy had established credit.

The proprietor was an old friend of Kennedy's, a tall angular Scot who had known the Quaker some years before in North Carolina. "So ye're working for John Kennedy, eh, lad? Ye don't know the luck ye're in, working for as fine a man as old Quaker John."

The storekeeper talked continuously about his former relations with Kennedy, but David heard scarcely a word. His eyes were fixed on a rifle on the wall behind the Scotchman, a brand new rifle, its barrel dull blue with the ramrod shining in the light from the street.

" That rifle for sale? "

" Aye, it is. For twenty dollars ye can have it, and dirt cheap that is, too."

"But twenty dollars is all the credit I have to spend."

" I have another one, just as good as new, I'll let ye have for ten."

David looked long at the used rifle which the man held out to him, but finally turned away. He could feel the ragged shreds of his coat sleeves dangling against his hands. " Let me see your hunting shirts, sir."

The storekeeper led him back in the rear of the room, where a dozen or more leather hunting shirts were suspended from a rafter. David selected one with a red and blue fringe along the sleeves and around the hem. The coat was a perfect fit about the shoulders, but it was too long, he thought, reaching almost to his knees.

" Here's a pair of britches to go with it, good deerskin they are, too, with a leather lash for fastening the bottoms in bad weather, so as you won't be a-needing leggings."

" How much? "

" Well, let me see." The Scotchman shut one eye and looked up at the rafters. " Take both of 'em, and they're yours for thirteen dollars."

" And how much is a good pair of moccasins? "

" Four or five dollars, depending on the leather."

David was turning his fingers down one at a time, counting. " That will make about seventeen dollars. Too much."

" Too much! " The Scotchman's forehead wrinkled up suddenly and his blue eyes turned bright as flames. " Why, lad,

I'm offering these articles to ye for what they cost me, just because ye're working for my good old friend, Quaker John. And ye tell me they're too much." He turned his back on David and walked back toward the store entrance.

"I mean they're too much for me to have the gun, too," David explained hastily. He was still turning his fingers down, trying desperately to count. He started after the storekeeper, and then, remembering that he was still wearing the new hunting shirt, stopped suddenly.

"I know," he cried. "This shirt, a pair of moccasins and the old gun! For twenty dollars credit?" He was thinking of his worn breeches; he ran his fingers hopefully over the ravels at the seat. He had an idea that he could perhaps persuade Nancy to fasten a patch on the seat, and with the long shirt hanging over it nobody would be the wiser.

The old storekeeper had turned sharply around, and to David's surprise was smiling broadly. "Lad, ye can't beat the Scotch-Irish for driving bargains. Ye're a real Scotch-Irish, all right, queering me out of two whole dollars at the least, ye are, but I can't stand here making argument with ye all day. Let me fit a pair of moccasins to those big feet and run ye out of here before ye take my whole stock."

With his old coat and moccasins rolled up in a bundle, David stepped out on the Knoxville street, expecting every person in sight to stop and stare at his new hunting shirt. But the passers-by scarcely glanced at him, at his store-bought hunting shirt, or his new gun. Somewhat disappointed, he turned and walked down past the tanneries, paused to peer inside the inn, the Sign of the General Washington on the corner. Then he walked down toward the river, stopping for a while in front of the old stockade. The squat blockhouses still served as dwelling places, but the solid posts of the fence were beginning to sag from the effects of weather and the tugging of horses which had been hitched to them.

He walked through an opening in the fence, following a zig-zag path that led down to the river. A log raft was tied up to the shore, but nobody was aboard. Holding his gun carefully, David walked out on the raft. He wished for some powder that he might try the gun out by shooting across the water.

Leaning over the edge of the raft, he saw himself in the water, the blue and red fringes of his coat sleeves dancing in the tiny waves. He put his gun carefully down on the logs, and leaned far out in an effort to learn if his long shirt looked peculiar reaching as it did almost to his knees. Stretch as he might, however, he could not get his body into a position where he could see the hem of the shirt. He was almost ready to abandon the attempt when a sudden sound of laughter and a girl's voice set him off his balance. He danced madly on the edge of the raft, finally falling forward on his knees, safe but indignant.

"Davy Crockett, what in the world are you doing out there?"

He stood up dusting off the fringes of his new shirt, his mouth opening slightly when he saw who she was. "I wasn't thinking to see you—you."

It was Margaret Elder, with two other girls, her sisters, and the three of them were stepping timidly out upon the raft. "Did you float down the river on this thing, Davy?"

He blushed, stooping to pick up his precious rifle. "Nah, no—I just now walked down here, looking around, kind of."

Margaret had walked near to him, stumbling slightly, catching at his shoulder. "I almost fell, too, didn't I?" David took his arm slowly away from her waist, his nostrils filled with the sweet scent she wore on her dress.

He swallowed hard. "You're mighty dressed up. Your sisters, too," he added hastily. The three girls giggled excitedly as they tiptoed about the raft.

"I thought you was working for the Kennedys," Margaret

said, after they had started back up the path toward the town. She looked up at David, her dark eyes smiling at him, as they had that first night in his father's tavern.

"Well, yes'm, I am, but I just come over to Knoxville. Starting back tomorrow, if I can catch a wagon."

Margaret looked at him quickly. "Whyn't you go back with us? We're starting first thing in morning. Pa will let you go if I say so." She smiled, her shoulder brushing against him as they walked over the edge of embankment, and he smiled back.

That night David slept in a log shed next to the old block-houses, a place filled with clean hay and pine-straw. Margaret's father and several other farmers from the back country also stayed there, and late in the night, half-asleep, David could hear the older men talking about a quarrel between Judge Andy Jackson and old Nolichucky Jack Sevier, about a letter Andy Jackson had published in the Knoxville *Gazette* accusing Nolichucky Jack of land swindling. To David, Nolichucky Jack was a legend, a tall storming man who had married his mother's sister; and often he had heard his Uncle Joseph Hawkins tell of Andy Jackson, another great man, perhaps even greater than Nolichucky Jack. He could not imagine why these great men should quarrel, or fight a duel as some of the farmers said they probably would.

On this night, however, David had other things to think on, the sweet scent of Margaret as she had brushed against him on the raft, the long ride home with her tomorrow, all day with Margaret, riding in her father's wagon.

Tom Elder's wagon was a new Conestoga, with the red and green paint still fresh on the body and wheels. The sway-backed canvas cover flapped in the cool morning wind, as David and the three Elder sisters crawled into the back end, scratching comfortable hollows in the soft hay. David and Margaret sat close together at the end, letting their feet swing outside, jolting together as the wagon rolled away from Knoxville.

The sun was just rising; cool mists, blue in the early light, curled up from the river bottoms. Tom Elder and his brother-in-law sat up front, hidden by piles of supplies, and but for the two sisters David and Margaret would have been alone.

For an hour or so David watched the sisters impatiently. As he had hoped, both of them finally began to drowse, rocking back and forth with the movement of the wagon. Cautiously he let his arm drop around Margaret's waist; her head turned quickly the other way, but she leaned closer against him. He squeezed her roughly, kissing her suddenly on the cheek, and then her lips turned toward him. They kissed until a rough bounce of the wagon clicked their teeth together, and then they sat apart. The roughness of the road had wakened the sisters, who were giggling behind them. Embarrassed, David turned his attention to his rifle, lying in the straw beside him. He drew the gun across his knees, rubbing the barrel with the palm of his hand.

Margaret also looked at the rifle. " It was made in 1789," she said.

Surprised, David turned to her. " How do you know when it was made? "

" There it is, 1789, on the barrel. N-O-C-K, 1789."

David looked at the markings on the barrel where Margaret's finger lay. He dropped his head, and then blurted out abruptly: " I'm going to school this winter and get some learning. Save some money, too, working for Kennedys." He turned his head around to see how close the sisters were to them. Leaning toward Margaret's ear, he said softly, " And the next spring—how about you and me ——"

Covering her face with the spread fingers of one hand, Margaret smiled enigmatically at him. One of the sisters behind them was chanting: " Davy and Margaret are a-courting

[39]

Davy and Margaret are a-courting." The other sister joined her: "A-ah-ah, Davy and Margaret are a-courting, a-courting, a-courting."

Through the afternoon and into the purple dusk of the long July day, the Conestoga wagon rolled slowly along the valleys. They stopped overnight with old friends of the Elders, but were away before dawn the next morning. Late in the evening when David reached the Kennedy place, there was still light enough for Nancy to step outside the cabin for an examination of the new store-bought hunting shirt.

John Kennedy came in late from the fields, but the old Quaker had David light up a pine knot so that he, too, might see the shirt. "It's a good coat, lad. Should be giving thee service for some years. But the rifle—had I known thee was in mind of buying a rifle I shouldn't have advanced thee credit for that."

As the autumn approached, David dreaded increasingly the thought of going to school. He decided, however, that this would be the last winter he would have an opportunity to learn from books, for in the spring he would marry Margaret Elder. He had made up his mind to that, even though Margaret had been noncommittal on the subject.

After the crops were put by, he informed Kennedy that he wanted to go to school; the old man was pleased of course. "Good, good. My married son will be glad to teach thee. Thee will learn quickly, I know that."

The Quaker's married son, Edmund Kennedy, had moved to a small cabin only a mile and a half from his father's place, and several children were attending his school. David was the oldest pupil, which was embarrassing to him the first few days. Under the arrangement with the Quaker, David was to attend school the first four days of each week, and work on the farm the last two days. He thought the first day of school would never end. But the next week, he was eager to start again.

Already he had learned the letters of the alphabet, and wanted to begin putting them together so as to make words.

Edmund Kennedy resembled his brother, William, physically, but his mind was much more alert than William's, and unlike William he enjoyed talking. David soon got to like Edmund; he thought there was nothing the young schoolmaster did not know. Several nights, instead of returning to the Quaker's place to sleep, he sat up late with Edmund, talking, and then slept the night out on a floor pallet. Edmund seemed as excited as David when the latter was able to read from the Knoxville *Gazette* an acount of Andy Jackson's duel with Nolichucky Jack Sevier. Edmund was opposed to dueling, but he talked long of Jackson, of how he had attained greatness against many obstacles. Another favorite topic of conversation between the two was the expedition of Lewis and Clark; both David and Edmund agreed that someday, they, too, would explore some of the vast territory west of the Mississippi.

"This east Tennessee land is poor," Edmund said. "A man must go west to prosper. If I were single as you are, Davy, I would go now, anywhere, west."

David did not speak of Margaret Elder. Perhaps a man might marry and also go west. Several Sundays, he slipped away from the Kennedy place for visits with Margaret. Always she was gay and smiling, always she was eager for courting. Even when the ground was frozen she would go with him, wrapped in a heavy cloak, to the dark places in the cedar woods near the Elder cabin. Yet always was she evasive when he spoke of marriage, and on his return home late at nights through the crisp frosty woods there was a nameless fear in his thoughts, a longing for the unattainable.

As it does when men's minds and bodies are filled with new experiences, time flowed by with incredible swiftness. Winter was gone, spring was come again, and Margaret had not given her promise.

[41]

On a Sunday in April he started for the Elder cabin, crossed the creek, and turning up the hill met Jesse Wilson. It was the first time he had seen Jesse since the day he had returned Abe's rifle; David was surprised to see considerable changes in his appearance. Jesse's face was clean, and he was wearing new clothing, a hunting shirt much more elaborate in its decorative effects than David's. Unconsciously, David had looked down at his own shirt, comparing it with Jesse's, reluctantly admitting to himself that Jesse's was the more elegant of the two.

Neither spoke. Jesse walked rapidly, grinning at David, his two front teeth thrust out, turning his head, still grinning as he walked on down the hill.

When David reached the Elder cabin he was surprised to find Margaret alone. The others had gone for a visiting, she explained.

She was strangely silent, sitting across the room. David was irritated; this was a most excellent opportunity for courting, having the cabin to themselves. When he walked across the room, touching her, she drew back.

" We could walk, then, down by the cedars," he suggested later.

" No," she said.

He looked at her quickly. " Tell me. Was Jesse Wilson here? "

" Supposing I don't say? "

" Was he here? "

She nodded. David did not even say good-bye. He got up and walked out the open door, holding his coonskin cap tight in his hand, walked slowly down the hill past the cedars. He could hear her calling his name, but he did not look back.

For a month he did not see Margaret Elder, a month made more torturous for him than it might have been by the romantic activities of Nancy and William. It was the month of their

[42]

wedding, and the preparations and whisperings surrounding the marriage were constant reminders to him of his own wrecked plans.

But there was a day in May when Nancy and William came to him in the field, William blushing more furiously than Nancy, to tell David that he and Margaret were to wait on them at their wedding.

" She is now at the house," said Nancy.

David dropped his hoe. " She has come to the house? "

" She said you were angry with her." Nancy smiled. " But you'll make up, won't you, for our wedding? "

Jerking his head forward in quick assent, he followed after them, impatient at their slowness. When he met Margaret he pretended indifference; his vanity was touched that she had come to the Quakers' house to see him.

The wedding of Nancy and William was a simple affair. Their two attendants were much more gaily dressed than they. David had carefully brushed his hunting coat, and had cleaned the red and blue fringes until they looked as fresh as when the coat was new. As for Margaret she wore a dark red dress gathered so tightly at the waist that John Kennedy gave her several disapproving glances.

In the evening there was a marriage feast with plum pudding and cider. David saw that Margaret was impressed with the ceremonies, and he realized that the time was advantageous for him to suggest a like occasion for themselves. To his surprise she agreed, and for a moment he was elated. " But David, you have nothing, not even enough to buy the marriage license, or build a cabin."

" I have a rifle," he said quickly. " I can soon get enough furs to buy a dozen marriage licenses. And I can build us a cabin myself."

Margaret smiled at him. " When you've done it, we'll be married."

It seemed to David that for years he had been wishing his life away, wishing for time to pass so that he might achieve something that was obscured always in the future. All the summer now, he marked the passing of the days. Furs were of little value if caught before the snow fell, and he must have furs to sell before he could marry Margaret.

But when cold weather did come, he discovered that long trips were necessary if he hoped to secure good furs, two- or three-day journeys back into the Clinch Mountains. Also John Kennedy seemed to begrudge him the time he used for hunting, and finally forbade his taking the rifle out Sundays.

The Quakers in the neighborhood had begun holding services at their various cabins, and David was expected to attend. Several times he begged off; once when the services were held at the Kennedy place he told Kennedy he was ailing, went up to his new sleeping room in the attic, slid down a pole, and ran off through the woods to see Margaret. He stayed with her in the cedars until both of them were blue with cold. When he started back home snow had begun to fall, and the next day he was sick with a cold. He was certain that he was going to die, that he was being punished for sinning, but Nancy's asafetida and hot water treatments made him well again in a few days. For two successive Sundays he attended the Quaker services, resolving that he would never again disobey the commands of John Kennedy.

As spring did approach again, he found himself beginning to wish it would not come too quickly; he had so few furs that he was afraid to calculate their value. He owed several dollars for gunpowder, and after that amount was deducted he knew he would have little money left, scarcely enough even to buy the marriage license. He was prepared, therefore, when Margaret demanded an accounting of his savings before she would set the wedding date.

[44]

"Are you aiming to marry me, or what I've got in my sock?" he asked.

She only laughed.

He went off furious not only with her but with the whole world; both seemed always to ask for more than they were willing to give.

The restless summer passed. In August he was twenty years old, and there was a birthday dinner for him at his father's tavern. But he was wretched through it all, wishing for money, wishing for Margaret.

On an October night he was with Margaret in the cedars. They lay on crackling leaves that had just fallen from the surrounding oaks, with the moonlight like silver on the cedars. It was she who said they would be married. "I reckon we'd better," she said. "Purty soon, now."

The next day he went to the settlement below his father's tavern; he passed the blacksmith shop, whistling, walked briskly up to the log-cabin courthouse.

It was a nerve-wracking business, this purchasing a marriage license, signing your name to a paper promising to the Governor of Tennessee on your bond that you would marry Margaret Elder. He wondered why the Governor was mixed up in the matter; marrying must be even more serious an affair than he had thought.

David gave all the coonskins he had for the flimsy piece of paper that entitled him to be wed. He thought the fee rather high, but he was of no mind to dicker. He had waited long enough for marrying.

Margaret had set the time for the wedding on the following Thursday. The preceding Saturday, John Kennedy had David up before daybreak husking corn. He worked very badly, sometimes sitting quite still for five or ten minutes with a shuck in one hand and an ear of corn in the other, staring at the blank wall of the barn. Around noon, he suddenly remembered he had not spoken to Margaret's parents about the wedding.

" I would like to go for the rest of the day," he said to Kennedy.

The old Quaker looked at David solemnly. " What reason have thee, lad? We've a sight of husking to be done here."

" I've just got to go."

" Well, in truth, if thee work no better the rest of the day than thee did work this morning, thee might as well go."

But when he saw David come out of the attic room with his rifle in hand, he spoke to him sternly: " Would thee be going to the shooting match down road, Davy? "

" No, sir," David replied quickly. " No, sir. I thought I might see some deer in the woods. They're right much plentiful this year."

He had not intended to go to the shooting match. In fact, he had forgotten about the match. But as he walked through the forests toward the Elder cabin, he began thinking of how it was right on his way, if he cut back to the road, and how he might win the prize, something he would be needing now that he was going to be a man with a wife to keep.

The shooting match was just beginning when he arrived at the clearing where it was held. Under the rules for the day two marksmen were required to form partnerships for the competition. A young boy who had attended Edmund Kennedy's school with David agreed to join him in the shooting.

Although most of the competitors were much older than the two boys, they survived the first elimination, and before anyone could realize it they were out in front. David himself was surprised at his accuracy, and, even had his partner been a poor shot, they would have won the prize, which was a fine fat beef.

The crowd milled around him, offering congratulations. " How much am I offered for my half? " he cried. " I'm going to get married and need the hard cash."

"Glory be," a grizzled old man with black whiskers sprouting like porcupine quills slapped him on the back. " I'd oughta knowed you was handy with the gals from the way you hit them pegs with yore rifle." He laughed uproariously, louder than the others. " The beef ain't worth more'n three dollars, but since you're marrying, here's five." He opened a leather pouch and dropped two gold pieces into David's opened hands.

This was indeed a wedding gift for Margaret. And he was not afraid now of Tom Elder or his wife. No doubt he, David Crockett, was the best marksman in Tennessee, a highly desirable son-in-law. Whistling loudly, jingling the gold coins merrily in his pocket, he hurried along the road and turned off at the creek, running at a dog's trot. He noticed that a cabin had recently been completed near the road. Remembering that Margaret had said one of her uncles was moving there, David stopped, looked up at the sun, and saw that the afternoon was yet young. Since Margaret's uncle was soon to become his uncle, why not, he thought, introduce himself. I, David Crockett, sir, your nephew to be, and if I do say so, the best shot in all Tennessee.

Yellow leaves and hickory nuts were swirling and thumping down in showers from the trees as he walked into the yard. The afternoon was warm, Indian summer, and the door to the cabin was swung wide in the sunlight. For a moment, he thought that it was Margaret he saw inside, but it was one of her sisters.

" How you, Jane? " He jerked off his cap, swinging gaily up the gravelly pathway.

Jane had come to the door, her hands fluttering up to her face, down to her apron strings. Her mouth opened, but she could nót speak.

" Is it all well at home, Jane? "

As he came closer, she stepped back, hands still moving nervously. David chuckled, reached out with his arms, pre-

[47]

tended to box her ears. "Whyn't you speak? Scared of me 'cause I'm going to be your brother-in-law? "

Abruptly Jane began sniffling, soon was crying so loudly that David looked inside the cabin for some clue to the girl's surprising behavior. In the shadows of the room he could see a tall gaunt woman, with a face devoid of all emotion. The woman's mouth was moving. " Go on, tell him, Janey. Tell him."

" Davy, Davy." Jane finally stopped sobbing long enough to look up at him. " It's Margaret. Margaret's run off from home."

He caught her shoulders roughly. " What you mean, what you mean, Jane? "

" She run off with Jesse Wilson."

He did not believe; he could not let himself believe. This was a fine joke they were playing, a fine joke. He looked at Jane, trying to laugh at her, but Jane was weeping again, and the gaunt woman in the doorway stared at him with eyes that lacked all sympathy or pity.

Once when he was very small he had fallen from a tree; the sudden contact with the earth had crushed the breath from his body, and he had remained stunned and speechless for several minutes. This, he tried to think, was a repetition of that long forgotten experience. High he had climbed, looking down upon the lowly earth from his safe perch in the tree, and then, there he was stunned upon the ground.

But on this Indian summer's day, with the gold and yellow leaves spinning around his head, he was standing safely enough, it seemed, upon his two feet. There was no sense to any of it, at least he could make no sense of it. The world had come to an end, and here were three people trying to make sense of it.

There was no point in talking about it. He turned and walked away from the cabin, the small gravel crunching and slipping under his moccasins. Jane followed after him, bab-

[48]

bling incoherently. *Would he come back with her to their house? She would go with him. Her father and mother preferred him. Jesse Wilson was a no-good nobody. You might even break off the match.*

But he walked on to the creek, not bothering to step upon the dry rocks, splashing his feet in the water, Jane's voice growing fainter and fainter, her words rolling around and around in a void like stones in a barrel.

★ 5 ★

" There's as good fish in the sea as has ever been caught out of it." Katrina Dykeman was laughing at David from behind the rail fence that separated the Kennedy farm from the Widow Dykeman's new cabin.

This was the third or fourth time that Katrina had spoken to him about fish in the sea, and David, his back turned to her, did not bother to reply. He calmly continued picking the dried field peas, dropping them methodically into his sack, wishing Katrina would go away. If she, with her homely square face, thought she was a good fish in the sea, she would wait a long time if she was counting on him to throw out a line.

He was convinced that all women were creatures set on the earth by the Devil to plague the men; he had resolved to have as little as possible to do with them for the remainder of his natural life.

Katrina was still laughing at him in that deep throaty voice of hers. He was thinking that everybody in Tennessee must know about his being jilted, and with the marriage license in his pocket, too.

It was too much for mortal man to bear.

He stood up straight, stretching his arms slowly up to the blue autumn sky, and then spoke to Katrina Dykeman. "You

[49]

womenfolks are all pieces of deceit," he said with the finality of a man of experience.

" Maybe it is too easy for you to lose your heart," Katrina replied.

" No," he said solemnly, " I am a man born odd. God forgot to make a mate for me."

Katrina clucked her tongue, and laughed loudly. Looking at her, David thought he had never seen so homely a creature in his life. She had crossed her plump elbows on the top railing of the fence, her wide mouth stretched in a grotesque grin. " What would you say if I told you I knowed a gal who'd make a fine match for you? " She twisted her head to one side. " And purty as a pitcher, she is, Davy, so purty she can't be talked of along with the one you're pining away for."

David shook his head. " Margaret may be a little varmint, all right, but she's the purtiest piece of flesh and blood in Tennessee, I'll lay a bet on that."

" Stop yore talk. Remember there's as good and better fish in the sea. You just come to the reaping over at Squiers' place next Saturday, and you'll be whistling another tune. This little gal that's going to be there is just the one for you."

He shook his head again. " I'm born odd, I tell you. There's no mate for me."

Facing the bright autumn sun, Katrina's eyes were drawn down to a squint. " Come to the reaping anyhow, Davy. There's good dancing afterwards. Old man Squiers has got two nigger fiddlers."

His eyes brightened. " I'm kind of fond of fiddle music."

" And I'll bet you're the dancingest and singingest fool in the country." She was laughing her husky gurgling laugh again, her wide mouth twisting.

" Maybe. But no one gal for me. I'll dance with all of 'em, kind of a lone wolf." He laughed softly, for the first time in days, feeling much better. " For sure, I'll be at the reaping."

[50]

Albert Squiers could not have picked a better day for the reaping; the air was dry and crisp and still, the bright sunshine just warm enough to be comfortable.

David was surprised that John Kennedy objected to his going. " It would be best that thee stay at home, lad. There will be much bad company at this reaping. Good folk say the Squiers are too much given to riotous pleasures."

" But I've promised to be there, sir."

" Thee should be more careful of promises. A man's name is his fortune, and of late thee've frequented with folk whose names are not as good as the name of David Crockett."

" Thank you, sir, I'll remember that," David replied hurriedly. While he crossed the Kennedy field and started across the ridge to Squiers' place he thought about the Quaker's words, and was not sure that he knew what John Kennedy meant by riotous pleasures. He wondered if Kennedy had ever attended a dancing party, or was merely content to judge them by what he had heard others say about them.

Albert Squiers' farm was one of the best in the valley, and as David walked down from the wooded ridge he looked with pleasure upon the still waves of golden wheat and flax glittering with tiny dots of morning dew. Squiers was a good farmer even if he did not have a reputation for sobriety.

Already a good-sized crowd of boys and girls and a few older persons who enjoyed reaping parties were gathered around the Squiers cabin. Albert Squiers, a rotund red-faced man with short bowed legs, was passing around gourds filled with cider. His face was wrinkled with smiles. Every time he laughed his fat belly would shake violently until he slapped it sharply, an action which seemed always to bring it to rest.

"Hell-o, Davy." Squiers thrust a dripping gourd under David's nose, and he drank the sour cider in a quick gulp. " Come over to find another gal, eh, Davy? Well, there's goin' to be some purty little fillies here, some purty little fillies."

[51]

" Not looking for no particular gal," David replied softly.

" Heh, heh, that's what you say, that's what you say." Squiers moved on with the cider jug.

In a few minutes, sickles and cradles were passed around to those who had not brought tools. Although David wanted a cradle, there were only a few, and so he had to take a sickle. With a cradle a man could cut a wider, cleaner swath through the wheat without bending his back half as much as when he was using a sickle.

Some of the younger and more inexperienced reapers started off with a great display of energy, slashing at the yellow grain as if it were a mighty tribe of Indians which must be exterminated immediately. But David kept back with the older men who swung their sickles in slow rhythmic curves. They were soon gaining steadily on the advance group, and began taunting them.

" Look at their britches sweat! " Recognizing the voice of the porcupine-whiskered fellow who had given him the gold pieces at the shooting match, David turned his head quickly. He grinned at the man and shouted: " Them britches'll be dragging the stubble afore we cross the field."

When they caught up with the front line, David badgered a tall red-haired youngster until the latter agreed to give up his cradle for David's sickle if David was first to reach the end of the field. David won the race by several yards, grabbing the coveted cradle jubilantly. The sun was shining hot on his back now, and he stopped for breath, perspiration dripping off the end of his nose.

Starting back, the reapers had to turn sharply to avoid a clump of black fire-scarred trees. Here they met a group of late starters.

Bounding along in front of them, swinging his sickle with a graceful rhythm, laughing his deep rumbling laugh—was nobody else but Joseph Hawkins.

[52]

"Uncle Joseph!" David tossed his cradle aside and was running, leaping through the thick grain like a deer. He was laughing so hard he was crying when he caught his uncle's ham of a hand and tried to outsqueeze him.

"By the eternal," roared Joseph Hawkins. "Davy, you're looking as peart as a young coon dog."

"I thought you was gone to Nashville, Uncle Joseph."

"So I was, boy, but when Albert Squiers has a reaping party, you can bet your last ounce of powder that Joseph Hawkins 'll be there, ah-hah-hah."

Except for a few streaks of gray which had appeared in his long black mane of hair, Joseph Hawkins had not changed in the few years that had passed since David had seen him. "Come on, Davy, join up with us, and we'll trade some talk."

As they swung down the field, Hawkins began a lengthy recital of his various adventures in Nashville. "With my own pair of eyes, Davy, I saw Andy Jackson, old Andy. Been fighting another doo-el, he has. And this fellow, Aaron Burr, was high-stepping around Nashville with him. Ain't got much use for Aaron Burr, myself."

"I never heard tell of him," said David. He had paused for a moment, leaning on the cradle handle, catching his breath.

"A mean man, greasy as a fresh cut hog. Killed Alexander Hamilton in doo-el. Lots of talk back in Nashville about him trying to set up a new gov'ment across the Mississippi River somewhere."

"Is Andy Jackson going to help him?" David was thinking that perhaps he might join in the adventure, fighting Spaniards and Indians, some place, where there were not any women around to plague a man.

Joseph Hawkins wiped his face on his sleeve; his forehead wrinkled in a dark frown. "The good Lord knows, boy. Old Andy's a quick-acting man. But I hope he don't mix up with this Aaron Burr." He broke out in a sudden laugh. "But what in tuck we worrying about such things for? Why, look at all them purty gals behind us! "

Following them was the first group of girls, gathering and binding the wheat into sheaves. " Lord a-mighty," said Hawkins. " Do listen. A-chattering like crows after corn, they are."

" If they can dance as well as they cackle," said David, " we'll be well paid tonight for our sweating."

His uncle looked at him admiringly. " You talk just like a Hawkins, boy, ah-hah-hah."

At noon they ate a hasty dinner served on the ground in front of Albert Squiers' cabin. But they were soon back in the fields, eager to finish the reaping before darkness fell. The sun was still high above the line of hills to the northwest when the last swath of wheat went down before the shining sickles. Now the men joined the girls, teasing them about their slowness at binding. With loud talk and songs and laughter, the binding was finished before the shadows grayed out into twilight.

The Squiers family had already prepared a grand feast beside the cabin, on the hard-packed earth that would later serve as the dance floor. Logs had been brought up for seats, and a huge fire of leaves and brush was burning to one side.

" There'll be frost on the moon tonight," said Squiers, thumping his belly. He was passing around a platter of roasted chestnuts still warm from the fire.

David sat alone at one end of a log, watching the sparks fly up from the fire, the sweet smoke from the brown leaves blowing in his face.

" Evenin', Davy," Katrina Dykeman's deep voice brought him back to earth.

" How you, Katrina? "

" Fat as a bear, Davy, and feeling fine and dandy. I want you to meet a fine lady, a Mrs. Finley." Katrina moved to one side as David slid off the log to his feet. A large moon-

[54]

faced Irishwoman stared at him with her steel-blue eyes until he felt his face burning in embarrassment. " Pleased to meet you," he mumbled.

Mrs. Finley thrust a huge stringy hand stiffly toward him, and he shook it awkwardly. She said not a word, nor did she take her eyes from his face. Removing a black oak twig from her mouth she dipped it deftly into a bladder of snuff she was carrying in her apron pocket. Thrusting the twig back in her mouth, she rubbed it back and forth between her teeth, and then spat suddenly upon the ground.

" He's got mighty purty red cheeks, ain't he, Katrina? "

David's cheeks turned more crimson than ever now; he was hating Katrina with all his heart for bringing this woman to meet him. Who was she to poke fun at him? He hated all the women in the world.

" Katrina, I think I never did see a boy with such purty cheeks. Mister Davy Crockett, I think we got a sweetheart for you."

He dropped his head, looking at Mrs. Finley's feet, wishing he had listened to the Quaker and stayed at home. Katrina was laughing, way down in her throat, nudging him with her elbow. " Better speak up, Davy. She's the mother of the little gal I was telling you about."

Mrs. Finley had turned her back, shading her eyes, peering across the yard. " Now where is that young-un? Polly! Pol-ly! " Her voice shrilled up when she called.

David was thinking that if Mrs. Finley's daughter was no more pleasing to the sight than her mother, he would rather die than meet her. And when he saw Katrina start after Mrs. Finley in the search for the missing Polly, he ran quickly behind the blazing bonfire, sneaking around to the other side of the yard.

Here he was relieved to find Joseph Hawkins engaged in a violent argument with Albert Squiers. What they were arguing

[55]

about was of no concern to David; he was satisfied merely to stand beside them, safe from the jibes and tricks of women.

In a few minutes, Squiers' two Negro slaves came out from the barn, bringing two stools and their fiddles. Squiers immediately set about lighting the pine-knot torches hanging in the trees around the yard. As the lights blazed up, David stood with his uncle, watching the Negroes tune their fiddles.

" Squiers says his niggers can beat any fiddlers in Tennessee. I told him he was a lunatic. Why over in Nashville ——" Joseph Hawkins rambled on, his words pleasant to David's ears. He watched the Negroes' faces, their round close-cropped heads bobbing and jerking as they squeaked a few notes on their instruments, their heavy lips rising over white grinning teeth.

Apparently out of thin air Joseph Hawkins had produced a jug of whiskey. " Here, take a snort of this, Davy. Squiers has got barrels of cider all over the place, but I say there ain't nothing like a few snorts of red-eyed moonshine to set a man's feet loose for dancing."

The liquor burned David's throat; then he could feel it spreading out slowly in his stomach. The Negroes were still scraping away with their bows, producing vague melodies, ending in sudden raucous notes. The pine-knot torches fluttered in the quiet breeze. Across the yard coming out of the cabin, he saw a group of girls, one of them holding her skirts daintily as she tripped out a mock dance. She wore a gay blue handkercher around her head.

Beneath one of the pine knots, just across from him, she stopped, her mouth half open in expectancy as she watched the musicians. The light played upon her face.

David stared, the warmth in his stomach flowing all through his being. He watched every move of her slender restless body, her eyes, gay with the excitement of the evening, turning about the crowd. He had forgotten everything, the time, the place, everything but this girl.

"Ah-hah-hah." Joseph Hawkins' laugh was subdued. " Ain't she a purty one, though? "

David said nothing. He knew that almost everyone in the crowd was watching this girl. Her excitement was transmitted to them and they too were becoming excited.

Suddenly the Negro fiddlers drew out a full and vigorous call to the dance, and Albert Squiers popped into the middle of the hard-packed earthen square like a jack-in-the-box, patting his fat belly in a fast rhythm. The crowd began applauding, shouting and clapping hands.

" Hands all around, set-to, and face your pardner," cried Squiers. In the sudden bustle of movement he spilled his gourdful of cider on his waistcoat, and everybody laughed. " Get your pardners, balance all! " he shouted.

" Well "—David felt his uncle's bristling chin close against his own—" ain't you going to ask her to break-down with you? All these clods are scared of her, she's so purty. Go grab her quick."

Stepping between the swinging lines of dancers, David crossed the yard quickly, bowed, and reached for the girl's hand. He did not speak. He was too frightened at first to look at her face; he could feel her resist slightly, but then she followed him, and they swung out into the midst of the swirling jumping mob of dancers.

It seemed they had scarcely started when the music stopped and Albert Squiers was out in the middle of the yard again. In his hands he held a leather-covered cushion, which rested at a ludicrous angle upon his abdomen. When they saw the cushion, several of the boys and younger men began shouting, for it was only at Albert Squiers' place that they were allowed to dance the cushion dance.

[57]

David was still holding the girl's hand, but all of her fingers except one had slipped loose. He turned to look at her. She was looking at him sidewise, smiling slightly. He felt fine, warm all over when he saw her smile.

"Here y'are, Davy." Albert Squiers shoved against him with the cushion. "Here, here, you dumb ox, take this cushion." Already the music had started, swift and antic in its movement. The dancers had formed a wide circle, scuffling slowly around him and Albert Squiers and the Negroes; Squiers had withdrawn to the side of the musicians where he might watch the proceedings.

For a moment David was terrified. He realized that a great favor had been bestowed upon him by Albert Squiers, and he knew what he was supposed to do with the cushion. Out of the corner of his eyes he could see Squiers begin clapping his hands; the crowd around him followed the host's example. The merry music, the rhythmic clapping in concert of hands, the warm liquor spreading through his body—all combined to restore his confidence.

His feet skipped lightly along the ground; he held the cushion balanced between his hands. As he circled the ring his eyes met the eyes of the girl for an instant; but she looked quickly away from him. Suddenly he remembered he did not even know her name. Again he danced around the circle, saw Katrina Dykeman grinning at him, danced on until he was rubbing his elbows against Albert Squiers. "What's her name?" he whispered. "What's her name?"

"Heh? What say?" The noise was growing louder in volume, and Squiers leaned closer against him.

"What's the gal's name, the one I was dancing with?" David saw Squiers nod; then he danced around the circle again coming back to him. Squiers' cidery breath blew in his face. "Her name's Polly Finley. I thought you knowed her name."

Polly Finley! That old moon-faced Irishwoman's daughter? He could not believe it. He had stopped dancing, and the boys were hooting at him to select a girl. Polly Finley.

The shouts of the dancers rang in his ears. He swung around the circle clumsily, found the girl's face in the blurring crowd, and dropped the cushion at her feet.

Instantly the music stopped, the hand clapping faded out quickly like a swiftly passing shower. The silence was so sudden David almost forgot his words; then he blurted them out: " This dance it will no further go! "

Albert Squiers' voice echoed back in the crisp air: " I pray you, good sir, why say so? "

" Because, because "—he looked straight up into the girl's face—" because Polly Finley will not come to! "

" She must come to whether she will or no," cried Squiers.

With the toe of his moccasin, David pushed the leather cushion closer to the girl and kneeled before it. He could see her eyes wide and bright in the light from the torches. Then she was kneeling on the cushion, her lips quivering in a shy smile.

" Welcome, Polly Finley."

He should have sung the words, loud for all the crowd and Albert Squiers to hear, but his voice was soft and husky. " Welcome, Polly Finley," he repeated, and shut his eyes and kissed her on the lips, a breathless kiss on the lips, while the circle of dancers made smacking noises and screamed like panthers.

Now the music was going again, slow and rollicking, and he could hear Albert Squiers: " Up, up, finish the dance, give somebody else a turn." The girl and he were dancing around the circle again, holding the cushion between them. " Prinkum, prankum is a fine dance, and shall we dance it over again? " They tried to sing together but he finished last, Polly laughing and nodding assent at the same time. She had the cushion, swinging around the circle which David now joined. For him all time had stopped, and the others in the circle had become wooden puppets making sounds and movements; he was dizzy with watching her skip around the circle until she found him and dropped the cushion in front of his feet. The kiss was even briefer than the first, for the circle dissolved around them while Albert Squiers set about selecting another worthy dancer.

In the confusion he became separated from the girl, moving back into the semi-darkness of the outer yard. He stood staring up at the stars. Above the sounds of the music he could hear wolves howling in the hills to the north. A twig cracked beside him, and he turned, and she was there. Somehow, before he saw her, he knew she would be there. He touched her hand, and they stood quite still for a few minutes and then without speaking went back to one of the log seats, where they sat down, watching the circle of dancers begin a repetition of the cushion dance.

" How'd you know my name was Davy Crockett? " he asked.

" Katrina told me. We saw you in the wheat today. She talks about you all the time."

" Uh-huh. She lives over by Kennedys'."

" You work for Mr. Kennedy, don't you? "

" Uh, yes'm."

She punched him with her finger. " Yes'm," she mocked. " My name's Polly."

" Polly."

They looked straight ahead at the dancers, at their grotesque shadows bobbing on the ground. Then a larger shadow fell across their faces, and in front of them was Mrs. Finley, hands on hips, her feet spread wide.

" Hell fire in the mountains," she said, tossing her head to one side. " I been searching all over the Holston valley for you two rapscallions so as to make you acquainted to one another.

[60]

And then what—I find you setting together on a log a-courting like a pair of coo-birds." She stopped to catch her breath. "You young folks work too fast for an old lady such as me."

"He's a good dancer, ma," said Polly.

"I bet he's the dancingest fool in the country." She sat down beside David, breathing heavily. "Well, son-in-law, what you think of my daughter?"

David was at a loss for words until he felt Polly squeezing his arm reassuringly. "I'll be telling her that in private, thank you, ma'm," he said quickly.

Mrs. Finley shook with laughter. "A bodacious feller, ain't he, Polly? And ain't he got the purtiest cheeks, though?"

David was positive the old lady was trying to make a joke of him. He would trust Polly, all right, but not Mrs. Finley. Most women were treacherous beings and he was on his guard. He was glad when he saw Joseph Hawkins coming toward them a few minutes later, for Mrs. Finley's sharp tongue was about to get the better of him. "Uncle Joseph," he called. "Polly, this is my Uncle Joseph Hawkins. And Mrs. Finley."

"A lovely daughter you have, Mrs. Finley," said Joseph Hawkins, bowing.

"I reckon she's fit for my new son-in-law," she replied tartly, pinching David's arm.

"Ah-hah-hah-hah," roared Joseph Hawkins. "Would you be dancing this next dance with me, Mrs. Finley? Or is your husband about?"

"Lord no, he's home, likely drunker'n a coot-owl. I ain't much for dancing, but I'll run a set with you, Mr. Hawkins."

While they were talking a young man with black hair combed tightly back from his forehead walked up to Polly. When David turned back to her she was walking away with the stranger to join the dance.

Disconsolate, David sat down on the log. Mrs. Finley and Joseph Hawkins had left him. All he could think of was Polly

[61]

Finley dancing with the slick-haired boy, and then of how she had kissed him. He drew his knees up, hugging them tightly with his arms.

" Davy Crockett, what in thunder you doing setting out here, on this log? " Katrina Dykeman shook a fat forefinger at him. " Letting that Luke Powell take Polly away from you."

" She went," he said.

" And Mrs. Finley gone, too. You better be good to Mrs. Finley. Salt the cow to catch the calf." Katrina laughed and walked away.

Later he found Uncle Joseph, and asked immediately for another drink. " Well, boy, if this wasn't a mighty fine dancing party I'd say no, no more drinks. But since it's the dagfiredest dancing party I ever seen, here's the bottle."

He drank long and thirstily. With his throat choking him he turned and walked back to the dancers, seeking out Polly Finley in the haze of smoke and shadows. He saw but dimly the dark face of Luke Powell when he swung Polly out in the swirling mass of bodies.

The reaping parties of Albert Squiers never ended until break of day. But even the sturdiest of the dancers were weary by the time the stars began paling in the sky. The pine torches were fluttering out one by one and, in the gray light, scattered around the yard beside the logs and flat upon the ground, were the casualties of the dance, brought low by sleep or too much drinking. Joseph Hawkins, his head resting upon a log, was one of the loudest of the snorers.

There were many, though, who trooped joyously into the Squiers cabin for the final event of the party, the blindfold game. David managed to get Polly Finley for a partner, but was scarcely able to look at her for casting triumphant glances at Luke Powell who sat glowering at him from a stool in one corner. However, David was dismayed when he learned that Polly and her mother were going home in Luke Powell's wagon. "His folks are neighbor-people to us, over by the Big Gap," she said.

When the blindfold game was ended, the party rapidly began to break up. Couples left on horseback, or on foot. Luke Powell had hitched his horses to his flat wagon, pulling it up to the front of the cabin. David helped Mrs. Finley and Polly upon the wagon bed, watching Luke Powell standing to one side, his dark Indian-like face twisted in a scowl.

He had turned and started across the yard to rouse his Uncle Joseph when he heard a sudden stealthy movement behind him. Luke Powell had caught his arm in a powerful grip.

"Look a-here, Davy Crockett. I don't know who you be, and don't give a damn, but I'm telling you this. Don't ever let me see you around my gal agin. Polly Finley is my gal." Powell's face was close to his, his dark skin appearing even darker in his anger.

David twisted his arm loose. "You can go sit in hell." He turned his back on Luke Powell. His head was spinning with all the madness of the dying night, and he cared little what Luke Powell might do. He never had any luck with women anyhow. There was always someone else, somebody lurking in the shadows.

But he heard Luke's footsteps retreating toward the wagon, and then, in front of him, the sound of Uncle Joseph snoring. He wheeled around, watching Luke Powell's wagon roll away to the east, but the sun was already up, blinding his eyes so that he could not see Polly Finley waving her blue handkercher to him in the wind.

★ 6 ★

Edmund Kennedy's school had so increased in enrollment this autumn that he could scarcely find time to attend to the ordinary odd jobs around his farm. His fences needed mending, his woodpile needed replenishing, and oftentimes his stock went hungry while he helped his pupils with their lessons.

One day he asked David if he knew of any boy who would like to work through the coming winter for his keep.

" What would you be willing to add to the keep? " asked David.

" Well," said Edmund, " you know as well as I do that I can't give any money. My pupils all pay in kind, a slab of salt meat, or a sack of meal."

"You've got an extra horse, now." David looked at Edmund slyly.

" Old Tom, yes."

" He's getting old," said David. " But Tom's still a good horse. I'll work for you all winter for Old Tom and my keep—if your pa's willing to let me leave him."

As cold weather was coming on, John Kennedy decided that he and William could attend to most of the tasks around the farm, and agreed to David's going to Edmund's place for the winter. David was pleased with the change. While John Kennedy had always been kind, David thought he was too much inclined to give advice and issue orders. With Edmund it was different; he considered David an equal, giving him complete freedom as long as he kept things ship-shape around the farm.

He had thought he might soon forget Polly Finley, but instead he found himself unconsciously planning his future with Polly as the center of it all. He sometimes wondered, while he was splitting logs or watering the stock, how he could have suffered a single moment of unhappiness over the loss of Margaret Elder. He had an idea that some unknown power had rescued him from Margaret. The fact that she had chosen Jesse Wilson was proof enough to him now that she did not have the brains of a wild rabbit, and he wondered why he could not have seen it that way at the time the thing was

[64]

happening. One day he caught himself laughing aloud, thinking of Margaret running away with Jesse Wilson, and promised himself that if he ever met with Jesse again he would shake his hand and tell him he was the best friend he ever had.

But then he got to thinking about Luke Powell, wondering if Polly preferred him, with his dark ugly face and his black hair slicked tightly back from his forehead. He decided he had to know, had to see Polly and find out, for good and ever, where he stood. He did not intend to spend the remainder of his life mooning around, thinking about a woman.

Early on a Sunday morning, a few weeks after he had begun working for Edmund, he put a bridle on Old Tom and started for the Big Gap. This part of the Holston valley was new territory for him. As he knew only the general direction of the Gap, he had to stop several times to make inquiries along the way.

Before starting on the journey David had borrowed some of Edmund's bear grease, slicking his hair down like Luke Powell's. However, he had left his shabby old coonskin cap behind, and the wind tousled his hair into greasy knots. The condition of his hair worried him for a time, but after he reached the Big Gap neighborhood he became so concerned with the business of finding the Finley cabin that he stopped thinking about his hair.

It was mid-afternoon before he found the place, a low, rambling cabin built snugly against a sharp rock cliff, almost surrounded by a curving brook foaming with rapids. The Finley farm widened out triangularly up the stream. Polly's father evidently made his living mainly from trapping, for hides were nailed all over the outer walls of the cabin and some even hung grotesquely from the trees.

A brown-bearded man thrust his head out of one of the windows as David guided Old Tom across the noisy brook. By the time he had dismounted and fastened a halter to a tree

[65]

limb, the brown-bearded man was out in the yard, looking at him with friendly sparkling eyes as brown as his beard.

"Hello," said David. "My name's David Crockett."

"I reckon I've heard the name." The brown-bearded man approached, walking with a slight limp. "That gal of mine has been saying Davy Crockett this, and Davy Crockett that, for the last two or three weeks."

David couldn't help grinning when he heard this. "Suppose you must be her pa?"

"Yep. Old Billy Finley, that's me. Come in and set a while. Polly ain't t'home yet. But here's the old lady."

Mrs. Finley was standing in the doorway, her long skinny arms akimbo. "Hell fire in the mountains," said she, "if 'tain't Davy Crockett."

"Yes'm, it's me," said David.

The inside of the Finley cabin was filled with all sorts of hickory furniture, turned and polished with remarkable craftsmanship. He sat down on a wide bench that was a twin to another on the opposite side of the stone fireplace. Both benches were piled high with indigo-colored pillows, thrown indiscriminately along the seat and over the arms.

"Mighty soft setting," said David, feeling of the pillows.

"Polly made 'em," said Mrs. Finley. "Right smart gal, Polly is."

Neither Mrs. Finley nor her husband had offered an explanation of Polly's absence. David decided it was none of his business, but he hoped she would come home before Mrs. Finley got to talking a blue streak. She was already relating incidents that had happened at the reaping party, declaring it was a pity Mr. Finley had stayed at home that evening drinking from his bottles.

"Well, Jeannie, you might explain to the lad as how bad I was with the rheumatics. He might get the idea as how old Billy Finley is a sot."

[66]

"And he wouldn't be much wrong at that," retorted Mrs. Finley. "It's either a-drinking you are from a bottle, or a-sipping one of your nasty-tasting herb potions."

Mr. Finley was stroking his thick brown beard with one hand and rubbing his ailing rheumatic knee with the other. "Maybe David would be liking to see my herbs and teas?"

David did not know what Mr. Finley had reference to, but thinking that perhaps it might be an opportunity to escape temporarily from Mrs. Finley he pretended interest in her husband's herbs and teas.

"Well, well. Come on in here." Mr. Finley was up, hobbling across the low-ceilinged room. He pushed a door open, and followed David into a tiny room; a rough workbench ran the length of one wall, and above it was one long oil-papered window. Mr. Finley pulled an extra stool up for David, who was puzzled by the strange collection of articles in the room. On a workbench was the queerest assemblage of jugs, bottles, and pewter pans he had ever seen. Hanging from the walls, heaped untidily in corners and beneath the bench were bundles of dried roots, barks, and leaves. Assorted pungent odors seemed to drift in layers about the room.

Mr. Finley was already absorbed in his collection. "This here now is a new remedy for rheumatics," he said, lifting an earthen jug, shaking it back and forth. "Made out of peach seed pits, slippery elm bark and wild cherries. Tastes like something the Devil might've brewed, but it's a mighty help to my knee."

"You make potions out of all this stuff?" David had picked up a bundle of mullein leaves.

"Yep. There ain't nothing like mullein tea for asthma."

"How'd you know all these things? You must be purty smart."

"You're the first one ever said that. Most folks think I'm tetched in the head." Mr. Finley's brown beard wagged from

[67]

side to side when he talked. " It's a fact, too, as far back as they go, the Finleys was all a mite tetched in the head. Take Macbeth—I don't know much about him myself—he was a chief or somebody in Scotland. He was the first of the Finley clan, so my old pa used to say. My old pa used to could say off words and words about Macbeth." He threw his head back, his beard thrust up toward the window: " For brave Macbeth, well he deserves the name."

His brown eyes glistened when he looked back to David. " My old pa was a remarkable man, but I reckon he was some tetched in the head, too. Had a pile of books, he did, but when the Indians burned his cabin, he lost 'em. Most broke his heart, that did."

" Always running off with your tongue, you are, Billy Finley." Mrs. Finley must have been standing in the doorway listening all the time. " Whyn't you let Davy tell about his ancestors? "

Mr. Finley had picked up a piece of bark, rubbing it between his fingers. " She's a mite jealous of my lineage, Davy. The old lady can't trail her clan back further'n a stubble-bearded Irishman in Maryland."

" My folks come from Ireland," said David.

He saw Mrs. Finley wink at him. " Now will you be talking too fast about the Irish, Billy Finley? "

" But he's Scotch-Irish," Mr. Finley countered. " You can tell it in the litheness of his muscles and the fine shape of his nose."

The verbal battle between Mr. and Mrs. Finley continued for some time, then was adroitly diverted by the latter to David's past and future prospects. She seemed disappointed when she learned that David's father owned no farm, but was dependent upon his run-down tavern for a living. She was just beginning to offer comment about the difficulties of young

[68]

folks who married without owning property, when they heard voices and the noise of horses' hoofs splashing in the stream.

" Reckon that'd be Polly." Mr. Finley opened the window, thrusting his head outside. " Yep. Polly. And Luke's with her. Jeannie, it looks as if we might have a sociable git-together this evening."

" They been to revival meeting down the creek," Mrs. Finley explained, as she leaned forward to look out the window.

For a moment David was ill at ease; he had not expected to meet Luke Powell here. Then he remembered Luke's threat when he was leaving the reaping party; his anger rose, and with it his courage. He sallied out into the yard, ahead of the Finleys, watching Polly's eyes widen when she saw him.

" Why, Davy, it's you! "

He was helping her from the horse, his back turned to Luke Powell. As his hand touched her fingers he remembered the two kisses in the cushion dance; his face colored slightly.

" Kind of surprised to see me, Polly? "

Her eyes turned in a coquettish sidewise glance. " No," she said softly.

" You knew I was coming to see you? "

She nodded.

He heard Luke's footsteps behind him, as the three walked slowly to the cabin, Luke frowning darkly at David.

" You young-uns come in to the fireplace and set," said Mrs. Finley. " The old man and me'll go out to the smokeroom for some venison."

David was disappointed when Polly sat with Luke Powell on the fireplace bench opposite him. He leaned back luxuriantly in the blue pillows, however, propping his moccasins up against the edge of the fireplace, his face turned sideways to Polly and Luke. For several minutes the conversation was forced, Polly doing most of the talking, recalling incidents at the reaping party, which from the expression on Luke's face must have been painful remembrances to him.

When Mr. Finley stamped back into the room, David made a place for him on the wide seat, but he shook his head. "You young-uns go on talking. I got to work on my herb potions. I'm fixing up some honey and buttermilk for Polly's complexion that'll make her so danged purty the house 'll be over-running with young fellers day and night." He paused a moment in front of the door. "Polly, your ma might like you to help her a minute with that venison."

With the room empty except for themselves, David and Luke sat stiffly, staring at one another, Luke's dark face twisted in a malignant scowl. When he spoke the words seemed to writhe out venomously. "Davy Crockett, you remember what I said about Polly? You're just barking up the wrong tree when you come around here. She's my gal."

"She's not married to you yet, Luke Powell, not by a long sight. And so long as I'm around here, I aim to stand up to my rack, fodder or no fodder."

They said nothing further. When Polly returned she brought a pewter plate, and they played at spinning it until Mrs. Finley brought in some potatoes for them to bake in the coals. David was so busy looking at Polly he let his potatoes burn. Immediately Mrs. Finley unleashed her tongue. "Davy Crockett, you're a careless good-for-nothing. Can't even tend to potatoes. Takes a good steady young man such as Luke to do things right."

David had no reply to make; he looked at Luke whose lips curled in a complacent expression that reminded David of a proud tomcat. He did not mind the scolding particularly, because Mrs. Finley also asked Luke to turn the spit on which the venison was fastened. While the turning meat crackled out drops of grease that turned to little flaring spurts of flame in the coals, he and Polly sat quietly looking at one another.

Although he could feel that Polly's mother was drawing other unspoken comparisons between him and Luke, he made up his mind to make no further overtures to Mrs. Finley. It was Polly he was courting, after all, and if Polly liked him that was all he wanted to know.

It was late in the afternoon before the meal was served. After offering a secret potion to his guests from a yellow jar, Mr. Finley began carving the smoking venison. With his long knife raised in a gesture above the table, he squinted one eye and began reciting:

> " I have no pennies pullets for to buy,
> Neither geese nor pigs; but two green cheeses . . .
> And yet to say, by my soul, I have no salt bacon . . ."

He cleared his throat loudly. "That's what my old father used to say, only he knew a lot more words." Mr. Finley saw that Luke was impatiently eyeing the venison, and with a half-guilty expression on his face he set about the carving again. " Queer folks, the Finleys. Tetched in the head, I reckon."

They ate heartily, becoming more talkative as their stomachs filled. David was telling, with animated gestures, of a recent encounter with a wolf in the lower part of Edmund Kennedy's cornfield, when he chanced to look at Mrs. Finley and saw that she was sound asleep, her head nodding forward.

" Lord a-mighty, Davy. You're the first one I ever saw could beat the Finleys at talk. I never was able to talk Jeannie to sleep. 'Twas always the other way round." Mr. Finley pulled at his beard, rocked back and forth in his hickory chair.

Later, after Mrs. Finley had awakened and cleared the table, David and Luke and Polly were left together in front of the fire. Again Polly sat on the bench with Luke. David, sitting alone, wondered if his rival would ever leave. Luke talked forever about his father's farm, and how before long he would have a farm of his own and be somebody.

Finally David got up and walked to the door. It was almost dark outside, the stream like a black ribbon in front of the house. He could see Old Tom stomping impatiently, shaking his mane. " I reckon I better be riding for home," he said suddenly, loudly.

Polly was up from the bench, walking quickly to the door. " You can't go home tonight, Davy. It's a long piece to Kennedys'."

" I ought to started long ago."

She was touching his arm lightly. " Stay the night." Her voice was almost a whisper, so low he knew Luke could not have heard; she had not meant for Luke to hear. He walked with her back to the bench, and she sat beside him this time, her shoulder against his arm.

A log dropped in the fireplace, showering sparks, and when the resulting flames lighted the room, David could see Luke's eyes on him. When the flames died again only the eyes were visible, and he thought of Luke as a wildcat sitting in a tree. He laughed suddenly, shaking the pillows.

After a long while Luke stood up, smoothing his slick black hair. " Well, time I get to home, it'll be bedtime. I ain't one for galloping around all the night. Sunday is the day of rest, as the preacher-man said today."

" Sorry you're leaving so soon-like," said Polly. David was exultant. She had not asked Luke to stay the night.

While the two went to the door, he twisted the pillows, wishing he might leap up and dance around the room. Polly preferred him; he knew it now.

He could never forget this night, he would never forget the firelight on Polly's face, and her eyes when she looked at him just before he kissed her with his arms tight around her.

Absent-minded though he was, Mr. Finley was at times a thoughtful man, for he made a great ceremony of opening his door around midnight, banging it again and again with an awful clatter. David moved over to the farthest corner of his side of the bench, sitting up straight with exaggerated dignity.

"Time for bed —— Well, where's Luke?" Mr. Finley peered around the room.

"Gone home, long ago," said Polly.

"Well, I reckon you'd better put your horse in the barn, Davy."

"My what—my ——" He had forgotten he had a horse, forgotten where he was.

After Old Tom was turned loose in the Finley barn with a handful of hay for munching, Mr. Finley showed David up to a bed in the loft. "I'm taking this candle back down now, boy," he said softly. "You can undress in the dark. You got stars in your eyes, and you're liable to drop a mere candle in the bed straw."

The next morning as Polly Finley told him good-bye, she whispered in his ear: "If you don't come back to see me next Sunday, I'll send a witch to haunt you."

When David turned Old Tom sideways at the edge of the stream for one last look back, he saw Mrs. Finley standing in the doorway, hands on hips, feet wide apart. No witch, not even Mrs. Finley, could keep him from seeing Polly again.

★ 7 ★

Early Tuesday morning, Edmund Kennedy roused David from a sound sleep. "Wolves in the pigpen," he explained. "Get your rifle, and let's go after them."

Hurriedly David slipped into his cold clothing, picked up his rifle, and followed Edmund out toward the barn, his eyes straining to see in the half darkness. The wolves had slaughtered several of Edmund's finest pigs, leaving their bloody

[73]

carcasses strewn about the pen. Against the side of the barn was the dead watchdog. Edmund turned the animal over with his foot; the throat was torn to ribbons. " I guess we're too late, Davy. They've got away."

After they had buried the dog and the remains of the pigs in a deep hole, they went back to the house. They ate breakfast in silence. David knew the loss of the pigs was a severe blow to Edmund; he had been counting on them for the winter's supply of salt pork.

" They say the wolves are worse this year than ever." Edmund's shoulders drooped in dejection. " Whole packs of them roaming the Holston valley. If they're starting in this early on stock, it won't be safe for human folk first thing you know."

David dipped his corn pone in his milk, then began chewing slowly. " Maybe we could have a big hunt, everybody in the valley, and kill the whole pack off at once."

" That's a good plan," said Edmund. " Somebody ought to do something, for certain."

About the middle of the morning, Edmund came running out to the barn where David had gone to shell corn for the fowls. " Say," shouted Edmund, " Albert Squiers' oldest boy just come in for his lessons. Says his father lost two calves last night. Wolves."

" Two calves! "

" That's what he said. Why don't you go over to Squiers' place right now and talk up that wolf hunt you had in mind this morning? "

David needed no further urging. Ten minutes later he was astraddle Old Tom, off for Albert Squiers' farm.

Wednesday was the day set for the hunt. Word of it had been passed all through the neighborhood, with instructions to meet at Albert Squiers' place at the crack of dawn. It was a gloomy morning, with a chilling dampness that foreboded rain.

Albert Squiers had a huge fire roaring in his fireplace when David and Edmund arrived, but the growing crowd of men and boys and dogs soon overflowed into the yard where another fire was started. Everybody carried a weapon of some sort.

"Reminds me of the times when the Indians was making raids hereabouts," Squiers said grimly. "And I reckon the wolves are getting just as bad as the Indians was."

With a sharp-pointed stick Squiers drew off a rough map of the river bottoms, ordering the men to gather around him. "We start from here," he said, making a tiny circle with the stick, "spreading out gradually as we move up the valley. If we don't separate too far apart we ought to clean out every wolf in the brush."

Edmund and David walked together for a mile after they left Squiers' place, but then, following instructions, they separated. Across the wide meadows, David could see the line of men on either side of him, advancing like an army, spreading fanwise. They then entered the forest. In a few minutes even the sounds of distant voices faded; he might have been alone in a vast wilderness.

On through the morning he walked, his gun slung loosely on one arm. Again and again he saw squirrels darting in and out of hollow tree trunks. He was tempted to fire but, thinking the noise might warn away the wolves, he would drop his raised rifle. The sun which had shone but dimly through the haze of clouds soon entirely disappeared, and a faint cold drizzle sifted down through the trees. When he became hungry he stopped to eat his portion of the food Edmund's wife had prepared for them. He drank from a stream that bubbled down through the rocks, the water so cold it set his teeth to aching.

Not a trace of a wolf did he see. The territory he was traversing was higher ground, to the left of the main body of hunters who were in the river bottoms. Late in the afternoon he heard firing and the baying of dogs from that direction; he changed his course slightly, hoping to encounter any wolves which might flee toward the hills. However, he saw nothing but squirrels and an occasional raccoon.

Meanwhile the clouds were thickening, the rain making a rattling noise on the dead leaves around him. These were the shortest days of the year, and he knew he would have to travel rapidly in order to get back to Squiers' before night. Cold and wet as it was, he had no desire to be out after dark. Suddenly he realized that he did not know in which direction to turn. When he did make up his mind as to which was the southeast, he was certain that he was wrong in his guess, and turned to walk in the opposite direction.

The forest seemed somber and merciless, the trees so thick together that he could not see for any distance. Sudden rustlings in the brush would make him turn his head in alarm, and when a wild hog snorted across his path, he jerked his gun up in quick fright. He was scared. It had been so long since he had known fear that the sensation was strange. He tried to laugh it off. The misery of the cold and dampness helped him forget fear for a time, but it came back upon him again, an unseen, overpowering force.

When he heard a rustling noise again, up ahead, he stood still, stopped breathing, for this time he knew the sound was of footsteps. Perhaps a deer, he thought. Here the trees were tall and straight so that in certain places he could see for several yards. His rifle was ready for firing, when the gray shape of a human being darted in front of him, not twenty paces away, then concealed itself behind a tree.

" Hallo," he called. There was no answer. If it was one of the other hunters, he would surely have replied. An Indian? The tribes were all far to the south. As David took a step forward, he heard the sound of running feet. Evidently this unknown person was afraid of him. He started immediately in

[76]

pursuit. He did not intend to lose the trail, for, he reasoned, wherever there are human beings there must be shelter and warmth. He ran with renewed energy.

When he next saw the gray shape, he was surprised to see that it was a woman. As loudly as his short breath would permit he called out again: " Wait! I'm lost! "

The figure turned, hesitant, still moving slowly away from him in the deepening darkness. " Wait. I'll not harm you." His voice sounded queer, echoing in the trees.

" Davy! " Suddenly the strange woman in wet gray linsey-woolsey had shouted his name, running to him, and he was holding her by the shoulders while she cried and laughed in sudden relief from fear.

" Polly, how did you get here? "

" I wish I knew," she said, turning her face up, so that the rain was running off the tip of her nose. " I'm lost too."

They laughed so loudly that again echoes rang back at them from the trees. " You make me a promise," he said. " Right now, promise. We won't ever tell anybody about being lost. They'd laugh us out of Tennessee."

Both were shivering from the cold. " What direction you suppose is the Big Gap? " he asked.

She shook her head.

" This is powerful funny," said he. " I start out looking for wolves and find Polly Finley."

She laughed. " I was out looking for a horse and found you."

They walked on, laughing in the cold rain. There was a quick fluttering of wings as a bird streaked out of the underbrush, and Polly drew close against him. " Just a red bird," he said. " More scared 'n we are."

" A red bird flew across my path." Her eyes sparkled when she looked at him. " You know what that's a sign of? "

" It's a sign you're going to be kissed before dark," he said.

[77]

"And it's most dark already." The rain beat in their faces while they kissed.

Suddenly David drew back from her, his head up. "Look there. Over there!" He pointed toward a thinning line of trees, beyond which was a cabin, its roof line merging into the gray-black sky.

They ran down the slope, crossing a small ravine in front of the cabin. In the background was a small field, the black stumps and dead trees scattered like a retreating army.

David banged his fist against the door, which swung inwards. "Hello," he cried. There was a smell of mustiness coming out of the room.

"I guess nobody lives here," said Polly.

By now David's eyes were growing accustomed to the darkness; he could see the black square of the fireplace at one end. Holding tightly to Polly's hand, he walked slowly across the uneven puncheon flooring, bent forward to feel along the edge of the hearth. After he had made a small heap of dry twigs and bark he soon got a fire going. The tiny blaze threw a dim light around the room. They could see cobwebs hanging from the rafter logs and in the corners, but the cabin's roof and walls were tight and dry. From the side of the wall he pulled the remains of a split-log shelf, dropping it on the fire, and then went outside for more wood.

In a few minutes the fire was roaring up the chimney, and they sprawled in front of it on the floor, their damp clothing steaming in the heat. "My folks will be about crazy if I don't get home," she said.

"They'll think you stopped at a neighbor's place out of the rain. Wouldn't be much sense of us trying to find the way on a night like this."

Now that he was comfortable, David had begun to realize what had happened. Here they were, alone for the night, free to say, free to do what they pleased, safe before a warm fire while the rain poured outside. Often he had dreamed of some

[78]

such situation, had colored it with all sorts of romantic trappings. But now that the thing had happened, unexpectedly, almost miraculously, it all seemed quite ordinary, quite natural that he should be here with Polly. It was as if it had happened to both of them many times before; each knew exactly what to do, what to say.

She had spread her thin cloak on the floor, and they sat on it, their arms around each other's shoulders, looking into the blazing fire. " You believe in signs, Davy? " Polly's voice was soft and warm, like the fire.

" Sure, why? "

" I saw a spider web over our door this morning. That's a sign my lover is never coming to see me again."

" For sure," he said. " I believe in that sign. Only that spider web wasn't for me. It was Luke Powell's spider web."

For hours they must have sat there, saying very little, until both were nodding sleepily. The rain had stopped, and the wind was blowing up outside, moaning and whistling around the corners of the cabin. When Polly went to sleep against his shoulder, David held her for a time; then he let her head drop gently down on the cloak. He removed his old hunting shirt, spreading it over her shoulders, and then stood up, back to the fire, looking down at her face. As she breathed, the hunting shirt moved slowly up and down. He got to thinking of the day he bought the shirt in Knoxville and how proud he was wearing it down the street, and how Margaret Elder had found him on the raft admiring his reflection in the river water. In his sleepy brain Margaret Elder's face became confused with Polly's. Always it had been Polly. He slept for a time, his back resting against the edge of the fireplace, but toward morning he got up, stretching his stiff arms and legs, and tiptoed outside. Into his face the wind slapped, cold and sharp, but he stood in the doorway for a while breathing deeply, watching the big stars pale out as the sky grew lighter.

When Polly awoke, her teeth were chattering from the cold.

He stirred up the fire; and she turned around and around in front of it until she was warmed. Although the sun was up now, neither of them seemed eager to go, to leave the cabin.

"If I wasn't so hungry," said David, "I'd as soon stay around here all day. It's a good cabin."

Her back was turned so that he could see the strands of her hair twisting down the back of her neck. He caught her tightly in his arms.

"You would as soon stay all day, Davy? I would stay forever, and ever, and ever." She slipped out of his arms. "But I reckon we'd better go now. My pa will be searching all over the valley."

"Some day we'll come back," he said.

With the sun as their compass, they walked northwestward until they came to a trail familiar to Polly. "It's only a mile or two," she said, "to the Big Gap." In the cold her cheeks had turned red as new apples.

"You're right purty," said David. "I'll walk you to home."

"Go on with you. If we both turned up together, we'd have to get married."

He chuckled. "We're a-going to get married anyhow."

"You better ask me that Sunday." Polly had turned quickly, and was running swiftly along the leaf-strewn trail. He followed her a short distance, then stopped, watching her until she became a slender gray figure swinging out of sight over the top of the hill. He was whistling a crazy sort of tune.

★ 8 ★

The following day David learned from Edmund that the wolf hunt had been fairly successful; many of the participants reported that they had killed more than one animal. During

[80]

the week, however, David slept out in the corn crib in order that he might foil any further attempts on the stock.

Late Saturday afternoon a wagoner stopped at Edmund's cabin with a message for David. His father was seriously ill, and his mother wanted him at the tavern as soon as he could come.

David was undecided as to whether he should go at once, or wait until Monday. He had promised Polly he would see her Sunday, and yet, thinking of how feeble his father had seemed on his last visit, he knew he should go immediately to the tavern. Finally he asked Edmund if he would try to send word to the Big Gap; he was certain that if Polly only knew the cause she would forgive his absence.

When he arrived at the tavern and saw his father's pain-drawn face he was glad he had come when he did. John Crockett reached out a thin pale arm, the blue veins corded like vines along the wrist and hand. " Time you was a-getting here, Davy." His voice was very weak. " They think I'm a-going to die, don't they? "

" You told me once the Crocketts are hard to kill."

His father tried to chuckle, but choked up with tearing coughs. Elizabeth came running, shooing David away with her apron.

The next day two of his brothers, James and Willson, arrived, James bringing his wife. David had not seen either of the brothers for several years. The illness of John Crockett thus brought about a family reunion, which in turn seemed to act as a tonic for the old man. Several times each day, John Crockett would summon his daughter, the three boys, and James' wife to his bedside. He would look at them proudly. "A fine family, the Crocketts," he would say. " James looks more like the Hawkins folks, I reckon, but Davy and Willson are real Crocketts."

David enjoyed the renewed association with his brothers.

[81]

James was as strong as an ox, and in an impromptu wrestling match out by the barn he succeeded in throwing both David and Willson together. When it became evident that their father was going to recover from his illness, Willson demanded that David go with him on a bear hunt. For a day or so, David put him off with vague excuses; he was waiting to hear from Polly Finley. At last Edmund Kennedy came to the tavern late one evening, riding his young mare. After inquiring about John Crockett's health, he handed David a letter.

It was from Polly. David was so excited he almost tore the rough paper unfolding it. To his chagrin, he found that he had forgotten most of the words he had learned in Edmund's school, and for fear he would misunderstand the exact meaning of Polly's writing, he went secretly to Elizabeth. His cheeks reddening with embarrassment, he listened while Elizabeth read through the final closing phrase: " I am yours forever, Polly."

As she folded the letter, Elizabeth smiled at him. " Davy, Davy, is she purty? "

" Purtiest gal in Tennessee," he said, running from the room. He sought out Willson immediately, telling him to get ready for a big bear hunt in the Clinch Mountains; he had to do something to celebrate.

After three days of hunting, they returned with four bear-skins, and a huge buck which David shot on the return journey. Burdened down with their spoils, the two brothers arrived at the tavern door to find their father sitting out in the bright winter sunshine, his cheeks flushed with health again. " If you boys had put off that hunt another week, I'd 'a' gone along and showed you some real b'ar hunting," he chuckled.

David looked at him, grinning. " Does you good to have a spell of sickness, pa."

That evening they feasted on the fresh venison, and David chose an appropriate moment to announce his intention of

[82]

marrying Polly Finley at the first opportunity. James suggested he wait until summer. "The winter is a hard time for marrying," he said.

"You ought to know," replied David. "You married in a January blizzard."

It was a good idea, though, he thought, waiting until summer. Now that he was sure of Polly's feelings toward him, he was anxious to have more worldly possessions to offer her. When he returned to Edmund's the following day he asked him if he would take his rifle as final payment on Old Tom. "I'd like to go back to your father's farm for the remainder of the winter and spring, to earn a little money." Edmund agreed to the trade, though he was disappointed over losing David's help with the chores.

"But won't you need a gun as badly as a horse?"

David winked at him. "My pa has an old rifle he never uses any more. When I get married I'll ask him for it."

"You're sly as a fox, Davy. Got everything figured out ahead."

He thought Sunday would never come. Before dawn he was riding Old Tom across the Holston bottomlands, headed for the Big Gap, and it seemed an eternity before he reached the brook in front of the Finley cabin. Polly had been watching for him, and was down at the brook's edge before he had forded halfway across. Leaping to the ground, he caught her in a tight hug.

"Wait a minute," she said breathlessly. "Ma will raise Cain, us carrying on like this in broad daytime."

To avoid Mrs. Finley's disapproving glances, David suggested they walk down the stream for a short distance. Although it was a wintry day with a raw wind cutting down from the hills, they walked along as carefree as though it was the first day of spring.

[83]

"I been thinking," said David, "about that cabin we stayed in all night."

"I think of it every day," she said softly.

"I mean," he said, "thinking about us living there—soon's we get wedded, that is. How'd you like that?"

She kissed him full on the lips.

His face brightened, then became serious again. "I reckon it'll be summer 'fore I can think of starting out, though, with you."

"I'll wait, I'd wait a long time, for you and that old cabin, Davy."

It was he who kissed her this time.

Quaker John Kennedy was not sympathetic toward David's plans for a marriage. "Thee'd best wait, lad. Starting out empty-handed at farming is a mighty task." However, he agreed to pay David in cash for the spring work.

In March and April he plowed and sowed in friendly rivalry with William, and was often reminded of that other spring when he had thought to marry Margaret Elder. Philosophically now, he reflected on that long dead spring, wondering at the miracle of love, its power over a helpless fellow such as he.

He worked hard and saved every penny, yet it was late July before he felt that he could ask Polly to set the date. "Soon or late?" she asked.

"Sooner the better," said he. It was a hot Sunday afternoon, and they were lying in high green grass that rippled in waves down to the edge of the brook. "Give me time to go see my folks at the tavern—and I owe John Kennedy one more week of work."

"I want to be married on a Thursday," she said, looking up to the puffs of clouds hanging motionless above them. "A week from Thursday," she said.

"A week from Thursday," he cried, lifting her up by the

[84]

waist. " Let's go wading." They splashed barefoot into the pebble-strewn stream.

Saturday he went to the tavern, calmly announcing that he was to be married on the following Thursday. " Glory be," said his father. " The Crocketts will soon be thicker'n the woods in Tennessee."

" We'll have an infair for your wife, son." His mother embraced him, weeping copiously, while Elizabeth stood by, hands folded, smiling.

They promised to send the news to James and Willson, and David stayed the night, explaining that he would be up before daybreak to make an important journey to the Big Gap. " You see, I been putting off asking Polly's ma and pa. And her ma is a cutter, she is."

Mrs. Finley was standing in the doorway, chewing slowly on her long snuff twig when David splashed Old Tom across the brook. There was scant welcome in her voice when she bade him enter. And the absence of both Polly and Mr. Finley seemed to him to be a portent. As he stepped inside the doorway he felt that he was walking into a trap.

" It's a hot day, ma'm," he said.

" Hot enough, I reckon. Makes the corn grow."

" Yes'm. It does make the corn grow." He shifted his weight first to one leg, then to the other, watching her fidgeting with her snuff pouch.

" Well, Davy, draw you up a chair and set. If you got something to say, say it."

David was abashed; he knew Mrs. Finley knew what he had come to say. After all, he and Polly had made no secret of their plans. " There's no point in running in circles," he blurted suddenly. " I'm aiming to wed Polly, and I thought I should speak with you first, ma'm."

[85]

She looked at him sternly, her snuff brush jutting from one side of her mouth. " Who said you was a-going to wed Polly? "

" You knew I was sweet on her."

" It takes more'n just being sweet on a gal to wed her."

" You object, ma'm? "

" For certain, I object. You little more'n just a no-account bound boy, without a measly thing to offer Polly—course I object."

David stared at her feet for a minute, then stood up quickly. " You remember the reaping party, ma'm? You called me son-in-law that night. That was a long time 'fore I thought of speaking to you as mother-in-law."

She was standing now, her sharp eyes flashing. " You— you ——"

" Where's Mr. Finley? " he demanded.

" None of your concern. Now you go along, go along, you ——"

" Is Mr. Finley nearby? "

" No—he wouldn't care for to speak with you if he was— now go along with you."

David heard the door creaking behind his back, and then the slow easy voice of Mr. Finley. " Now, Jeannie, maybe I should be a-caring for to speak with Davy. How'd'ye, Davy? "

" Hello, Mr. Finley."

" Get out, the both of ye," Mrs. Finley shouted so vehemently that her snuff brush fell to the floor. As she bent forward to pick it up, Mr. Finley pushed David out of the doorway, following after him.

" Her temper is like a fever today, Davy. Best we remain outside." Mr. Finley's brown eyes assumed a comical expression. " Are you certain, Davy, you'd like to have her for a mother-in-law? "

David grinned, feeling much better now. " You have no objections, sir? "

"Lord, no, Davy. Don't know a finer feller to have for a son. You know I've no son of my own. Always wanted a son, too."

"Yes, sir." He felt more confident now, his faith in himself restored. When she had called him a no-account bound boy, Mrs. Finley had struck a blow at his pride. But he guessed Mr. Finley was as good a judge of character as his wife.

Mr. Finley was pulling nervously at his brown beard. "Step down the stream aways, Davy. Surprise her. She's down there. Been fishing with me." He slapped David lightly on the shoulders.

Polly heard him, crashing through the high reeds, and held up a string of perch for him to admire. He thought she was more beautiful than ever, standing there in the sunlight, her auburn hair blown in the wind.

"We'll never go hungry, anyways, Polly, long as you've got a fishing line."

"You spoke to ma yet?"

"Sure did." He grinned. "She was hard-headed as a treed 'possum. Your pa was mighty agreeable though."

"We'll be wed then?"

"For sure, we'll be wed. But not here. Not the way your ma thinks about me."

"I'm sorry about ma. She's kind of hot-tempered, that's all. She likes you, Davy, she just won't say it."

He hugged her. "Next Thursday I'll come with an extra horse, bridled and saddled for you. You be ready. Tonight I'll go by Albert Squiers'—he's a justice of peace—and arrange for him to tie the knot. Then we'll go to my folks' tavern. They're going to have an infair for you; everybody in the valley will be there. You'll see, we'll have a fine wedding."

On the morning of David's marriage day, the dew was thick and heavy as summer raindrops, sparkling but briefly as it evaporated in the hot August sunlight. He guided Old Tom along the forest path with extreme care, lest his wedding attire become disarranged. In the growing humidity, his new buckskin coat was uncomfortably hot, and he envied his companions who wore much lighter clothing. Yet he felt so good he was almost afraid to think of realities for fear everything would evaporate with the suddenness of the dew.

James and his wife, riding their gray horse, followed close behind the stallion David had borrowed for Polly, and after them came Elizabeth and Willson on separate mounts. Somewhere behind them, out of sight in the thick trees, were Edmund and William Kennedy. David was pleased to have such a large escort, even though he was embarrassed by their frequent remarks. He rode stiffly upright, so that they might show more respect for the dignity of his mission.

As they approached closer and closer to the Big Gap, David began showing signs of nervousness. Sometimes he pulled so sharply on the bridle that Old Tom would stop still, turning his head back with an air of extreme annoyance. Although he tried to think on other matters, the image of Mrs. Finley kept rising before him like a specter; he dreaded the meeting with her.

When they were within two miles of the Big Gap, David turned his horse in toward the valley road. Several hundred yards ahead was a strange cloud of dust, which at first he thought must be a small August whirlwind. Instead of a whirlwind, it turned out to be a group of men and boys on horseback, galloping toward them. A few seconds later he recognized the horseman in the lead, his thatch of silver-streaked hair streaming in the dusty wind, his laugh booming along the road, echoing against the trees.

" Uncle Joseph! " Surprised, David pulled Old Tom up sharply.

" It's Uncle Joseph, all right," said James.

Joseph Hawkins was singing, roaring out hoarse words as his huge horse jerked to a stop in front of David:

> " A gentleman came to our house,
> He would not tell his name,
> I knew he came a-courtin'
> Although he were ashamed.
> O, although he were ashamed! "

As he stopped singing, the powdery dust blew slowly away from him. " Davy, my lad, so you thought you'd wed without your Uncle Joseph around to see it well done? "

David removed his cap, dusted it, then set it carefully back in place. " I had thought you might be here 'fore 'twas over." He laughed shyly.

" Ah-hah-hah-hah, you couldn't wed without me, lad." Uncle Joseph had leaped to the ground; he walked over and patted David's knee. He spoke softly: " I hear tell the old lady is mighty wrathful this morning. Says there'll be no wedding."

David leaned forward, flipping Old Tom's mane back and forth with his fingers. " She's a high-tempered old lady, Mrs. Finley is."

Joseph Hawkins cleared his throat awkwardly, and spoke softly again. " I ain't one to borrow trouble, lad, but you know your Uncle Joseph. I'd pull the whiskers off the Old Devil hisself to help a friend. And as for you, lad, well, there ain't nobody I'd rather ——" He stopped, and then looked sharply at David. " Whyn't you stay right here for a time, and let me go ahead and swap some talk with the old lady? Remember, she kind of took a cut to me at the reaping party? "

David nodded silently.

His uncle winked reassuringly. " Maybe James and his wife better come, too. They look like respectable folk."

While James and his wife prepared to go with Joseph Hawkins, the crowd milled around David, congratulating him,

[89]

joking about the wedding. Surprised to see Abe Wilson among them, he leaped off his horse to shake hands with him. Abe's protruding teeth had turned even more yellow in the years that had passed since David had worked for him.

" How're you, Abe? "

" How're you, Davy? Heard you was going to be wed, so I thought I'd come."

" Jesse come too? "

Abe's teeth seemed to lengthen as his lips widened in a grin. " Nope. Jesse went away to Virginny."

" He wed one of my old sweethearts," said David.

" Yeah. He did, didn't he? " Abe sniffed. " Reckon you're glad now he did."

David nodded. He moved restlessly among the members of the crowd, watching up the road for a cloud of dust that would signal the return of Uncle Joseph. He wondered what Mrs. Finley would have to say to him.

Sooner than he expected, the cloud of dust rolled back down the road, and Joseph Hawkins, far ahead of James and his wife, jumped off his horse and came over to David with a brown bottle in his outstretched hand. " Wedding gift for you, lad. Sent by your father-in-law. A fine old gent, Mr. Finley, and makes good drinking stuff, too."

As calmly as he could, David raised the bottle, and swallowed deeply. The stuff burned his throat, and he turned, offering drinks to the others.

Uncle Joseph leaned close to him. " The old lady says no," he whispered. " A hell cat, she is."

David was not surprised. However, the gift from Mr. Finley was reassuring. He set his jaws firmly as he walked across the road to his horse. " Let's go," he said, " to the wedding."

As the party moved slowly along the road, David took several swallows from the brown bottle Mr. Finley had sent him. But the liquid was less productive of courage than of perspiration, which trickled down his cheeks until the dress scarf around his neck became a twisted soggy rope. He removed the scarf and loosened the broad silver-buckled belt that was a wedding present from his father, and felt much relieved.

When he came in sight of the Finley cabin, he slapped Old Tom's flanks sharply, urging the horse into a trot. Splashing across the stream, he swung the horse up to the open door of the cabin, with the borrowed stallion following closely behind.

Polly was there, waiting, in a dark blue homespun dress, her gray eyes bright with excitement, a scarlet kerchief like a brilliant flame at her throat.

" Are you ready? " He shouted the words above the noise of the splashing horses behind him.

She opened her mouth to speak, then nodded quickly.

" Light on this other horse, then. We're going to Albert Squiers' place." He reached out his hand, caught hers, and swung her neatly up on the borrowed stallion. Turning about, he saw Mr. Finley standing directly in front of them, his fingers nervously combing knots in and out of his brown beard.

" 'Morning, Davy."

" 'Morning, sir."

Mr. Finley's eyes appeared to be slightly moist, yet there was good humor in them.

" Would you be taking my daughter away before making her wife? " he asked.

" My intention was to go to Albert Squiers' place."

Mr. Finley slowly twisted his beard. " Mr. Squiers could come here, I reckon."

" He could, sir. But your wife—she ———"

" She has too much tongue in her head? "

David's face reddened. " Excuse me, sir, but she has."

"You shouldn't be a-minding her, son. After all, it's Polly you're to wed, not my Jeannie."

" Yes, sir."

[91]

"If Jeannie 'd be asking you to stay and marry at our house, you'd be willing then?"

"For sure, sir, I would."

Mr. Finley turned hastily toward the door, where his wife stood watching the crowd in stern silence. He whispered something. She started as if to reply angrily, then followed her husband out to one side of the cabin, where they remained facing one another for several minutes, talking so low that none of the crowd could hear their words, she gesticulating violently with her long arms, he tugging nervously at his beard. Gradually her gestures became less violent; she turned her head once or twice to look at David and Polly who sat on their horses exchanging embarrassed glances. Finally Mrs. Finley turned and walked across the grounds straight to David's horse; she stopped and stared hard at him for so long that he felt he must surely look away. Then she smiled slightly, thrusting her long stringy hand up toward him. "I reckon I'm asking your pardon, Davy. Well, you see, Polly's my only child, and I just couldn't bear thinking of her being wed and going off." She was squeezing his hand tightly. "Now get off them horses, you two, get off. Come on in this cabin this minute." She swung around, waving to the others with a swooping motion of her long arms. "Come on in, everybody. We're going to have the finest wedding ever in Tennessee."

While a messenger went galloping off for Albert Squiers, Mrs. Finley bustled about, tidying the room. She had donned a white cap and a lace scarf and her tongue seemed to wag incessantly. "Makes me recollect my wedding day, it does, Davy. This scarlet kerchief, now, Polly is a-wearing. I brought that from Baltimore on my wedding journey."

Mr. Finley had passed around innumerable bottles of his potions, and the crowd was becoming exuberant. Uncle Joseph was singing again:

[92]

"A gentleman came to our house,
He would not tell his name.
I knew he came a-courtin'
Although he were ashamed.
O, although he were ashamed."

Finally, Albert Squiers arrived, dressed in a big black coat which would not button over his plump abdomen. He regarded the merrymakers with a beaming face and a nod of approval, yet he declared that the knot-tying part of the wedding was a solemn occasion, and ordered all hilarity to cease while he performed the ceremony.

"Who's to wait on you?" he asked David.

"Edmund Kennedy, he's to wait on me."

"Very well," said Squiers. "You and Polly, her parents, and young Mr. Kennedy may remain in the room. Everybody else out in the yard—well, you *can* look in at the door, but quiet must prevail herein." Thumping his abdomen, he stood waiting until his orders had been carried out; then he fastened on his spectacles, and took up his Bible.

To David, the silence that fell over the room was like a sudden shock of cold water. When he walked out of this cabin again he would be wed to Polly. He turned quickly, saw that her head was bent forward as if in a silent prayer; he reached awkwardly for her hand. Clasping her hand he felt queer but happy inside. He glanced at Edmund, whose mouth twisted slightly in a smile.

Albert Squiers was reading: "We are gathered together here in the sight of God to join together this man and this woman." David tightened his grip on Polly's hand, jerking his head sidewise, looking once out of the door at the faces, some solemn, some grinning, peering in at them. "Will you have this woman for your wedded wife?" Squiers' spectacles slipped down his nose as he looked at David.

[93]

"I will." His voice sounded so unnatural he wondered if he had actually spoken the words.

Now it was Polly who spoke in answer to Squiers, her voice firm and strong: "I will."

He heard Mr. Finley's boots scuffing on the floor as he stepped behind Polly, and then Albert Squiers was joining his right hand with Polly's right hand, and Polly was leaning close to him, and they kissed briefly, so lightly, he was reminded of their first kiss on the night of the reaping party.

Now the crowd was clapping hands, shoving and pushing into the room, everybody wanting to kiss the bride, and David was so flustered that he slipped against the wall and knocked down a row of Mr. Finley's rare and precious drying herbs. Mr. Finley was too busy passing his bottles around to bother with the herbs, and if Albert Squiers had not had the presence of mind to toss them up into the loft they would have been trampled into dust.

David was surprised to find Edmund Kennedy pressing a small paper packet into his hand. "A wedding gift from my father to you and Polly," he said.

"The good old Quaker," said David. "What is it? You know?"

"It's an order to the store for fifteen dollars."

"Fifteen dollars! That's a fortune to me."

"There's a condition," laughed Edmund. "Polly must do the spending of it."

Immediately David sought out Polly in the crowd, pushing against Albert Squiers who was shouting in his ears: "I'm sending off for my two nigger fiddle players." All who heard Squiers set up lusty cheers.

Before the fiddlers arrived in the cool of the August twilight, the party was already in full swing. The merrymakers were beating on pots and kettles, blowing queer noises out of Mr. Finley's emptied bottles, and singing so raucously that even the frogs in the stream and the crickets in the grass seemed to have retreated in a baffled silence.

Somehow, Mrs. Finley managed to produce food for every member of the growing crowd of merrymakers, and after they had dined there was a brief lull in the uproar. Several times David and Polly attempted to slip away for a moment, but escape was an impossibility. They became resigned to their fate, and sat down in the doorway, trying to look as prim and proper as they thought married couples should look.

"The cushion dance," somebody yelled suddenly. Albert Squiers needed no further urging. He skipped clumsily out into the yard, waved his fiddlers to a log seat, and began beckoning a circle to gather around him.

David, of course, was awarded the first cushion. As he went through the steps, he lived over again that first night at the reaping party; he had thought then that no kiss could be so sweet, yet tonight Polly's lips were even more tantalizing. And she was his, forever.

The music of the fiddles squeaked on and on. The night seemed endless, filled with summer stars and the green white dots of fireflies flashing and a warm wind that came from the south.

At last even Albert Squiers grew weary; the musicians were nodding over their instruments; the crowd, hot and perspiring, had scattered along the cool edge of the brook. Mr. Finley came to David and Polly, his voice thick from the drinks, his eyes a bit sad. "Time for bed," he whispered loudly. "You two, slip up in the loft, you'll be safe there."

Polly dropped her head against David's shoulder. Surreptitiously he kissed her ear, and then they stood up. They went quietly into the house, and up the ladder to the loft. A candle was burning beside the bed. He was undecided for a moment about the candle. Then he walked over to it, blowing it out quickly.

[95]

At the head of the bed was a small window through which a burning pine torch in the yard below threw a wavering tree shadow against the rafters. He could see Polly in the dark grayness sitting on the white counterpane of the bed, moving her arms above her head, and then she was under the covers, leaving her blue dress a dark circle on the floor.

From outside came a sudden clatter of pots and pans, and then the deep bass voice of Joseph Hawkins baying a final chorus:

> " He was weary of the livelong night,
>   He was weary of his life,
> If this is what you call courting, boys,
>   I'll never take a wife.
>   O, I'll never take a wife!
>
> " Whenever he goes in company,
>   The girls all laugh for sport,
> They say, there goes a ding-dang fool
>   He don't know how to court!
>   Oh, he don't know how to court! "

David heard Polly laughing softly at the words of the song. He walked quietly to the tiny window and looked outside. The noise was fading out now; he could see sleeping forms sprawled like ghosts in the grass below. In the sky the stars were blurred by the late summer's haze. The night, it was a promise of reality, of always tomorrow. But he knew there could never be for him such another day, such another night.

O<small>N</small> *a June day in 1807 outside the port of Norfolk, Virginia, the Leopard, a British man-of-war, fired on an American vessel, the Chesapeake, killing or wounding twenty-one men. This incident was the most serious of several similar occurrences in that year, and President Jefferson immediately demanded an apology from England.*

When it became evident that no apology would be forth-coming, citizens' committees began forming up and down the coast, organizing boycotts against British goods. In a few weeks war fever was spreading like a fire. Alarmed, Jefferson and his agrarian supporters from the South and West sought means of averting war by a policy which Jefferson called " peaceable coercion against all of Europe." At his recommendation, the Congress passed in December, 1807, the Embargo Act, pro-hibiting the exportation of any merchandise whatever from the United States by sea or land.

Within a few days after the act went into effect, the seaport towns, crowded with idle ships and famished seamen, began feeling the first effects of the embargo. When corn and wheat and tobacco dropped rapidly in price, all the cities of the nation saw starving men begging for food in the streets.

This was America's first economic depression. While these hungry citizens begged for bread in the Eastern cities, helpless farmers in the South and West let their corn and wheat rot in the fields for want of markets. When land values collapsed soon afterwards, even the most remote frontier settlements felt the effects of this stagnation of trade.

By 1809, even Jefferson reluctantly admitted that complete national isolation was impossible, did not protest when Con-gress killed the Embargo Act, substituting the Act of Non-Intercourse which forbade trade only with England and France. As a result of his Embargo Act, Jefferson's private for-tune in Virginia land had been completely wiped out. During the final years of his life he would have to live from the charity of friends, would leave a debt so vast that even his only surviv-ing child would be evicted from Monticello without a cent.

His attempts to prevent war finally culminated in the War of 1812, and not until after this war was ended did the economic depression run its course.

Thus the years from 1807 to 1814 were harder years than most on the isolated frontier, where life was not easy even in times of peace and plenty.

PART TWO

★ I ★

ONE July morning, almost a year after his wedding day, David Crockett awoke early and left the cabin where he and Polly had established themselves as share-renters. It was the same log house in which they had found shelter late that night long ago when he had come upon Polly lost in the forest. After the wedding, both of them had agreed that no other place would be so desirable for a home, and so David had sought out the owner who agreed to let him have it for a share of the crops made on the land.

Even so early in the morning the air was warm, and he knew that by noon the sun would be blistering the fields. He walked slowly across the yard, stopped to pick up an axe beside the rail fence, and looked back toward the house, wondering if he should awaken Polly so that she might have breakfast ready when he returned. He shouted: " Polly! " There was no reply. He tossed a stone against the side of the wall. The cabin remained silent in the warm dawn.

He laughed, thinking of Polly lying in the bed asleep, and how she would jump up and bustle about the kitchen when she awoke and found he was gone.

He passed the pen where he had kept the hogs before they had broken through the fence and escaped to the woods. He was thinking of the hogs, how he had fed and watered them for weeks, and now they were gone, more than likely for good, and he and Polly would be lucky if they had enough venison for the winter as scarce as deer were nowadays. As he walked through the corn, parched and stunted by the drouth, his face became serious. He wondered if the future was as bright as they had believed it a year ago, or if always they would have to live one day ahead of hunger.

Two hours later when he came back to the cabin, his shirt soaked with sweat, his long black hair hanging damp over his forehead, he was surprised that he could hear no sounds of movement inside or see smoke coming from the chimney. He wondered if Polly had prepared breakfast already, and was waiting for him.

He walked into the shadows of the cabin, cool after the heat of the sun. There was still no sound.

" Polly! "

He heard a low moan, and ran quickly through the door. She was twisting on the bed like a wounded deer, her head drawn back, her nightgown knotted over her knees.

" Polly, Polly." He had never known her ill before.

" Davy, it's time, I reckon." She was breathing slowly. " Go for ma. She'll know—what to do."

So it was that, already. It was queer, he hadn't given it a thought for days, he was so used to seeing her go about the place, big like that. He brought her a gourdful of water, and then started on a run for Finleys'. The distance was four miles; he did not stop running until he splashed across the stream in front of the Finley cabin.

" Hell fire in the mountains, Davy, what's matter? " Mrs. Finley was sitting barefooted on the doorstep.

" It's Polly. It's her time."

Mrs. Finley stopped only long enough to put on her shoes. They saw Mr. Finley coming up the creek; he shouted at them, but they didn't wait for him.

All the way back to the cabin, David kept urging Mrs. Finley along, clutching at her arm until she would shake him loose. She pretended to be quite calm, but David noticed that whenever he slowed his steps she would accelerate hers.

Polly was lying quietly in the bed when they arrived. She tried to smile, but there was pain in her gray eyes and great beads of perspiration clung around her tight mouth.

" You git out in the yard and start a fire under the caldron, young man." Mrs. Finley was shaking out a clean sheet with one hand and ripping one of David's old undershirts with the other. " You git out now and stay out. I'll tend to Polly."

He had a great fire going under the cauldron when Mr. Finley hobbled through the yard gate. " Gone plumb crazy, David? Sun's hot enough to bile water already."

" I reckon maybe it is," said David, adding more wood to the blazing fire.

It was almost an hour before Mrs. Finley called for a jug of hot water. Mr. Finley shouted at her: " I ought've brought some of my potions," said he. " But Lord knows, everybody is so excited, I didn't think ——"

The day was long. David and his father-in-law whittled, chewed tobacco, threw rocks at targets, but the hours passed like so many centuries. Occasionally they would hear Polly moan, and they would look at one another uneasily, saying nothing. About dusk, there was a sudden shrill screaming in the cabin; David decided he would wait no longer.

He started through the open door, but drew back when Mrs. Finley stood in his way, a bundle of rough linen in her arms. " Here he is, Davy," she said. " You must of knowed from the way he hollered he was a man-child." He glanced briefly at the squirming red face and then went inside and kissed Polly. After a while he came out and sat on the doorstep alone.

A half moon was over the tops of the trees. He looked at the moon, thinking about Polly and that wrinkle-faced baby, lying beside her, in his place in the bed. He started to grin, thinking about it, and didn't even notice Mr. Finley when he walked up beside him.

[103]

" I declare, Davy," said Mr. Finley, " you look just like an old proud 'possum, sitting there, grinning at the moon."

★ 2 ★

They called the boy John Wesley. At a church meeting Polly had heard an itinerant preacher tell the story of John Wesley and she had liked the sound of the name so well that she wanted her firstborn to bear it. David never told John Crockett that his grandson was not named for him.

During the winter, which was a hard one for them, two events occurred to break the monotony of the chill gray days. Mrs. Finley fell ill with a pain in her chest and died before any of them could realize what had happened. Mr. Finley was a pitiable sight, walking about his farm by day, too sick at heart to return to his empty cabin at nightfall. David and Polly tried to persuade him to come and live with them, but he would always refuse with a sad shake of his shaggy head.

Then in early February they had a surprise visitor. David's brother, Willson, arrived at the cabin late one night, singing at the top of his voice. David got out of bed, shivering with cold, to open the door, and Willson caught him in a bear hug.

" Willson, you old polecat, where'd you come from? "

" The cold weather drove me out of my holler log," said Willson, offering David a drink from his jug. He took a swig, and then set about building a huge fire in the fireplace. Polly was up and dressed, showing Willson the baby, which was rubbing its eyes sleepily with clinched fists.

" He's just like old Davy, always wanting to sleep," said Willson, laughing.

David took another drink. " Tell us where all you been. Pa said you went off to the Chickasaw country."

" Didn't get that far. Been down in the Duck and Elk River

[104]

valleys. Man, you never saw such country. As good a rifle shot as you, Davy, you wouldn't never have to work a lick. Just live off the country. It's running over with deer and turkeys."

David's eyes were bright in the reflected firelight. " I'd like that. This rent farming, it's not what it's cracked up to be. Stay here all our lives, we'll never have nothing."

" It's a good cabin," said Polly.

" Yeah, it's a good cabin, but I could build a better. Maybe on land we could call our own, too."

" Why don't you go down to Elk River? " Willson poked at the fire, making the sparks fly up the chimney.

" How far is it? "

" Oh, I reckon a hundred, a hundred and fifty mile. Purtiest country you ever saw."

" Many Indians? " asked Polly. She was rocking the baby quietly in her arms.

" Few. Good Indians though. Don't bother nobody."

David took another swallow from Willson's jug. " Well, I'm ready to quit this and cut out for some new ground."

They talked long into the night, and the next morning David insisted that Willson go with him to Mr. Finley's cabin. Mr. Finley was ready for any new undertaking which might take his mind off his wife's recent death, and immediately agreed to accompany David and Polly on a journey to the south.

Within a week, both of them together managed to persuade Polly that such a move would be for the best. They set the latter part of March as a good time to go; most of the cold weather would be over by then, and they should arrive in the new country in time to plant a few things before summer.

They packed Old Tom and the two colts with their most precious belongings, and Mr. Finley agreed to carry Polly's dismantled spinning wheel on his horse. For nearly two weeks they journeyed leisurely southward, following the rough trail through the thickening forests. After the first few days, they passed no more settlements, and it was miles between the lonely cabins.

David was delighted. " This is the best country in the world down here," he repeated again and again.

Two or three times they were caught in sudden thunderstorms, but the raindrops were warm, and they dried themselves out comfortably in front of fires after each shower. On the coldest night of the journey they were lucky enough to be the guests of a settler and his family who heaped a great pile of corn husks in one corner of the cabin for them to sleep on during the night.

" You're in Lincoln County now," the frontiersman told them the following morning.

" I think I'll settle near here," said David. " This is the best country in the world, I reckon."

The next day they selected a place at the head of the Mulberry fork of the Elk River, and David and his father-in-law started constructing a one-room cabin. As the weather was warm, they did not bother to chink the logs. Mr. Finley girdled a few trees and planted some corn in the damp black soil while David roamed up and down the river valley shooting enough deer and squirrels and turkeys to keep them in a plentiful supply of meat. On a two days' journey several miles to the west, he came upon a scattered group of cabins. These were his nearest white neighbors, a friendly group of settlers from North Carolina.

In July, Mr. Finley decided to return to his old home. " In-laws got no business overstaying their time with sons and daughters," he said, and no amount of talk would bring him to change his mind. David was genuinely sorry to see him leave; it was a lonely place there in the dark forest, and with his father-in-law away he did not feel as free to go on long hunting trips, leaving Polly and the boy alone.

For weeks they would see no human being except an occasional roving Indian. One day, David was a mile or so from home, looking for turkeys. Finally he bagged one with a difficult shot through the underbrush that clipped the bird's head neatly away. A moment later a tall Chickasaw stepped out in front of David, making a friendly gesture with one arm. " White man shoot straight," said the Indian.

David stood still, wondering what he wanted. The Indian's black hair hung in long plaits over his naked shoulders; his clothing consisted simply of a pair of buckskin breeches and moccasins. He took one step forward. " Tall Grass shoot straight, too." He waved his arm as if to encircle David. " We good friends? "

David extended his hand, and the Indian gripped it awkwardly. " My name is Davy Crockett."

" Davy Crockett good hunter," said Tall Grass, showing his long teeth in a quick smile.

From that day Tall Grass was David's most dependable friend in all of Lincoln County. Although the Indian detested work, he made a willing effort to assist David and Polly when they began chinking their cabin in the autumn. After the work was finished, he looked at David and said: " Today we work." He pointed over the horizon. " Tomorrow we hunt."

The next morning Tall Grass brought his two young sons to the cabin. " Tall Grass's sons. Sons shoot straight." Tall Grass carried an ancient musket, but his solemn-faced boys were armed only with reed blowguns about ten feet long. In bags slung over their naked shoulders they carried a few small darts tipped with sharp stones. As they walked away from the cabin, a rabbit darted across the pathway, stopped still with ears up sharp beneath a bush. David saw the older boy fill his cheeks suddenly; then the dart streaked in front of him, pinning the rabbit dead and quivering to the earth.

" Good aim," said David.

[107]

"Look, look me," said the younger son, glancing over his shoulder. He was creeping along ahead of the others, listening to a faint rustle on the left; suddenly he puffed his blowgun, and ran into the woods, bringing back a quail.

Tall Grass turned proudly to David. "Some day big chiefs, huh?"

"Both big chiefs," agreed David. He knew he would have to shoot straight that day if he intended to keep his reputation as the best shot in Tennessee.

Some months later, after the winter had come and gone, Tall Grass once more proved a good friend. Polly was pregnant again, and David knew of no neighbor woman within forty miles. He spoke to Tall Grass of his problem.

"Tall Grass' squaw dead. But other squaws over hills. Tall Grass bring squaw." Two days later Tall Grass arrived with a grimy-faced Indian woman, who spoke no English, but who knew what it was like to bear a child. She stayed in the Crockett cabin for a week. In that time she learned only one English word. It was a proper noun, William, the name of David Crockett's second son.

During the following weeks, David made little efforts toward farming; he found hunting so easy that he collected a great pile of skins, bundled them together, and carried them over to the settlement of North Carolinians. He was disappointed that none of the men had any money; he knew the skins were worth several dollars if he could but find a buyer.

"There ain't no money a-tall in Tennessee no more," one of the settlers told him. "Some says it's account of the 'bargo act, whatever that is."

He finally traded the skins for some gunpowder. The man who agreed to the trade, a ruddy-faced Irishman named Tom Patton, promised to visit David and go for a hunt a few days later.

When Tom Patton visited the Crockett cabin the next week,

[108]

Polly came out in front to sit and talk with the men. "You know, Mr. Patton," she said, "it's been most a year since I talked to any white folks."

"That's a mighty shame, Mrs. Crockett. Maybe sometime my wife, Liza, might come over to visit with you. She's strong as a ox, Liza is. She could walk it over here easy in two days."

David was lying on the ground, facing his wife. He had been staring at her while Tom Patton was talking, realizing for the first time the loneliness she must have felt during the past months. "I'll tell you," he said, leaning back, resting his head on his hands. "We're a-going to move right soon now. I used to think I'd like it way off from everybody. But a man can't live by himself. Got to have some talk, some neighbors, to help out one another with, sometimes."

"That's right, Davy."

"I hear tell Franklin County is a good place. When I was over to your settlement last week I was talking to that young feller from Beans Creek, what's his name ——"

"Young George Russell, yeah, a mighty fine lad he is—bygod, say, Crockett, it's a funny thing, but I been thinking to move, too. Liza's crazy to move."

"Well, whyn't we go together?" David was sitting up now, looking at Polly. She was nodding her head, smiling.

A few days afterwards David and Tom Patton visited the Beans Creek neighborhood and selected sites a few miles apart for their new homes. On their return trip they stopped off at Winchester settlement to visit George Russell who insisted that they stay for a week in his father's huge log house.

"Davy, I hear you're the best shot in Tennessee," George said. "I'd like to go for a hunt to see if it's so."

David agreed to go for one day's hunt; when they returned in the evening George admitted that he'd never seen a better marksman. "I'll promise you, Davy, as soon as you and Tom get your families over to Winchester, I'll call everybody in

[109]

the neighborhood together for a double house-raising. We'll end up with another hunt afterwards. Maybe you was just doing some lucky shooting today."

"Naw he wasn't, son, naw he wasn't," Tom Patton declared. "I ain't never seen him draw a bead yet but what he dropped his game for fair."

Tall Grass was at the cabin the day the Crocketts moved away, his dark lined face emotionless as ever. "Davy Crockett good friend. He go far from here. Tall Grass not glad." He touched his chest. "Hurt here."

David regretted leaving his friend, and told him so, but Tall Grass only shook his head and said, "Bad, bad." He was still standing there in front of the cabin when David and Polly looked back for the last time.

"He is a good Indian," said Polly.

"A damn good Indian," said David, holding John up to wave back to Tall Grass.

The next day they joined Tom Patton, his wife Eliza, and their two children; they were all packed and ready to go. Eliza was a large muscular woman, with a hearty laugh that was contagious to the entire party. Before they had gone a mile, Polly was laughing as merrily as a child, her cheeks flushing in the fresh spring air.

"Mr. Crockett, you sure did pick a purty wife," Eliza said, looking at Polly.

"I reckon I'm no better wife picker than Tom Patton, ma'm," he replied gallantly.

"Aw, go on with you, you flattery-tongued thing."

Although it was a long journey to Winchester, they were still laughing gaily when they arrived at the Russell home. George, followed by his father and mother, came running out to meet them; they had spare beds and pallets laid out for the entire party.

[110]

"I declare," said Polly, "these must be the best people in the world."

"That's right," David agreed. "I never knew a finer young feller than young George Russell. We're going to like to live down here, I'll bet you."

The next morning nearly twenty men joined the caravan at the Russell home to welcome the Crocketts and the Pattons to Franklin County. "We'll have your cabins up in a couple days," George said, after the handshakings were all over. "Bibe Jones is coming along to organize; he's the organizingest man you ever saw."

Bibe Jones was a lawyer; his head was round and bald, set on a scrawny neck. As soon as the party reached the chosen site of David's cabin, Jones gathered the whole crowd around him and made a short speech. In ten minutes he had the work laid out so that every man knew exactly what he was expected to do. The trees began falling to the right and to the left, and the cabin was rising before Polly had her belongings untied from the horses.

"That Bibe Jones is a talking fool," David said to George Russell, between blows of his axe. "I wish I could make a speech like he did."

"Someday maybe you will," said George.

MANY *months before the War of 1812 was a fact, a sharp-brained Shawnee Indian chief in Ohio saw it coming, and laid plans to turn the conflict to the advantage of his people. The Shawnee's name was Tecumseh. As a youth he had attacked settlers going down the Ohio River, for he had no illusions about the ultimate destiny of the Indians if the westward migration of the white race was not halted.*

Tecumseh's hatred for the new American nation was not softened by the Indian policies of the United States govern-

ment after 1800. He saw his strong brothers bribed, his weak brothers coerced; he saw his tribes goaded into committing overt acts which might be used as excuses for seizing more lands; he saw the debauchery of his people by United States agents who traded whiskey for lands; he saw injustices legally committed against Indians in all the courts of the frontier.

By 1804, Tecumseh had gathered a few wise chieftains together in Ohio and Indiana, had formed a communal organization of tribes, had begun systematically teaching his people the arts of agriculture.

By 1811, he was planning to combine all the Indians from Canada to Florida into one democratic federation to resist the imperialistic encroachment of the whites. He made long journeys to Florida, to Alabama, to Tennessee. In Alabama and Tennessee he found the Creeks divided. But Chief Red Eagle listened to Tecumseh's eloquent plea to fight for the preservation of the Indian nation. The Creeks, already pushed back from their best hunting grounds, were suffering hunger after two years of drouth which had withered their crops and driven the wild game far into the west.

Weeks before June 18, 1812, the day of the official proclamation of war between the United States and England, the British were running guns and ammunition into all the Creek villages south of Tennessee, and for a year after that date the patriotic preachments of Tecumseh spread slowly from tribe to tribe.

In the summer of 1813 when the Creeks began daubing war paint on their copper skins, the white settlers of central Alabama gathered for protection on Lake Tensaw where a pioneer farmer named Samuel Mimms had built a stockade for his cattle. From Louisiana militia came to the improvised fort, and the 553 settlers felt safe enough behind its walls.

But at noon on August 30, 1813, while the occupants were at their dinners, one thousand berserk Creeks poured suddenly through the gate and over the walls. By nightfall all but twelve of the 553 men and women of Fort Mimms were dead or dying. As the news of the massacre spread northward through the settlements, there was no longer any doubt that the War of 1812 had at last penetrated to the farthest outposts of the United States of America.

<h1 style="text-align:center">★ 3 ★</h1>

On Christmas morning in 1812, Polly gave birth to her third child, a girl. Tom and Eliza Patton had spent Christmas Eve in the Crockett cabin, staying awake most of the night with David, awaiting the child.

" I'm mighty proud it's a' girl baby," said Polly. She was pleased, too, that the child was born on Christmas day.

" I reckon it's the best Christmas present we could've had," David agreed. They named her Margaret Finley, but David insisted on calling her Little Polly.

With two Pollys in the family and John and William old enough to talk and run around the cabin, David decided he would have to turn back to farming in order to provide food for all of them.

There were two natural clearings near the place, and he found the fertile soil could be turned easily with a wooden plow. Then Mr. Finley paid them a brief surprise visit in April, bringing a cow and calf which he had led all the way from the Holston valley, and while he was with them he helped David sow several acres of corn and beans. Polly was strong enough now to work in the fields; she planted and tended a vegetable garden close to the cabin.

By early summer the Crocketts had all the food they needed, and David felt that he could spare the time for a hunt with Tom Patton and George Russell. Although they hunted for three days they could find little game. As Tom Patton said:

" Danged if there ain't more Indians than animals running through the woods nowadays."

Shortly before dusk of the third day, David returned home to find Polly sitting on the front steps with the three children, watching for him, a look of anxiety upon her face. " I'm glad you've come, Davy," she said. " Lots of Indians been passing here today."

" I saw right many redskins myself back down the river. I reckon they don't mean no harm, though. What you got for supper? "

" Beans and potatoes and corn pone."

" That all? I'm hungry as a she wolf. Been eating so much fresh meat on this hunt, I reckon I'd like to taste some salt pork." He picked John up from the step, paddling him affectionately. " Johnnie, whyn't you run bring your old pa a slab of salt pork? We'll have a big feed and then I'll tell you about that bear we treed."

John ran excitedly into the cabin for the meat while David set a fire to blazing under the kettle which hung from a tripod in the yard just in front of the doorway. In a few minutes the kettle of meat was bubbling merrily, the wind blowing the odorous steam back into their faces. The sun was already down behind the trees, and it was warm and pleasant out on the stoop. The cow, Bessie, was grazing near one corner of the house; her calf, tied to a nearby tree, was snorting indignantly because it could not reach her full udders.

David leaned back against Polly. John and William hung on to his knees, and the baby behind him was pulling at the long strands of his hair. " I guess I got no cause to complain," said he. " We're fixed now, I reckon, Polly; we'll stay here, won't we? "

" It's a good place," she said.

There were footsteps from the farther side of the cabin, soft footsteps made by moccasined feet.

[114]

" Who could that be, the Pattons? " asked Polly nervously.
" No," said David, sitting up straight. " Indians, I'd say."
Three Creeks appeared in the shadowy side of the building,
walking in a wide semicircle away from the place as soon as
they saw David and his family.

" They're the same Indians who walked by here today,"
Polly whispered.

He laughed. " They won't hurt you. They're no worse'n lots
of white folks I know."

A few moments later the Indians stopped, began talking
among themselves; then they turned and walked quickly up
toward the door stoop.

" How do," said the tallest one.

" How're you." David stood up. Their faces were not
pleasant, he had to admit, their eyes sharp and cruel in the
semi-darkness. They looked hungry.

" Want food," said the tallest Indian.

" All right. We got potatoes and beans and corn pone.
We'll share."

" Want meat, too. Indians heap hungry, walk long time,
no eat. White man give meat."

" Sure. You can have some meat, too. Got a kettle full
there. Sit a while, till it's done."

The Indian made a facial gesture expressing extreme disgust.
" Salt meat no good. White man eat salt meat. Indians no
eat." He turned, waving his lean arm toward the calf. " Eat
calf. Good meat."

" No," David replied firmly. " We're not going to eat that
calf. Calf grow to cow, give milk, make much more meat.
We won't eat the calf."

The Indians stepped closer, their eyes gleaming in the light
from the fire. " You kill calf," the tall one said. " You half."
He swung his right arm across his body as if to cut it in two.
" You half. Us half."

While the Creek was talking David had reached inside the doorway for his rifle, at the same time pushing his two young sons back inside. Polly had dropped the baby on the bed, and was outside now, running across the yard, untying the calf. While she led the frightened animal inside the cabin, David cocked his rifle and started moving toward the three scowling Indians who backed slowly away from him.

Darkness was dropping rapidly over the little valley, and he wondered how many more unfriendly Creeks were hiding out in the forest beyond the field. He walked only to the trail that passed in front of the cabin, then stood there a while watching the three Indians skulk away into the night.

Until morning came, he stayed awake inside the cabin, wondering if the visitors would return. Polly slept fitfully all night, occasionally talking out suddenly in her sleep, and the calf made so much noise with its sharp hoofs dancing back and forth on the log flooring the children began to turn and whimper in their bed. Long before daylight he led the calf outside. He did not want to have three crying children on his hands if anything happened. But nothing did happen.

The next day, the encounter in retrospect appeared of such little importance to him that he changed his mind about going up the trail to tell Tom Patton about it. Before noon, however, Tom Patton was dashing down through David's cornfield, his round Irish face ruddier than usual from exertion and excitement.

" Crockett! Crockett! Where in thunder are you? "

David was lying asleep in the grass against the rail fence, but he heard Tom coming and sat up, blinking his eyes, surprised at his friend's excitement.

" Damme, so that's the way you farm, Davy. Lord take pity on the little Crocketts with a father lazy as you, man."

" Hell, I didn't get no sleep last night, Tom. Indians been acting ornery."

"How'd you know? What you heard about Indians?" Tom was mopping his damp scraggly beard with his sleeve.

"Haven't heard nothing. Three Creeks tried to steal my calf last night, that's all."

David could see that Tom had something to tell him. "What you know about it?"

"Mebbe you don't know how lucky you are, Davy Crockett. Four families was wiped out in cold blood west of Winchester last night. A redskin name of Little Warrior was the leader. It sure looks bad, Davy."

David whistled. "Damn if it don't, Tom. I can't figure it out myself. Most the Creeks I know seem to be peaceable enough critters. I can't figure out why they're acting so ornery."

"Me neither," said Tom. "But they sure are stirred up about something."

During the next few weeks David kept his rifle loaded and ready beside his bed, and every evening he tied his cow and calf to the front door so that any noise outside would awaken him. No more Indians appeared, however.

Then, one morning in September, while he was piling corn in a shed beside the cabin, he heard excited voices in the yard. He thrust his head outside, sneezing suddenly from the corn dust.

Tom Patton and a dark-bearded stranger dressed in a dirty buckskin coat were standing outside. "Why, 'morning, Tom. Where'd you come from? Glad to see I'm going to have some help harvesting my corn." He stopped talking when he saw Tom's solemn face; then he looked at the stranger who seemed vaguely familiar to him. "What's matter? Something happened?"

"Sure, and something has happened," said Tom. "The redskins just wiped out a fort, Fort Mimms, down south aways. Hurricane Ned, here, was just telling me about it, passing through. Thought maybe you'd like to hear the word, straight from him."

"They killed five hundred settlers, Mr. Crockett," said Hurricane Ned. "I was by Fort Mimms day after it happened. Never saw so many dead folks, I reckon, in all my put-together."

"Five hundred! I reckon then nobody's safe a-tall now."

"That's right," said Tom. "Ned's on his way to Nashville to see Andy Jackson. Everybody says Old Andy is the man to put a stop to it."

Hurricane Ned had only one eye; where the other should have been was an empty scarred socket. When he spoke his good eye twisted and strained as if it too would leap out. "Old Andy'll raise an army and clean out the whole fired mess," he cried. "The damned British are to blame for it, bringing in guns and gitting the redskins drunked on whiskey. It's turning into a war, that's what it is."

David was looking at Hurricane Ned, trying to remember where he had seen him before. All at once he remembered. "Say, Ned, was you up in the Holston valley about ten years ago?"

"The Holston country, up past Knoxville? Sure, I used to go up there about every year."

"Remember a man named Abe Wilson?"

"'Course I do. Old Abe Wilson made the kickingest whiskey in Tennessee."

"I used to work for him. I remember one night you was there, telling about how you lost that eye in a fight, and old Abe's boy tried to gouge mine out after you left."

Hurricane Ned laughed, opening his wide toothless mouth. "He did, did he? Well damn my soul."

"I haven't got any whiskey strong as Abe's, but maybe a little swig won't hurt you none before you start trailing up to Nashville. Come on in the house and drink."

While Hurricane Ned drank from David's largest jug, Polly and the children sat together on the bed listening to his vivid description of the Fort Mimms massacre.

After the old Indian fighter had gone on up the road toward Winchester, David walked back and forth around the cabin, unable to put his mind to his work, wondering what would happen next.

He stopped once in the doorway, talking to Polly who was even more excited than he was. " Hurricane Ned said this was going to be a war, Polly. All my life I've heard about wars from the old folks, but I'm kind of like Old Quaker John Kennedy; I ain't much in favor of a war. I like a good private fight, all right, but there's not much sense to a war. That's what Old Quaker John always said."

" Men get killed in a war," said Polly, " and their womenfolks have to suffer for it."

" Yeah, but this Indian massacring, maybe it's not a war. They been doing most the killing so far. If the settlers, me and Tom and George Russell and all the others, get together and have Andy Jackson to tell us how to go about stopping the redskins—if we don't do something now after Fort Mimms, no settler on the Tennessee border can sleep safe nights—if we go about it together, kind of like a big hunt, maybe it won't be a war, but just a private fight."

The following day, Bibe Jones, the Winchester lawyer, rode up to David's cabin on his white horse. " No time to talk much now, Davy. I'm riding up and down the whole slope, passing the word. All the settlers aim to meet at my place next Saturday to raise volunteers to fight the Indians. We'll be looking out for you." He rode away as quickly as he had come, his horse kicking up clouds of dust with its great hoofs.

Friday night, David greased his rifle. Polly was sitting on the bed, watching him, her eyes round and bright with fear.

"Whyn't you stay home tomorrow, Davy? Let the men who got no families do the fighting."

"Not enough single fellers. Besides it's the family men who ought to be most consarned about the Indians." He continued rubbing the barrel of the gun.

"But if you go away, I don't know a soul nearby, 'cept Liza Patton, and she's five mile off. And who'll tend to the place, and the children?"

"I know it's bad, Polly. It's going to go mighty hard with you, but think about all them people at Fort Mimms, five hundred of 'em dead. The next thing you know they'll be up here a-scalping you and Johnnie and Willie and Little Polly, if we don't go and stop 'em right now. If every man waited till his wife got willing for him to go to fight, there wouldn't be no fighting done till we'd all be killed in our houses."

"But maybe it's different with us, no close neighbors, no big children to help about the place."

He went over to the bed and patted her shoulders. "I reckon I'm able as any man in Franklin County. Ain't I the best shot in Tennessee? I guess it's kind of my duty to go; as old Hurricane Ned said, it's a war, a private kind of war, and I'm bound to be part of it."

"I reckon there's no stopping you, Davy."

Before noon Saturday, David was in Winchester. A drizzling rain had begun falling sometime during the night, but the narrow slippery clay street between the log buildings was filled with a restless mob of settlers who came from all parts of the county, eager to learn more news about the Indians. He found Tom Patton and George Russell already there, standing in front of one of the stores.

"Hello, George, hello, Tom, anything you heard?" Tom's face was flushed with excitement. "We know there's going to be a fight now. A militiaman just rode in early this morning from Nashville. Colonel Coffee is already on his way down here, and Andy Jackson is going to take command in a few days."

"Old Andy just got out of his bed," a stranger declared. "Jesse Benton almost shot his shoulder off in that doo-el, you know."

"Yeah, I hear Old Andy can't even wear his epaulets," said George.

David laughed. "That'd be a pity now, wouldn't it? Old Andy going out to shoot Indians without his shoulder ornaments."

The talk continued for hours; then about mid-afternoon Bibe Jones appeared on his white horse, riding up and down the sticky red street. "You men all line up two by two," he yelled. "Everybody, two by two. We'll march down to the meeting house and have some talk."

Almost without exception the members of the crowd lined up in irregular formation. Several women stood in the doorways of the houses watching them walk along through the misty rain, down the muddy street to the big meeting house. The long single room filled rapidly and stragglers had to stand outside in the wet, their heads thrust through the open windows.

Bibe Jones and two men in militia uniforms together with Herbert Julius, the Winchester pastor, sat at the rough hickory table at one end of the room, waiting for the hubbub to cease. Suddenly Jones was on his feet, pounding the table, and the room became silent.

"Reverend Julius will lead us in a prayer," he said briefly.

For several minutes the pastor prayed, reciting the good deeds of the settlers and the evil deeds of the Indians. David thought he made out too good a case for the settlers, and he knew all the Indians were not red devils, but he supposed it was too late now for fair argument.

As soon as the prayer was ended, Bibe Jones was standing

[121]

up again, introducing the two members of the militia, one the lieutenant who had just arrived with the good news from Nashville, the other a Major Gibson who was traveling from settlement to settlement helping to organize the various companies.

" Now," shouted Jones, shaking his round head so savagely that it seemed in imminent danger of leaping from his scrawny neck. " Now, I ain't going to make no long-winded talk. I know how you all feel about this matter. We got to fight, we all know that now. And we got to do the fighting ourselves, you and me, all of us. The gov'ment army is fighting in the East, and no hired soldiers are coming down here to do our fighting for us. And we don't need gov'ment soldiers. In two months' time we can clean out every painted redskin in the Creek nation. I offer my services to Major Gibson and Andy Jackson, our leader. How many you boys aim to join me? " He shouted out his final words, pounding upon the table.

David stepped forward immediately, holding up his hand. Several others, including George Russell, reached the table at the same time he did. They shook hands with Major Gibson. Then, while David was withdrawing to make room for the others, he saw Tom Patton off to one side, chewing on his lower lip, his blue eyes blinking indecisively. " Come on, Tom," he cried. " We can't go on a fighting march without you along."

Tom grinned sheepishly, and then began pushing through the mob toward the table. " I was just thinking a little about Liza and the kids, wondering about them," he said.

David could hardly wait to get back to the cabin to tell Polly that he had signed up to fight. He rode along with Tom, who seemed worried, and not at all anxious to reach home as Davy was.

" I'll bet Liza was agin his going to fight," David told Polly later. " I'll bet she talked him blue last night."

"I don't blame Liza," said Polly. "It's them that stays behind that suffers most in times like these."

He returned to Winchester Monday, when the volunteers met to elect a captain. Bibe Jones, naturally, was the unanimous choice, and he made a stirring speech of acceptance, David listening to every word, watching every gesture the long-necked lawyer made. Already orders from Colonel Coffee had been received in Winchester; they were to march south on the following Monday, leaving them only one week in which to make preparations.

The week passed swiftly, for he had many tasks to complete around the cabin. Polly cooked a huge batch of hard cakes, patched up one of his old hunting shirts and knitted a woolen underjacket. She would have packed a large bundle of supplies but David refused to carry anything except absolute necessities. "If I get into an Indian battle, I don't want to be pestered with any unnecessary plunder," he said.

Early Monday morning he joined the column of volunteers when they passed along the trail in front of his cabin, telling Polly and the children good-bye as soon as he heard the men coming. Polly's eyes were dry, but he knew she would cry as soon as he was out of the yard. He slapped John affectionately on the shoulders, jumped on his horse, and rode out to meet the column. In the lead was Captain Jones, dressed in a brand-new blue coat.

David was surprised at the number of men; there were more than a hundred, a long line mounted on horses, reaching almost as far back as he could see up the valley. He waited, speaking to each man as he passed, until he saw George Russell, then fell into line in front of him. George was carrying a new rifle, which his father had given him that morning. "He says it's as good as the ones the British have been giving out to the Indians," laughed George.

Tom Patton joined them when they passed his farm. Liza

[123]

was out at the rail fence, waving at the men, tears streaming down her broad face.

All that day and the next they rode until they reached Beatty's Spring, where they joined a smaller company already encamped. For several days they stayed there, other troops joining them almost every day until there were over a thousand men in the camp.

"I never saw so many settlers together in one place in my life," David remarked one day while they were eating dinner under the trees.

Tom was chewing noisily on an ear of boiled corn. "Damned redskins ain't got a chance against all us, now, have they?" said he.

"If they ever set eyes on that red beard of yours, Tom," George Russell said, "they'll throw down their guns and quit."

"He's grown a mat of whiskers, all right," David agreed.

"You got quite a mess yourself, Davy. But look at mine, not even enough fuzz to hide my dimples." George rubbed his chin ruefully.

That afternoon Major Gibson arrived, immediately calling all the company commanders together. News soon spread through the camp that an army of Indians was gathering below the Tennessee River, and that Colonel Coffee would reach Beatty's Spring in a few hours to lead them into battle.

As soon as the consultation between Major Gibson and the company captains was ended, Bibe Jones sought out David and led him over to meet the major. The officer was dressed in regulation uniform, a blue tight-waisted long-tailed coat covered with brass buttons, which made him appear conspicuous among the buckskin-clad volunteers.

"This here is Davy Crockett," Captain Jones said, pushing David forward.

The major nodded slightly. "Your captain tells me you're the best shot in his company."

"Some folks say I'm the best shot in Tennessee," replied David, grinning.

"That may be," said the major brusquely. David decided the officer was not a man for joking; so he straightened up stiffly and waited for him to have his say.

"I'm looking for some good woodsmen to join a small scouting expedition with me. We're going to make a quick dash down below the Tennessee River to find out the lay of the land. What do you say to it?"

"For certain, yes, sir. You can count on me." David was pleased that he had been selected; a scouting party was just the thing he had wanted to organize days ago.

"All right, Crockett. Could you select a couple of mates to go with you?"

"Yes, sir." He looked around at the faces of the group of men who had gathered to see what was happening. "Tom Patton." Tom stepped forward, his forehead flushing redder than his beard.

"He looks like a good man," said the major.

"And George Russell."

When George pushed forward, Major Gibson frowned slightly, turned to David, speaking softly: "We need men, not boys, for this journey."

David looked straight into Major Gibson's cold gray eyes. "I reckon I know George Russell purty well, sir."

"But this boy, he has scarcely any beard."

"I didn't know the militia measured a man's courage by his beard," David drawled. "By that light, I reckon a goat would have the preference over a man."

Major Gibson snorted. "Be ready early in the morning for the start," he said shortly, turning his back and walking quickly away.

They left before dawn, on horseback, with nine other scouts selected by the major. After crossing the Tennessee River, the

[125]

party separated, David and his two friends and two other scouts heading south, while Major Gibson and his group went west. At dusk they came upon a cabin in a broad clearing, and a huge raw-boned settler ran out to meet them as soon as they appeared. "Boys, I'm damn glad to see you. My name is Radcliffe. I knowed you was scouts soon as I saw you coming."

Radcliffe had married a Creek woman, yet his wife was very friendly and his two half-breed sons asked if they might join in the fighting against the Indians. While David and his men ate large portions of their host's corn and potatoes, they listened to his remarks about the actions of the neighboring tribes. " You're in mighty dangerous territory right now. Ten warriors painted red as blood was here this morning mad as hornets. I made out I didn't know nothing about any army coming to fight 'em."

David was surprised to learn that only about one-half of the Creeks were arming. " Why, there's a whole Creek village down the trail who'll be just as happy to see you as I was," Radcliffe declared. " They're more 'fraid of the fighting Creeks than some of us whites are."

" Whyn't we go by that village tonight? " David looked at George Russell who nodded approval; his mouth was so full of boiled corn he did not take time to speak.

" We might learn something there," David added.

They rode through the forest in bright moonlight; the autumn air was fresh and sweet with the odor of dry leaves. " I ain't felt so good in a dozen years," Tom Patton shouted, galloping his horse along in the lead, his red beard flowing around his chin.

At the Indian village they were welcomed noisily, but the chieftains warned David that if they were discovered there by a roving war party the whole village would probably be wiped out.

[126]

"If just one red stick shows hisself," David replied, "I'll carry his scalp back home with me to make a moccasin."

The Indians who understood English laughed loudly, and the others joined in. David was laughing too. "Suppose'n you fellers teach me how to shoot a bow and arrow?"

Pine torches were set up, and David entered a shooting match with bows and arrows underneath the huge oak trees which surrounded the village. The Indians, however, were too adept for him; he lost one of his best powder horns in the final match to a young Creek whose eye seemed unerring.

About ten o'clock Radcliffe left for his cabin. Withdrawing to one end of the village, the scouts rolled up on the ground for rest after the day of hard riding. But David had scarcely put his head to the ground when a sharp scream cut across the still night air.

An Indian had rushed into the camp; he was running up and down between the shelters, jabbering and screaming as if in mortal terror. At last, David learned from one of the old chieftains that the excited runner brought news that a war party of Creeks had been crossing the Coosa River all day at the Ten Islands, some miles to the south. In ten minutes, the village was emptied of all its frightened inhabitants.

"We better ride like hell back to Beatty's Spring and let Colonel Coffee know what's coming." They were soon on their horses, heading back north. Although it was a seventy-five-mile ride, they rode into Beatty's Spring before ten o'clock the following morning, sore and hungry.

Colonel Coffee, in a resplendent blue coat and skin-tight trousers, was sitting in front of his brush shelter, smoking a twisted black cigar. David had never seen him before, but he knew from his uniform that he must be the famous colonel.

"Colonel Coffee?" he said. His eyes were bloodshot from the journey, his voice sounded rusty even to himself.

"I'm Colonel Coffee."

" I have to report, sir, that an army of Creeks crossed the Coosa at Ten Islands yesterday."

" And who are you, man? "

" David Crockett, sir, a scout."

" By whose authority do you make this report? "

" By my own authority. I rode out of here under Major Gibson."

" When Major Gibson returns I'll listen to his report," replied the colonel sharply.

David turned away angrily.

"By God, Tom," he said to Patton when he rejoined his companions, " d'you see any smoke coming out of me? I'm so damn mad I'm burning inside like a tar kiln. That old colonel is a sniveling bearcat, that's all there is to it."

Major Gibson returned to the camp early the following morning with the same report David had brought in twenty-four hours earlier. The Creeks, he said, were massing forces above the Coosa at Ten Islands.

Within a few minutes pandemonium broke loose at Beatty's Spring. Colonel Coffee mounted his horse, riding up and down the camp, ordering all the troops to begin throwing up breastworks a quarter of a mile around the spring. At the same time an express rider dashed away for Fayetteville with a message to General Jackson urging him to send his regular troops marching immediately. The Indians were coming!

" I'll be damned," said Tom Patton, " I thought we was aiming to go fight the Indians, not wait for them to come to us." There was also considerable grumbling among some of the volunteers about the breastworks. Bill Matthews, a man from Shoal Creek, one of the scouts who had gone with David, was disgusted. " We signed up to shoot," said he, " not to pile up a heap of rocks and logs and dirt."

" I bet old Andy Jackson won't set on his tail and wait for 'em," said David.

"Nah, Old Andy'll go right after 'em," George agreed.

Late the next day, when Andrew Jackson, his wounded arm in a sling, arrived at the head of his uniformed troops, he was greeted with lusty cheers from the waiting volunteers. As the cheers echoed in the trees, David ran out with the others, pushing forward to see General Andy Jackson. At first he looked for an officer in a uniform more elegant even than that of Colonel Coffee, but the man leading the troops was dressed in a frayed blue cloak and high unpolished boots which knocked against his bony knees as he rode slowly along. He was waving a worn leather cap at the shouting line of volunteers.

" Is that Old Andy? " David asked George Russell almost incredulously.

" Sure, that's him," whispered George.

David looked again at the tall emaciated man with the bear-trap jaw and sharp nose, and just then Andy Jackson looked at him briefly with eyes that were cold and sharp as flint rock. " That's Old Andy, all right," he said to himself, watching the general slide off his horse and stagger painfully across the ground to greet Colonel Coffee.

Jackson's troops were so weary they dropped flat on the ground when the command was given for them to fall out. Half of them were suffering from blistered feet after the long forced march; and in a few minutes an order was issued for them to rest for twelve hours. All night the volunteers stood guard while the militiamen slept.

Early next morning, Jackson called the volunteers to order, and walked down the line, shaking hands with each man. After the inspection, he explained tersely that they were marching at once for the Coosa River.

" I told you Old Andy wouldn't set on his tail and wait for 'em," David cried. All the volunteers were excited; days of waiting at the spring had begun to pall on them. Rifles were polished quickly, powder horns were filled, and the march began.

Only scattered bands of Indians were sighted on the march, some of whom were taken prisoners without resistance. Village after village they found deserted, and David began to doubt that there were any fighting warriors when they reached Ten Islands without even a minor engagement. However, after they had set up a crude fort at the Islands, a scouting party soon brought back word that the Creek warriors had gathered in a town south of the Coosa and were preparing to march against Jackson. David had wanted to join the scouting expedition, but because of his reputation for marksmanship he was sent instead down the river to shoot any game which might be used for food. Supplies expected from Fayetteville had failed to arrive, and the men were suffering from hunger; only small portions of parched corn were doled out to them each day. The foraging party headed by David brought back only a few wild hogs and a deer, which when divided only served to whet the appetites of the starving soldiers.

After the quick repast, Jackson issued an order. " We'll make a surprise march against the Indian village," he said.

It was a sunny day in early November, so warm that after they had marched for an hour David removed his hunting shirt, tying it around his neck. He walked along with Tom Patton for a while, and they talked quietly about their families.

" Our two months is most up now," said Tom. " I sure'd like to see Liza and the little 'uns."

" I feel the same," said David, " but I want to finish up this fighting, if there's going to be any fighting."

They crossed a section of swamps, beating a pathway through the yellow dried canes that grew taller than their heads, then came out upon a green pine-covered slope. Over a rolling hill they could see wisps of smoke curling; the rangers, on horseback just ahead of them, had stopped. Andy Jackson,

[130]

in his ragged blue cloak, was riding back down the line issuing orders to the captains.

A minute or so later, Bibe Jones shouted back at them: "That's the village over that hill. Thousand redskins piled up in there waiting for us. Split ranks, don't pay no 'tention to marching any more, left line go left, right line right, every man for himself now. We're going to tie 'em up in there, and then wait for the rangers to give the signal for attack."

The rangers held their horses still while the men on foot went forward, half of them to the left, half to the right. David was alone now, except for a uniformed militiaman a few feet ahead of him, and a youngster in buckskin some yards behind him. There was no sound, only his moccasins padding softly on the brown pine needles. Now the village was to his right; he could still see faint traces of blue smoke floating high in the hazy November sky.

After a while the militiaman ahead stopped and turned, fingers to his lips; the two lines had met on the other end of the village; a circle of men was strung completely around the enemy. David squatted on his haunches, patting the barrel of his rifle, keeping a close watch through the green pines toward the town. After a few minutes he heard the rangers, riding over the hill, shouting and firing their guns. This was the signal for the marchers to run toward the town. David was on his feet, every sense alert, dodging from one scrub pine to another. He could see the outside huts of the village now, and a few Indians in scarlet paint and bright feathers running toward the end of the town where the rangers were advancing. But already the horsemen had turned about, racing back out of rifle range, giving the militiamen and the volunteers time to reach the edge of the village while the attention of the inhabitants was attracted to them.

David came out suddenly in the open, amazed at the number of warriors gathered in close formation at the north edge of the town where they had rushed to meet the attacking rangers. Automatically he raised his rifle and fired blindly into the group; simultaneously firing began on both sides of him, several Indians in the mob falling to the ground. Taken by surprise, the Creeks fired hastily in return, retreating back into the town in confusion. When they realized they were surrounded, several rushed out toward the attackers begging for mercy. David was reloading, when a skinny brave came dashing out toward him, his hands over his head in a gesture of supplication. "Lie down, you damn fool, and I won't shoot you," David cried, but at that moment the youth on his right fired a bullet into the Indian's skull.

"Wasn't no use for that," David said, under his breath. "That one wasn't aiming to fight any more."

As the army drew closer and closer to the village, the distance between each man lessened so that they were almost shoulder to shoulder. When he approached the first line of huts, David saw a group of Indians crowding into one of the doorways. He fired into them; one fell. The militiaman on his left had lighted a torch, tossing it into a heap of bedding against one of the buildings. Squaws were rushing toward them, weeping, catching at the volunteers' hunting shirts, begging for their lives.

Now he could see the opposite line of soldiers coming in from the woods on the other side of the village. "Hold your fire short," he yelled at the men on either side of him. "Our boys are coming in over there."

The Indians were firing so recklessly that few shots took effect; he had seen only one man hit, a bearded fellow who went down on his knees clutching at his shoulder. Then as he hurried across a bare space near the middle of the village, he saw twenty or more braves crouched against a wall, preparing to make a rush against the invaders. Out of the corner of his eye he saw Tom Patton and several others of his companions firing into the group. David reloaded quickly, but held his fire as the Indians had turned, trying to take cover in a mud-chinked log building nearby. From the windows guns were already spitting fire, and a bullet knocked dust up a few feet ahead of him.

" Let's take that house," yelled one of the lieutenants of the militia.

" Here we go," David answered. They ran boldly across the line of fire, until they reached cover beside a heap of old logs. Several others followed them without mishap.

In the doorway of the besieged house, a squaw suddenly appeared. She sat down calmly on the step, staring at the men behind the logs. Behind her in the shadows was a churning mass of warriors, firing from chinks and windows.

" If we can take that house, we've got 'em whipped," David said. He looked quickly at the faces of the men around him, expecting to see Tom Patton, but he was not among them.

The leathery-faced squaw was still sitting defiantly in the bright sunlight that fell across the doorway, a bow and arrow resting in her lap.

" They can stay in there all day, snipe shooting at us," said David.

" Yeah. We'll have to set fire to it," the lieutenant said. He had already lighted a torch, and as it flared up he ran over the heap of logs, tossing it onto the low roof of the building. But before he could drop back to cover, the squaw had placed her foot against the bow, drawing with all her strength, streaking an arrow into the lieutenant's abdomen before any of the men knew what was happening. He fell writhing in the dust, his uniform turning black with dirt and blood as he rolled over and over. Instantly almost every man behind the heap of logs had risen, firing into the doorway, ripping bullet holes through the Indian woman's body until she fell face forward, motionless.

[133]

David's stomach sickened. He had never seen a man killed by an arrow; nor had he ever seen a woman killed by a hail of rifle bullets.

But now the straw roof of the hut was blazing furiously, and three or four Indians dashed out, running but a few feet until they all fell dead from the steady firing of the attackers. The others stayed inside the burning building, while the roof and blazing logs crumbled rapidly in upon them. David and the others rushed forward, surrounding the building, firing bullets into the doorway and windows.

The heat was so terrific David drew back a few feet, stumbling over the dust-covered body of an Indian who was trying to crawl away from the flames. He crouched down, expecting resistance, and saw that the warrior was a boy of about fourteen, the side of his face burned severely, one arm crushed, his thigh torn open. Perspiration streamed out of the boy's coppery skin; his mouth, closed tightly, held back cries of agony. David stepped back, his own face blistering from the heat, reminded suddenly of a deer he had once found in the woods, its leg torn away, and how he had shot it to end its misery. He looked once more at the crawling Indian boy, raised his rifle, fired blindly. Quickly he turned and ran down through the lines of blazing huts, sick with disgust.

Except for occasional bursts of firing off in the woods, the battle was ended. He wandered about aimlessly, looking for Tom and George. He found George, his face black with cinders from the burning huts.

"Old Tom may be back down at that big hut where we roasted the redskins," David said wearily. "Last place I saw him." When they reached the burned building, half of one wall had fallen away, and in the smouldering ruins they could see half-charred bodies standing or leaning grotesquely against the logs.

Some of the soldiers had already discovered that a potato

cellar was underneath the building, and were jerking away
the smoking flooring, trying to get at them. David had forgotten the pangs of hunger in his stomach, but the sight of
the vegetables brought back the desire for food with increased
agony. He grabbed a handful of the potatoes when they were
handed up to him by one of the men inside the cellar. He
ate ravenously two of them and then examined the others in
his hands; they were covered with slimy grease which had
dripped down upon them from the burning bodies of the
Indians above. Quickly he dropped them to the ground, where
they were picked up by a hungry soldier before they stopped
rolling. Hearing his name called, he pushed through the crowd,
remembering that George Russell had been with him a minute
ago.

" Hey, George, where're you? "

" Davy! Davy Crockett! Come over here."

He saw George now, near one of the heap of logs where he
had sought shelter during the fighting. George was leaning
over something in the runway, something that looked like one
of the logs, but was a man.

" For God's sake, Davy, it's Tom. It's old Tom."

David stumbled forward, feeling for Tom's chest under his
thick mat of a beard. It was no use. Tom Patton's face was
as white as the dust around him, and David knew it would
never flush red with life again.

★ 4 ★

Returning to Fort Strother at Ten Islands after the battle,
the army rested for several days. Food and supplies were expected daily until the seasonal rains began falling; then the
men realized that weeks might pass before any outside resources could reach them.

[135]

Several foraging parties were sent out, but except for an occasional starving deer the hunters were unsuccessful. The small stores of corn that remained were being rationed out in handfuls to the men who parched or boiled the grain before eating it. Sickness began to spread; General Jackson himself was suffering from acute attacks of dysentery.

The men in David's company had signed up for sixty days; already they had served ninety days. Their clothing was worn to shreds after the long marches through the brush. Many of their horses had died from starvation. After several days of talk, a small group led by David and George Russell went to Bibe Jones and told him they were ready to leave for home. Captain Jones' long face was solemn for a moment. "Well, I'll tell you," he said slowly, "Old Hickory says he aims to strike another blow afore winter. But I know how you boys feel. I got a family back home myself."

"We don't need to kill every last one of the Creeks," said David. "I figure we've taught 'em their lesson now."

"Mebbe so," replied Jones thoughtfully, "mebbe so, but General Jackson thinks different."

"Well, by God, if we aim to lick 'em proper we got to have something to eat, and some more clothes and fresh horses. We couldn't whip a squaw army the way we are now." David stopped, waiting for some of the others to speak.

"I think Davy's right," said George Russell. "If we can't get supplies we can't do much fighting in this country. If General Jackson will give us leave to go home and fresh up, we'll come straight back and fight another battle, if he thinks we got it to do."

Several of the others spoke then, Jones nodding slowly as each man had his say. "Wars ain't ordinarily fought like this," the captain said finally, "but I'll pass the word on to the General. Mebbe you boys don't know that me and some of the other cap'ns been having the same ideas. Fellow by name of Jim Matthews from up Shoal Creek way, just been made a cap'n, says all his men are rarin' to go home."

"I know Cap'n Matthews; he's all right. Went on that long scout with me," David said.

"Well, I'll go get him and mebbe a couple other cap'ns, and we'll go see Old Andy right now."

A few hours later, Jones reported that General Jackson had emphatically refused to grant leave to any of the men. David was defiant. "Old Hickory Face can go kill all the Creeks he wants to," he cried, "but Davy Crockett is going home. I volunteered for two months, I've stayed three. I'm not a militiaman, I'm a settler, with a wife and three children to feed. It'd be different if the redskins was raising hell still, but they ain't. They're licked."

"I'm with you, Crockett," said Captain Jim Matthews. "And so are most of my men."

"I don't like to walk out on Old Andy, but count on me, Davy," George Russell said quickly.

"Well," interrupted Bibe Jones, "I'm aiming to stay, but any of my men can do what they please. I'd like to go, but I've made promises to Andy Jackson I can't break right now."

That night almost a hundred men prepared to leave, making no attempt at secrecy. When morning came, those who had horses strapped their belongings to their animals' bony backs. Then, in a straggling group they moved down toward the log bridge that led from the island fort across the rocks in the river to the opposite shore. David and George and Captain Jim Matthews were in the lead.

Although they had expected Jackson to make some move, they were surprised when they came to the bridge to find it blocked by a small cannon and a guard of uniformed militiamen. Andrew Jackson was leaning against the side of the stockade, stroking his long nose with his fingers, his face as gray and forbidding as the cold December skies.

Matthews stopped still, but David jerked at his arm. " Let's call his bluff. If we don't, he's got us licked for good. Then we'll be here all winter." He paused just long enough to pick his flint and prime his gun. " If they fire on us," he added, " we'll fight our way through."

" Or all die together," said Matthews, stepping up even with David.

" I don't like what we're doing," George said huskily. " If it was anybody else but you, Davy, I wouldn't carry it through."

As they came nearer the bridge they could hear the militiamen cocking their guns. One of the men beside the cannon had lighted a flame to touch off the fuse, but when he saw that the insurgents were not going to stop advancing, he threw the flame in the stream, at the same time beckoning them to come on. Immediately some of the other militiamen dropped their guns and raised their bright caps in the air in friendly salutes. At this show of camaraderie the volunteers began cheering.

Passing close beside the stockade, David could see Jackson's eyes moving jerkily from one man to another, as if imprinting each face permanently upon his mind. They marched jauntily on across the bridge, the militiamen standing aside to make room for their passage. David and Matthews stopped when they reached the end of the crossing, waiting until the last volunteer had stepped down to the ground.

David turned, looking back toward the camp. Jackson had walked over to the opposite end of the bridge and was standing there, his hands in his pockets, his steely eyes glaring after them.

" Good-bye, General," cried David. " We'll see you again soon."

Jackson raised his fist cursing. " Ye're the damnedest volunteers I ever saw in all my born days," he screamed. " You volunteer to go out and fight, then you volunteer to go home when the notion strikes you. Go on and be damned, you—volunteers!"

After a week of hard travel through mud and rain and across flooded streams, David and George finally came in sight of Tom Patton's little cabin, looking snug and warm against the dark sky.

"I wonder if the news has come to Liza yet," said George.

"I don't know," replied David. "I'd hate to have to tell her."

They knew that Liza had heard as soon as they saw her; her square face was wrinkled with grief. She caught at David with her lumpy hands, wanting to know how Tom had died and if they had buried him properly.

"How's Polly?" he asked after a few minutes.

"She's kind of peaked, Davy, worrying about you. She'll be mighty grateful to see you. I was over to your place, day afore yesterday."

After a few minutes more of painful conversation, he and George were on their way again, anxious to reach their own homes. Although David's horse was so lame that he had to walk most of the remainder of the journey, after he saw the chimney of his cabin with its lazy curl of smoke he could hardly keep himself from running. Polly met him at the trail, and he knew she had seen him coming from a distance; probably she had been looking up the trail for him all these many days. He hugged her tight, and then turned to shake hands with George who was eager to ride on to Winchester before nightfall.

It was good, being back inside the cabin, with its clean flooring, and warm fire on the hearth, and the smell of food cooking, and the sound of Polly's voice, and the children romping about and jerking at his leggings. He sat down in the old

hickory chair, pulling Polly across his lap. He kissed her again
and again, with John standing there laughing at them.

"My goodness," said Polly excitedly, "we can't sit here
loving one another all day. Why, you look plumb starved,
Davy." She felt his sides. "Your ribs are sticking out like a
pore mule's."

She jumped up and started another kettle of food to boiling over the fire. "We've got a smidgin of grape jam. I've
been saving it up for you 'cause I know you like it. Johnnie
climbed trees and brought down piles of sour grapes, but we
didn't have any way to keep them."

"Yeah, I sure do like grapes," said David, stretching his legs
slowly. "Polly, there just wasn't nothing to eat down there
where we was, just nothing."

"We looked for you a month ago."

"I wanted to come then, too, but we couldn't right then."
He started to tell her he was going back soon, but there was
no need yet, he thought. It might spoil things for her if she
knew he was going back again.

"Did you kill many redskins, pa?" John was straddling his
knee, his gray eyes round and big like Polly's.

"Nah, not many, Johnnie. Indians not such mighty fighters.
I'd rather kill a bear any day."

"Did you kill any bears?"

"Yessiree, one old big brown bear."

"Did he growl at you?"

"He sure did. Like this." David imitated the bear's growl,
and John and William both scampered back behind the bed,
screaming with mock terror and delight.

Polly brought out the pewter dishes she had saved from her
mother's things; they had never used them before. In a few
minutes the table was covered with steaming food. David ate
for almost an hour, until his stomach felt tight. " This is the

[140]

best I've had since I left here, Polly. Never knew what a good cook you was till I went away."

They sat in front of the fire until late. He felt warm and lazy and sleepy, watching the flames rising and falling. When she saw the cake of grime on his feet, Polly hastily poured him a pot of warm water. " I never saw such dirty feet," she said. " You must have walked barefooted."

" Just the same as," he replied, showing her the holes in the bottoms of his moccasins.

He thought the children would never go to sleep they were so excited over his return. But finally they began to nod, and he helped Polly put them under the covers in the wide bed in the back room. Then as the fire died down, leaving only red coals glowing on the hearth, she blew out the candle; they began to undress in the darkened room. Polly was slipping her nightgown over her head, but he drew it away gently, picked her up, and carried her over to the bed.

" Remember the night we got married, Polly? "

" It is 'most like that night," she said.

The following day was fair and cold, with ice films on the pools of water near the cabin. When David saw the size of the woodpile he was glad he had returned when he did; there was not enough wood to last another week. And as yet, the winter had scarcely begun.

With his young sons as interested spectators, he cut down two large trees, an oak and a dead pine, and spent the next three days chopping the limbs and logs into firewood. John began stacking the pieces into neat piles against the wall of the cabin, but when he learned that his father was going on a hunt the next day, he lost interest in stacking wood and demanded permission to go hunting too. David agreed, and they returned in the evening with a deer, a coon, and several squirrels. The coon was brought down by John, after David

[141]

had drawn a bead on the animal for him. " We'll make a cap from its fur for you," said David.

The deer was young and tender, but Polly was disappointed because they had brought back no turkeys. " Next week is Christmas, and I wanted a turkey to fix."

" Next week is Christmas? I'd clear forgot. Little Polly will be a year old, won't she? "

" She will." Polly's face was suddenly sad. " I always think about pore old Tom Patton, how funny he was last Christmas when Polly was born. Whyn't we ask Liza and her two young-uns over for Christmas dinner? "

" Sure, and we will. I'll go over tomorrow and see how she's making out."

He found Liza more cheerful than when he had seen her last, and she seemed quite pleased at the invitation to Christmas dinner. David looked about the place; repairs were needed everywhere. The roof was so bad with holes he could see the sky in several places. Before he left for home he hewed out a few crude slabs and fixed the worst crevices.

" That'll help some," he told her, " but soon, you'll be needing a new roof."

" Lord have mercy on me." She threw up her hands. " I'll be needing more things than a roof, I'm thinking. I don't know what is going to become of us."

All the way home, David was thinking about Tom. It wasn't worth it, the whole Indian mess, it wasn't worth the life of one such a man as Tom Patton. Yet he knew he would have to go back into it again, himself. The business would have to be finished. And if he was going back, he would have to go soon. He didn't mind the going; it was telling Polly, watching her face when he told her he was leaving her again.

The day before Christmas he rode up to Winchester on his young pony to see George Russell. As he expected, George had received news direct from Fort Strother. " Jackson has got some new reinforcements," George told him. "And he's planning to strike out for New Orleans or Florida maybe, to try to get at the British themselves."

"That's the way I been thinking all along," said David. "Stop the British and we've stopped the Indians."

"Well, when are you going back?" asked George after a minute of silence.

"When are you going?"

"Next week."

"I'll go with you," said David.

George declined his invitation to come and spend Christmas day with him, as he wanted to stay with his father and mother as long as possible.

On the way home, David bagged a fine turkey hen, and rushed into the cabin waving it under Polly's nose. She plucked the fowl, stuffed it, and started cooking it at once.

Early Christmas morning, Liza and her two children rode over on their old mare. There was much merriment all day. None of them spoke of Tom, although David and Polly could feel that Liza was thinking about him all the time.

"I'm mighty glad," Liza said, after they had finished the dinner, leaving the turkey bones picked clean on their plates, "I'm mighty glad you're safe home to stay, Davy."

He looked at Liza sharply, then stood up, pushing back his chair. "I reckon I might as well tell you all, I'm not home to stay." He glanced at Polly, then turned away, seeing her face turn pale with shock. "I've got to go back. The fight's not over. I can't quit now, I just can't."

He wished he hadn't told them, just then; a minute ago they had all been happier than they had been for weeks, sitting there full of good Christmas food. And then he had had to tell them. He looked at Polly's face again, watching her hands moving nervously, brushing her forehead.

As he backed away from the table he stumbled over Little

[143]

Polly; she started crying, and he picked her up and carried her out in the yard on his shoulder. He felt low as hell.

★ 5 ★

The day before David and George were to return to Fort Strother, Captain Jones arrived in Winchester to reorganize his company. He informed them that if they signed again as volunteers they would have to agree to stay six months, as General Jackson was intending to march to Pensacola in Florida as soon as the weather permitted.

"This time we're going after the British," said Jones.

Although the term of enlistment was longer than he had expected, David decided to go. Several weeks passed, however, before Jones was satisfied with the number of his recruits and was ready to start.

When the new company reached Fort Strother the men found only a few guards left there. Jackson had already started south, and reports had come back the day before that Chief Red Eagle of the Creek war faction had surrendered. "Good, we'll take the British next," cried Captain Jones. "Let's go on to Pensacola now, boys."

The officer in command of the fort warned them not to take their horses, as there was insufficient forage on the route south. It would be a long march, but they shouldered their guns and blankets and provisions, and started out, hoping to overtake the main army. But when they reached Pensacola, days later, Jackson's men had already captured the town and fort. "Damn our luck," said Bibe Jones. "I wanted to be in on the fighting against the British."

That evening, David and George went down into the town, walking along the narrow street until they could see the British fleet lying at anchor far out to sea. "First time I've seen ships since I was a boy long time ago in Baltimore. I almost ran away to sea, then," said David.

"Well," said George, "they look mighty quiet out there. I guess they're afraid of us."

"Yeah." David was looking into the dingy window of a grog shop. "Whyn't we get some liquor and have a drink to celebrate?" They went inside and bought a bottle, pooling their last coins for the transaction. They took several drinks before they walked back to the camp, where they finished the bottle and stayed up all night, singing songs and telling stories. The next morning when they were suddenly ordered to start marching they were still so drunk they could scarcely walk straight.

"What're they marching us away from here for? I like it here," said George. "It's warm and the wind smells good."

"They say Old Andy is heading for New Orleans," David replied sleepily. "Cap'n Jones says the British are moving over there."

Reaching old Fort Mimms, they encamped for three days inside the rotting stockade where hundreds of settlers had been slain less than a year before. On the third day, Jackson and the seasoned veterans moved out for New Orleans; the later volunteers, including David and George, were ordered back to Florida.

"News just come that Washington City fell to the British. Jackson's afraid they might have another try at Pensacola," Captain Jones explained to his disgruntled followers.

For days they marched, back and forth, whenever rumors came of activities along the coast line. Some weeks before his enlistment term was up, David was back with a small detachment near Fort Strother, but as there had been no engagements or any signs of hostilities, he and several other family men were dismissed by Captain Jones. A month or so earlier, George Russell had transferred to Jackson's army near New

Orleans, and so David had to make the journey home alone. He spurred his horse on unmercifully as he had become anxious about Polly and the children. For almost six months he had heard not one word of them.

Arriving at the cabin in mid-afternoon he was surprised to find a young woman he had never seen before, washing clothing in his front yard. Evidently she had already seen him riding up the road, and she met him near the doorway, wiping her wet hands on her apron. " You must be Davy. I'm Martha, your brother's wife."

" Pleased to know you," he stammered. " But who—what brother? "

" Oh—Willson! "

" Willson! Is he about? "

" We live nearby now."

" But Polly, where is she? "

" Inside. She's ailing." Martha smiled faintly. " I think mostly for you. She hasn't heard in so long."

He stepped inside and spoke Polly's name. She sat up quickly in the bed, and then he was across the room, crushing her thin body in his arms. " It's been such a long time," she said, hugging his shoulders.

" I'm here to stay," he promised. " Here to stay for good, now, Polly. You got to get well now." John and William and Little Polly appeared suddenly from nowhere, swinging onto his legs.

" Little Polly walking," he said, grinning. " She looks just like you."

That evening Willson came for a visit, talking and looking so much like their Uncle Joseph Hawkins that David could hardly believe it was actually Willson instead of his uncle. Until after midnight the cabin was filled with laughter and talk; then after Willson and Martha had gone home, David crawled into bed beside Polly, hugging her tightly. " I'm going to kill that fattest beef of ours tomorrow," he said, " and feed you on beef tea until you're strong as a she wildcat."

Although he kept his promise and slaughtered the beef and prepared beef tea potions after a formula he had learned from Mr. Finley, Polly did not seem to recover very rapidly. After a few days she did leave her bed, but she was so weak she had to lie down several times during the day.

But as the autumn days came on, she seemed to grow stronger, and one night in October when the moon was full and round as one of the pumpkins in the field, she went with David for a long walk, deep into the pine woods. The air was fragrant with the tang of the pines, and the needles were soft as a carpet under their feet. He held her close against him once, kissing her. " I oughtn't have run away to fight Indians leaving you home to work yourself to skin and bones. You got to get good and well now. I couldn't live without you, Polly, I couldn't live without you."

" I guess I felt the same 'bout you since that night we danced the cushion dance, Davy."

After the fall harvests were over, he saw Willson quite often. With John, who was seven years old now, they made several long hunting trips back into the hills, bringing back enough meat and skins to keep them all through the winter. Almost every Saturday the two brothers went to Winchester, to stand around the general store and talk and chew tobacco and swap drinks from their jugs. David missed George Russell and wondered how long it would be before he returned from New Orleans. There was much talk about the British and Napoleon and the possible end of the United States.

One Saturday in January, David and Willson rode their horses through a deep snow all the way to Winchester, arriving not long after a courier brought the news of Jackson's smashing defeat of the British at New Orleans. Everybody in

[147]

town was celebrating by drinking, guns were fired off in the street by some of the more exuberant celebrants.

David had been thinking a good deal about the war of late; he knew there was no longer any danger from the Indians, but he had been torn between a desire to go to New Orleans to rejoin Jackson and his fear of leaving Polly alone again. The relief of knowing that the business was over for good was almost too much for him. He drank such quantities of raw liquor that he fell off his horse several times on the way home. Each time Willson had to dig him out of the snow and start him on his way again.

It was late night when he reached home. A candle was still burning, and Polly was lying on the bed, coughing violently. Half sobered, he stumbled over to her, carrying the candle. Red blood splotches were all over her chin and on the neck of her gown. He went quickly to the door to call Willson, but his brother was already out of sight down the snow-covered trail.

Neither he nor Polly slept that night, but the next day she closed her eyes in exhaustion, and that afternoon when she awoke she seemed much better. He built a great roaring fire on the hearth, and told funny stories to the children loud enough so that Polly could hear him, hoping to keep her mind off her illness.

She scarcely left her bed all through the remainder of the winter. Each week Martha came over to sweep and wash and mend the children's clothes, and while the weather was cold David stayed in or near the cabin so that Polly was not lonely. Ill as she was, David thought she had never been so beautiful; her gray eyes were bright and full of life and her cheeks seemed flushed with health, yet her body was pitifully thin, and almost every night she suffered from paroxysms of coughing.

While he was in Winchester one Saturday, David had asked Bibe Jones to help him write a letter to Mr. Finley. He had

[148]

sent it off by a wagoner who promised to leave it at one of the taverns beyond Knoxville in the hope that it might be delivered. In the letter he asked his father-in-law to come as soon as possible and to bring some of his herb remedies. Weeks later he received a reply from one of the Holston valley tavern keepers; Mr. Finley had turned suddenly feeble and was almost blind, but he had dictated a letter in which he included some herb recipes. David scoured the countryside for the herbs, and finally made up a dark horrible-tasting potion which Polly swallowed bravely. Yet she grew no stronger.

Then one day in early April when the leaf buds were already swollen bits of green on the trees, he walked into his cabin after a day of ploughing to find Polly lying on the floor near the doorway, unconscious. Her arms were outstretched toward the door, as if she had been reaching for something. He picked her up and placed her on the bed, brushing her long hair back from her face with his earth-stained hands. Then he called the children from the yard, and sent John running over to Willson's cabin to tell them to come at once.

Soaking a cloth in water, he mopped her face with it until she was able to open her eyes. She was still too weak to speak, but she pushed one hand out from the covers and he caught at it, squeezing it so that she would know he was there. As darkness came on, he sat there thinking about Death and God and Heaven. William and Little Polly were running up and down outside in the yard, playing at Indian fighting, and he thought about the squaw he had seen shot full of bullets in the Indian village, and how she had toppled over on her face and never moved again, and that was Death. He couldn't stand thinking of Polly dead, and he tried remembering the few preachermen he had ever heard praying, and what they had said to God in camp meetings, and he mumbled a few words to God, half aloud. He asked God to make Polly well and not let her die.

Then Willson and Martha came in quietly, tiptoeing and whispering. Willson tried to reassure him. He had brought a bottle of corn whiskey, but David refused to drink.

"Come outside and drink," said Willson; "it'll do you good."

When David tried to withdraw his hand, Polly's fingers tightened slightly. "I'll hold her hand," Martha said.

When the brothers stepped outside, the stars were out in the sky, and it was so quiet and still they could hear a wagon rattling along the trail across the ridge five miles away. David wondered if God had heard what he had said to Him about making Polly well; he wondered where God was and if He was listening all the time to what people had to say to Him. He had never had occasion to speak to God before, and was not certain what he should do. The preachermen always kneeled and spoke quietly, but he wondered if God wouldn't hear better if messages were shouted heavenward.

"I'll be back in a minute," he said abruptly to Willson, and went walking swiftly off toward the hills. When he had gone a couple of miles he was in the pine woods where he had walked with Polly the previous autumn; he stopped there, raising his head up, looking at the stars sparkling through the sharp-bunched pine needles. "God, make her well again," he cried. "Don't make her die."

Walking hastily back to the cabin he found Willson nervously pacing up and down in front of the door. "Where you been, Davy? Martha says she's been wanting you, to hold her hand."

David looked at his brother, "She's bad off, ain't she, Willson? She's bad off." When he went inside he stared into Martha's eyes, trying to read what was in her mind, but she said nothing, only shook her head.

Around midnight David was sitting beside the bed still holding to Polly's fingers. Willson was near the fireplace, slumped in a straight hickory chair, and Martha was sleeping in the big bed with the children. Suddenly he felt Polly's fingers slip away from him; he reached down for them in the darkness. The hand was cold to his touch. He picked up the guttering candle from the floor at the end of the bed, and leaned over his wife, shading the light with his hand so that it fell full upon her face. Her eyes were shut, but her mouth was drawn in a tight open slit across her white teeth. She was dead.

He blew out the candle, and went quietly outside, walking slowly across the bare earth of the yard. A chill fog had risen from the ground, but he could still see the stars dimly. He was thinking about that Indian squaw again; he didn't know why he kept thinking about that Indian squaw. He didn't mind so much seeing a man die, but a woman was different. He wondered if Polly and the Indian squaw would know one another in Heaven, and what kind of place Heaven was. And then he realized he would never hear Polly's voice again, would never hear her laugh again, or see her face again, or see her gray eyes smiling at him. And he knew he would never sleep with his arms around her soft breasts again, and he'd never feel the touch of her skin or her hair or her lips. He wanted to cry and scream and rage at God, but he just sat there on a stump in the yard, scratching at the dead bark with his fingernails.

Martha dressed Polly in the blue dress in which she was married, and David asked her to find the red kerchief her mother had given her and tie it in a bow around her forehead. Willson brought some flat boards from Winchester, and he and David built a box coffin. Alone, David dug the grave on a round knoll not far from the cabin; he dug it deep into a bed of gravel, and then went back to the house, where they had put Polly into the box. He stared at her face for a long minute, and but for the paleness of her skin she looked to him the same as on the day they were wed, lying there still in the blue dress with the red kerchief about her forehead.

Liza Patton was there, sobbing so loudly that John and William and even Little Polly joined in without understanding. David stood silent, watching Willson move toward the coffin and place the top boards over Polly's body and start nailing them down with a hammer.

On their shoulders the two brothers carried the coffin out through the yard and on to the knoll, where Herbert Julius, the preacher from Winchester, said a few words. Then Willson began shoveling in the red gravelly earth, packing it tight, leaving a mound that looked so small and lonely there under the wide blue sky that David wanted to cry, but he could not.

That night he was restless, sitting in the cabin with Willson and Martha and Liza, watching the children who could not understand the things they had seen that day. He slept with Willson, drawing his legs in a tight knot, staring at the blackness of the night until dawn came.

In the morning he went alone to the grave, piling a few chunks of stone at the head of the mound. Birds were singing in the trees nearby, for it was spring. It was spring, and there was work to be done in the fields. That day and each day following for a week he worked so hard and so long that body weariness brought sleep forcefully to him in the lonely nights.

Willson and Martha, who had no children, offered to come and live with David so that Martha might care for John and William and Little Polly. "That's mighty good of you two. I reckon I can't say no, though I know as soon as you and Martha have young-uns of your own, you'll wish you had a place of your own."

"We'll keep our cabin up," Willson replied. "If we ever need to go back there, we can."

"For certain," said Martha, "I'll only be too glad to see

after your children, Davy, no matter how many of my own I may have."

Though neither of them had told him so, David knew that Martha was already pregnant. He knew that for the time being she would care for his children as if they were her own, but he also knew that the arrangement could not continue for long.

He would have to find another mother for his children.

★ 6 ★

Through the summer David spent most of his free time at Liza Patton's place, repairing her roof and fences, and sometimes ploughing in her fields. Liza was a good cook, and David told her more than once that a single one of her meals was more than fair payment for a day's labor on his part.

He said to her one day at the dinner table: " Liza, you and me are in the same boat, kind of."

" How do you mean, Davy? "

" Well, here you are a widow woman with two children to feed, and me a widower with three to take care of."

Liza looked up from the chicken she was slicing, her eyes sparkling. " I'm managing, all right, I suppose, as is."

He changed the subject abruptly, but a week or so later after he had finished ploughing her corn patch, he was sitting at her table again and she made a remark which gave him an opening to speak further.

" Davy Crockett," she said, " you're about the best man I know, working in that hot field all day just to help me out. You're a good man, Davy Crockett, and the Lord will reward you for it."

He stopped chewing his food, swallowed hastily, and said: " You think I'm not such a bad one, then? "

[153]

"Now go along with you, I should be throwing compliments at your head."

David laughed. "You're getting to be like your old self, Liza. Why, you used to be the laughingest woman I ever knowed. Remember when we all moved on here from Elk River? You laughed and hollered your head off all the way over. I thought then you was one of the purtiest women I'd ever seen, and I still do."

"Stop such talk, Davy Crockett, before my two children."

David grinned at George and Margaret Ann, the two Patton children. "You two remember, don't you?"

George nodded bashfully, and Margaret Ann giggled.

David finished his berry pie in silence, and then spoke again: "You know, Liza, I'm not thirty year old yet, lacking a year. Are you older or younger'n me?"

"Davy Crockett, such a question! You know a woman is always the younger."

That night, all the way home David kept thinking about Liza. She was not a pretty woman, her face was quite plain and she knew it; but she was a good woman, and strong and healthy and a hard worker. He didn't know a better mother woman in Tennessee. At home watching Willson and Martha whispering in a corner, Martha large with her unborn child, he began making up his mind.

The next day he went early to Liza Patton's place. She was evidently surprised to see him back again so soon, but said nothing of it. On some pretext, David sent George down into the field, and then drew Liza out of the house onto the ramshackle porch so that Margaret Ann would be out of earshot. "Liza Patton," he said slowly, "I want to make a bargain with you."

"If I can get the better of it, it's a bargain," she replied.

"I got three children, you know, and you got two children."

"Seems to me we spoke about that before."

"Well, that's so, we did." He stopped, at a loss for words.

"Well, what's the bargain? You want to swap children?" She was laughing at him, her large-muscled body shaking with mirth.

"You know well enough what I mean, Liza Patton, you know well enough. Here you are living over here, trying to make out a living, and me over yonder trying to do the same, both of us just getting by at it—that is, we could do better ——

"Go ahead, Davy." She stopped laughing, and sat down on the doorstep beside him.

"Well, I'm not thirty, and you said you wasn't, and well, we're young enough to ——"

She shook his shoulder with her huge flat hand. "You're the beatingest man ——"

"What you think of me, Liza?"

"I like you well enough."

"I like you the same. We could do better, both of us, not have to work so hard—together."

She looked at him, her large face solemn now. "Wonder what Tom and Polly would think of us ——"

"I reckon they'd say it was the best thing could be done. When'll we be wed, Liza?" His face was crimson, and as he wiped the sweat from his face with his shirt sleeve, he turned toward her, his mouth twisting in a smile. "It took a long time to get up to that."

"We'll be wed any day you say."

"And move over to my place."

"If we wed, I go wherever you say, Davy."

"Then it's done. We'll go to Winchester tomorrow and have Preacher Julius splice the knot."

The wedding was a quiet affair, with only Willson and Martha present. David had wanted George Russell to be there, but George was in Nashville on a business mission for his father. Willson and Martha had already gathered their belongings together, and seemed relieved now that they were free to return to their own place.

All of Liza's best household furnishings were brought over in the wagon, and two new beds were set up in the second room for the five children. They all seemed quite pleased with the new arrangement. Margaret Ann appointed herself as a mother to Little Polly, and the three boys were overjoyed with each other's company until the time came to decide which one was to sleep alone. They finally compromised by all sleeping together, leaving the second bed empty.

"We'll have to build an extra room, won't we, Davy, with such a family?" said Liza.

"Such a family," cried David, "such a family! Why, Liza Crockett, we haven't even started yet!"

Liza had produced a jug of cider from the heap of stores she had brought from her cabin. After the children were asleep they drank it together, trying to keep from laughing too loudly. She was still laughing her deep contagious chuckle when he lost consciousness in undisturbed sleep.

The months passed swiftly after the wedding, for both of them worked hard at knitting together the two broken families, and there was little time for thinking of the past. Although he told Liza often that he had no love for farming, he could see no other occupation for a man with a family. And, said he, if farm he must, he was determined to make the best farm he knew how. He ploughed up new ground and built new fences, and swapped corn for more cows and horses.

A year after the wedding, the Crockett farm was one of the best in the valley. He was proud of it, and satisfied that now he was settled for good and ever. He was also pleased to learn from Liza that they were going to have a new member in the family.

[156]

The child was born in the midst of a hot summer, a boy, and they named him Robert Patton Crockett.

Not many months after he had made up his mind to continue working his farm near Winchester, David began to realize that it would not be long before he would have to seek new land. Rich and productive as the soil had been when he first began tilling it with his plough, it was now deteriorating so rapidly that his summer crop of corn was scarcely sufficient for his stock.

The winter after Robert Patton was born, there were several weeks of heavy driving rains which ripped gullies through his fields, baring wide scars of sticky red clay. When spring came belatedly, he waited weeks for the earth to dry before he started ploughing; even then great hunks of clay clung to his ploughshare, and after he had covered the seeds the sun baked the ground surface until it was brick hard. The sprouts which did push through to the sun were so spindly that he knew they would make scarcely any fodder, and no grain.

In addition a bog had formed at the farthest end of the farm, and hosts of mosquitoes swarmed up, making life miserable for the Crockett family through the hot summer nights. Fever and ague brought the children, one by one, down in their beds, until only he and Liza were able to continue at the daily tasks.

A young physician had recently settled in Winchester, and when Little Polly became so ill that her sallow skin hung like parchment to her thin body, David went into town and brought the doctor back to examine the entire family.

" This is a sickly country right here," the doctor told David after he had dosed the children with strong physics. " Low sickly country. I noticed when I was living in Virginia that folks who lived near low swamps was most likely to be sick of fever and ague. Mountain folks not so apt to get sick that way." He slapped at one of the mosquitoes buzzing around his ears. " I suppose it must be the mists rising off the bogs makes folks fall sick of fever."

" Well, if that's so," said David, " I reckon we'd better find a new place to live. I don't aim to have sick young-uns on my hands every year. And the land is no good for farming any more, either."

That fall, after he had harvested his small crops, David told Liza he was going out to look for a new farm site. " What do you think of the matter, Liza? "

" Whatever you say is right, Davy. Whatever you say, we'll do."

Alone, he started out toward the northwest, riding one of his prized stallions. He had heard that the Chickasaw country around Shoal Creek was now open for settlement, and that some portions of it had not yet been marked off by the land speculators in Nashville. Remembering his old friend, Captain Matthews, of the Fort Strother insurrection, he made inquiries along the way until he finally found Matthews' place, a low ramshackle log farmhouse at the head of Shoal Creek.

Matthews was at home, nursing a wounded leg. " Bear almost bit it off last week," he explained. Evidently he was glad to see David, and they talked for an hour or more about their " victory " over Andrew Jackson at Fort Strother.

" He was so danged mad," said Matthews, " I bet he still cusses us out every night before he says his prayers."

After a while David remarked that he was seeking a new homesite. " My family has growed so big," he said, " I'll need plenty of room."

" Well, now, we've sure enough got room hereabouts. Land grabbers ain't got here yet. And folks like me will be mighty

[158]

glad to have a man like you come in here, too. So danged many bad characters, horse thieves and murderers and outlaws from the East been flocking in here, if we don't get some good honest white men in here, a man's life won't be worth a bad penny."

" Don't you have any law? "

" Nah. No laws in this Chickasaw purchase. No such thing as law and order."

David let his fingers slide along the barrel of his rifle. " Well," he said, with a grin, " I can get along as well as anybody else without law and order."

Matthews expressed his regrets that he could not go with David up the creek to search for a farm site. " My leg's too bad. Got to set still for a few days more. But I'll tell you— 'bout five miles up is a good friend of mine, Abram Henry. Kind of queer like a duck, but as honest a neighbor as a man could ask. Back of him it's open country, some good meadow ground and rich for farming. Tell him I sent you by, and he'll help you lay out a spot."

Abram Henry was a red-haired young man in his late twenties. Dark brown freckles were splotched all over his angular face. His wife was as red-haired as he, but her face was fair, her eyes blue, and her breasts large and buxom. Abram scarcely ever smiled, and he talked slowly as if thinking over the meaning of each word before uttering it.

David had talked with the Henrys but five minutes when he decided that he had never known such friendly folks before in his life. Abram was only too eager to go with David to plot out a farm. He had been practicing on his fiddle when David arrived, and he was so anxious to help and show the way that he carried the fiddle along with him when they started out.

" This is fine country," said David. " Finest country I ever saw."

" Yessiree, I like it myself," said Abram. He stopped beside the creek to let his horse drink, and began playing a sprightly tune upon his instrument.

"That's purty music all right. You have many dances hereabouts?"

"Not so many. Too many shootings when we do."

"Matthews told me there wasn't any law as yet."

"Nope, don't need laws."

They continued for a mile along the stream until they came to a high flat meadow, protected from the creek by a natural rock embankment. The meadow ended against a thick wood of tall oaks. As soon as he saw it David said: "That's where I'll build my place."

"As good a place as a man could ask for," agreed Abram. He dropped off his horse and began playing his fiddle again, hopping around on his long bird-like legs. David remembered what Matthews had said about Abram Henry being "queer like a duck," and smiled to himself. He liked Abram though, and was glad to know he would be his nearest neighbor.

Abram stopped fiddling for a moment, looking at David's stallion. "Say, Crockett, that's a fine looking stallion you riding. Now I got a mare in heat, what you say——"

"I say let's breed 'em. After all, some day maybe I might want to borrow the colt!"

Shortly after the Crocketts had settled on Shoal Creek in a large four-room house which their new neighbors helped construct, David borrowed enough credit from Captain Matthews to build a small gristmill on the side of the swift-running stream near his farm. There was plenty of corn to be ground into meal, and the tiny mill soon proved to be a profitable investment.

With each passing month the valley welcomed additional settlers until finally David had to increase the size of his gristmill in order to grind all the grain which his neighbors brought

[160]

to him. Liza now had to spend half her time helping about the mill, but she seemed to enjoy the work, meeting and talking with the customers, and she was so strong she could lift the heavy bags of corn as easily as if they had been stuffed with cotton.

Soon there was considerable demand for a distillery in Shoal Creek, as most of the newcomers had no time for making liquor, and after Captain Matthews agreed to stand half the expense, David and Abram Henry set out for Nashville to purchase a small vat and a supply of kegs. They enjoyed the trip keenly. While they were in the town, the new steamboat which had just been put in service was docked at the landing, and consequently there was a carnival spirit in the air.

When they returned to Shoal Creek, the settlement seemed dull and uninteresting by comparison. " This ain't much after Nashville," said Abram as they rode up to the gristmill.

" Some day maybe this will be as big a place as Nashville," David replied. " You never can tell."

" Look," cried Abram, " the mill's closed."

" By God, it is. Liza must be sick, corn stacked all over the place. I'll ride over home and see what's wrong."

Reaching his cabin, David found Liza confined to her bed. But she was not seriously ill. A few days later, there was a second daughter in the Crockett family, born oddly enough on Christmas day as was Little Polly. They called her Rebeckah Elvira, but the name soon proved to be too complicated for the busy Crocketts. After the first week, Rebeckah Elvira Crockett was known simply as Sissy.

★ 8 ★

By the following summer, David had completed the installation of his distillery and soon was able to buy back Captain

Matthews' share of the equipment. Matthews was so pleased that he invited the Crocketts to have a pot-luck dinner with his family the following Sunday. Charlie Matthews, the captain's son, had recently married and the family was celebrating. By noon, relatives and friends were all over the place, but Captain Matthews finally drew David out near the road for a talk.

"Got something I been wanting to tell you, Squire Crockett. You know old Colonel Jones over by Winchester died not long ago and nobody's been elected to take his place as head of the district's regiment. The first major's place is vacant too. Now, I had a letter from Nashville urging me to set up as a candidate for colonel, and, well, thinking as it might be a good idea to have you for my first major I thought I'd ask you to put up for major afore I announced for colonel."

David pondered a minute before replying. "I'm a purty busy man right now, running the mill and distillery and tending court between times. And besides, Cap'n, you ought to know as well as me that I ain't much for military fighting. I had my share in the Creek War."

Matthews laughed. "You ain't no busier man than I am, Davy Crockett. And you know danged well there ain't a-going to be no more fighting of the Indians. Military offices in this district are just the same as political offices in other places, you know that. Why, man, it's a chance for you to get into politics, easy."

"Politics?"

"Sure, politics. If ever a man was cut out for politics, you're him. Everybody around Shoal Creek knows you and respects you and likes you. If you'll put up for first major, I'll support you, and at the same time you can put in a good word for me for colonel."

"I'll do it," said David. "Can't do me no harm, can it? When's the election come off?"

[162]

"Not till fall. We got plenty time."

Late in September, Captain Matthews invited the entire neighborhood to his farm for a corn husking. His was the largest farm in the valley, and that year his corn was tall and heavy with large solid ears.

David brought his family, including the babies, Robert and Sissy. They arrived early on the crisp sunny morning, crossing the fields which were blue with early autumn mists. Several of the Matthews' close neighbors were already there, bringing in baskets of corn which would be shucked later in the day.

Abram Henry touched David on the shoulder as he passed one of the smokehouses, and David noticed that his slow, easy-going friend seemed more animated than usual. "Davy, I thought you said Matthews was supporting you to be major of the district regiment."

David grinned. "Yeah, he aims to be colonel, and me major. If we can get enough votes between us."

"Ain't you heard about his boy, Charlie?"

"What about Charlie?"

"Well, Charlie is aiming to run agin you."

"Who told you that?"

"Charlie did. Said his old man was encouraging him, too."

David stopped, catching at Abram's sleeve. "Why, that squirrel-faced little runt! Abram, I reckon you know I don't give a damn about being major, but if old Cap'n Matthews is aiming to try to sneak Charlie in over me after begging me so hard to offer my name —— Well, by God, you know what I'm ——"

"What?" Abram was carelessly thumping the strings on his fiddle, apparently no longer interested in the matter.

"I'll run for colonel myself, against old Matthews, just to get even for such a trick, trying to put Charlie up for major. Why, that boy can't even shoot a rifle straight."

As soon as he left Abram, David sought out Captain Matthews and asked him point-blank if Charlie was intending to announce for major. "That's right, Davy. Don't know why I didn't think of Charlie before. He needs the job. Me and Charlie both hate having to run against a man like you, Davy, but politics is fair game for anybody I guess. Yes, sir, Charlie almost wouldn't put up because he thinks so much of you."

"Well," said David abruptly, "you can tell Charlie he needn't worry any more about running against me. Because I ain't a-going to run for major."

"Not run for major? You can't back out of it like this. Of course if ——"

"I'm not backing out. I'm aiming to run for colonel against you."

Captain Matthews threw back his head and laughed loudly. He thrust out his hand then and shook David's briskly. "Come on out to the yard. We'll make a speech to the folks right now."

Standing on a block of wood against the corncrib, Matthews quieted the crowd and told them he had a few words to say before the husking commenced. "I guess you all know I'm up for colonel of the district regiment, and you all know Davy Crockett has been up for major. Well now, my boy Charlie is aiming for major and Davy is withdrawing his name."

There were sudden cries: "Why? What's wrong with Crockett?" But Matthews quieted them with a wave of his hand. "My friend, Squire Crockett, is now offering to run for colonel against me," he finished with an air of sarcasm. Then he smiled broadly and stepped down from the block.

"Davy Crockett! Davy Crockett!" somebody was shouting. "Make us a speech, make us a speech."

David was excited, at the same time smarting inside from the manner in which Matthews had attempted to dismiss him as a candidate for colonel. He jumped upon the block. "I reckon you all might want to know why I'm changing over from major to colonel in this election. Well, I just found out

[164]

this morning about Charlie Matthews running against me for major, and I says, well, since I got the whole danged Matthews family to run against, I might as well levy on the head of the mess. I figure I'm as good a man as Cap'n Matthews any day of the week, and I figure I've got just as many friends in this crowd as he has." Cheers sounded suddenly in his ears, the many voices startling him. He had never known before this moment that there could be such power in words. He grinned suddenly. " Well, now that's over, I reckon we might as well start gathering in the Cap'n's corn. After all he's not such a bad feller."

Politics was soon forgotten amid the noisy excitement of the husking. Long lines of men were carrying baskets of corn into the huge crib, where the women were already at work removing the shucks. Before noon one end of the crib was stacked high; a second pile was started in the yard, growing gradually into a small mountain of brown ears.

In a pit behind the smokehouse, Matthews was roasting a huge ox. The fragrant odor of the barbecued meat floating tantalizingly in the air served to speed up the movements of the men going back and forth to the fields. They knew that as soon as all the corn was in, Matthews would give the signal to slice the juicy meat for serving.

By mid-afternoon the cornstalks were stripped of all their ears, and the men and boys crowded into the yard.

" Barbecue! barbecue! Anybody want barbecue? " Captain Matthews shouted. There was a wild rush for the pit, where the ox lay on the green saplings, oozing delicious juices. Matthews began slicing the meat, serving it out piece by piece to the hungry crowd.

As soon as they had finished eating, cider bowls were passed around, and then everybody moved back to the crib. The real fun of the husking was now to begin. All the boys and younger men were grinning in anticipation, for according to the un-

[165]

written law of the husking bee, any man who found a red ear could demand a kiss from any girl in the group. Shucks were torn loose in lightning-like movements.

" Old Matthews ain't got nothing but yellow corn this year," Abram complained to David after he had shucked a hundred or so ears. " I'm going to get my fiddle and play some music for the others."

Abram had scarcely started playing when a lad near David discovered a bright red ear. Tossing it in the air gleefully, the boy grabbed for the nearest girl; there was a shrill scream, a flurry of skirts, a loud smack, and laughter. The other young men redoubled their speed, encouraged by the success of the first boy.

It was David who found the second red ear. He did not quite know what to make of it at first. Liza was inside the crib, and here he was outside. He looked around at some of the other women, half-concealing the red ear under his hands. Then he saw Little Polly, sitting across from him, working busily and earnestly, her face for the moment exactly like her mother's.

Abram Henry was fiddling merrily behind him, and the situation was so similar to that of the reaping party so many long years ago that he felt a sudden stab of nostalgia for the lost evening of happiness. He walked over to Little Polly, dropped the red ear in her lap, and kissed her loudly. She ducked her head and looked sidewise at one of the small boys beside her, and everybody laughed. " I reckon you're my best girl, Little Polly," said David, backing over to the heap of corn where he had been working. It was queer, he was thinking, how her eyes were so much like Polly's. After that, he couldn't keep his mind on his work for long; finally he got up and walked away to the side of the barn where he had concealed a small barrel of whiskey, brought from his distillery for Captain Matthews to serve later to his hard-drinking friends.

He opened the bung, and drank a long drink. He had forgotten all about the coming election.

But some weeks later, when the elections were held, David received the surprise of his life. When the votes were counted, he had been given twice as many as Captain Matthews. He could not understand it; he had opposed Matthews for no. other reason than that his ire had been roused. And as much as he disliked the military, he was now the commander of the entire district regiment. He was, in fact, Colonel David Crockett, miller and distiller of Shoal Creek, Tennessee.

★ 9 ★

David was talking with Captain Matthews about the news of Daniel Boone's death which had just come from Missouri, when for apparently no reason Matthews said: " I hear tell you're going to put up for the state legislature this coming year."

David was flabbergasted. For weeks he had been basking in the glory of his colonelcy, and now to have it said that he was planning to run for the Tennessee legislature—well, things were moving too fast for him. " Why, I don't know anything about it," he said.

" Well," Matthews continued, " some of the boys in the store last night was just talking about it. Asked me if I was going to run. I said, Lordy no, not me. Then somebody said, What about Crockett? He'd be a good man, I said. So we all agreed that you were the man."

David did not know whether or not Matthews was making a joke. " I'll think on the matter," he said quietly, and then went straight to Abram Henry, sounding him out, telling him exactly what Matthews had told him. " I'd just like to know if old Matthews was trying to hornswoggle me or not. I wish you'd inquire around and see what my friends got to say about it."

"Sure, I'll find out." Abram took his fiddle from the wall. Although he walked slowly and deliberately from the mill it was plain to David that even stolid Abram Henry was excited about the possibilities of his running for the legislature.

When Abram came back next day to report, his eyes were glowing with suppressed jubilation. "Well, Davy," he drawled, "I ain't found a man yet who's agin you. I'd lay my best studhorse against a counterfeit dollar that you'd get the vote of every honest man in Shoal Creek valley."

"Yeah," said David, laughing, "but how many honest men are there in Shoal Creek valley?"

A few days later he learned that he would have an opponent, Ed Whalley, who lived in Hickman County, the other half of the district. "I reckon I better get over to Hickman County soon as I can and make myself known to the folks," he said to Abram. "You know anybody over there? I don't believe I know a soul."

"Sure, I know a feller real well, used to live nearby here. Jud Hunnicutt's his name, a big strapping man with black hair all over hisself, but as good as gold. Ain't seen him for some time, but he lives over by Vernon settlement. He's a rouster and he'll know everybody that counts in Hickman County, you can lay to that."

David found Jud Hunnicutt's place without any difficulty. Everybody he met along the way seemed to know Hunnicutt, and oddly enough when he told these strangers his own name he found that most of them had heard of him. "So you're Davy Crockett? We heard you was up for office. Mighty glad to know you," they would say, and he would ride off down the road, puzzled as to how they had known about him.

Jud Hunnicutt also had heard his name. "We was expect-

[168]

ing you over, Davy Crockett," he boomed, and he led David into his low-roofed cabin, shooing chickens away from the doorstep. " Ed Whalley, who's got his name up agin you, was by my place last week. Told me he'd never heard tell of you, but I told Ed I'd heard of you; folks say you're the dad-blastedest shot in Tennessee. Old Ed now, he lays claim to know Latin and Greek, had some school larning back in the East afore he come out here, but I bet he couldn't plug a dead horse at four paces."

Hunnicutt put a bridle on his horse and rode with David around the neighborhood, introducing him to all his friends. Most of them evidently had heard his name before, and though none said so, David was almost certain that all the settlers preferred him to Whalley. At Hunnicutt's suggestion, some of the men returned with them to the cabin for supper. " We'll do some palavering," said Hunnicutt, winking one sharp black eye at David.

After the meal, Hunnicutt brought out a jug of corn whiskey and some black twisted chewing tobacco, and they sat out in the yard in the cool of the spring night talking of politics. " We all got one question we want to ask you," said Hunni-cutt. " We want to move Vernon town, which is about ten mile from here, up to high ground, but the legislature's got to act afore we can take the spot we want to move on. Now what is your idea on that, Colonel Crockett, are you agin it or in favor of it? "

David took a chew on one of the tobacco twists, tearing the bitter leaves with his teeth. " Well, if it's a good thing," he said, " I'm for it." He spat on the ground. " But if it's a bad thing, I'm agin it."

Hunnicutt laughed loudly, the others joining in. " By God," said Hunnicutt, " Old Ed Whalley couldn't of made a better answer. Davy Crockett, you're sure some politician."

" We heard you was a champeen hunting man," spoke up

[169]

one of the younger men. "Whyn't you come to our squirrel hunt on Duck River next Friday?"

"Sure," Hunnicutt interrupted. "He's coming. Going to tie up right here with me till then, ain't you, Colonel Crockett?"

"Well, if you put it up to me like that, I can't say no," replied David.

"Maybe you'll make us a speech at the barbecue afterwards?"

"Maybe," said David. His heart sank, thinking of making a speech. Perhaps he could avoid speaking, instead just talk around with some of the men. It was easier, and quicker to make friends, just talking around.

Friday the Duck River folk gathered near the Hunnicutt cabin for the squirrel hunt. Jud Hunnicutt and David were at the meeting place early, moving among the crowd, shaking hands, and talking. The leaders decided to divide the group into two parties, each side to hunt all day Friday and half of Saturday and then to return to Hunnicutt's place for an accounting of the squirrel scalps. It was agreed that the losing party would pay all expenses of the barbecue and frolic to be held on Saturday night. "Davy, you're going with my party," Hunnicutt declared. "With you along shooting, we'll bring back all the squirrels in the woods."

"My aim might not be so good," replied David. "I'm kind of excited about all this politics."

"Aw shucks, let's forget politics, and think about squirrels. We want a free barbecue, don't we?"

Squirrels were plentiful along the Duck River bottoms, and as his group spread out fanwise, David found himself so busy aiming, firing, and reloading, that he scarcely had time for talk. His aim was never better; as soon as his eye caught a streak of fur in a tree, his gun was up, and almost without exception a squirrel would tumble dead to the ground.

"You can beat anybody I ever saw, barking a squirrel,"

[170]

Hunnicutt told him. "Why, half of your squirrels don't have a drop of blood on 'em."

When they returned to Hunnicutt's place the following afternoon, he was still talking about David's marksmanship. "Danged if I ever seen anything like it," he told some of his friends who had gone with the competing group. "Davy just bangs away and the squirrel falls dead, either scared to death or just stunned dead. There ain't one scarred animal in Crockett's pack, and man, there's a mess of 'em there, too."

As Hunnicutt had predicted, David's party was victorious; they had far more squirrels in their bags than their opponents. But the losers were game; immediately they set about preparing a barbecue, laying green poles across a ditch and building a huge fire of dried maple and beech wood underneath for roasting the meat. A dozen fiddlers were hired, and a place was smoothed on the ground for dancing.

"I bet it's going to be a tip-top frolic," said David, as he walked about the place with Jud Hunnicutt, continually shaking hands with new acquaintances introduced by his host. As they neared the barbecue pit, they found a small group gathered around a short, heavy-set man, who was dressed in a neat linsey-woolsey suit, his fat reddish face perspiring freely.

"Why, it's Ed Whalley," said Hunnicutt. "Mr. Whalley, meet Colonel Crockett, your opponent for the seat in the legislature."

"Pleased to meet you, Colonel Crockett," said Whalley, offering a pudgy, perspiring hand.

"The same to you," said David.

"I suppose you'll soon be making us a speech, Colonel Crockett, so as we'll know your views."

"Sure," Hunnicutt cried, "he's going to make us a speech."

David wanted to back away; he started to stammer something, but he saw Whalley staring keenly at him. He swallowed hard.

[171]

" Let's have some speeching right now," somebody shouted
loudly.

" Sure, let's have a speech before we eat! "

" Well, gentlemen," mumbled David, " I ain't much a one
for speech-making."

" Oh, come, Colonel Crockett," Whalley spoke up loudly,
" you shouldn't be such a modest fellow. We'd like to hear
what you have to say."

David would have liked to punch Whalley's fat face. He
knew the man suspected his ignorance of the intricacies of
politics, did not even take him seriously as a candidate. He
guessed, too, that Whalley could twist long words out of his
mouth, words that he'd never even heard before. But as the
cries of " Speech, speech," increased in number and volume
around him, he realized that he would have to go ahead and
leave it to chance as to what words came from his mouth.

Mounting upon a large log nearby, he removed his cap and
ran his fingers nervously through his hair. All about him were
faces, waiting expectantly.

" I think I've shook hands with most of you all, and by now
you ought to know what I've come here for. But if some of
you ain't guessed yet what I've come for, I reckon I might as
well tell you. I've come for your votes, and if you don't watch
mighty close, I'll get 'em too." He could hear a gentle rumble
of good-natured approval when he paused. But they were
waiting for something else, something about the government
probably.

He tried to recall some of the things he had heard other
speakers say about the government, but he couldn't remember
a single word. It was late evening and the faces around him
were gray in the twilight; they seemed as blurred as his own
mind, standing there with eyes and mouths and ears opened,
waiting for him. One or two unintelligible words he spoke,
and then he ducked his head and grinned, and said: " I reckon

I'm kind of like a feller I saw down the road not long ago. He was just a-setting there, beating on an empty barrel as I rode up, and I stopped and looked at him a minute and says, ' What you doing that for? ' ' Well,' he says to me, ' there was a little bit of cider in this barrel a while ago, I know because I drunk it. I'm just a-beating on it now, trying to see if it's there any more, but if it is, I sure as hell can't get to it.' I reckon I'm like that feller's barrel. There was a little bit of a speech in me a while ago, but I sure as hell can't get to it now."

Slowly at first a few guffaws swept across the crowd, then they were laughing mightily. He felt good, standing there on the log, looking at the men laughing, and he started in to tell another story about a preacher and a bear. They laughed again; then as silence spread gradually among them he said quickly: " I don't know how you all feel, but I'm dry as a powder horn myself. I think it's high time we all wetted our whistles a little." He jumped down from the log, pushing through the jostling crowd, Jud Hunnicutt at his side, thumping him on the back. They walked straight up to the liquor stand beside the barbecue pit, the men in front of them parting for them to have room, and then David was rubbing his belly against the stand, his body quivering with excitement.

Huge quantities of rum and cider and buttermilk were arranged in containers in front of them. " What kind of cider you got? " boomed Hunnicutt to the girl behind the stand.

" Apple and peach," she replied timidly.

" A couple of peach brandies for me and my friend, Squire Crockett, your next legislator from our district," he cried, then added hastily, " And buttermilk for Ed Whalley! "

David was grinning so hard that he felt he must look like a 'possum. He straightened himself up and assumed a serious mien. Later, while the music and dancing further enlivened the group, he kept thinking back on his speech. Everyone had told him it was a good speech. But he knew Ed Whalley did

[173]

not think so, for he had said not one word about government matters, and he wondered how long it would be before the individual members of the group realized, as Ed Whalley did, that he had only told them a few funny stories.

As the day of the election approached, David was so busy with his mill and distillery that he had no time for speech-making in his own county. A man from New England had just moved to Shoal Creek, bringing some machinery for making gunpowder, and he had persuaded David to let him set the equipment up in the mill in exchange for a share of the profits.

All these business matters kept his mind from politics, so that election day came before he had made a single speech in the Shoal Creek neighborhood. As he saw his friends trooping to the polling place in Matthews' store, he wondered if they would vote for him.

But when the votes were counted, he no longer had any doubts as to the loyalty of his friends. He received more than twice as many votes as Ed Whalley. Now he was Colonel David Crockett, miller and distiller, honorable member of the Tennessee state legislature.

The first days of the legislature were more exciting for him than any experience he had undergone since his runaway trip from home when he was ten years old. He loved the endless palavering, the banging of gavels, the pompous manners of the clerks.

Most of the time he spent listening, hours on end, to speeches, and then returning to his room in the little hotel, he would repeat over and over the points he remembered. He began to see the hollowness and insincerity of many of the speakers, and after he had tried a time or two to use some of the ornamental phrases he had memorized, he abandoned such words altogether. " Grammar," he said one evening to a friend in the barroom, " is nothing at all. It is nothing at all in spite of all the fuss made about it."

One day while he was sitting in his chair near the middle of the legislative chamber, he heard a commotion near one of the side doors; turning he saw Abram Henry standing there, his red hair hanging in loose strands over his ears, his freckled face quite distraught.

David was up on his feet immediately. He caught Abram's hand, and moved out into the hall. " What're you doing here in Murfreesboro?"

Abram shook his head sadly. " Something mighty bad has happened, Davy. None of your family," he added quickly. " It's the mill."

" What! I bet that damned gunpowder blew up sky high!"

Abram tried to smile. " No. Floods, Davy. A freshet tore down Shoal Creek, smashed everything all to pieces. Cap'n Matthews lost most his store, but the mill got the worst of it. Just ain't nothing left a-tall, Davy." Abram wrinkled his freckled face and seemed about to burst into tears.

David took out a plug of tobacco and bit it savagely. " Just as I thought everything was riding high, too." He spat on the floor. " Wait a minute here, Abram. I'll go tell the clerk I'm heading for home. I may be a legislator, but I'm a sunk duck so far as money goes, if my mill's gone."

The mill was gone, there was no denying that fact. Broken boards and logs were scattered for a half mile down the creek's sides, hanging in trees and piled up against rocks. Twisted from its foundations, the equipment was ruined, some of it buried under sand and gravel.

After he had looked at the wreckage for some time, David went on to his house. He was glad to find Liza cheerful.

" Well, I guess we're pore again, Davy."

[175]

"Yeah, it'll take all we got to pay for some of that stuff we bought on credit that's now buried in the creek."

"Seems a pity. But I always say, pay up what you owe long as you got a bit's worth in this world, then everybody'll be satisfied, and we can always scuffle for more."

"That's just the talk I want to hear, Liza. We can always scuffle for more."

That night, tossing in bed beside her, he laid his plans. Always before, when difficulties had mounted, he had moved on to another place. Could he do it again? It would mean giving up all that was left of his property, his office in the state legislature, his friends.

But in the morning, while the family ate breakfast together, he announced his decision, looking straight across the table at his oldest son. "Johnnie," he said, "go and bridle two horses, one for you and one for me. We're going on a long trip. A man up at Murfreesboro was telling me about west Tennessee, up around the Obion river. Says it's the best country in the world, the best country in the world. You and me, we'll go and have a look at it."

PART THREE

★

★ I ★

WHEN Abram Henry learned that David was leaving for the west, he would not stop talking until he had persuaded his friends to accept him as a companion.

" There's not much left for me hereabouts, either, except the old farm."

" To tell the truth," David admitted, " I wanted to ask you soon as I made up my mind, but I figured as how you'd might want to cut loose from me since my spell of ill luck."

" Hell, no," said Abram, " if you'll have me I'll go."

They took four horses, an extra one to pack their provisions, and started out early in the morning. As far as Nashville the traveling was easy along the much-used trail, but after they turned west from there, bad weather set in to plague them the remainder of the way. Rain mixed with sleet fell ceaselessly day after day, and by the time they reached the canebrakes at the head of the Obion River all their clothing and food was sodden; it was almost impossible to dry themselves out sufficiently so that they might sleep.

Much to his chagrin John lost his father's axe somewhere along the way, but fortunately they met a party of hunting Cherokees who traded a steel-bladed tomahawk for some of their precious powder which they miraculously had kept dry.

As they drove further and further into the west the country leveled into a monotonous rolling plain of dried canes, broken by criss-cross trails, remains of old buffalo traces, and swirling creeks rising out of their banks after the rains.

For two days after they entered the river valley they saw no other human beings. Progress was slow through the cane-brakes; they could cover scarcely twenty miles a day.

At last they came upon a cabin set on a hill near the river. John, riding ahead, saw it first. " Somebody lives up there," he cried. They whipped their horses into a run and crashed through the brush into the clearing at the top of the hill.

The settler's name was Jeff Owens, a grizzly, gray-bearded man well over fifty, as delighted to see the travelers as they were to see him.

" Yes, sir, this is a great country," he told David. " Not many folks live here yet. My nearest neighbor is twenty miles down."

" That's fine," said David. " You don't mind if I settle in here, do you? "

" Shore be glad to have you," Owens replied. " Better pick out a hill though. Water backs up here mighty high sometimes. It's a-coming up right now, after all this rain."

The next morning they borrowed two axes from Owens and started on foot down the stream, crossing it with difficulty to a tree-covered ridge on the opposite side. Here they found an ideal site, with level grassland suitable for farming running back from the river.

They stayed on the ridge two days, David and Abram felling trees for their cabin, while John stripped the limbs off cleanly with the tomahawk. When they started to return to Owens' cabin on the third day, they were surprised to find the bottomlands flooded to the edge of the ridge, a slow-moving brown current which had erased even the river.

" If we only had enough to eat we could stay it out and put up our cabin ourselves," said David. "But we finished everything this morning, and there's not enough dry powder to blow a turkey's head off even if we could find one on this ridge."

" We can make it across," Abram said hopefully. " It don't look so deep."

" It's cold though," cried John, as he splashed ahead of them, his thin body shivering.

" Godallmighty, it is cold," agreed David.

Soon the water was up to their necks. To avoid falling into the deep sloughs that cut back from the river, David sounded the depths with a long pole as he pushed ahead of the others. John had to swim half the time, and his buckskins clung so heavily that he held on to his father's shoulders in the deepest parts. When they reached the channel of the Obion the current was so swift they feared to attempt swimming across.

Moving downstream along the submerged banks they found a fallen tree, but when they crawled out upon it, the trunk began bucking madly up and down like a wild buffalo. Finally David discovered a tall cottonwood, and while John and Abram helped to hold his legs steady in the slippery muddy waters, he slashed it through with the sharp-bladed tomahawk until it fell with a loud splash across the channel.

Even when they had succeeded in crawling across the raging stream they found the waters still deep and treacherous. For a mile they stumbled and slithered across the flooded flatlands, their bodies trembling with cold as they slowly emerged into the piercing wind. By the time they reached the Owens cabin, John's hands and face were reddish blue and he was shaking as if with ague.

Owens and two strangers were standing in front of the cabin, but without waiting for an introduction David hustled his son through the doorway to the fireplace, jerking his clothing off and wrapping him in a heavy blanket which old Mrs. Owens brought down from the loft. John was too cold to be embarrassed by his nakedness.

While David and Abram stood dripping water on the hearth, Owens introduced the two men. " This is Cap'n Carter and one of his men, Flavius Harris. Cap'n Carter just tied his boat up down on the river; it's the first big boat ever been this far up the Obion."

Captain Carter was so deaf David could not carry on a conversation with him, but he found Flavius Harris a talkative young man, not at all reluctant to tell of his adventures with the captain on a slave ship, and of their more recent journey down the Ohio and Mississippi Rivers. Flavius had a mischievous twinkle in his blue eyes, and at times it was difficult to determine whether he was telling the truth or manufacturing a magnificent lie for his listeners' entertainment.

"I've always had a hankering after boats and ships," said David. "I almost ran away to sea once when I was a boy."

"I've about had my insides full of boats," Flavius replied. "I'm ready for to settle down and find me a good woman."

While they stood there before the fireplace, David and Abram kept turning slowly around until steam was curling up about their heads. Jeff Owens brought out a tall bottle of corn whiskey and they took turns drinking from it.

"Lordamighty," said David after a while, "here I've gone and swigged off half a pint, and John my boy ain't had a taste." He poured a couple of spoonfuls into a wooden cup for his son. John drank it at one gulp, making a wry face. "Keep you from coming down with ague and fever, boy."

By the time their clothes were stiff and hot against their bodies, David was ready to visit the boat. "Let's go aboard," he shouted into the captain's ear. "Maybe you could use another man. Could you?"

The captain nodded quickly. "I'm right short of help. I sure could use another man or two to help us pull our way up to McLemore's Bluff. We're drawing a mighty big load."

"Count me on," cried David.

Later that afternoon, Owens rowed them down to the boat in a canoe, and they all went aboard. David was surprised at the enormous stocks of whiskey, flour, sugar, coffee and salt. " Man, I sure could use some of this stuff in my new cabin this winter," he told Flavius.

" Whyn't you make a trade with Cap'n Carter? He's standing to make plenty from this trip. The company is offering him five hundred dollars to get the stuff to McLemore's Bluff just to prove it can be done, and he's due for some high profits on the load on top of that."

David had left John at Owens' cabin in the care of old Mrs. Owens, and when Captain Carter suggested that he and Abram spend the night on the boat they willingly agreed. The north wind was shrieking furiously around the little craft, but after the captain ordered a barrel of whiskey tapped the cold was soon forgotten. Before morning David had managed to arrange an agreement with his deaf host to help with the boat for the remainder of the trip, for which he was to receive four barrels of meal, one of salt, a box of coffee, and ten gallons of whiskey.

The morning was clear and cold, and Captain Carter ordered the boat to start moving upstream. Before they had progressed five miles, however, they were stopped by a heap of twisted trees, swept across the stream by a recent tornado. It was obvious that days of hard work would be necessary to remove the obstruction.

Captain Carter walked up and down the boat, scanning the horizon and sniffing the wind as if he had been far out to sea instead of stranded in a shallow river deep in the heart of a wilderness. " It's going to rain some more," said he. " A six or eight foot rise would lift us over them trees, by God."

They dropped back downstream to Owens' place to await the rain, and to hope for more floods. As the captain had predicted, a slow rain began falling the following day, the wind changing to the southeast.

" Probably keep up a week," said Jeff Owens. He had in-

vited the captain and Flavius to his cabin for a pork dinner;
he had just finished butchering a hog.

"We'll wait a week," said the captain, "and then try to
run that harricane again."

Owens was pulling his gray whiskers thoughtfully. "While
we're waiting we might go over and help Crockett raise his
cabin."

"Sure," said Flavius. "I'd like to try my hand at building
a cabin."

As soon as they could make the captain understand what
they were talking about he became enthusiastic also, and sent
Flavious down to order all his crew out to help. They rowed
down to the ridge in canoes and skiffs, and the twenty men
soon had the cabin completed. Flavius insisted that David
build an extra room for him. "I want to board up with you
until I find me a gal and set up for myself." Flavius was so
excited at building his own log room that he jerked his shirt
off, and worked half-naked in the rain.

In three days the river was rising rapidly again. "I'd say it
was about crest time now," Owens shouted at the captain,
who nodded agreement. Before the boat left, David found time
to kill a deer and also swapped part of his corn meal to Owens
for a middling of bacon. He left these with John and Abram
at the new cabin, and then joined the boat.

The craft was cut loose at midday, but they did not reach
the fallen trees until about nightfall. Impatiently they awaited
the dawn, and then started moving slowly through the timbers.
They were about halfway through when Captain Carter
sighted a group of elk skirting the edge of the stream, and
having heard about David's marksmanship, he asked him if
he would like to shoot one or two for the boat's use.

David agreed readily, and started in pursuit, killing six deer,
but not until he had followed them for some miles. He had
to find his way back to the river after dark, fighting his way

[184]

through the sharp briers, almost missing the boat which had finally pushed through the timbers. The next day he and Flavius went back after the deer, and the crew feasted on venison for the remainder of the journey.

After they had unloaded the boat at McLemore's Bluff, Flavius informed the captain that he was leaving him. " I'm going to try my hand at farming with Crockett."

Captain Carter was reluctant to see them go. He presented them with a skiff and another jug of whiskey for the journey downstream. " Good luck to you boys. I'll see you next trip maybe."

By the time David and Flavius reached the ridge where they had built the cabin, the weather had warmed and the thin ice chips which had formed along the edges of the river were disappearing rapidly in the spring sun.

" Man, this weather makes me so lazy I won't be able to plow a lick," said David, as they ran the skiff up on the muddy bank of the river.

" Plowing can't be no worse'n poling a boat up a thousand miles of river."

To let John and Abram know they were coming up the ridge, David fired his rifle, and in a few minutes they heard them running down from the cabin. Abram's freckled face was twisted in a wide grin; he had unpacked his fiddle and was playing a tune for them.

" How're you, Cap'n Crockett? " he shouted. " How was the voyage? "

David grabbed Abram's shoulder with one hand and plucked his fiddle strings with the other. " Making music already, Abram? Now I know springtime's come to stay."

He turned to stare at John. His son was wearing a shirt of red and white stripes two inches wide. " Godallmighty, son, where'd you get that shirt? "

John's blond face turned pink as he looked down self-

[185]

consciously at the sleeves of the shirt. " I thought it was a right purty shirt, pa."

Abram drew a shrill scream out of his fiddle and said: " Old Mrs. Owens made it up for him out of a piece of petticoat she had. She was aiming to make me some pants from it too, but I said no."

" Boy, that's some shirt," David said, feeling of it with his fingers.

" It's a ringtooter, all right," Flavius agreed.

David winked at Abram. " I reckon it'll serve to scare off the wild varmints. We won't need to make us a scarecrow, we'll just put John out in the field."

" Don't pay 'em no mind, John," said Flavius. " They're just envious because they ain't got one like it."

John was grinning now, and David clapped him on the shoulders. They all started laughing, and then took turns drinking from the whiskey jug. Abram played *Who Will Shoe Your Pretty Little Foot?*, singing some ribald verses he had composed himself, and they all laughed some more and rolled on the damp ground.

> O, who will shoe your pretty little foot,
>   And who will glove your hand?
> And who will kiss your red rosy lips
>   When I've gone to the foreign land?
>
> I'll love you till the seas run dry,
> I'll love you till the day I die!

At last David stopped laughing. He stood up, dusted the dried leaves from his cap, and walked over to the grassy meadow that rolled away toward the canebrakes to the east. " Boys," he said, " this here heel-cracking won't make the corn grow. We're going to have to work hard from now on. Summer's coming early this year."

[186]

With only one wooden plow to turn the ground, the planting was a slow process. They had no time for fence building. As fast as they put the grains underground, the squirrels and rabbits were after them, feasting in the furrows before the sprouts were up. They spent hours throwing rocks at the multitudes of trespassing rodents.

As the corn finally did begin to grow up tall and fresh and green, David occasionally went out alone for bigger game, always bringing back either a bear or a deer so that they did not want for meat. Once, all four of them spent a night at bear hunting, but without success. " One man and one dog can get more bears any time than four men and four dogs," David said.

In July the corn was heavy with tassels. Flavius was so interested in the crop that he permitted scarcely a weed or blade of grass to grow in the field, and David and Abram decided that they could now spare the time to return to Shoal Creek for the Crockett family and Abram's wife.

★ 2 ★

When he arrived in Shoal Creek, David found his family eagerly awaiting his return. There were two letters for him. Liza had opened the one from his brother, Willson, which had come a few weeks after he started for the Obion. It brought news of the deaths of both his father and his mother. " I always intended to go back to the old tavern up the Holston and see my folks. Now it's too late."

The other letter bore an official seal. It was a summons from Governor Carroll to attend a call session of the state legislature at Murfreesboro. " I'll have to leave right off," he said after he read it. " But I can't make out why they want a meeting in such hot weather as this is."

[187]

Instead of waiting for the irregular stagecoach service he rode horseback all the way to Murfreesboro. Sweaty and dusty, he reached the town late in the afternoon to find a smoking ruin in place of the courthouse where the legislators were to hold their sessions. The little town was in confusion after the fire; the inns were crowded with legislators and curious strangers. He had to share a room with two other men.

He was lying on the straw cot assigned to him, resting from the long journey, when his two unknown roommates walked in upon him. They were both well-dressed, one of them extremely tall, a man whom David had seen in Murfreesboro during the previous winter session. The other man's face he suddenly remembered as he sat up. It was James K. Polk.

" Mr. David Crockett, I believe," Polk said. " It seems we're going to be quite close together here."

" That's right."

" Do you know Mr. Houston? "

" I never met him," said David.

" The name's Sam Houston," said the tall man quickly, bending his long neck forward.

They talked for some minutes about the courthouse fire. " I understand we'll have to hold our meetings in one of the churches now that the courthouse is gone," said David.

" A suitable enough place, considering the main subject of the session," Houston commented dryly. He had sat down on the opposite cot, his long legs bent up like a grasshopper's.

" I hope I don't appear too ignorant—I been back in the canebrakes of west Tennessee since last spring—but what is the main subject of the meeting? "

" Ostensibly," replied Polk, " to adjust some of the hard-times emergency laws ——"

" But actually," Houston finished, " to announce Andy Jackson as candidate for President of the United States."

" Andy Jackson for President! " David stood up in surprise.

[188]

" Well, why not? " Houston returned quickly.

David walked slowly over to the dingy window, his hands in his pockets. " I reckon he'd be as good as any other," he said. He was grinning when he turned back around.

A few days later, David returned to Shoal Creek and made preparations for moving his family to the Obion. They started off on the hundred-and-fifty-mile journey in high spirits, the trip turning out to be quite a contrast to the rain-drenched expedition of the prevous spring. Only once were they discommoded. A few miles west of Nashville, one of the wagon wheels was broken when they crashed into a boulder along the trail; they were two days repairing it.

Before they could pull the wagon up the ridge to the new cabin, David and Abram and Ben worked for hours in the hot August sun, cutting a road through the thick growth of new canes. Flavius Harris and John heard the creaking wheels of the wagon long before they reached the cabin; they came running down to meet them, Flavius blushing like an adolescent when he was introduced to Liza's daughter, Margaret Ann.

The weeks which followed were golden ones. Although there was much work to be done on the new farm, Abram and Flavius, as well as David's two oldest sons, were willing toilers, and by mid-December all the crops were gathered and stored for the winter.

One evening just before Christmas, David announced that they would go for a hunt early the next morning. " We need some Christmas meat," he said.

That night, rain fell in torrents, drumming against the log walls of the cabin like a continual cascade. David's legs ached even under the warm covers; he slept fitfully, waking once or twice after strange nightmares.

By morning the rain had turned to sleet, rattling in upon

his head through a crack in the window. He jumped out of bed and crawled up to the loft to awaken Abram, who was curled up with his wife. "Get up, you sleepy 'possum," cried David. "This'll be a good day for hunting, after that rain."

Flavius was already up, greasing his gun. "Going after a turkey for Christmas dinner, I am," he said.

When they started, sleet was still falling, glistening in the wind. David walked ahead of the others, watching the lead dog flick its tail as it leaped over a low mound; then the animal disappeared, barking furiously, and David started running. The dog had stopped still, its eyes fixed on the trunk of a large oak; it whined, then raised its head to the sky, baying triumphantly. David searched the tree up and down, circling it twice, but he could see nothing in the bare branches except clinging bits of ice.

"Come on, you old fool, there ain't no bear up that tree." The dog had started running circles and then wheeled off toward the upland. In a few minutes he was out of sight, baying again.

They were almost out of the forest; the canes, bending low with their coats of ice, knocked against his body as he ran through them to the open stretch of grassland. Jerking his head up into the sleet, he stopped abruptly. Twenty paces ahead of him stood the largest bear he had ever seen, snarling, feinting with his paw at the excited hound.

At first David stepped back, thinking his imagination had got the better of him. The animal looked more like a huge black bull than a bear. Even the dog appeared to be nonplussed; it was backing off nervously now, its hair stiff and straight like a porcupine's. Quickly the bear turned and started lumbering off sideways through the trees.

David immediately was in pursuit, breaking the frozen canes ahead of him with his rifle butt. The hound managed to trail the huge animal to a black oak which the bear ascended clumsily; the baffled dog stood scratching at the bark and whining softly until David was close enough to shoot.

"Look at him," he whispered. "What a bear he is, setting up there with his chest poked out. One piece of lead wouldn't likely do more'n a bee stinger would do to him."

He put fresh priming in the gun, packing it, then raised the weapon, taking careful aim at the beast's breast, and fired. The bear snorted, raising his paws, slumping in the tree crotch. As quickly as possible David loaded again, firing into the same vital spot. Down the beast came, crashing into the ice-brittle brush; the dog set up a fearful howl.

With his tomahawk in one hand, his long knife in the other, David ran forward to find the bear crouching over the dog, its eyes gleaming horribly. As soon as it saw David, the bear released the dog which limped away, whimpering. Retreating slowly, David picked up his gun which he had dropped in the excitement, reloaded and fired at the slowing advancing animal. The bear dropped dead.

For some minutes, David walked around and around his kill, measuring it. The size of the beast was almost unbelievable. Already he was wondering how he would ever get it back to the cabin.

The hound was still whimpering, and he examined it to see if it was severely injured; the dog had suffered only a few scratches, and when David started back for home, it followed after him, still limping.

It was late afternoon when he got home, but the sky was beginning to clear and darkness was yet a few hours away. Luckily, Abram and Flavius had already returned, with half a dozen turkeys. Taking all four of their horses, they hurried back to the bottomlands, following the blazes on the trees which David had marked as he had come out.

Both Abram and Flavius were astounded when they saw the bear. "Biggest one I ever saw," said Abram. "And I seen some plenty big ones too, back in the Tennessee River bottoms."

As darkness approached, David built a huge fire so that they might see how to work. They skinned the animal carefully. "Nobody else will ever believe there was such a bear unless we keep the skin whole," said Flavius.

"How much you think it weighed?" asked Abram.

"I'd lay a wager on six hundred pounds," David declared.

They were all night hauling the butchered animal back to the cabin, Liza coming to the door in her night shift to let them inside. "Landsakesalive," said she, staring at the heaps of meat, "how many bears did you boys kill?"

O N *the second day of December in 1823, near the end of his seventh year as President of the United States, James Monroe addressed the assembled Congress in Washington.*

In those seven years of Good Feeling that had passed since his inaugural, many a sectional barrier had collapsed. The East, still politically all-powerful, was at last beginning to respect the potential strength of the West. With the 49th parallel already running across the maps, the United States had developed a national consciousness.

Therefore it was not remarkable that President James Monroe should say to the Congress on that day in December 1823 that henceforth the American continents were "not to be considered as subjects for future colonization by any European power." For good and all, the ties between the new world and the old were to be severed.

This Monroe Doctrine was no brilliant brain child of the man who gave it a name. Indeed, it grew out of a proposition made by Great Britain to Thomas Jefferson twenty years earlier, a Great Britain anxious to maintain a flourishing trade in the young nations of the Latin Americas. Thomas Jefferson, distrusting everything British, turned the plan down flatly.

[192]

*Twenty years later, James Monroe read a modified version
of that British proposition to his Congress, and although to
this day it has never been made an official part of United
States foreign policy, from 1823 onward the Monroe Doctrine
represented an attitude of mind that was significant.*

*For in 1823 the United States was no longer a straggling
tier of loosely connected coastal states, reaching feelers out
over the Alleghanies; it was instead a lusty young nation,
already facing the western plains beyond the Mississippi, beginning to beat its sturdy chest, disrespectful, if not contemptuous, of all the nations across the Atlantic.*

*Concurrently with this rise of national consciousness, rose
the spirit of the frontier democrats. If the United States is a
mighty power, said they, then we too are a mighty power.*

*Since the days of Thomas Jefferson, the rumblings in the
West had been growing steadily in volume. After December
2, 1823, the West slowly began to erupt.*

<h1 style="text-align:center">★ 3 ★</h1>

In 1823, the town of Jackson, Tennessee, was one long
street, with half a square beginning to form in the center. In
dry times the street was powdery gray dust; in rainy weather it
was thick gummy mud. More than a dozen unpainted frame
buildings of various ages, some still new, others black and
dilapidated, faced each other across the rutted street. Back
from the line of business structures were the dwelling houses,
standing at different angles as if tossed into position by a
careless dice thrower. Most of these were plain log cabins;
three or four were more pretentious, embellished with rough
columns.

The town was an important stop between the trade center of
Nashville and the thriving Mississippi River village of Memphis.

To the south and west, new settlers by the hundreds were plowing the virgin black soil, planting it into cotton; to the north and east other settlers still trapped and hunted for skins and furs. It was to Jackson that many of these new settlers turned for supplies, trading their cotton or their pelts for coffee and sugar and salt and tobacco.

Above the largest of the frame business houses a crude sign, swinging from wires in a crosspiece, announced to the passers-by that Mack Davidson, Prop., was a trader in both animal skins and cotton.

On a late February day, this sign was twisting sharply in stiff gusts of wind when three strangers entered the town, treading carefully to avoid the deepest holes of mud in the street. The man in front was laden with bundles of furs, his back bent so low that he had to turn his neck upwards to read the swaying sign. In one hand he carried his rifle as a sort of balance. His face was almost covered with stiff bristles of dark brown beard.

The second man, also bent forward under a load of skins, was lean and freckled, red hair straggling out from under his cap. Instead of a rifle he carried a battered fiddle, almost colorless with age. The third stranger was a boy, thin and wiry. His dark eyes, resembling those of the man in front, were wide and filled with curiosity.

They entered the general store, dropping their bundles on the greasy floor, breathing simultaneous sighs of relief. In the mud fireplace at one end of the store, a slow smoky fire was burning; around it several men were sitting or standing, most of them chewing tobacco, spitting occasionally into the fire. The conversation that must have been in progress died out quickly when the three strangers entered.

" Howd'ye," said the first man, pushing his hand up inside his cap to scratch his head.

An old man with a bald copper-colored skull stood up from

behind the counter. The frizzled patches of hair around his ears and the pointed beard on his chin were almost snow white. He was wearing a leathern apron, like a blacksmith's. " Good evening, strangers," said he.

" You're the proprietor of this here store? "

" Yup. I'm Mack Davidson."

" Mack Davidson, eh." The man with the furs scratched his head again. " Let me study a minute. Mack Davidson. Fought with Andy Jackson agin the Indians in the Creek War, didn't you? "

• " Yup."

" Went down to Pensacola, didn't you? "

" Shore did."

" My name's Davy Crockett. Remember me? "

The bald-headed man smacked his lips open in a quick laugh. " Damn if I don't. You was always raising hell about something. Well, well, you live hereabouts now, I reckon."

" Forty miles up'n the Obion. I brought you down some furs for to trade. I want you to meet Abram Henry. He was too far up in the hills to come out for the Creek War, I guess, and this is my boy, John."

Suddenly David felt the presence of someone close behind him; he turned quickly and was face to face with a handsome, well-dressed young man. The young man's mouth dropped open just as David slapped him on the stomach. " George Russell! Well, skin me a coon. Daggonit, I almost didn't know you with that plow-handle moustache and them yellow-striped pants! "

George Russell had changed considerably since David had seen him last in Winchester, seven years before. His shoulders and his boyish face had filled out and he looked more prosperous than any other man in the store. " Last I heard tell of you, Davy, you was over in Shoal Creek country. Got elected to the legislature, didn't you? "

" Yessiree, it was Colonel Crockett this and Honorable Mr. Crockett that, back there. But hell, that's all done with now, George. I'm having me a fine time, just a-hunting a little, and a-farming a little. None of that highfalutin stuff out here on the Obion. What you do out here, yourself? "

" Cotton," said George. " My father got a head start out here before he died, growing and trading in cotton. Keeps me kind of busy going from place to place, tending to business."

" Making lots of money, though, ain't you, George? I notice you sort of got a fancy rig on there, boy."

George smiled, somewhat embarrassed. " I'm about to get used to these outfits now. It's pretty near necessary in my business, dressing up, but many's the time I've felt like I'd rather have on buckskin again."

They moved over toward the clay fireplace; the slow flow of talk had commenced again, most of it emanating from a moon-faced man sitting in a big rocking chair. The man wore a tall beaver hat which he occasionally removed to stroke his silvery hair. His paunch was enormous, spreading out in great folds of flesh, almost enveloping his knees.

" Colonel Alexander," George Russell was saying to the moon-faced man, " I'd like you to know my friend David Crockett from up on the Obion. He was a member of the last Tennessee legislature, from Shoal Creek." He added for David's benefit: " Colonel Alexander is the United States Congressman from west Tennessee. He's paying us a short visit."

Colonel Alexander leaned forward with great effort, breathing heavily, limply shaking David's hand. " Mighty proud to know you, Davy Crockett. You aiming to get into politics out here? "

David had been looking at three printed posters on the wall just above Colonel Alexander's tall hat. " Well, sir," he replied, " judging from them three announcements, west Tennessee don't need no more politicians." He read aloud: " Robert Butler. Major Lynn. Jack McEver. All for the same seat in the Tennessee legislature, too."

" And all mighty fine men," Colonel Alexander put in hastily.

" Well, I'm aiming to stick to bear hunting." He caught at George Russell's arm. " Say, boy, I want to show you a bearskin I got last winter, the biggest daggoned bear I ever shot yet."

David unrolled his pack, spreading the dark bearskin out on the floor; he could scarcely find room for it between the barrels and the counter. Before he had flattened the skin out, the talk around the fireplace had ceased altogether. When he stood up David was surprised to see that all the men were turning to look at the enormous bearskin, forgetting for the moment their distinguished visitor, Congressman Alexander.

" Where'd you kill him, Colonel Crockett? " asked a tall cotton planter, who had been sitting quietly listening to the talk.

" On the Obion. And there's plenty more up there like him."

" By God, you must be some bear hunter."

Mack Davidson, the store proprietor, was dancing about, measuring the skin with his long arms. " Jehoshaphat," cried he, " what a bear, what a bear! "

" And what a bear hunter," added George Russell, laughing, prodding David in the ribs.

Unnoticed, Abram Henry had tuned up his fiddle; he broke out suddenly into a lively tune, the men clapping hands to keep time. U. S. Congressman Alexander pursed his lips and frowned. This small audience, which a few minutes ago had been listening so attentively to his words, was no longer his.

George Russell had produced a small flask, offering David a drink. " How long you staying in town, Davy? "

" Leaving tomorrow. Got to get back and start my spring plowing."

[197]

" Couldn't you wait long enough to meet three acquaintances of mine? "

" Maybe so. Who are they? "

George pointed at the political announcements on the wall.
" Robert Butler, Major Lynn, and Jack McEver."

" You mean you want me to vote for one of 'em? "

" Why not? "

" Which one? "

"That's up to you," said George, taking another pull from
the flask.

In the morning early, David completed his trade with Mack
Davidson, loading down his packs with coffee, sugar, powder,
lead, and salt. Seeing Mack's display of rifles on the wall, he
suddenly remembered his boyhood journey to Knoxville when
he had purchased his first rifle.

" Hey," he cried. " Hey, John! "

John crawled out from behind a pile of furs, where he had
been watching people pass by on the street.

" John, how'd you like a gun? "

Mack Davidson broke into a sudden roar of laughter.
" Davy, the lad's already beat you to it. He traded me his
'possum pelts for a rifle last night while you was a-talking your
head off about your bearskins."

David laughed, dropping a paper note on the counter board.
" Give him an extra load of shooting lead then, Mack." He
poked his son playfully in the chest, and went out to join
George Russell at the inn.

The town's only tavern was an unprepossessing structure, an
old log house reconstructed with earth and stone. The windows
were too small and the fireplace drew badly; as soon as he
entered Davy understood why the local citizens preferred to
meet in Mack Davidson's store instead of at the tavern.

He found George Russell and Colonel Alexander sitting in

a dark corner by the fire. " Hell," said David, " it's warmer outdoors than it is in here."

" Nevertheless," replied Colonel Alexander, " I much prefer to stay in here where I may sit."

David did not blame the Colonel, considering his weighty paunch, for preferring to sit. While they waited for the stage-coach, the innkeeper poured a round of drinks. The whiskey was raw, but it warmed his stomach, and he felt invigorated immediately.

He was in a talkative mood when the stagecoach arrived, bringing the three political candidates from the south. It seemed that they were all friends; they were running for the legislature because they had little else to do.

Robert Butler was the first to leave the mud-stained coach. He was wearing a long-tailed striped coat, and a tall hat was pressed down on his black curls. " He's the one that married Andy Jackson's niece," George Russell whispered to David. " Got everything he wants, big plantations and plenty of slaves."

Major Lynn was an older man, with long side whiskers grown to conceal a slight facial jerk which gave him a comical expression. The third man, Jack McEver, was a rough Irish-man, swearing at everybody, smiling all the while. David liked him as soon as he saw him.

After they were all introduced, Colonel Alexander took complete charge of the meeting, frequently referring to David as Colonel Crockett of the Tennessee legislature. David had to explain twice to the three candidates that he had changed his residence permanently and was no longer interested in politics.

He tried to excuse himself before they returned to the tavern, explaining that Abram Henry and his son were waiting for him.

" Oh, come along, Davy, and take another horn with us at least, before you go," George insisted. " Perhaps it'll be a long time before we meet again."

[199]

"Sure, I guess I could take another drink." He had not realized before how different he was from the others. They were all well-dressed, their hair and beards neatly clipped and oiled, while he in his worn buckskins, and his whiskers dirty and scraggly, must have appeared quite ordinary to them. More than once he was conscious of Butler's piercing eyes appraising him from head to foot.

They sat down in the chilly tavern. David gulped his drink at once. Robert Butler was tapping the table top with his long soft fingers. "So you've had enough of politics, eh, Colonel Crockett?" he asked abruptly.

"Yes, sir, I have."

"Really, I think you should offer your name again here. Major Lynn and McEver and I would relish a battle. Between us three it's not much ——"

"I live forty miles from here," David interrupted. "Not enough voters around my neighborhood to count for anything."

Colonel Alexander appeared bored. He belched, muttered something about high tariffs and low tariffs. There was a pause in the conversation, and David stood up, shook hands around, inviting them to visit the Obion country. He hurried out of the gloomy tavern, glad to be on his way back home.

Two weeks later David was hoeing out grass with Flavius Harris in the upper part of the field, when he heard a horse galloping over the ridge; he turned and saw the horseman heading down along the fence in their direction.

"Some stranger, I'll bet," said Flavius. " I never saw that black horse around this neighborhood."

In a minute the horse was near enough for David to recognize the rider from his striped yellow pants thrust in high boots. "Hyah, George," he yelled. " Get off and grab a hoe! "

It was George Russell, all right, his long moustaches rising in a grin. " You better get out of that field and start campaigning, Davy Crockett. I just talked to one of your neighbors five miles below and he never even knew you was up for the legislature."

" What you talking about, George? "

A wrinkled newspaper came hurtling through the air, landing at David's feet in the freshly dug earth. He picked it up, unrolling it, still thinking George was making a joke.

" Look at the bottom corner," said George, swinging down off his horse.

Suddenly from one of the columns at the bottom of the tattered sheet, his own name flashed before his eyes. " Candidates for Tennessee legislature," he read aloud, " Jack McEver, Major Lynn, Robert Butler, and David Crockett! "

He looked up at George, his eyes wide with astonishment. " How is this—where'd you get this newspaper? "

" It's about ten days old," replied George, as he crawled over the fence. " I saw it a few days after you left Jackson. Didn't you have the notice printed? "

" Hell, no! " David dropped his hoe. Flavius stood open-mouthed, not understanding what the conversation was about. Finally David remembered to introduce his two friends, and they went on to the cabin. Liza was pleased to see George Russell again, though she was not quite at ease with him because of his tailored clothing.

In all the excitement of reunion, the political announcement was soon forgotten. All afternoon David and George re-lived the Creek War, outdoing one another with wild recitals of battles to the great delight of Flavius who wound up the day with a series of tall sea tales. At bedtime, David's youngest sons who had been listening were reluctant to turn to their pallets in the loft.

In bed with Liza, David mumbled and tossed for so long a

time that she finally got up and lit a candle. " Now, tell me what's eating on you, Davy, so's we can both go to sleep."

" It's politics," he said rubbing his eyes wearily. " You saw that piece in the paper George brought—about me being up for the legislature from this district ——"

" Well," said Liza, " ain't you aiming to be elected? "

" That's what's bothering me. The whole danged business is a joke. I'll bet you that feller Butler, Andy Jackson's nephew, I'll bet he put my name in there just for a prank on me. But all the same—well, this part of Tennessee ain't like Shoal Creek—too many plantations—all scattered out—only the squatters up around here would vote for me."

Liza leaned back in the bed, closing her eyes sleepily. " Folks is all the same everywhere, Davy. Folks everywhere take a liking to you soon's they know you."

He kissed her suddenly on the cheek. " I reckon you're right. You know what I'm aiming to do, Liza, I'm a-going to give that Butler feller, or whoever it was put my name up, I'm going to give him his money's worth. I'm going out and make some speeches, you'll see ——"

The next morning at the breakfast table he told George that he was going to make a campaign for the legislature.

" That's the way to talk," cried George. " I wish I didn't have to go back to Memphis—I'd sure like to go along with you."

David noticed that Abram Henry was looking at him, his freckled face as attentive and expectant as a bird dog's awaiting a word from a hunter. Abram's long jaw was sagging; he finally spoke: " I guess maybe you'll have to be away from the farm a good part of the spring and summer."

" Yessirree," replied David. " I'm going to have me a time canvassing the country."

" Then Flavius and me and the boys will be right pressed to keep the crops going."

"Aw, hell, Abram, you know damn well I couldn't campaign without your fiddle. Flavius knows a feller over across the river working in staves—he'll help for shares. You and your old fiddle are coming along with me." Abram's grin spread so wide he could hardly finish eating his scrambled eggs.

Before breakfast was ended, David had a hundred things in mind to do. Not since the Crocketts had moved there had the big cabin seen such a hustle and bustle as went on during the remainder of that day.

Although it was early March and the election day was almost five months away, David decided he would start traveling immediately. With Abram and his trusty musical instrument as faithful supporters, he left home the following day, traveling up and down the Obion valley, circling the small communities around Jackson, then moving over to McLemore's Bluff for a celebration arranged by his old friend, Jeff Owens.

Printed handbills carrying his name and a phrase " the man from the canebrakes " appeared mysteriously from somewhere. Some good friend, he guessed, must have stood the expense for them.

Just after he finished his speech at McLemore's Bluff, he stopped by the local inn for a drink. George Russell was there waiting for him.

" I got here too late for the speechifying, Davy, but I figured you'd head over this way to wet your whistle so I came here direct."

He was glad to see George. " Man, this politics is the thing for me. Lots more fun than hoeing corn. Say, George, what're the folks up around Jackson saying about Davy Crockett now? "

" They're saying plenty, Davy, about that old wild bear hunter from the Obion. I guess you knew your three opponents are calling a caucus at the Saturday court—to pick the strongest man, the other two to withdraw. I figure it'll be Doc Butler."

"Yeah. Him, with Andy Jackson backing him up. I'll bet he'd give his eye teeth not to have put my name up as a prank the way he ——"

"So you think it was Butler did that?" George swallowed his whiskey suddenly.

"Who else could it've been? Major Lynn is too close-fisted, and Jack McEver is not the kind of man to pull pranks."

They finished their second drinks. "Whyn't you go over to Jackson with me tomorrow and stay until your opponents hold their caucus?" George suggested.

David shook his head. "Abram and me, we've got to head for home now. He's lonesome for that plump little wife of his, and I'd mighty like to see my old woman and the young-uns. We've been gone most a month."

"I'll tell you what I'll do then. Soon as I find out who's the man you got to beat I'll ride up to your place and tell you ——"

"We'll be looking out for you," said David, "with a big keg of corn right beside us."

On the following Monday, George arrived at the Crockett cabin with the news. McEver and Lynn had withdrawn their names. To win now, David would have to defeat Robert Butler, Andrew Jackson's nephew, the wealthiest man in Madison County. David looked straight at George, squinting one eye almost shut. "Tell me right off, George, you think I could beat Doc Butler?"

George rubbed his long moustaches slowly with his forefinger. "Butler has quite a number of friends, all right, big landowners most of 'em. But remember this, Davy Crockett, Doc Butler never shot a bear in his life."

David started to laugh. "You mean I'll get votes according to the number of bears I've killed?"

"It's not so simple as that," said George. "But you know what I mean."

"I reckon I do," said David, nodding his head. "I reckon I do. Abram, play us a tune."

In June, David journeyed to Jackson to see George Russell before beginning his tour in the southwestern counties. As a result of his business dealings, George knew a number of important men in that part of the district, and he had promised David to accompany him on a trip through that section in July.

Arriving late in the afternoon, he and Abram took a room at the inn, where they found Colonel Alexander was also listed as a guest. The innkeeper informed David that the Colonel was at that very moment making a speech down at the open end of the town. As soon as they could stow away their packs, he and Abram hurried down the street to hear what the Congressman had to say.

Colonel Alexander, however, had just completed his oration. Judging from the beaming faces of the crowd surrounding the corpulent old gentleman, David guessed that the Congressman's seat in Washington would be in no great danger in the autumn when he would be up again for election. Leaving Abram and his fiddle somewhere behind in the press, he pushed through to the Colonel's side.

"Howd'ye, Colonel Alexander," he said. "That must've been some speechifying. Looks like everybody in west Tennessee is here."

Colonel Alexander chuckled, shaking his fat shoulders. "They're just hanging around waiting for a free drink," he whispered in David's ear. A makeshift bar had been set up beside the speaker's platform, and liquors were pouring over the slab counter. "Have a drink yourself, Davy. Here, Tom, I want you to meet my friend, Davy Crockett, the man from the canebrakes, yessir, sure enough it's him, Tom, old bear-killing Davy." In a few minutes David had met several strangers, all evidently close friends of the Congressman. "Don't forget," the Colonel kept saying, "Davy Crockett is electioneering too—and by damn, I'm glad it's not me he's running against."

As the supply of liquors ebbed, so did the crowd. Suddenly, in front of him, coming from the opposite side of the street, was Robert Butler, his opponent for the legislature. He was certain that Butler saw him, but the man gave no indication of recognition and walked straight on toward Colonel Alexander. For a moment David was inclined to remain silent; then he turned toward Butler. "Hey, Doc Butler!"

Butler turned quickly, looked at David and nodded with frozen dignity. David was feeling good; the June air was enough to make a man kick up his heels like a spring colt. He stepped jauntily over to the group around Butler and the Colonel. "Well, Doc," he said, "I suppose the election is all skinned and stretched out to dry now—since you and McEver and Lynn had your caucus. A feller was telling me just t'other day how the election was all over last March, but I said to him to lay around a while, till August maybe ——"

"Damn it, Crockett," cried Butler with forced cordiality. "Is that you?"

"Be sure it is, but I don't want it understood as how I'm electioneering. I just crept out of the canebrakes to see what discoveries I could make among the white folks." David noticed that the crowd was increasing, gathering closer around him and Butler. Butler appeared to be nervous; he kept fingering the brim of his tall hat; obviously he was trying to think of something to say. "That's a fine hunting shirt you have on there, Crockett," he suddenly blurted out. "Is that the latest style in electioneering shirts?"

David pushed back his long hair and grinned at Abram who

[206]

had suddenly appeared at his elbow. "Yessir, I had this shirt special made; these here two pockets will hold a peck apiece." He raised his voice so that it would carry out through the crowd. "In one pocket I carry a big twist of chewing tobacco, in the other my bottle of corn. When I meet a good man, out comes my bottle for him to take a dram. Course then he's got to spit out his quid of tobacco in order to drink, but soon as he's taken his drink, out comes my big twist of tobacco from my other pocket, and he gets a good fresh chew. You see, Doc, everybody I meet is on as good a footing when I leave him as when I find him. Have a swallow, Doc?" David flipped open his left pocket and withdrew a long bottle, offering it to Butler.

To his surprise, Butler laughed. It was the first time he had ever heard him laugh. The other men were laughing too. Butler drank briefly and returned the bottle. "Crockett," he said solemnly, "you can beat me electioneering all hollow."

"We'll wait till August to find that out, I reckon. After all, it ain't just Davy Crockett you got to beat. You got to beat my seven young-uns, and, man, they're the seven loudest-talking young-uns in west Tennessee. And you got to beat my four coon dogs, they'll be hunting every night till midnight supporting my election."

Butler was still laughing. Colonel Alexander's rotund folds of stomach flesh were quivering with mirth. "Abram," said David, winking, "hit up a tune."

At dusk of that day, George Russell arrived on the Memphis stage. He brought news that two men from the southwestern counties had just announced their candidacies for the state legislature. "Don't give it much worriment, though," George said. "If anything they'll only cut into Butler's votes among the planters. The ordinary folks, Davy, are all for you."

"But they've never even seen me down south of here."

"Politics travel fast, Davy. Everywhere I been down there,

[207]

people are talking about that bear-hunting Davy Crockett from the canebrakes."

David's face was serious with wonderment. "And they never even seen me?"

He was anxious to be off to the southern counties at once, but he waited three days until George was ready to join him. All through July they traveled through the rich rolling country south of the Obion, George arranging meetings, Abram fiddling merrily, and David talking.

In August the people voted. When the count was ended, David Crockett had a majority of 247 votes over his three opponents. He was now Colonel Crockett, bear hunter extraordinary from the canebrakes, for the second time a member of the Tennessee state legislature.

Robert Butler, arriving early at the Jackson inn, was one of the first to congratulate him. " You're a born politician, Davy. You could turn a funeral into a political speech-making."

Colonel Alexander was there, repeating over and over again to everybody who would listen: " Davy moved clear across the state without losing a session—that's politicking."

" A fool for luck, and a poor man for children," David said, for no reason at all.

" You're no fool," said George Russell.

" There's one thing I would like to know," David said, looking straight at Robert Butler. " Why did you have my name put in that newspaper as a candidate?" Butler stared at him, incomprehension written across his face. " Didn't you do it?" David added quickly.

George Russell placed himself squarely in front of his friend. " If you knew who had your name put up, Davy, what would you be inclined to do to him?"

" Well, if I'd known who it was when I first heard about it, I'd 'a' been aching to kick him where he sets. But if I knew now, I'd offer him a long drink."

[208]

"Then let's have that long drink," George said, laughing.
"I did it."
"Well, skin me a coon!" David reached for his bottle.

J OHN QUINCY ADAMS *was a lonely man, in his own words*
" a man of reserve, cold, austere, and forbidding." His face
was like cold marble, draped along the jowls with white side
whiskers, his forehead high and round.

Late in the presidential election year of 1824, few Ameri-
cans thought of John Quincy Adams as presidential timber.
Instead they were debating whether their next President would
be William H. Crawford, Henry Clay or Andrew Jackson.

But before the year ended, William H. Crawford was
already out of the race, and Henry Clay of Kentucky had
bowed before the chosen leader of the western democrats,
Andrew Jackson. John Quincy Adams' star was rising fast,
and when Congress assembled in February 1825 to elect a
President, there were those who thought he had a fighting
chance to snatch the White House from the thundering
Jacksonians.

One man who thought so was Henry Clay of Kentucky, no
friend of Jackson. With the aid of clever Martin Van Buren
of New York, he swung that state's votes to Adams and pulled
the trick.

And though the rising tide from the West failed in its first
great sweep, as it ebbed slowly back to gather new strength,
it attracted to itself many a dissatisfied American from North
and East and South.

The ideas of Thomas Jefferson and Thomas Paine, so re-
pugnant to John Quincy Adams, were still abroad in the land.
Bitterly did the new President write in his little diary note-
books, sadly did he bemoan the rise of the " vulgarians."
But the " vulgarians " cared little for John Quincy Adams'
opinions. Ahead of them were four years of waiting, four
restless years of waiting, for the day when finally their chosen
hero, Andrew Jackson, would be their President.

★ 4 ★

David went to Murfreesboro in September for the opening of the legislature. As the new courthouse had not been
completed, sessions were called in the Presbyterian church.
There was some talk of moving the capital, but the conflict of
choice between Knoxville partisans and Nashville partisans led
to a postponement of final action.

During his first days in Murfreesboro, he stayed in his
small tavern room much of the time, reading all the newspapers he could find. He purchased a new suit, with a fancy
waistcoat which worried him at first because it was cut so
short and the pockets were so much smaller than those he was
accustomed to have in his hunting shirts. Try as he would he
could not master the art of tying his new black neckpiece, and
finally he decided to let it hang loose.

As soon as Andrew Jackson had been elected to the Senate,
the legislature adjourned, and David returned to the Obion,
dressed in his buckskins, his new suit and neckpiece tied up
neatly in a bundle. He wondered if he would ever have occasion to wear them again.

His family received him with a specially prepared dinner,
and immediately afterwards Flavius Harris proudly brought
out a bearskin almost as large as the one David had sold the
previous winter. " Boy, I'll be glad to go on a hunt again,"
David told him.

Hunting, however, did not satisfy him as he had thought it
would. In three or four days he grew restless, and started for
Jackson, finding George Russell there as he had expected.

" Well, Davy," George said, after they sat down in the
tavern for drinks, " what you going to do now? "

" Go back home and hunt some, I guess. I was sort of

counting on you coming up on the Obion for a long bear hunt with me."

" I'd like mighty well to do that. But I expect to be too busy these next two months, and I'll bet you'll be busy too, because it's on account of you that I'll be so damned busy."

" What you talking about, George? "

George called the tavern keeper, ordering more drinks for David and himself. " You heard folks around here talking about the tariff, haven't you? "

" Sure, Mack Davidson says the tariff's ruining the cotton business. And I heard a couple of cotton planters say they was going to lose money on account of the tariff. I'm not sure I know what the tariff is, but I hear everybody damning it from kingdom come."

George clinked his glass against the bottle on the table. " Some claim it's keeping prices up on all the things we buy from the East, and keeping prices down on everything we sell in the East. I don't know whether that's so or not, but that's what folks are saying. And at the same time everybody is raising Cain because Colonel Alexander voted for that tariff law."

" He did, didn't he? "

" Sure he did. And that's why you and me are going to be so busy the next few weeks."

Suddenly a broad smile of comprehension spread across David's face. " You mean you think I'm going to run against Colonel Alexander for United States Congress? "

" Sure. You can beat him easy, with all your friends that voted you into the legislature behind you, added to all the big cotton planters mad as hornets because of the Colonel's tariff vote. He won't have a chance."

David, still smiling, shook his head slowly. " I couldn't stand to that. Being a Congressman to Washington City—that's a step above my knowledge. I don't know a damn thing about Congress matters."

[211]

George leaned back, looking at the ceiling. " What about the Colonel? You think he's got more knowledge than you? You wouldn't own to that, would you? "

David got up and walked over to the dingy tavern window. He could see several men standing across the street, talking together. " George, I can count eleven men over yonder. I guess four or five of 'em are right smart fellers. Why not ask one of them to run against the Colonel? "

George had just taken a fresh chew of tobacco from his long twist; he spat the entire quid indignantly into the cuspidor under the table. " I'll answer to that. If I'll go over and ask these eleven men if they'll vote for you for Congress, and six say they will, you've got to offer up your name. Is that a wager? "

" I'll lay to that," said David.

In less than a dozen long strides, George crossed the street, kicking up dust as he walked. David watched him wave his arms violently, then point once to the tavern. As he turned, eight of the men started after him. David knew all of them. He was pulling nervously at his cap when they entered the tavern.

" By God," cried George, " eight of 'em say they'll vote for you against the Colonel."

" Then I reckon I lose the bet," David said, shaking hands around.

" But you ain't going to lose the election," spoke up one of the men. " We don't like Colonel Alexander's tariff a-tall."

" If Andy Jackson can be made President," George declared loudly, " then Davy Crockett can be one of his Congressmen."

The campaign began immediately. Every moment seemed precious because of the nearness of election day. So instead of returning to the Obion for Abram and his fiddle, David sent a messenger with orders for Abram to join him, and for his son John and Flavius Harris to make a tour through the river bottoms to spread the news among his neighbors.

Before Abram could catch up with him, David had made three speeches in as many settlements. Though he used his old technique of telling simple stories rather than delivering political orations, he was always careful to mention the tariff law, pointing out the low price of cotton and the high price of store-bought goods. " I'm aiming to vote for Jackson for President if I'm in Congress this winter, and I'm asking you to vote for me so as I can vote for him. That's a fair swap-out, ain't it? "

But he lost the 1825 campaign.

✶ 5 ✶

For months the idea of becoming a United States Congressman remained uppermost in David's thoughts. Money was the thing he needed most—not much, but enough to enable him to travel rapidly, to pay printing bills, and to buy drinks for the voters. He had only a few dollars to his name, and they were disappearing rapidly. There was no money to be made from farming, he knew that. And prices on furs and skins had dropped so low that trapping was no longer profitable. He resolved to try something else.

It was Flavius Harris who gave him the idea of shipping a boatload of staves to New Orleans. The previous autumn a stave-cutter had worked with Flavius on the farm while David was campaigning, and from what he had been told Flavius believed there would be money in the project.

David soon became enthusiastic about the staves. If one boatload would bring them money, why not ship two loads at one trip? He talked to all his neighbors, and early in the fall of 1825, about twenty of them started to work, first building two crude flatboats of split logs, then cutting oak staves to fill them. Before they had been at work many days David realized the task was a gigantic one; they would be all winter at it. The edge soon wore off his enthusiasm, and the first frosty day in November he slipped away for a bear hunt with Jeff Owens. They killed three bears in two days, just enough to whet his desire for more hunting.

The staves no longer interested him. He could think or talk of nothing but bear hunting. A man from Virginia, Zach McDaniel, who had just joined forces with the stave-cutters, was a willing listener. McDaniel had never killed a bear in his life, and David enjoyed telling him tall tales about his hunting trips.

The week between Christmas and New Year's Day was declared a holiday period for the stave-cutters. David took advantage of it, and with John as a companion went far up into the lake country to the north. Before they returned home, they killed seventeen bears, bringing in all the skins as proof of their exploit.

As soon as Zach McDaniel saw the bearskins, he insisted that David take him along on his next hunt.

" Well," said David, " I'm afraid the bears are all gone in for the winter, now. You see, soon's they get fattened up in the fall they go into a hole, or in a holler tree, or a log, or a cane-brake, and lie up till spring like frozen snakes. They just lie in there sucking the bottoms of their paws all the time."

McDaniel appeared to be so disappointed that David finally agreed to try one more hunt. They decided to take a week for it, going up into the Reelfoot Lake section, where, he had been told, the bears were as plentiful as rabbits. They rode horseback. John went along to take care of the horses while David and McDaniel were hunting.

They made camp when they reached a section where trees and canes had been twisted to the earth by a hurricane. " You always find bears in a hurricane in winter. They find lots of places to hole up in there." A few minutes after they had stopped they discovered tracks; the dogs soon got the scent and began tugging at their leashes.

As soon as they could get the horses tied, they were off, the dogs dashing ahead of them into the tangle of canes and brush. John stumbled into a deep rutted hole, and when David reached his hand down to lift him out, he let out a sudden exclamation. "That's the damn queerest hole I ever did see. It's just a big crack running off into the cane."

McDaniel stepped closer, examining the narrow fissure intently. "You know what that is, Crockett; that's where the earthquake was up here, some years ago. A settler was telling me about it not long ago."

"Sure, I've heard about that earthquake. It drained a lot of lakes and filled up a lot of dry holes, shook everything up. But that was a long time ago. This hole looks kind of fresh to me."

"Sure enough it does." McDaniel shook his head, puzzled.

They went ahead, occasionally stumbling over more fissures concealed by the vines and leaves until the nearness of the baying dogs warned them that a bear was in front of them. McDaniel crashed through, ahead of David, his gun ready, but David saw the bear first, twenty yards off to one side, and he fired, clipping the animal's shoulder.

Growling with rage and pain, the bear spun around. "Let me get him, let me get him!" McDaniel had turned and approached within a few feet of the crouching beast, firing point-blank.

"Man, you don't know much about bears, walking up that close," David cried. "Next time you may not be so lucky. They're quicker than you'd think. You sure got him this time though."

McDaniel wanted to skin the bear immediately. "It's my first one, you know."

"Sure, you stay here and cut him up. John, you better get

back to the horses. I'll go on up ahead and see if I can get another bear."

He had noticed that it was growing much colder as night fell, and he hurried his steps as much as possible, for he had no desire to be away from the camp after dark. But the woods were rough and hilly, covered thick with hard canes. Logs twisted into the earth by the hurricane tripped him frequently, and the cracks made by the earthquakes seemed wider and deeper. He fell so often that he began to fear for the safety of his rifle, already loose in its stock.

The dogs led him across a narrow creek, up a grassy hill, then down into a dark ravine, where they stopped running and began barking like mad. It was almost dark now; he could scarcely see in the ravine. He passed the dogs by once, turned back and found them around a large forked poplar, the bear sitting in the fork, a vague round ball against the somber sky.

It was so dark he was not sure of his aim. He fired. The bear did not move. He reloaded, fired again, but still the bear did not move. As he bent forward to load again, he heard the bear drop into the midst of the excited dogs. One of his dogs was white, and in the darkness the white dog was the only object he could distinguish. But all around him was movement, snarling dogs, a wounded, maddened bear, tearing at any adversary within reach. He was glad he had on his toughest leather breeches, and resolved to stand still until the bear stopped leaping about. Finally the animal slipped into one of the earthquake fissures, the dogs bounding in upon him. With his gun, David poked into the crack, judging it to be about four feet deep. He moved forward, calling softly to the dogs, until he could feel the gun's muzzle against soft flesh. Not certain whether it was bear or dog, he withdrew the gun. He believed the bear was caught in the fissure, and he dropped down into it at a safe distance, approaching slowly, his long hunting knife drawn back. Quickly he felt out in the blackness with his left hand, brushing the bear, then stabbed quickly, leaving the knife behind as he leaped out of the ditch. The bear was dead, almost instantaneously.

It was too dark to attempt a return to the camp, so he spent the night in the ravine. The intense cold seemed to settle over the hollow. He had to run back and forth to keep warm. Several times he climbed the poplar tree, sliding down its smooth trunk, the friction warming his arms and legs.

Next morning he returned to the camp, joining his two companions, picking up a new trail as soon as they had eaten breakfast. Before the week was ended David had killed nine more bears. When McDaniel asked him how many bears he had killed since he had been living on the Obion, he figured up the total as best he could remember at one hundred and five.

On the last night of the hunt, all three of them were awakened at the same instant by a frightful rumbling. David jumped to his feet, thinking that an invisible monster had him by the shoulders shaking him violently. He kicked up the fire at their feet, and as the light blazed up, John pointed to a new earthquake fissure which had appeared a few yards from their grass pallets.

" Let's scat from here," David cried. " The ground might take a notion to swallow us up like the big fish did Jonah."

With the first spring freshets, they were ready to start for New Orleans, their two flatboats loaded tight with thirty thousand staves. David appointed Flavius Harris pilot, and with a dozen men to each boat, they floated down to the Mississippi River. Here, they decided to lash the two boats together, in order to keep them from being separated on the way down.

Most of the men had never been on the Mississippi and the river was so wide and so deep that even Flavius, with all his experience, appeared to be nervous at times. Lashed together, the two boats were so cumbersome and heavy that it was almost impossible to guide them; half the time they were floating helplessly with the current.

John, who was now eighteen, and William, two years younger, had been included in the crew, and as darkness fell on their first day out on the Mississippi, David began to regret bringing his two sons. The journey which had first appeared a joyous lark was turning into serious business. Anything might happen on this river.

At dusk, two Ohio boats swung alongside, and David shouted questions at the pilots. He wanted to land for the night, but the Ohioans advised against it. " With this current," they shouted, " you'll break up."

A few minutes later they were swept around a narrow bend. " This must be the Devil's Elbow," David told Flavius. " I've heard tell it's the most proper named place in the big river." They were soon swirling in circles, the men poling frantically into the deep channel, trying to keep off the sharp bits of driftwood along the dark river bank.

After swinging around the second bend, their speed slowed. On the shore directly in front of them, a few torches were fluttering. " That's the woodyards," somebody shouted from out of the darkness.

" Let's try for land," David shouted. He megaphoned his hands, screaming at the pine torches: " Hey, there, woodyards, we want to make land." He could see the lights waving a welcome. Men were running up and down the bank, shouting encouragement. He took up his pole to help the crew edge in to shore.

It was useless, he soon admitted to himself; the current was churning them into the hard graveled banks. They would be wrecked if they moved any closer in the darkness.

" Let 'er go," he finally shouted. Rapidly the two clumsy boats moved out into the river, the current clutching at them like monstrous fingers, dragging them downstream. He dropped down into the makeshift cabin where he found Flavius poring over a charcoal map, a tallow candle illuminating his bearded face. A smudge fire was burning on a heap of stones. " Flavius, ain't we got ourselves into a hobble, though? I'd ten times rather be a-bear hunting on hard land than floating along on the water, where you got to go ahead whether you will or no."

He pulled a burned potato out of the fire, eating it slowly. Flavius got up after a minute and crawled out through the hatchway. The water was slapping violently against the logs beneath him. He could feel the boat beginning to tremble, then suddenly the entire cabin seemed to leap upwards, twisting sideways, and the pinnings crashed down, water hissing into the fire.

David had fallen flat on his face, and when he tried to stand up his head struck a log beam. Logs were piled up in crazy criss-cross fashion. Through the cracks he could see a half moon, serene as ever in the sky. He could hear footsteps pounding overhead, men shouting in confusion. He swung around, feeling for the hatchway, but water was pouring through it. The boat was slowly turning under.

He remembered a tiny hole they had cut in the side of the cabin for dipping water out of the river, and he turned toward it. In the darkness it was a frame filled with a dozen stars in a square of sky. To reach it he had to crawl over and under the log beams, bruising his ears in his haste. He got his head through the opening, but his shoulders banged against the sides; the hole was too small. The cold river water was sucking at his knees and he could feel the boat edging slowly over.

Against the star-filled sky he could see men leaping off the boats, and guessed that they must have touched land. He cried out sharply, and in a few seconds Flavius and John were tugging at his wrists. Others quickly joined them.

"An axe! We'll have to have an axe," Flavius shouted. " Get an axe, somebody! "

"No time for that. This water's up to my crotch now. Either pull my arms off or take me through." He spoke rapidly, breathing the spring air, which seemed suddenly sweet. " Jerk like hell, damn it."

They gave a violent lunge, and he came through, his shirt tearing to ribbons, his skin scraped off all along his sides. Warm blood was running off both his hips.

Flavius gave him a boost off the sinking boat, and they dropped down on a heap of drift logs, shivering, watching their staves sucked under in the foaming water. " Where's William? " David asked as soon as he had regained his breath.

"All right; everybody got off all right," John said. " They're looking around to see if we're on land or just on an island."

" Looks to me," said David, " like we're on a heap of drift logs and nothing else."

They were on a small island which had been buried under collecting driftwood. Not until dawn did David discover that he was barefooted. Then he remembered having removed his shoes while he was sitting in the cabin.

Shortly after sunrise they hailed a passing boat, which took them off on a skiff and carried them down to Memphis. One of the boat's crew gave David a pair of old shoes, so big he could hardly keep them on while he scaled the bluff to the business street of Memphis.

He remembered having met a Major Winchester, a Memphis merchant, during the political campaign, and searched for his store. The Major was dumbfounded when he saw David, and listened sympathetically to his story of the accident. " I suspect you must feel quite disappointed at your loss, Colonel Crockett."

" No, sir, there never was a happier moment in my life than that night I set on the driftwood, thinking of that miraculous

[220]

escape I'd just made. I reckon the Almighty intended I should go on and be a Congressman, and stop trying to get rich."

Major Winchester advanced sufficient credit for David to outfit himself and all the crew. David would have gone directly back to the Obion with his sons and neighbors, but Flavius insisted that they try to recover part of the staves. The two of them made a futile trip to Natchez, where they learned that one of the boats had been seen floating on its side some miles below where they had crashed, but most of the staves had been swept loose.

All the way back to the Obion from Memphis, David made frequent stops, talking with acquaintances and friends about the coming political campaign. He still did not know where his finances were coming from; he had not a cent of his own in the world, and was considerably in debt now to Major Winchester in Memphis. But he felt more confident of the future than ever before.

MARTIN VAN BUREN, *a mutton-chopped little Dutchman from New York State, guessed wrong when he picked William H. Crawford to win the presidential election of 1824. With Henry Clay he had finally sidestepped nimbly to swing the votes to John Quincy Adams, making him President, but he had little confidence in the newly elected leader's political abilities.*

Van Buren was nobody's fool. Not many weeks after the Adams inaugural he was busily engaged in ferreting out the likeliest candidate for 1828. Adams, he was certain, could not repeat. The various factions of the nation's one-party government, cracked wide apart by the Adams election, were rapidly consolidating into two sharply opposed groups, the Whigs and the Democrats, and Van Buren decided the Democrats were going the fastest and the farthest. He became a Democrat.

Of all the Democratic factions, the Jacksonians were un-

doubtedly the strongest. So Martin Van Buren became a Jacksonian Democrat.

In 1827 he journeyed to the South and West. Before he had traveled many miles he knew the South and West would vote almost to a man for Jackson. Purposely he avoided Nashville, for he knew that Andrew Jackson resented his old trade with Henry Clay. But he sought out all the Friends of Jackson he could find, who relayed his messages to the man in the Hermitage.

Returning home he wrote letter after letter to Andrew Jackson. New York and Pennsylvania were doubtful states for the Jacksonians, and Andrew Jackson knew it; he also knew well the power of the little Dutchman in the East. An alliance was soon formed, Van Buren advising his candidate to say nothing and sit still while he brought the East over to his side.

To clinch a victory in New York State, Martin Van Buren offered his name up for governor, and then sat back quietly to await the outcome, this unofficial driver of the Andrew Jackson backwoods bandwagon, this calm little dandy with a penchant for snuff-colored coats, white trousers, lace-tipped cravats, yellow gloves and morocco shoes. Now he had picked a winner, and he knew it.

★ 6 ★

On an early summer's day in 1827, David Crockett rode his horse into the town of Jackson, hitched the animal to one of the wide-spreading limbs of the full-leafed oak in front of the new tavern, and stepped jauntily inside.

" Hello, Davy." George Russell, in a resplendent new suit, got up to shake hands.

" Hyah, George."

" Thought you wasn't going to get here," George said, swinging one leg up on the table in front of him.

" Had to make some stops on the way. Politicking." David grinned.

" I'll bet you been doing some loud talking. How's the campaign moving? "

" Well," said David, " according to the newspapers Colonel Alexander and General Arnold are running a close race. But a feller down the road told me he had a friend named Crockett he was aiming to vote for."

" There's a man sitting right in front of you feels the same way. Let's have a drink on it."

They drank slowly, neither of them saying a word. George threw his other leg up on the table, and leaned back. " How much money you got, Davy? " he asked directly.

" By God," said David, " I ain't got a red."

" That's what I thought. Lots of people in the south counties don't even know you're running again. They've been asking me, ' What's happened to old bear-hunting Davy? ' "

David stood up to remove his coat. It was warm in the inn. " I'm aiming to make a tour down that-aways purty soon now. Then they'll know I'm up and raring again."

" Davy, you got to have some money. I'll make you a proposition. I'll lend you a small sum. It'll be like a bet." He dropped a roll of notes in the center of the table. " I'm betting that amount on you to win."

David looked at the money for several moments, then pushed it back across the table. " Don't be a damn infernal fool," George said softly. " There ain't another man in the world I'd offer this to. You know as well as I do that most the folks who know you and want to see you elected don't have a red either, to help you along. They can't help you. And you got to have a little money to get around. It's not much. I been a lucky trading man; that little amount comes easy."

" Suppose we call it a loan? " David asked.

" Call it anything you like," George said brusquely. " It's

yours. When I get up from the table it'll still be there. From now on it's yours to take care of, you stubborn old jackass."

David dropped the money into his shirt pocket, then reached out his hand to his friend. "Well, George, up to now I just been hoping to win this election. Now I *got* to win it."

When he went outside the tavern to the street, the July sun shone down hot on his back, and he moved into the shade of the dust-covered oak. A teamster was leaning against the tree trunk, whistling quietly to himself. "You vote in this district?" David asked casually.

"I reckon I might," said the man.

"Who you aim to vote for?"

"For the best men, I reckon." The teamster spat against the dirty board sidewalk.

"And who might they be?"

"Sam Houston and Davy Crockett," said the man shortly.

"Why?"

"Say, mister, you're a damned curious varmint. But I'll tell you why. I'm voting for Sam Houston for governor because he's a fighting man and a friend of Andy Jackson. And I'm voting for Davy Crockett for Congress because he's a cantankerous bearcat from the canebrakes."

"You're a smart feller," said David. "Let's go and have a drop of whiskey in the tavern."

Several weeks later, the campaigning was over, and with a majority of 2748 votes, he became the Honorable David Crockett, United States Congressman from the state of Tennessee.

★ 7 ★

As summer passed into autumn, David's jubilation over his victory was somewhat tempered by thoughts of having to leave

[224]

the Obion for so long a period of time as a Congressional session. Colonel Alexander informed him that the Congress would open the first week in December, and as the journey to Washington City was almost a thousand miles in length, he began making preparations for it in October.

To save expense, he had decided to make the journey on horseback. Carrying only his rifle and a small bundle of clothing, he galloped down the trail, skirted the small settlement of Trenton, and was off on the main route to Nashville. In that city he stopped to have his horse shod, and spent a day walking about the streets, stretching his legs and listening to the talk. He overheard Andrew Jackson's name spoken more than once, and there were whispered sentences about his wife, Rachel, and rumors of Old Andy's threats to duel Henry Clay if the lies about his wife's virtue were not stopped.

At Staunton, Virginia, he sold his horse and took the mail coach to Fredericksburg, there boarding a new steamboat which chugged slowly up the Potomac to Washington.

It was muddy where the boat docked, tying up to a rough board wharf built above the quagmire along the river's edge. A coachboy attempted to seize his bundle, but he turned aside and followed some of the other passengers who elected to walk into the town.

Passing numerous hovels and shanties which seemed filled to overflowing with Negroes, he finally reached the edge of the Capitol grounds, and paused in front of a cheap weather-beaten boarding house. He spoke to a slatternly woman who was leaning on a fence. " Could you tell me where Gadsby's Tavern is, ma'm? "

The woman looked him up and down with her rheumy eyes. " Gadsby's is on the Avenue. You go up to the Capitol and then down the hill and there it is. But if you don't mind my saying so, Gadsby's is a place where quality gentlemen puts up."

[225]

David was grinning when he turned his back. As he walked through the grove of trees, bare of leaves in the December sunshine, he examined his clothing. His homespun suit was tattered from travel; his leggings were coated with mud and grime. No wonder the woman had warned him about Gadsby's.

He came out suddenly in an open space, facing the Capitol, two square flat-topped stone buildings joined tight together with a cleavage in the middle it seemed, though it actually was a single structure. A row of short posts for hitching horses formed a semicircle around the front and sides. Picking his way carefully across the flat grounds to avoid the deepest mudholes, he passed around the building, and now from the hill he could see the town of Washington, dirty and cold even in the sunlight. Pennsylvania Avenue ran straight as an arrow away from him, long lines of sharp-tipped Lombardies on either side. He could see people and cattle and hogs moving about in the street.

Below the line of trees on the left was a narrow cobblestone sidewalk, built above the muck of the street, and as he walked rapidly along it he could see the squat rows of brick kilns to his left, their laborers' huts off to one side almost in a state of collapse. On the hill to his right were a few dwelling houses, scattered far apart, their privies and pigsties and cowsheds and geesepens cluttering the background. All the people he met along the narrow sidewalk were ill-clad, their faces sharp-pinched and hungry, the Negroes shivering in their cotton clothes. This Washington City was no golden dream, he could be sure of that; he tried to remember the time he had traveled through the town thirty years before when he went on his jaunt to Baltimore, but he could remember nothing of these things he saw now. Even the hogs wallowing in the middle of Pennsylvania Avenue presented a picture of destitution; he could not help comparing them with the fat acorn-stuffed boars on his farm back on the Obion.

[226]

After he had walked a short distance along the Avenue, the buildings appeared more pretentious. He could see the signs of several taverns and boarding houses. Nearby, one of the tall Lombardies had recently crashed into the street, and a wood-cutter was standing knee-deep in the mud, chopping away at the trunk.

" Good day, stranger," said David. " I'm looking for Gads-by's Hotel."

The man leaned his axe against the fallen tree, swinging half around, pointing up the street. " Over there, sir."

" Thank you." David would have gone ahead, but the man, who was eyeing him with some curiosity, asked: " You come from out west, eh? "

" Sure do. The name's Crockett, Davy Crockett, Congress-man from Tennessee."

" You don't say! " The woodchopper's mouth opened wide. " You ain't rigged out like a Congressman, but then you western folks never put on much folderol. You take these Con-gressmen from up Phillydelphy and New York aways, they wear lace cuffs and fancy shirts and strut like monkeys."

David dropped down on the edge of the cobblestones to rest his legs. The man talked freely, evidently glad to have an audience. " These Lombardies, now, right purty trees, ain't they, but don't stand up, rotten to the core. Lightest kind of wind cracks 'em open. President Jefferson had 'em planted, I remember the planting myself, I was just a young feller then. Jefferson, now, he was a good President, but he didn't know much about trees."

" What do you think of Andy Jackson for President? "

" He's going to be the next one, they say they ain't much doubt of that. All my kinfolks over in Virginia, they think Old Andy is the greatest man ever lived. I expect maybe he is, at that. We've had enough gentlemen in the President's House. Time we had a good commoner. President Adams, now, I've seen some of him, he ain't such a friendly man, carrying his head up in the skies' when he sees the likes of such a one as I am. This wood I'm chopping up is for the President's House. They got a dozen fireplaces up there, and thirty servants. Some place, it is. You seen it yet?"

"No," said David, standing up, "but I'm heading up that way now. I reckon I'll put my things up at the tavern first though, kind of dress up a little too. Nobody looking at me thinks I'm a Congressman."

Gadsby's Hotel was a pleasant enough place, with a well-fitted taproom and comfortable seats for the guests. David's room was small, divided off from another space by a curtain, but there was a pitcher and bowl and a cake of yellow soap, which he set to immediate use. The rates, however, were higher than he thought he could pay regularly.

On the following morning he made inquiries as to the whereabouts of Jacob Isaaks, a man he had known slightly in Winchester, who had been elected Congressman from that district two years before. Isaaks was staying at Brown's Indian Queen, and as soon as David learned the rates there, he changed his lodgings. With Isaaks, he spent his second day in Washington City walking around the White House, where they watched the well-dressed people of the town ride past in their carriages. They could not help laughing aloud when a dandy in tight fawn-colored trousers rode past on horseback, holding a parasol daintily above his head.

In the afternoon they walked up the winding three-mile road to Georgetown, where a number of Congressmen made their residences while in the capital. Georgetown, David thought, was too far from the legislative chambers, so he decided to stay indefinitely with Jesse Brown, the host of the Indian Queen.

Jesse Brown's Indian Queen was an unusual tavern, as David soon discovered. No guest was ever considered a stranger; it was the host's custom to treat everyone as if he were the

[228]

most privileged member of his family. A huge dinner gong, so loud that it shook the windows, was sounded before every meal, and then Jesse Brown, himself, served the food from the head of a long cloth-covered table, singing out remarks about the victuals.

At the beginning of his first dinner at the Indian Queen, David was startled to hear the host sing out: " Here's a rare slice for Colonel Crockett." Embarrassed at such special attention he was about to offer his thanks, but already Brown had turned to another guest: " Ah, a nice bone cut for Major Stamm." Then quickly, still singing: " Congressman Isaaks, can't I help you to some more pigeon pie? " All through the meal the host continued to sing out extemporized verses, while buxom Negro wenches dressed in white cotton shifts were carrying steaming platters out from the kitchen.

The day before Congress opened, Senator John Eaton called on David at the tavern to inquire if he would like to visit the Capitol with him and meet some of his colleagues. Eaton seemed to have forgotten the Murfreesboro incident in which David had figured as the chief opponent of the Jackson forces. He was extremely affable, joking with David about the state of politics in Washington City.

At the Capitol they joined James K. Polk and two other new Tennessee representatives, and after they were introduced to the House clerk, David learned that he could draw on his future salary if he so desired. Though he had several dollars remaining from the hundred he had borrowed from George Russell, he asked for an advance of three hundred dollars. As soon as he left Eaton and the others he went to a bank, where he arranged for two hundred and fifty dollars to be sent to a Nashville bank to the credit of George Russell. That night he wrote George a note, thanking him for his many favors.

Next morning he was quite excited when he walked up

Capitol Hill, dressed in the suit which he had bought back in Murfreesboro. His leggings, even after a thorough scrubbing, showed signs of mudstains, and his coonskin cap was in need of repairs. That most of the other Congressmen wore heavy leather boots and beaver hats was a fact which had not escaped his attention, and he had resolved to buy a pair of boots and a hat at the earliest opportunity. But this morning there was little time to think of how he looked.

Somewhat self-consciously he edged into the chamber to take a seat on the aisle where he could see all that happened. Amidst all the turmoil and movement surrounding the opening ceremonies he was beginning to realize that in Washington even a Congressman is not such a great man. To attract notice in Washington, one must be a great man indeed. He took a dip of snuff from the box in front of him, and sat back to wait, but it was some minutes before the chamber quieted sufficiently for the speaker on the platform to make himself heard. Then just as the man began to speak, there was a sudden flurry of whispers, heads were turning toward one of the entrances, and David looked around to see the cause of the interruption.

A man wearing riding clothes, his saturnine face bent forward, one fist clenched to his side, the other clutching a long whip which he kept flicking against his boots, was striding down the aisle, looking neither to the right nor the left. He continued down to the front row of seats, followed by a Negro boy carrying a huge flagon of porter.

The man sat down, leaning heavily on the side of the chair, his lower lip thrust out belligerently. " He's John Randolph," somebody whispered. The Speaker of the House stared at Randolph for a full minute, then began reading again from his paper. Randolph was sipping his porter, apparently oblivious to the presence of all others in the chamber.

Shortly afterwards there was another disturbance, this time

[230]

from the gallery. David had been aware from the first that there were others in the chamber besides the Congressmen, spectators seated on a curving gallery a few feet above the level of the floor. Two men were bringing in a short heavy-set gray-haired woman, whose right foot was wrapped in heavy bandages. As soon as she was comfortably seated the men retired, and there was a sharp sound of hissing from one side of the gallery, evidently intended for the woman. Ignoring the hissing, the woman waved and smiled to one of the Congressmen on the floor, flashing her white teeth, and David saw her blue eyes fixed on his face for a moment, eyes as young as a girl's.

He nudged one of his neighbors: " Who is she? "

" That's Anne Royall, she makes up books about people. Didn't you notice some of the Congressmen get up and leave when she was brought in? She writes about them in her *Black Book*. She says what she thinks about everybody, particularly Congressmen. Somebody pushed her down a stairstep not long ago and broke her ankle. That's why she's still crippled. You better watch what you say when Old Annie's in the gallery."

David heard scarcely a word of the opening speech. Between watching John Randolph sipping his porter and Anne Royall jotting down notes on her pad, he had little time for thinking on governmental matters.

A third commotion, well toward the end of the speech, was created by a tall white-haired, blue-eyed man with a high forehead, who entered from the rear of the chamber and stood near the wall, one hand resting on the chair adjoining David's. Though the man had entered quietly, he had not stood there five minutes before every man in the House knew of his presence. David had no idea who he was, but he had an opportunity to study his features for some minutes. His nose was large and blunt, his mouth unusually large, and once when he stepped across the back of the room to shake hands with an acquaintance, David noticed that he wore yellow shoes instead of the customary boots, and that he walked with his feet straight ahead of him like an Indian.

A few minutes later, the Representative sitting beside David whispered a suggestion that they step outside in the corridor for a drink. As they pushed through the door, the tall white-haired man joined them. " I can tell from your expression, gentlemen, that you're in search of liquors." The man wrinkled his high forehead and twisted up one side of his wide mouth in friendly fashion.

David smiled broadly. " I'm new here, but I'll stand to a dram of the people's liquor, I reckon."

Standing beside the bar where drinks were issued without charge to members of Congress, were James K. Polk and Jacob Isaaks and one of the other Tennessee Congressmen. Polk stepped aside, nodding coldly to the tall man, who turned suddenly to David: " Name your drink, Mr. ——"

" The name's Crockett, Davy Crockett of west Tennessee."

" Well, I'll be damned," said the man, stepping back. " I'm Henry Clay." He extended his hand. " Davy Crockett, the only man in Tennessee with enough backbone to stand up against Andrew Jackson."

Henry Clay! David turned slowly around to see James K. Polk disappearing through the nearest doorway. He could well imagine what Polk would soon be saying to Senator Eaton and all the Jackson supporters—a Tennessee Congressman fraternizing with the Secretary of State, Henry Clay, hated Judas of the West.

After they had finished their drinks, David offered his new friends his plug of tobacco. The Congressman accepted, but Clay refused. " No, thanks," said he. " My lips are so formed I never learned to spit. A man can't well chew tobacco without spitting."

When they parted, Clay shook hands again. " We'll have to have a talk sometime, Colonel Crockett."

[232]

The talk with Henry Clay came sooner than David had expected. The supporters of John Quincy Adams planned to gather unofficially one evening in Gadsby's Hotel, and David received a special invitation from Henry Clay delivered by a Negro messenger from the State Department. At first he was of a mind to decline the invitation. After all, he had pledged himself to support Andrew Jackson in the presidential campaign. However, when he learned that several of the expected guests were not Adams men, and that Martin Van Buren, the leader of Jackson's eastern supporters, had accepted a courtesy invitation, he sent a note to Clay informing him that he would be present at the affair.

On the appointed evening, Gadsby's Hotel was brilliantly lighted with three fireplaces filled with flaming pine knots. When David entered the decorated meeting room, acrid smoke from the fires and the sharp tang of expensive liquors swirled into his nostrils. He saw several Congressmen he knew to be Adams supporters, but he searched in vain for any of his colleagues from Tennessee. At the end of the room, Henry Clay was seated before a large oaken table, talking rapidly from one side of his wide mouth, his voice ranging from deep bass up to a high falsetto when he emphasized his remarks.

Daniel Webster, his jet black hair combed back tight on his high smooth forehead, his round face somber in the shadows, sat beyond Clay, gravely folding and unfolding a piece of paper, obviously a duplicate of others which seemed to be attracting the attention of recent arrivals in the room.

As Crockett approached the table, Clay picked up a heavy decanter and poured several drinks into a row of glasses. " Evening, Colonel Crockett." He pushed a drink across the table.

" Good evening, Secretary Clay."

Clay gulped his wine. Setting the glass down firmly, he brushed his mouth with the back of his hand, and turned sud-

[233]

denly to Webster. "Dan'l, have you met Davy Crockett, the Tennessee bear hunter?"

As he stood up, Daniel Webster's face became less grave; his dark gray eyes, large and prominent, searched David keenly up and down. "Very glad to make your acquaintance, Colonel Crockett."

Then as Webster was turning to sit down again, he dropped the handbill, which he had been holding, onto the top of the table, and David looked at it briefly. Six black coffins ran across the top of the sheet in a row. Above them in heavy black letters were the words: Some Account of Some of the Bloody Deeds of General Jackson.

David looked up to see Henry Clay smiling at him, his blue eyes sparkling. "What do you think of that, Davy? You fought with Jackson in the Creek War, didn't you?"

"Well, I don't know what all this says here," David replied, running his finger down the sheet to a cartoon of Jackson who was depicted as running his sword through a defenseless man who had stooped to pick up a stone. "I reckon it's a mess of lies though if it's the same stripe as some of the other things you hear and read about Andy Jackson these days."

Clay had stopped smiling; he held the stem of his glass between his fingers, twirling it slowly. "I've heard it said that you left Jackson in the lurch during the Creek War."

"That may be true," said David quietly, "but I was only a volunteer and I didn't leave till after my enlistment ended. I didn't leave till I knew we had the Creeks running with their tails dragging. And when I found out the British was mixed up in it, I went back again and stayed through till I was told to go home."

Clay shrugged his shoulders as if to pass over the matter, then turned to face David again. "But you did fight Jackson good and proper on the floor of the Tennessee legislature when his name was up for Senator." Clay's voice had risen to that

[234]

strange falsetto which betrayed him when he was excited. He set his glass down quickly on the table. " If you thought then that he was not fit to be a Senator from Tennessee, then you must think now that he's not fit to be a President of the United States."

David was watching Webster's face, immobile in the half shadow of Clay's tall body. He wished he might have the eloquence of Webster for just this brief moment in order to reply to Clay. " If I should be talking to you as one man, as Davy Crockett alone, I might say some things about Andy Jackson. But I'm not just Davy Crockett a man, I'm a representative of the people of west Tennessee, a part of the people of the whole West. And the people of the West, Mr. Clay, of whom you are one, want a voice in the government, and to their minds Andy Jackson is the man to give it to them."

" Granted," said Clay quickly. " But they have chosen the wrong leader."

David banged his hand down on the table. " They've made up their minds. All right, according to the way I understand our government, the people pick their own rulers. They've chosen Andy Jackson. Last election, he should have been made President according to the people's will. Maybe you and me think Old Andy's not the right man to lead this government, but the people think he's the right man. And by the Lord Almighty, from what I've seen of fancypants Easterners around Washington City, I think any honest man from the West could do a better job of governing than the ones in power today."

A faint smile crinkled the corners of Daniel Webster's dignified mouth, then it faded quickly. The wide door at the end of the room had been thrown open; sounds of violins and a harpsichord mingled with the voices of women.

" Well," said Clay, pouring another glass of wine, " I suppose the dancing is about to begin."

David turned so that he could see the dancers. Women in

[235]

flowing satin dresses and men in tight breeches and lace shirt fronts and cuffs were forming opposite lines. Then to the stately classical movements of the minuet they began to dance.

Clay had risen to his feet again. " I suppose I'll go and join them, gentlemen. I see Van Buren is already out there." He walked across the room, his body moving as gracefully as a deer's.

Daniel Webster shifted over to Clay's chair. " Colonel Crockett, excuse me, but in what ways do you find Easterners so grievously at fault? "

David moved his hand in a wide semicircle, taking in all of the crowd in the adjoining room. " That dancing is a good place to start in. Call that dancing? Man, you never saw a dance till you get out into Tennessee. All these polite minuets and lace and finery. And look around you at Washington City. 'Tain't much of a city, yet already it's more'n half full of starving folks no good for much of anything."

Webster nodded his head solemnly. " It's long been a belief of mine that our democracy cannot endure if men gather into cities. Democracy must have the soil to grow in. But I disagree entirely with your contention that the people must have all governmental power. The bulk of the people do not yet know how to use that power. They must depend upon a group of democratically chosen leaders, men of wisdom, to guide them, and I regret to say I do not believe your Andrew Jackson is a man of sufficient wisdom to be a leader of the people's government."

" The people," said David slowly, " will tell Andy Jackson what to do. And do not be fooled, Mr. Webster, the people are smarter than you think. We built this country, didn't we? We're still building it, and be damned if we're not going to rule it, too! "

PART FOUR

DUFF GREEN *was a political adventurer from St. Louis, a shrewd imaginative man, who felt more keenly than any editor of his time the possibilities of the press as a political force. It was John C. Calhoun who first discovered the genius of Duff Green, but it was John Henry Eaton who asked him to set up the Washington Telegraph, a journal which was to serve as a mouthpiece for the Friends of Jackson.*

Eaton took Duff Green to the Hermitage where Andrew Jackson gave him an official benediction. In parting, Old Hickory said to Duff Green: "Truth is mighty and shall prevail," a maxim which the wily editor followed only when it was politically expedient to do so.

Duff Green got the Telegraph going in March 1826, and not long afterwards his copy was being reprinted in more than fifty other back country news sheets, unofficial Jackson organs.

But the Adams forces did not sit idly by. Even while Duff Green was planning his dazzling campaign, a mysterious old Englishman named Day, probably in the employ of Henry Clay, was ferreting out documents and court records dealing with Andrew Jackson's adulterous relations with Rachel Robards. Woven into a lurid legend, these were printed in John Quincy Adams' paper, The National Journal. And so began the dirtiest journalistic battle in American political history.

Duff Green immediately retaliated with a fabrication of a story of premarital relations between John Quincy Adams and his wife.

For the remainder of the presidential campaign, readers of the Adams newspapers were told that Andrew Jackson was a low-class cold-blooded murderer who went about ruthlessly shooting down all his opponents, his wife a loose woman who continually smoked a clay pipe.

To readers of the Jackson newspapers, John Quincy Adams was a lustful drunkard, who kept concubines, misappropriated public funds, and while serving as minister to Russia sold beautiful American girls in slavery to Russian aristocrats.

Thus flourished freedom of the press. Power-drunk, the newspapers soon destroyed their own influence through repeated falsehoods.

By midsummer of 1828, the American people knew what they wanted; no printed lies could bring them to change their minds. In November they elected their first west-of-the-mountains president, Andrew Jackson. And so fell the aristocratic dynasty of the East.

★ I ★

TIME for David Crockett never passed so swiftly as during the weeks after he left Washington City for the Obion. The presidential campaign was an infectious plague of excitement that let no man rest in Tennessee. There was but one thought uppermost in everyone's mind: Andrew Jackson must be elected President.

Late in November of 1828, when it was known for certain that Jackson had been elected, David started for Washington, stopping for a day in Nashville, where the townspeople were still celebrating the victory.

Arriving in Washington just before Christmas, he found scarcely any of his close friends there. Congress was in a doldrums, awaiting the arrival of the new President in March. One evening, he stepped into the almost deserted dining room of the Indian Queen, and saw two women sitting at the table. One of them he did not know. The other, a short sturdy woman with iron gray hair tousled over a youthful face, was Anne Royall, the woman he had seen in the gallery on that first day he had sat in Congress.

Her bright eyes turned toward him; he bowed and smiled. " Come and join us, Colonel Crockett," she said, beckoning with her spoon. " This lady is Sarah Stack, my partner. Sarah, meet Colonel Davy Crockett." Sarah acknowledged the introduction, then continued eating her bread which she was moistening by dipping it in her soup.

One of Jesse Brown's buxom Negro waitresses was hovering

[241]

in the background. " Bring me some of the pot-luck," David said. He sat down close to Anne Royall on the hickory bench.

" Well, Colonel Crockett," she said vivaciously, " when did you arrive from Tennessee? "

" Some days ago. Not much happening hereabouts, or I guess you'd heard me barking."

" No, there's not much happening, Colonel Crockett." Anne rested her elbows on the table and turned half around, facing him. She was well past forty, but her skin was as fresh as a young girl's, her teeth were white and even, her eyes bright with the keen interest she took in everything that passed her way. " No, there's not much happening. Washington is a sick town. The Secretary of the Treasury has a stomachache, the Secretary of the Navy hasn't been out of his room for three weeks, the head of the War Office is almost blind, the Attorney General has vertigo ——" She shrugged her shoulders.

David grinned. " I guess all the Adams men are purty green now that Old Andy's coming to town to take over the government."

" Even President Adams has quit taking his daily walk around the White House."

" I guess you ought to know," said David. " You know everything that's going on. You haven't been trapping Mr. Adams in swimming agin lately, have you, to get his opinions on the Bank? "

At this remark Sarah Stack let out a loud whoop of merriment. " That was a good one, wasn't it, Colonel Crockett? Anne catching Mr. Adams swimming in the Potomac and making him give her a statement before she'd give him his clothes."

" I always thought that story was a little stretched," said David.

Anne punched him sharply in the ribs. " A little. Things like that make folks buy my newspapers, though."

[242]

A few days later, dozens of strangers began appearing on the streets of Washington, men who were dressed as David Crockett had been dressed on the day of his arrival in the capital, men in coonskin caps, men in homemade jeans, men in checkered shirts, rough hairy men, used to the fields and woods, men who chose to walk down the middle of the muddy streets rather than use the sidewalks.

Members of Washington's polite society, who were staying close to their firesides during the cold wet winter days, watched these strangers through their lace curtains, wondering if this growing throng of commoners would seize their city even before President Adams' term was ended. Rumors ran up and down the streets from the Capitol to the White House to the secluded mansions on the Georgetown heights. General Jackson's wife was dead. The President-elect had threatened the lives of his political foes for bringing on her death. And there were rumors that General Jackson's health was failing rapidly.

One day in early February the city was nervous as a cat over rumors that General Jackson had suddenly died.

Daniel Webster arrived in the city, his face thrice as somber as usual. "When the new President arrives," said he, "he will bring a breeze with him. Which way it will blow I cannot tell."

President John Quincy Adams paced the floor of his study, unable to write in his journal, unable to read a line in one of his many books.

Long before daybreak of February 12, a Negro servant was pounding on the door of David Crockett's room in the Indian Queen Hotel, pounding, pounding, until the sound sleeper jerked himself upright in bed.

"Who's there?"

"Mistah Crockett, you is wanted downstairs by a gen'man."

"Gentleman, hell," said David. "No gentleman would rise me out of bed on a cold night such as this."

[243]

Shivering in the unheated dampness of his room, he pulled on his trousers and boots and dashed down to the front entrance of the hotel. A lantern hanging from a carriage illuminated the gray mist, making it appear as a curtain over the blackness of Pennsylvania Avenue.

" Hey, there," David shouted.

" That you, Crockett? "

He recognized the voice. John Henry Eaton. " What's up, Senator Eaton? "

A tall figure, swinging another lantern, appeared out of the gray mist. The rays lit up the lurid painted face of Pocahontas that hung over the Indian Queen's entrance. " Sorry to disturb you like this, Davy. But I need a Tennessean, and you're the handiest one I could find. How're you at driving a carriage? "

" I can handle horses better a-setting on 'em, but I guess I can handle 'em from a cart."

" Come along then. We're going after General Jackson."

" General Jackson? He's almost here, and still alive? "

David was vastly relieved when Eaton assured him that Old Andy was very much alive. As the carriage swung up the muddy street past the White House, the mists curled away from them and they could see stars bright in the sky. With Eaton silent at his side, David got to thinking about the old General. İt would be a catastrophe indeed if anything happened to Andrew Jackson now, the hopes the people had in him.

They drove for hours, taking turns at the reins, until they were several miles into Maryland. Finally in the darkness ahead they saw lantern lights, and then suddenly in the cold starlight was a caravan of coaches, moving toward them, and behind the vehicles were horsemen, and behind the horsemen were men on foot, vague forms in the ghostly light.

" Looks like an army," said David.

Eaton said nothing. He pulled the carriage to a stop, leaped

[244]

down from the seat and ran over to the first coach. He spoke to the driver, who stopped his horses immediately; then a man's head was thrust out of the coach in the lantern light, a grizzled gray thatch over eyes sunken and staring. A bony hand reached out to clasp Eaton's. Then the coach and the carriage were side by side, and Andrew Jackson stepped over into the carriage without touching the ground. Eaton swung over into the seat beside Jackson. " Let 'em go, Davy," he cried. " Fast as they'll gallop."

They rolled swiftly back toward Georgetown, and as the carriage climbed the hills into the town in the sunrise, Eaton stepped over to the driver's seat. He touched David's shoulder. " There's one more thing I got to ask you, Davy, that's to drop off now and make your way down to the river road where the cannon and the crowds will be waiting. Tell the people you just got word the General will be here in a few minutes more. I'm going to take the back roads into the rear of Gadsby's Tavern and put him to bed. He's a tired man. You wait until the caravan comes in sight, then have 'em fire off that cannon. By that time, the General will be so sound asleep nothing will wake him."

It was broad daylight by the time David reached the river road. All the way as he walked he was wondering if Jackson remembered him, remembered the incident at Fort Strother during the Creek campaign when David had defied the command to stay in the camp. Old Andy certainly had aged in the years since that day. Still he must have asked Eaton who his driver was. And Crockett was not such a common name. He wondered too what the General thought of Eaton's marriage of a few days back, his marriage to Peggy O'Neale Timberlake. Already there was gossip. If Old Andy put John Henry Eaton in his cabinet now that he was married to the Georgetown hussy, there was certainly going to be some trouble.

On the heights, early as it was, the roads were lined with

people waiting for Jackson to arrive. David smiled, thinking of Jackson, in bed by now, in Gadsby's while all these people waited for him to arrive so that they might shout and cheer.

He saw Francis Scott Key coming out of his large house, and waved his hat to him. Key nodded a return greeting. " Quite a lot of excitement, eh, Colonel Crockett? "

" I reckon it's a time for excitement," said David, " with a new President coming to Washington."

Key was shaking his head solemnly. " I don't know what to make of it, I don't know. I never saw so many folks in Georgetown before. Their adulation of this man Jackson reminds me of accounts I've read of the Romans' worship of Julius Cæsar."

Though he had not read Roman history, David agreed. " I'm glad the common people have the power at last, but I don't like to see Andy Jackson bowed down to like he was a king."

They walked down to the cannon set up facing the river. A brawny sailor leaned against the barrel, complacently regarding the mob jostling around him. A few minutes later a cry went up far down the road, shouts swept back toward them. " He's coming, he's coming! Here comes his coach! "

" Fire off the cannon," David shouted. " Jackson's coming! "

The cannon roared, smoke flurrying back into their faces. A group of drummers standing nearby started up a rattle-rattle that was soon almost drowned out in husky shouts from the crowd.

David turned to Key. " I think I'll start moving back to Washington ahead of the mob." He walked swiftly away, half-running down the road that skirted Foggy Bottoms, passed the White House where another immense crowd was gathering, and proceeded to Gadsby's Tavern. He found John Henry Eaton sitting in the entrance room, talking quietly with his

[246]

wife. " I heard the cannon," Eaton said. " I suppose the crowd will be coming into town soon."

David sat down, breathing heavily. " You never saw such a passel of folks in your life. The whole damn back country has come to Washington."

" I'm afraid they'll soon be on us, Davy. And the General made me swear I'd haul him out of bed as soon as the folks found out he was already in town."

Within an hour the mob was sweeping down Pennsylvania Avenue, packing the street tight, circling Gadsby's Tavern until Andrew Jackson, awakened by their cries, stepped out to the front walk and valiantly shook hands with all comers until he was pushed back inside.

Peggy Eaton's arm assisted the President-elect as he climbed wearily back upstairs while Eaton and Jackson's young nephew pleaded with the crowd to depart. Daniel Webster, who had come down from his room, stood beside David watching the commotion. " The breeze is beginning to blow," he said solemnly.

Long before the fourth day of March, the population of Washington was doubled, tripled, then quadrupled. And still they came, crossroads lawyers, politicians, backwoodsmen, pioneers, immigrants, soldiers, editors, adventurers, all drawn by this champion of the common man who at last had attained supreme political power. Gadsby's Tavern was filled day and night, the lobby furniture was broken up, the stairway began to sag from the constant pounding of the jostling, exuberant throng.

David shared his room with four Irish iron moulders from Pennsylvania. Their holiday spirits were communicated to him, and every night for a week before inauguration, the five of them roamed the muddy streets, stopping at all the taprooms.

[247]

Whiskey prices had soared; some bars had closed because their supplies had been exhausted.

Barbershops advertised " Jackson haircuts." Clothing stores sold " Jackson neckwear."

Pennsylvania Avenue was choked with farm carts, and saddle horses were hitched all along the curbs.

Flurries of snow had been falling as February changed into March, but on the morning of inauguration day the sun came up warm and cheery, while cannon thundered up and down the Potomac.

By eleven o'clock Pennsylvania Avenue was a solid living mass moving slowly toward the Capitol. From every porch and balcony, from every window and door, human beings leaned outward, laughing and talking. David Crockett, pushing along the cobblestone pathway with one of his new Irish friends, was reminded of wild swarms of bees which he had seen and heard humming and soaring through the woods. In the street he saw a splendid coach almost overturned by a dirty farm cart; the face of an indignant bewigged aristocrat looked out for a moment at the bedraggled crowd, then disappeared hastily.

Across the street was Gadsby's, but David could not force his way through the mob. He waited. Then as Jackson and Eaton, with Major Lewis and Henry Lee forcing a pathway, walked out from the tavern, the crowd pushed inward, waving their caps and cheering. Jackson's head was bare, his gray-silver hair shining in the sun. His party turned toward the Capitol, the crowd swarming behind.

The sun was warm. The crowd milled and pushed and stumbled. David lost his Irish companion as he ran pell-mell up the west slope of the Capitol grounds. There were thin patches of snow still on the earth, and footing was slippery in places.

He caught a glimpse of Jackson as he was hurried into the Capitol, Major Lewis bending his back to give him a boost over a wall so as to elude the crowd that was running down from the other side of the building.

In order to reach a vantage point near the roped-off portico where Jackson would be sworn in, David tried using the name of his office. " I'm a Congressman," he said once or twice, but nobody seemed to care. Finally one hairy-faced woodsman grinned. " I'll bet ye're Davy Crockett."

" I am," said David. " Now can I come through? "

" You betcha," the woodsman replied; " ye're from Tennessee, ain't ye? "

By repeating his name instead of his office he made much better progress; he was standing in front of the portico when Jackson and Chief Justice Marshall stepped out from the Capitol. The cheers dinned into his ears until he began cheering too.

There was the people's earthly god, a tall, loose-limbed man against the sky, his blue eyes keen and electric with the excitement of the moment. He began reading the inaugural address, but his voice was dry and cracked, whether from emotion or weariness David could not tell. " About to undertake the arduous duties . . ." The voice died away. The crowd was silent and still, standing bareheaded in the March sunshine. " It will be my sincere and constant desire to observe toward the Indian tribes a just and liberal policy and to give that humane and considerate attention to their rights . . ." And David was thinking of a Creek village where so long ago he had seen Indians burn and die.

The speech was over quickly. Then Chief Justice Marshall was administering the oath and Jackson was raising the Bible to his lips.

" Sublime," a man whispered, and David glanced around to see his friend of the Georgetown reception, Francis Scott Key.

In a few minutes the President was riding on horseback toward the White House, his clean broadcloth and ruffles

[249]

contrasting with the worn mud-spattered clothes of the mob at his heels. Already there had been announced a reception at the White House, open to everybody for the first time in history.

All morning servants had been preparing long tables in the East Room, loading them with ice cream and cakes and orange punch. A group of men and women in expensive dress clothes, not wishing to join the rough crowds on the Avenue, had been standing for hours on the east terrace of the White House, and as they saw the new President come up the street, they began moving slowly toward the East Room for the reception.

Then as Jackson's horse passed through the gates, the crowd from the streets pushed past him, running for the White House. Like stampeding cattle they stormed across the porch. Men were fighting, cursing, elbowing, scratching, trampling into the well-dressed group ahead of them. A waiter passing the door with a tray of refreshments was bowled over, glass and china crashing to the floor where muddy boots were already stamping.

David Crockett, with several others, had leaped over the east fence, and reached the porch in the midst of the melee. Suddenly he saw Anne Royall laughing out at him from a barred window. He flung himself into the crowd until he was pushed through the doorway into the East Room. Just in front of him a woman fainted, but somebody caught her and lifted her up, ripping half her dress away. His own coat sleeve had been torn loose from the shoulder.

Men were jumping up and down on the expensive White House furniture; chairs were collapsing with noisy crashes. One of the Negro serving maids had fled into a corner where she was crouched, eating hurriedly from a jelly bowl with a gold spoon.

He saw Andrew Jackson, leaning against a window, his body listless from exhaustion. His young nephew, Andrew Jackson Donelson, was staring helplessly at the stormy crowd.

Then David saw two other men step forward. One leaped out the window, the other helped Jackson through to the man outside.

He searched the room for Anne, finally discovered her sitting under a table, trying to stop her nose from bleeding while dirty boots stamped dangerously near her knees. He reached down and caught her arm, and they scrambled over to the window through which the President had just escaped. " Think you can do it, with skirts on? " asked David.

" If Old Andy can do it, so can old Annie," she laughed. He held her wrist until she swung out and down, then he followed her, brushing against the shrubbery.

Darkness was coming swiftly, a furrow of gray-black clouds rolling up in the sky from the south.

" My nose has stopped bleeding, but I'm hungry," said Anne. " Let's go eat."

" The Indian Queen? "

" If we can get inside."

They found Jesse Brown's tavern packed with noisy cele-brants; the host with his white apron tied tightly around his belly was running frantically from table to table, trying to serve all his customers. The leisurely homelike atmosphere of the place had abruptly disappeared.

They managed to squeeze onto a bench at the end of a long table where people were throwing vegetables and bits of bread back and forth at one another. " There's old Davy Crockett," somebody shouted, and threw a boiled potato at him. He caught it and tossed it back.

Except for porter there was nothing left to drink in the Indian Queen.

" I never drink intoxicants," said Anne. " You ought to know that, if you've read any of my books."

" I told you I wasn't a book reading man. I'm just a wild horse from the canebrakes."

[251]

She put her hand on his arm. " You know, Davy, I always thought there was something almighty animal-like about you."

He turned and faced her suddenly. " I guess there is, ain't there, something purty common about me? "

" I like you for it. Most folks that know you like you; you're always full of fun and good spirits."

He drank his glass of porter slowly. It was bitter, almost rancid, but he felt fine, sitting there with Anne, with all these people at the table, laughing and having fun, the people asking him over and over to tell a funny story, and so he told them the one about the preacher and the bear and everybody laughed and started throwing potatoes again.

Anne was having fun too and she told a story about a girl and some ministerial students, and he had to equal it with one about a scissors grinder and a farmer's wife. But after a while she said she would have to be going home.

" I'll escort you," he said. " This is no night for a lady to be alone on the streets of Washington." And with the people at the table throwing pieces of bread after them, they escaped through the crowded doorway.

Outside, a cold breeze was blowing off the swampy Potomac.

PEGGY O'NEALE, *the beautiful daughter of a ne'er-do-well Washington tavern keeper, cared nothing for politics. Yet all her life she had lived in the nation's capital, where politics is as much a part of the environment as sunshine and rain. As a child she sat on Andrew Jackson's knee while he was serving his term as Senator from Tennessee. Even before her first marriage to a sailor, young Senator John Henry Eaton was in love with her.*

Politics bored Peggy O'Neale, but after her husband's death she married John Henry Eaton, and when Andrew Jackson was inaugurated it was in the cards that Peggy O'Neale should be the wife of a cabinet member.

[252]

Politics began to revolve around Peggy O'Neale early in 1829. Charges against her virtue were made publicly by two meddlesome clerics, but Andrew Jackson, remembering his wife's death, swiftly forced the accusers to recant.

Gossip, however, simmered and boiled while other cabinet wives snubbed the former barmaid. Mrs. John C. Calhoun led the petticoat attack, and even President Jackson's niece refused to receive Peggy Eaton at the White House.

Speedily involved were the members of the cabinet, Vice-President John C. Calhoun being the chief obstructionist. In a few months President Jackson found his cabinet in open revolt, with only Martin Van Buren supporting him in defense of Senator Eaton's rosy-cheeked wife. Cabinet meetings were suspended.

To break the deadlock, Eaton and Van Buren resigned, leaving Jackson free to force resignations from the others and create a new cabinet. But he could not be rid of John C. Calhoun, the elected Vice-President.

Thus was dissolved the first Jackson cabinet by Peggy O'Neale Eaton, who cared nothing for politics.

But even had there been no Peggy Eaton, the break between Jackson and his enemies would have come sooner or later.

The masses had elected their man Jackson, but already their Vice-President had gone over to the Opposition.

Gradually but surely after the Peggy Eaton incident, Andrew Jackson was forced into a vacuum, left with only a few close friends and unofficial advisers in his so-called Kitchen Cabinet, every one of whose members was a professional politician with an axe to grind. Andrew Jackson, the people's candidate, found himself alone.

★ 2 ★

In the autumn of 1829, David Crockett made a brief tour of his Tennessee district seeking re-election. As much as he enjoyed traveling and talking, he would have much preferred remaining at home with his family; he had seen so little of them during the past few years. Both John and William were past twenty, with beards on their faces, and Little Polly at sixteen was the prettiest girl in the valley. But he had scarcely won the election when he had to start again for Washington.

A few days after he arrived in the capital, James K. Polk visited him at the Indian Queen Hotel, and David received him in his room, suspecting the purpose of the visit. Polk evidently was uncomfortable; he sat on the edge of his chair, twisting his long pale hands on the chair knobs. "There's been some talk, Colonel Crockett, that you're not exactly satisfied with the administration's Indian bill."

"Hell, no," David replied sharply. "I'm not satisfied with any part of it."

"The administration, as you no doubt are aware, is facing considerable internal difficulty at the moment—the cabinet, the Vice-President, not to speak of the opposition of Mr. Webster and others in the Senate."

"I know it. But if you're asking me to vote on this damned Indian bill just to keep the administration's tail in the air, if you're asking me to follow Andy Jackson in all his motions and windings and turnings even at the expense of my conscience and judgment, then, by God, you're barking up the wrong tree."

Polk blinked his eyes, surprised at David's show of wrath, but he continued patiently: "The Georgia, Alabama, and Mississippi delegations will vote solid of course. We're anxious to have Tennessee vote solid likewise, as a gesture from the President's state. We'll need the South badly to block Eastern opposition on later measures. It's sort of a horse-trade, you know."

"The Jackson party," David said coldly, "is supposed to be the party of the common people. Now, there ain't no com-

[254]

moner folks than Indians. If we aim to treat the Indians worse'n dogs, then I can't see as the white common folks can expect much from us."

Polk shrugged his shoulders. He saw that he was getting nowhere, and after a few moments excused himself.

During the next few days, various members of the Tennessee delegation approached him, both on the floor of the House and in his room at the tavern, urging him to reconsider and vote with the administration forces. Felix Grundy, who had taken John Henry Eaton's seat in the Senate, was the most suave.

"You're fair to coming to be one of Tennessee's most famous sons," said Grundy. "Folks make as much of you sometimes as they do President Jackson. We Tennesseans are right proud of you, Davy, right proud. Now, if you up and vote wrong on this important measure, it'll be a bad mistake. The President's got his heart set on it, and you ought to go for it on that account."

David looked Grundy straight in the eye. "I believe it's an unjust bill, that's all. I'm going against it, let the cost be what it may. I'm willing to go with General Jackson on everything I believe is honest and right. Further than that, I wouldn't go for him or any other man in the whole creation."

"It may ruin you, Crockett."

"Look here, Senator Grundy, last year I was elected by a majority of 3,585 votes, honest votes, and most of 'em by honest men who wouldn't want me to vote for any unjust motion just to please General Jackson or anybody else. As I've said before, I'd sooner be honestly and politically damned than hypocritically immortalized. That's all I got to say, Senator Grundy."

As spring days came to Washington, David found himself in the thick of the fight to defeat the administration's Indian bill. Various forces in Congress opposed to Andrew Jackson were

[255]

attacking it, but David suspected that many of the politicians were engaged in the battle not because they wished to protect the Indians but because they were seeking an opportunity to strike a blow against the administration.

However, a group of Quakers visited the capital to file protests with the House and Senate, and after talking with some of the leaders, David was convinced more than ever that he was in the right. Since those days of his youth when he had worked for Quaker John Kennedy he had had the greatest admiration for the Friends. He felt that he was safe in fighting for any principles which they upheld. In April he was again gratified when a delegation of Chickasaws and Cherokees arrived in Washington, seeking him out as a supporter in the fight for their rights.

When the debate on the bill opened on the floor of the House, he was one of the first to leap to the floor. One of his fellow Tennesseans rose for a question. " I ask Mr. Crockett if he's representing the wishes of his constituents in opposing the administration's Indian bill? "

David banged his hand down hard on his desk. " I don't wish to represent my fellow citizens unless I can act according to my conscience. If any man has a right to be embittered toward the redskins, I'm the man. My grandparents were killed in cold blood by Indians. But I know, and every man on the floor of this House who knows anything a-tall about the Indians today knows they're living in peace in their villages, not harming nobody. They're trying to make an honest living at farming same as most the white settlers out there. We made treaties with 'em after we tamed 'em down, and a treaty according to the constitution is the highest law of the land. But there are those who do not find it so. They want to juggle with the rights of the Indians and fritter them away. It's all wrong. It's not justice. I would rather be an old coon dog belonging to a poor man in the forest than belong to any party that will not do justice to all. These Indians are the remnants of a once powerful people, and they must be fairly treated."

But he fought in vain. With only a handful of sincere supporters and a few insincere political sharpshooters to aid him, the debates dragged on until the bill came to a vote and was passed.

After Congress adjourned, he went home to the Obion where he found his neighbors too much concerned with other matters to sympathize with the plight of the Indians. They were up in arms against land speculators who were driving many of them from the farms which they had cleared and cultivated. Both the squatters and those who had taken claims which they had thought were legal were victims of concerted pressure from the land speculators who had bought up warrants and doubtful titles. And even those who had already moved back into the less desirable unappropriated lands were in danger of being dispossessed by the state of Tennessee whose legislature was recommending to the United States Congress that the lands be sold in order to raise funds for the state's treasury.

As delegation after delegation of his constituents came to his cabin to tell of their plight, David remembered what he had said to James K. Polk when the latter had asked him to support the Indian bill. *If we aim to treat the Indians worse'n dogs, then I can't see as the white common folks can expect much from us.*

He went back to Washington in the winter, fighting mad. He knew he would have to work fast. Of all his colleagues from Tennessee, only Tom Arnold from the eastern section was on his side. David had little use for Arnold because of his unfair personal attacks on Andrew Jackson's wife during the presidential campaign, and he would have preferred standing alone rather than having Arnold on his side.

But in the Kentucky delegation he found a friend, Thomas

Chilton, who was with the Jackson administration only when he thought it was in the right; and in the proposal to deprive the squatters of their land he could see nothing but wrong. He helped David plan his campaign, suggesting that they try to interest Henry Clay who was beginning his campaign to re-enter public life as a Senator from Kentucky.

Clay promised his support immediately, and intimated that he would ask Daniel Webster and John Calhoun to lend their influence. Thus, within a few weeks James K. Polk's proposition to sell the public lands out from under the west Tennessee squatters became a political issue, with all the anti-Jackson forces standing firm against the bill.

Anti-Jackson newspapers gave it considerable publicity, and David was not a little surprised to find his name mentioned frequently. One or two publications carried stories about his life, with exaggerated accounts of his adventures on the frontier. He was pleased when he read them, but was so busy preparing speeches and writing letters that he could scarcely realize the rapidity with which he was becoming a national celebrity.

Nor did he realize the rapidity with which the Jackson forces had been plotting his downfall in his district.

The following autumn, he lost his first major political campaign, and was voted out of Congress by his befuddled constituents.

A few days after election, George Russell visited him at his cabin. David was sitting out in his yard in the shade of a wide-spreading oak, in a hickory chair which one of his sons had made for him during the winter. On his knee was a sheaf of papers, and he was rocking back and forth nervously in the chair.

"Hello, Davy," said George.

"Hello, George." David stood up quickly. "Try setting in

[258]

my new chair. It sure suits me fine now that I've got two years for just setting to home in it."

George offered his hand. " Sorry you didn't win, Davy."

" It wasn't so bad as it might've been. Most of my real friends stuck by me anyhow."

" What you aim to do now, Davy? "

" I aim to spend the next two years telling my neighbors the truth about the Jackson administration and about what I did for 'em in Washington."

"You're aiming to break clean away from the Jackson party? "

" Can't do nothing else but. To tell you the truth, George, I wish I didn't have to. But there's no other way for me now."

George shook his head slowly. David looked at his friend for a moment, thinking how rapidly the years had run since he had first known George; his temples were turning gray and his underchin was filling out. " Say, George, how old are you? "

" Forty-three. Don't seem possible, does it? "

" I'm forty-five." He grinned. " Even my oldest boy, John, thinks I'm licked for good now. He was telling me this morning he guessed he would enter politics next year and try to carry on the Crockett name."

George took out a plug of tobacco, trimming off a piece with his long knife. " You ought to be satisfied, Davy. You been to Congress twice, you got a bunch of fine hard-working children, you even got a settlement named after you now. What more you want? "

David was looking out across the river toward the low ridge that was so green in the summer sun. " Damn if I know, George, damn if I know. Maybe I'd like to be President."

JOHN CALDWELL CALHOUN *was born an aristocrat. All his life he tried to do and say things which would make his class well thought of by the common folk, but his sense of timing was bad. He always said the right thing at the wrong time and did the wrong thing at the right time.*

His yellow-brown shiny eyes staring out from his ruggedly carved tragedian's face watched distrustfully Andrew Jackson's rise to power. Contemptuous of western pioneers, he called them infantile adults, escapists fleeing from the problems of civilization. Seeking power, he was glad enough to have his name linked with the people's hero, Andrew Jackson, but as soon as he became Vice-President, John C. Calhoun brushed his thick black hair defiantly back from his bony forehead and opened his attack on the rule of the masses.

Introspective rather than objective, Calhoun nursed his ambitions secretly; cold to intimacy, he could never build up a political following. As the anti-Jackson forces coalesced into the National Republican party and grew into the powerful Whig movement, his ambitions soared high. He burned with jealousy when Henry Clay got the upper hand and the nomination to run for President against Andrew Jackson in 1832.

Yet so bitterly did he hate Andrew Jackson and his followers, he smothered his ambitions and gave all his energies to the Whigs, that amazing group of conflicting elements which blazed brilliantly but briefly across America in the second quarter of the 19th century.

Daniel Webster, Henry Clay and John C. Calhoun—the Great Triumvirate. But who were the Whigs, what was their philosophy? Even John C. Calhoun, philosophic thinker that he was, could not have said. They were National Republicans, they were States Rights men, they were Anti-Masons, they were former Jackson men purged from the ranks. They believed in adequate protection for American industry, but John C. Calhoun hated American industrialists. They believed in states rights, but Daniel Webster had argued at length with

[260]

Robert Hayne on the floor of the Senate in a dramatic defense of a strong central government. They claimed to be the only true followers of the philosophy of Thomas Jefferson, but John Quincy Adams condemned Jefferson's ideas. They repudiated the Federalist doctrines of Alexander Hamilton, yet Henry Clay disinterred many of Hamilton's theories in his arguments for private control of the United States Bank.

Chief point for agreement among the Whigs was their opposition to extreme executive power at the expense of the legislative branch. Many a good Whig admired Andrew Jackson, but feared the growth of his power would deprive the people of their liberties. And many a good Whig hated Andrew Jackson because of fear that the common people were gaining too much liberty under his rule.

So it was that men of conflicting backgrounds and ideals found it possible to join forces in the Whig movement, fighting shoulder to shoulder for totally different objectives. And so it was that the Whig movement, in spite of its power, was doomed from its inception.

★ 3 ★

In November, 1832, David made his first trip to Jackson since his political defeat over a year earlier. Though he carried in a load of skins caught by his youngest son, Robert, the main purpose of his visit was to get the earliest possible returns from the presidential election.

He felt curiously aloof from the political arena. For a year he had passed his time making short easy jaunts to neighboring settlements, talking and making jokes, carefully rebuilding his political fences. But this national election, though creating considerable excitement in west Tennessee, did not stir his emotions as previous campaigns had. He did not believe Henry Clay could defeat Jackson; he did not particularly care one way or the other.

[261]

Even though President Jackson had not lifted a finger to save their lands, three out of four of his neighbors were voting for him. Trying to understand politics, he reasoned, was useless. He was beginning to doubt his own motto: Be sure you're right, then go ahead! Could any man ever be sure that he was right?

In Jackson, there was a hubbub of excitement. Half the people in the town were dependent on political patronage for their livelihoods and they feared Clay might win if he swept New England.

David found only a few old friends gathered around Mack Davidson's store; most of the important citizens of the town gathered at the tavern now. When the talk shifted from politics it was mostly of Texas. Sam Houston, who had deserted his wife and resigned as governor of Tennessee some months earlier, was now in Texas. " A good many of Sam's friends are going out there to help him take the place away from the Mexicans," Mack Davidson said.

" I'd like to move west myself sometime," David said. " Too many folks live in here now. Not like it used to be, not a-tall."

Not long after the first election results came in from Nashville, David returned home. He was not surprised that Jackson was defeating Clay two to one. Old Andy was still the people's choice.

Early in the spring a visitor came down from Kentucky— Tom Chilton, the Congressman who had helped him block James K. Polk's land bill. Chilton was wearing a long black coat, the tails of which kept twisting in knots underneath him in his chair. " So they named this settlement after you, did they, Davy? Folks hereabouts must still think a heap of you, to be naming the place for you."

" For sure, they like me. But they like Andy Jackson too."

He grinned, watching Chilton pull out his coattails. " I was mighty regretful," David continued, " to hear the same thing had happened to you as happened to me. I reckon your standing with me on the land bill might've had something to do with it."

" I'd still stand with you. They certainly froze us out of Congress, didn't they? But I'm coming back next year, the Lord willing."

" As a Jackson man? "

" Not Tom Chilton, no sir."

" Nor is Davy Crockett, either."

Chilton finally arose and took off his coat, spreading it on the back of his chair. " You know, Davy, I was in Baltimore when the Whigs nominated Henry Clay for President. Well, Henry Clay is all right, except for drinking a wee bit too much and gaming a lot, but he's not exactly one of the people. A good man from the people, that's what I say."

" Dan'l Webster? "

" No, Webster's not the man. I'll tell you, while I was in Baltimore there was a play at the theater there, *The Lion of the West,* they called it. Some of us went to see it. The main character was supposed to be a Colonel Nimrod Wildfire. All dressed up in coonskin cap and deerskin leggings. And you know, every one of us that went to see that play said the same thing when it was over ——" Chilton paused, picking up a twig, whittling on it. " Every one of us agreed that Colonel Nimrod Wildfire was nobody but old Davy Crockett to the life. And we found out later the play was meant to be about you."

David laughed. " I'd sure like to see it." He had attended several performances in the Washington Theater, and had liked all the plays he had seen. He could scarcely imagine what a play about Davy Crockett would have in it that would interest anybody.

" Well, the point I was trying to make," Chilton continued,

[263]

" is that folks all over the country are hearing about you. When I said we need a man to run for President who is a man from the people, I was talking about you."

" Well, by God," cried David, " afore I can think about running for President, I'd better try and get elected back to Congress."

And this he did, the following autumn, winning back his Congressional seat with a majority of 202 votes.

Eager to see Washington again after his long absence, David left home earlier than was necessary. A few days after his arrival, James Hackett brought his play *Colonel Nimrod Wildfire* to the Washington Theater. As there was no longer any secret that Colonel Nimrod Wildfire was Colonel David Crockett, David of course was invited to be the honor guest of the evening.

He wanted to dress in his best clothes, but Tom Chilton insisted that he wear his buckskin hunting shirt and coonskin cap. " Folks won't know you unless you dress the part," said Tom. To fill the four additional seats in his complimentary box, David invited Tom, Anne Royall, Jesse Brown, and Senator Hugh Lawson White. White was an administration supporter from Tennessee, but more than once he had stopped to chat with David on the floor of the House, and David liked him.

At seven o'clock, a few minutes before the curtain was to rise, David and his party arrived at the theater. A large crowd was moving around the front, unable to buy seats. Recognizing David, they started cheering, and the theater manager, a short fat man, rushed out to meet them. He pumped David's arm up and down, his round face beaming. " This way, Colonel Crockett."

As they entered the theater which was illuminated by new but smoky lamps, the audience went wild. " Go ahead, go ahead, be sure you're right and go ahead," a voice boomed from the balcony. Others took up the cry. "Go ahead, go ahead, go ahead," they shouted rhythmically.

Before they reached their seats the band started playing a new march tune. "That's Crockett's March, just been composed!" Tom Chilton cried proudly, turning to Senator White.

David waved to his friends. He saw Martin Van Buren sitting in the next box, smiling at him. The band was playing the march over again.

Then as the audience settled back into normal talk, he leaned over to Anne Royall. "I wish old Abram Henry was here," he said.

"Who's Abram Henry?"

"Abram's my fiddle-playing friend. He used to help me campaign. I'll bet he could play Crockett's March so it would make your toes tickle."

Boys were running up and down the side aisles extinguishing some of the lamps. In front of the stage, new lights flickered on, and then slowly the curtain rose.

A man was standing facing the audience, a man in hunting garb. He bowed respectfully to the audience, then turned toward David's box, and bowed again.

David stood up, returning James Hackett's bow. People were stamping their feet, whistling.

"Bless my soul," cried Jesse Brown of the Indian Queen, "if I didn't know for certain Colonel Crockett was sitting right here in front of me, I'd swear that was him out there on the stage."

David sat down, trying vainly to erase the grin which was spreading across his face. There was only one thing he wanted to do at that moment, and he felt that he just had to do it. Drawing in his breath suddenly, he let out such a yell as would have frightened all the panthers out of the Obion bottoms.

But nobody noticed. Everybody else was shouting too.

[265]

★ 4 ★

" The next move," Tom Chilton said to David one day as they walked off the floor of the House, " is for you to make a tour of the North and East."

" When? After Congress adjourns? "

" No, right now this spring. The debates on the Bank are going to last on into summer, you can bet on that."

" And I've already set my mind not to vote with the administration. I'll think about the journey."

" While you're thinking about it," said Chilton, " I'll send off some letters to my Whig friends in the North, to pass the word that Davy Crockett is coming that way."

David had not been feeling well all winter; he had been outdoors but little recently, and now Washington's damp spring weather seemed to depress his spirits. A physician who lived at the tavern advised him to travel. " You'd better get away from this climate and this continual political bickering, Colonel Crockett," the doctor declared. " Or else you'll come down to bed."

His writing desk was piled high with letters from unknown friends who had written him from all over the nation inviting him to visit them. He had standing invitations to speak before Whig societies in all the large eastern cities. With Congress in a jam over the Bank issue, he saw no reason why he should not leave Washington for a few weeks.

On April 25th, he packed a small bag, stuffing in a number of letters from the various cities he planned to visit, and left for Baltimore, traveling part way by rail, his first train ride. He stayed at Barnham's Hotel only one day, dining with a number of Whig politicians, and though they begged him to stay long enough to deliver a public speech, he declined. He was eager to see Philadelphia and New York.

On the steamboat running into Philadelphia, he paced back and forth along the deck, making friends with all the passengers, who seemed impressed when they learned that he was Davy Crockett. The captain was especially proud to have him as a passenger, and would accept no fare from him.

After dinner, just before they reached the city, David saw the captain hoisting three flags. " What does that mean, three flags? " he asked.

" Well, Colonel Crockett, I promised the citizens of Philadelphia that if you were on board this trip I'd hoist the flags so as they would know before we arrived that you were on board. They're planning a reception for you."

" You mean they're expecting me? "

" Sure, your visit has been the talk of the city."

He wondered if the captain was making a joke. How could the people of Philadelphia have known he was coming there, outside of the two men to whom he had written accepting their invitations to visit the city?

A couple of hours later as they moved into the wharf, it seemed to him that the face of the earth was covered with people, all staring at the incoming boat. He was standing on the bow-deck with the captain, who was pointing his finger at him, and the people started throwing their hats into the air when they saw him. That all these strangers could be shouting his name seemed queer. Why should these Philadelphians, so many of them, be excited over a backwoods Tennessean?

As he stepped out onto the wharf, a tall man wearing expensive well-cut clothes and a high hat stepped forward and caught his hand. " Give me the hand of an honest man," said the stranger cordially. He made a path for David through the pressing crowd, helped him into a polished barouche drawn by four horses, and they swung up the paved street, the horses' hoofs clop-clopping on the stones.

" I'm John Sanderson of the Young Whigs Club. We were

pleased to receive your acceptance of our invitation to Philadelphia, but it was on such short notice we scarcely had time to arrange a decent reception for you."

David mumbled a few words, staring up the street lined with people, people on the curb, in the doors, in the windows looking out at him as if he were some wild man suddenly transported from the jungle.

" Colonel Crockett, would you mind bowing to the people? They expect it here, you know."

He bowed to the right, then to the left, stiffly.

At a hotel on Chestnut Street where the barouche halted, the crowd swelled up behind them, running after David, many persons begging to shake his hand. Sanderson pushed him on through the lobby upstairs to a window overlooking the street. He took off his hat, waving it to the people. " A speech! a speech! " they shouted.

Sanderson touched his shoulder, whispered a few words to him. David turned back to the crowd, speaking almost mechanically: " I assure you I'm illy prepared to address this most enlightened people. However, gentlemen, if you'll meet me tomorrow at the Exchange at one o'clock I'll endeavor to address you in my plain manner."

He withdrew hastily. " What is the Exchange? " he asked Sanderson.

" That's where the bankers and merchants gather for business transactions. You are to address them tomorrow at one o'clock as I told you."

Late that night, after long hours of talking and shaking hands with important looking gentlemen who came to his room, he slipped out for a short walk alone. He could scarcely believe all that happened was true. This sleeping city that now was so quiet, with its tens of thousands of people that he would never know, but who knew him. It was a dream, these multitudes shouting his name.

[268]

Returning to his room he could not sleep, thinking of the day that had passed and then of the morrow when he must speak to these thousands of city strangers.

Next morning a group of politicians whom he had met in Washington visited him; he felt more at ease seeing people he knew even slightly. They scarcely allowed him to finish his breakfast before they took him for a tour of the new Philadelphia waterworks and the Mint. By the time he got back to the hotel, a carriage was waiting to take him to the Exchange.

He had not had time to prepare a speech or even to think about one. As he rode through the streets, he almost wished he had never come, but when a youngster on the curb shouted as he passed: " Go ahead, Davy Crockett! " he grinned to himself and decided to pretend that he was back on the Obion: he would talk as he would have talked to his people back there.

At the Exchange a guard of honor opened a pathway through the crowd surrounding the building; he was led up to the second floor to a porch where John Sanderson and a group of dignified bankers and business men were sitting. He took off his hat, bowed to the crowd in the street, and began talking about his visit to the waterworks and the Mint. " Before I came here to Philadelphia," he drawled, " I thought the only people who could make poor men into rich men were the President and the Congress. But since I visited your Mint and saw some real gold and silver coins instead of the paper we're handing out to the voters, I reckon Philadelphia is ahead of Washington."

He thought the crowd would not allow him to stop talking; the people laughed at every remark he made whether it was funny or not. When he sat down they were cheering and laughing at the same time. " I reckon I'm supposed to be a funny man," he was thinking, " and people think they're supposed to laugh at what I say because I'm said to be a funny man."

That evening after he had escaped from the Philadelphians for a few hours of rest in his room, the hotel keeper and Sanderson came up to escort him to the theater. " They have advertised that you will be in the audience," said Sanderson. " You'll have to be there."

" What is the play? "

" *Jim Crow.*"

They rode over to Walnut Street in Sanderson's barouche, the tavern keeper passing a bottle of expensive liquor around to the members of the party. When they entered the theater, the play was already in progress; a bandy-legged actor in burnt cork moving about the stage, speaking in very bad Negro dialect.

At the intermission the audience saw him in the box and started applauding. He stood up and bowed. During the second act he noticed that the people all seemed to be watching him rather than the actors. Every time he laughed the audience would laugh. For a while he was embarrassed, wondering if he were laughing in the right places. Jim Crow, he thought, was a character to be pitied, but the actor's legs were so crooked and his dialect was so bad that he wanted to laugh at him all the time.

The music bothered him; the musicians seemed never to play a tune.

" How did you like it? " Sanderson asked at the end of the performance.

" A very good play," said David.

" Everyone seemed to enjoy it."

" Almost as much fun as a country frolic. But not quite. You city folks have your theaters but you miss a might of fun by not having country frolics. You ought to see our boys and girls dancing out in west Tennessee. None of your straddling, mincing, sadying around for them, but a regular sifter, cut-the-buckle, chicken-flutter set-to. And when one of our boys puts his arm around his partner it's a good hug and you can lay to that."

Sanderson smiled, touching his waxed moustache gently with his finger. " Are you homesick already, Colonel Crockett? "

David grinned. " I reckon I'm just not used to big cities crowded full of people taken up with their own pleasures and their own business and with no time for caring about plain folks."

Next morning a delegation of politicians and newspaper editors visited the hotel to present him with a gold seal for his watch chain engraved with the words: " Go Ahead." This unexpected honor made him turn to Sanderson: " I take back what I said about city folks last night. They're just like country folks at heart."

" But the watch seal is not all," said Sanderson. " The Young Whigs have asked me to inform you that they wish to present you with a fine rifle to be made right here in Philadelphia according to your specifications."

He could not understand such generosity. " Surely," he said, " there can be no other city in the world like Philadelphia. And I reckon I owe most of this to-do over me to you, John Sanderson."

" You owe it not to me," said Sanderson, " but to the Whigs. You see, we're already thinking about a man to run for President in 1836."

✳ 5 ✳

As much as he had enjoyed his three days in Philadelphia, David was secretly glad to board a steamboat on the river and start for New York. He had never felt so weary in all his life. There was something about city crowds that seemed to suck all the energy out of his body. He longed to be lost in the depths

of a wilderness, a hundred miles from any human being; there
he might recover some part of his identity which had been
scattered among the crowds of the city.

He could not put out of his mind what John Sanderson had
said about the Whigs seeking a man to run for President in
1836. So that was the reason for the gigantic demonstration on
the wharf, the huge crowds at the Exchange, the gold seal, the
fine rifle? President? Well, who knows?

The April sunshine was warm, and he sat on the top deck
on one of a row of chairs, chewing tobacco, spitting over the
rail into the gray river water. Along the banks, trees were
bursting into leaf, the grass patches were dark green after
spring rains. He intended to ask the captain if he knew where
George Washington had made his famous crossing, but he
forgot it in the excitement of landing at the river town where
the passengers transferred to the Camden & Amboy railroad.
The train engine was puffing out great billows of black pine-
knot smoke, and the passengers disembarking from the boat
hastened over the stony landing to stare at it before boarding
one of the stages behind. On the Baltimore railroad David had
had little opportunity to examine the engine. He looked this
one over closely, the sharp plow-pointed nose which a man told
him was called a cow-catcher, the tall smoke-stack, the two
huge flanged wheels, the numerous chains and rods running
from end to end. He wondered what the folks back on the
Obion would say if such a monster came snorting out at them
from the forest. These engines might run very well along this
eastern flat land, but he doubted if they would ever get over the
mountains into Tennessee.

The train coachman was ordering the passengers to come
aboard. David stepped inside the last coach; the Baltimore trip
had taught him to keep as far away as possible from the flaming
cinders of the engine. They rocked along the uneven rails,
swaying from side to side. The second-growth pines along the

way seemed to move away from them in a semicircle as they went faster and faster.

"How fast you reckon we're going?" he asked the coachman when he walked by on the outside ledge.

"Twenty-five miles an hour," said the man laconically.

David whistled. A day's journey in an hour. He thrust his head outside the window, the wind and smoke whipping his hair. He spat; the spittle swept back stinging into his face. Twenty-five miles an hour! Up ahead he could hear the engine wheezing like a crazed animal. Twenty-five miles an hour!

At Amboy they stopped in the midst of a swampy field, transferred to horse-drawn stages for a short zig-zag ride between rail fences to a wharf where they boarded a ship for New York.

David's first view of New York harbor reminded him of huge clearings he had seen in the West, where acres of trees had been girdled, their naked dead trunks standing white in the sun and rain year after year. The number of ships with their masts and riggings high in the air was beyond his calculation. When his ship swung around to the wharf, he was startled to see a crowd as large as the one that had greeted him in Philadelphia. He quickly dismissed the thought that this crowd had also gathered in his honor. After all, New York was a large city; there were crowds everywhere in New York.

But as the ship jarred gently against the landing, he heard a cheer, heard his name shouted from a hundred throats. The captain on the upper deck was motioning down to where he was standing. Already three men, leaping onto the ship from the dock, were surrounding him.

"I'm Jack Walden," said the youngest of the three breathlessly. "Of the Young Whigs. And this is Colonel S. D. Jackson, to whom you wrote that very amusing letter. And William Webb. We're all good Whigs."

As in Philadelphia, he was led through a pressing mass of

[273]

human beings, shouting after him: " Go ahead, Davy! We're sure you're right, Davy! "

The reception committee took him to the American Hotel, New York's finest, into a large paneled parlor filled with bric-a-brac and sparkling chandeliers. Many well-dressed gentlemen, looking very important, were sitting in leather chairs smoking and drinking. After he was introduced to several of them, Jack Walden brought him a glass of bubbling champagne which tickled his nose when he drank it, but he felt quite exhilarated in a short time.

" I've heard it said you're something of a drinking man, Colonel Crockett," said young Walden. " If you can outdo some of the old sots in this room, you're some drinker."

Colonel S. D. Jackson cleared his throat, winked at David, and downed a glass of Scotch. William Webb, a middle-aged man with long graying sideburns, was drinking a glass of lemonade in which particles of white ice tinkled. Surprised to see ice in a drink in late April, David asked for a lemonade.

He was introduced to a hundred men in a few minutes, and could remember scarcely any of their names. They all looked very much alike, pink-faced, white-whiskered, plump of abdomen. Everyone apparently was trying to outdo the other at telling jokes about Andrew Jackson; few of the stories were funny, all of them reflected upon the President's morals and character.

It was evening before he realized it. His three hosts remained with him for a dinner of rich soups and meats, puddings, tarts and cheeses. Already they had informed him that he was to attend the Park Theater for Fanny Kemble's final appearance before leaving for Boston.

After the play, they drove through the streets of New York, David's head swirling from all the foods and liquors and lights and faces. Brighter than the flickering street lamps was the moonlight, silvering over the countless rows of houses.

[274]

As they turned into the American Hotel, there was a cry from up the street: " Fire, fire! " Other voices joined in, everyone along the street shouting: " Fire, fire! " David leaped out of the carriage, looking back for the others to follow him, but Walden was standing up, laughing. " Come back, Colonel, it's not near us."

" Ain't you going to help put it out? "

" No! " Jackson and Webb, too, were laughing at him. " We have fire companies here and we leave it to them."

David shook his head. " By God, gentlemen, I can't understand you city folks. Back home, I'd've jumped on the first horse at hand and rode full flight, bare-backed, to help put out the fire."

★ 6 ★

On board a steamboat bound for Boston, David Crockett was drunk. Surrounded by a dozen laughing men, he had come over the gangplank waving an American flag, and the captain, a grim-faced Norwegian, had solemnly shown him to the vessel's best stateroom, reserved by the Young Whigs for their departing guest of honor.

After the men had gone, David lay down on the bunk for a moment, but the stateroom began revolving. He watched the revolutions with interest until his stomach turned upside down, and then he sat up, his head in his hands, his elbows on his knees, staring at the criss-cross patterns on the rug beneath his feet. The past twenty-four hours blurred across his memory —the drinking party at the hotel. Be sure you're right, Davy, or I'll drink you under the table, no man alone can drink me under a table, I'm a wild buffalo from the canebrakes, I can drink a river dry. But Colonel, it's champagne, the best, imported, Colonel, under the table. For President, for President

[275]

the Whigs will drink you under the table, President Crockett, good evening, sir, the Bowery Theater's playbill for the evening says that Colonel Crockett in the flesh will attend, the real Crockett, sir. I never gave them my permission, no sirree, I'll not go, I'll drink you under the table first. Colonel Crockett, the head manager from the Bowery Theater, sir. I didn't come to New York to see a show, nor am I a wild bear for the citizens of New York to gaze upon. Tell him to go jump in the creek. Call me President, gentlemen, while I drink you under the table.

He raised his head, staring at the white walls of the stateroom. Better go on deck for some salt air, he was thinking, must be halfway to Boston by now.

He forced himself to cross the narrow room to the washstand, pouring a bowlful of water from the pitcher, ducking his head in the tepid liquid; then he combed his hair, and took a drink of brandy out of the bottle in his coat pocket, and set the bottle down on the stand. His knees felt weak and wobbly as he walked along the narrow passageway and up to the deck where mid-afternoon sunshine burned suddenly hot into his face. The boat was moving slowly across the front of a dock where a crowd of people were waving flags and cheering.

An aged man, with a long soft beard, turned and gave David a sharp look.

" Sir," asked David, " what port is this? "

The man's mouth parted slightly, his red tongue showing between his lips. " Why, it's New York, Colonel Crockett."

"New York! We're still in New York! " He waved his hand weakly to the crowd that was screaming his name. Then after a few minutes he stumbled back down the steps to his stateroom, falling across his bunk, sleeping in his clothes until dawn.

He woke up, his eyes focusing on a faint circle of pink light on the wall, remembering suddenly where he was. His head was hot, aching with fierce torturous throbs. In Boston, thank God, he knew not a soul. There he would wander about the streets unknown to all the passers-by, enjoying the sights, resting quietly in the evenings at some small hotel. The Bostonians, no doubt, had never heard of him anyhow.

He went on deck to watch the sun rise, breathing the cold breeze as if it were a precious life-giving substance. The captain was on the forward deck, walking slowly up and down. He nodded politely. The sun was small and red as an apple coming over the edge of the rippling horizon.

" How far from land? " asked David.

" Fort Juda's over there, sir. We'll pass right shortly."

They stopped at Newport but briefly, proceeding to Providence, where to David's dismay a delegation was waiting to carry him to the hotel for dinner. He declined as politely as possible, and boarded the fast stage for Boston, crowding into a seat beside the white-whiskered man he had seen on the New York boat.

The old gentleman seemed pleased to have David sit beside him, and proved exceedingly voluble, asking question after question about Washington and the Congress. " You know Cap'n Silsbee, I allow."

Yes, David knew Senator Silsbee, the Massachusetts senator. " Most folks think of Dan'l Webster as Massachusetts' senator, though."

" But Cap'n Silsbee, he's a friend of mine," chirped the white-whiskered gentleman.

David wished his companion would not talk so much; it seemed to him that he had done nothing but talk and listen to other people talk for days and days and days, ever since he had left Washington. He looked out at the stony face of New England, stones in the fields, stones in the fence rows, stones along the post-road knocking against the wheels of the swiftly-moving stage.

"Not far off there is Plymouth," said the old man. "The Pilgrims landed there."

"Seems odd," replied David, "they would've come all the way across the sea and not looked out for better land than this is."

"It was God's will they should stop here."

David chuckled. "I reckon so. If they'd had good land, they wouldn't've had to work so hard and bring up their children to industry and teach 'em how to make ducks and drakes of us ignorant folks out in the back country."

They came into Boston on a narrow clean street, the horses' hoofs beating a slower rhythm as they pulled up to a stop between two large buildings facing each other, the Tremont Theater on his left, the Tremont Hotel on his right.

The coachboy was already pulling the luggage down from the top of the stage, piling it on the sidewalk. "I reckon he means for me to stay here," David said, turning toward his companion, but the old man had hobbled away up the sidewalk, buttonholing an obvious acquaintance, pointing his walking stick at David.

"Well, anyway there's not any reception committee," he said aloud, and turned to follow a Negro servant into the Tremont's elaborate entranceway.

A broad-faced man with a forehead like Daniel Webster's was standing behind the hotel desk, nodding cordially to his new guests. In one hand he held a quill pen, dripping ink. "Your name?" he asked David politely.

"Davy Crockett, from Crockett, Tennessee."

The quill pen dropped on the bar-book, splattering ink in all directions.

"Davy Crockett! Welcome to you, sir!" cried the man. "My name is Dwight Boyden. We didn't know you were planning to visit Boston, though we've been hearing something of your visit to New York." He thrust out his hand. "Colonel

[278]

Crockett, you are the guest of the Tremont for as long as you may wish to remain with us."

David shook Boyden's hand. " I was kind of hoping for a quiet place for a day or two, no big speaking dinners and recep ——"

" This is the very place. Finest hotel in the world, if I do say so myself. The Tremont was built by a group of public-spirited citizens of Boston, and ——" David listened respectfully while the manager escorted him personally to the hotel's most elaborate double room, much better fitted than the one he had lived in while in New York. A few minutes after Boyden left him alone, a waiter appeared at the door with a napkin-covered tray of food.

That night, for the first time on his journey, David Crockett slept well.

★ 7 ★

Tom Chilton was delivering an impassioned speech against the administration's banking policies when David stepped into the House chamber and sat down quietly in his seat. Several members waved or nodded greetings, then Chilton, with a flourish of his long coattails, turned suddenly and saw David. He broke off in the middle of a sentence, his mouth wide open, then wound up his oration lamely, bowed to the Speaker, and stepped over to grab David's shoulder.

" Hang you, Crockett, you spoiled one of my best speeches, dropping in here so suddenlike. Come out here in the corridor and tell me all about the journey."

" Between you and the Young Whigs, Tom Chilton, I feel like a rabbit that's been chased clean across the nation by relays of houn' dogs." He took out his plug of tobacco, offering a chew to the Kentuckian.

"According to what I can hear from up there, you certainly were a hero, Crockett, you must've told 'em some whoppers."

"I reckon maybe I did." He pulled out his watchchain. "See this seal they give me up in Philadelphia. Real gold, a feller told me it cost at least forty dollars. In Boston I got a coat made out of India rubber that sheds rain. All I got in New York was too much drinking liquor."

"Maybe you think those trinkets are all you brought back." Chilton's gray eyes were twinkling merrily. "I'm thinking you brought back a good number of presidential votes."

"Pshaw. They'll forget about me in two shakes of a sheep's tail."

Chilton caught his arm. "We're not going to let 'em forget about you. We'll map out a speech-making campaign right now."

In his first speech in the new session of Congress, David brought up the Tennessee land question again. All during the autumn, while he was at home, his constituents had brought complaints of continuing injustices suffered because of faulty land titles. But he could get little attention from a Congress splitting into three political groups, Jacksonians quarreling among themselves, and Whigs watching and waiting for opportune moments to strike body blows at the crumbling opposition.

He protested several times on the floor against the interminable speeches. One day when a Pennsylvania Representative was haranguing at length on the low pay of Congressmen, his anger got the better of him, and he jumped up, demanding the floor. "Eight dollars a day is more than enough for such long-winded fellers as you. It's nonsense to talk about it being a sacrifice to come here. If it was a sacrifice, you wouldn't see

[280]

so many grasping to be members of Congress. Eight dollars a day is a-plenty."

On February 3, he delivered his last speech, a demand for 160 acres of free land for all American citizens who wanted to settle on it. He spoke very briefly. "You all know my sentiments, why say any more? I've heard so much windy talk on this floor, I'm beginning to believe silence is the greatest virtue."

Adjournment came early, it being an election year. At 3 A. M. Sunday, March 8, David walked out of the Capitol after a night of the customary revelry of a Congressional closing. Purposely the session had been dragged along past Saturday midnight, so that the members would be eligible to receive eight dollars extra pay, and a near riot was precipitated when a handful of Temperance Congressmen tried to persuade their colleagues to adjourn early and attend a temperance meeting nearby.

Back on the Obion once again, he rested a few days at home, then set off on horseback down the river valley to find his old campaign mate, Abram Henry. He found Abram on a tiny cotton farm, looking thin and hungry; his red hair was turning pink, and his freckled face was cut with lines like an eroded hillside. But he grinned broadly when David walked up the path to his door, turning and shouting to his wife to bring his fiddle out.

"Same old fiddle, ain't it?" said David.

"Sure, same old fiddle. When we going to start campaigning again, Davy?"

"Not till June anyway. Let old Adam Huntsman spill out his bellyful of lies first, then we'll go in and clean 'em up after him."

Abram rubbed his stubble-bearded chin with the edge of his bow. "They're sure a-gunning for you this time, Davy. They

[281]

sent me a Washington newspaper way out here full of stuff about you."

"Franked it through the mail, I'll bet. That's Gen'l Jackson's hand."

"Gov'nor Carroll's men are already out making speeches agin you, too."

As spring turned into early summer, the combined forces of Jackson's federal and Carroll's state administration were brought into play in David's district. His chief opponent, peg-legged Adam Huntsman, supplied with funds from the Union Bank at Jackson, was pouring liquor out by the barrelful at all his public meetings.

In June David opened his canvass at a crossroads community, drawing a large crowd of farmers. Abram entertained them for a few minutes, then David climbed on a raised log platform and began talking.

There was a sudden shout from the rear: "How about a drink first?"

"Sure, Colonel Crockett, make certain you're right afore you start talking. Politics is too dry without a drink."

David laughed, jumped down from the platform, and led the way into the crossroads shanty.

He knew the owner, Job Snelling. "Hello, Job, you old gander-shanked Yankee, let's have a quart of your best New England rum."

The lean, long-nosed proprietor turned slowly, pointing a bony finger to a crude sign above the bar: *Pay Today and Trust Tomorrow*. David's fingers twisted in his pocket; he had only two small coins. He knew that Abram had no money. "My credit's as good as the next man's. Better; why, I'm a United States Congressman." He could feel the eyes of the farmers shifting toward him. Somebody snickered. One or two men near the door moved back outside.

"Job is a Huntsman man; he'll never give you no credit," Abram mumbled huskily.

David's hand caught Abram's wrist. "Wait," he whispered, "you start playing your fiddle for 'em, play like hell. I'll be back in half an hour."

Abram started playing his instrument, the most rollicking tunes he knew, while David pushed his way through the tittering crowd, grabbed his rifle at the door, and ran off at a dog-trot into the woods.

He was back in half an hour with a coonskin, the fur still warm and dotted with fresh blood. The restless crowd, listening inattentively to the perspiring Abram's frantic music, followed curiously after him into Job Snelling's shanty. He slapped the coonskin on the counter. "There you are, Job. Coonskin's still legal tender for a quart of rum any day in west Tennessee."

Snelling's dark brows squeezed down in a frown; his lower lip drooped. Then, without show of emotion, he shoved a quart of rum across the counter, and dropped the coonskin down on the floor. But in five minutes the quart was gone, and half the men were still without drinks. David fingered his belt nervously, watching the grizzled faces in the room. He looked down, saw an edge of the coonskin sticking out beneath the logs supporting the bar. Surreptitiously he dragged it out with the toe of his boot, reached down quickly with one arm, suddenly slapped the pelt across the counter again.

"All right, Job, let's have another quart of same."

Snelling's round eyes bugged when he saw the coonskin; his lips pushed out suspiciously. But he caught up the skin without a word, and passed another jug of rum across the counter. This time he dropped the coonskin behind him, well out of reach.

Now the men behind David were chuckling; they had guessed his trick. They whispered the word along to those in

[283]

the rear. The little shanty began to rumble with their hoarse laughter. They were all with him now.

David's fury mounted, but he only grinned sardonically when he heard or read another story about his Washington activities. Of all his Congressional campaigns, he had never been so confident of victory as he was of this one.

He knew he would win. A few hours after the election was over, the first counts showed him so far in the lead, he went home from the polling place in the village to oil up his Philadelphia rifle. And with Abram and William, he went out for a two-day hunt. "No use to wait around for a final count. I've got to get some hunting in, so's I can start planning for some *real* campaigning."

"What you mean?" asked Abram.

"You wait and see, Abram, you'll be in on it. A real presidential campaign. A long time I been wanting to take you to see the sights in Washington and the big cities in the East."

When they came back home, Liza was waiting for him at the door. In her face he read tragedy. "What's wrong, Liza, what in tarnation's happened?"

"Davy," she said quietly, "they come and told me you didn't win the 'lection."

"Now, Liza, somebody's just been a-stringing you on."

But to corroborate Liza there was a sealed letter on his desk. Adam Huntsman had defeated him by 230 votes.

Outside the cabin, darkness was closing in, the end of a hot summer's day. William had gone on to the barn to feed and water the horses. Abram was somewhere out on the porch, squeaking dismally on his fiddle. Liza had lighted a candle, and it burned steadily without a flutter on the desk.

He stared at the knot holes on the rough wall in front of him; he looked down at his hands, flexing and unflexing his

[284]

fingers. Then Liza was behind him, her big knotted hands rubbing gently on his neck.

He raised his head. " Liza? "

" Uh-huh."

" You got some of that good cider you make anywhere around the place? "

" For sure, there's some cider."

" Let's have a drink, just you and me."

There was a delegation to see him Saturday night. Come down to the town and talk to us, they said. You're still a great man, Davy Crockett, even if you didn't win the election. No, he said. Just one more speech, they said, for old times. All right, I'll make you a speech, he said, I'll speak up my mind.

In the town that had been a wilderness of canes a few years ago, the street was filled with men and women walking in the dusty August twilight. In the town hall oil wicks sputtered along the walls, stinking in the heat, making shadows on the people's faces.

He talked slowly, searching in his mind for every word, but he could not find the right words. He had heard too many speeches, he had made too many speeches. Words meant nothing any more.

" We're all common folks, you and me," he said. " We want things, we want money, we want land. We know we've got to have a mouth in the government to get these things. In the last eight years we common folks have had a big mouth in the government. Your elected representatives have argued and quarreled about how we would do this thing and that thing, but we done 'em one way or the other. Now here's what I got to say. Watch out that we don't lose these things we've got. There was an Irishman I heard tell about, bet a glass of grog with a hod carrier that he couldn't carry him in his hod up a ladder to the third story of a new building. Well, the hod carrier took the bet and the Irishman set hisself down in the hod, and up they started. The hod carrier got up to the second story, but when he was halfway up to the third his wind was going fast and he started a-tottering. The Irishman was so tickled at thinking he was going to win the bet, he clapped his hands and crowed, ' By God, the grog's mine.' He made such a stir in the hod, I wish I may be shot if he didn't win the bet, but he busted his neck in the fall.

"Now, we common folks may win our victory, but unless we change the road we're going on, we'll all fall, you and me, and the country will fall with us."

In the hall there was a dead silence, except for the summer insects buzzing around the lamps.

"I'm telling you all now, I'm done with politics." The faces were all staring at him, yellow faces in the oil light. "I'm done with politics. You folks can all go to hell, I'm going to Texas."

PART FIVE

Just *how that shrewd Connecticut Yankee, Moses Austin,
was able to obtain permission to establish a colony of Americans inside the borders of New Spain probably will always
remain a mystery.*

*With the colony still a dream, old Moses died, but his
stubborn and persistent son, Stephen Fuller Austin, hastened
to translate his father's dream into fact. In 1821, the year
Mexico was busy winning her freedom from Spain, Stephen
Austin got his colony going at San Felipe on the Brazos River.*

*Three years later Mexico established its first republican
government, made Texas a state in the federation, let down
the bars to many another colony of Americans who modeled
their settlements after Stephen Austin's prosperous example.
And during the next decade, 30,000 Americans, adventurers,
hunters, farmers, insolvent debtors, broken shopkeepers, came
to Texas to settle along the rivers between Nacogdoches and
San Antonio southward to the coast. As the Mexican government demanded, they agreed to found towns, organize militia,
preserve order, become loyal subjects, and adopt Roman
Catholicism as their religion.*

*But by 1830, the Mexicans were beginning to show nerv-
ousness over the swift colonization of Texas by Americans;
on April 6 of that year, the Mexican Congress passed a law
stopping all further immigration. To enforce the decree, an
army moved northward across the Nueces River. Priests were
sent in to bring recalcitrant Texans into the state church. But
the earthy, good-humored colonists were not impressed; they
still sent word back to their friends in the states that there was
plenty of room in Texas. The land, they believed, belongs to
him who gives it value.*

*They also believed in democratic government, and in 1833
drew up a model state constitution which Stephen Austin
carried personally to Mexico City for ratification. At the same*

[289]

time in Mexico, Antonio Lopez de Santa Anna, under guise of liberalism, was rising to power. Austin reached the capital in the midst of revolution. When he wrote a letter back to the citizens of San Antonio de Bexar, advising a union of all Texas municipalities to defend their democratic rights, Santa Anna got wind of it, charged Austin with treason, clapped him into jail.

For two years, Stephen Austin was technically a prisoner in Mexico City, while Santa Anna, backed by a corrupt church and military, seized the presidential office, abolished the Congress, made himself dictator.

Free, and back in Texas late in 1835, Stephen Austin found his formerly peaceful friends raging at Santa Anna's dictatorial government. Drastic measures to curb the Texans—confiscation of arms, high import duties, military courts, orders to join the state church or lose their lands—only sharpened their anger. Already there had been skirmishes between the citizens and the military; at Gonzales the citizens had refused to surrender a cannon, had driven off an armed detachment.

Reluctantly, Austin accepted the chairmanship of the Committee of Safety, advised the immediate formation of volunteer companies for defense. By November his followers had pushed past him, demanding an immediate showdown with Santa Anna's government. A consultation was called, and the mild-mannered Austin was displaced as leader of the Texans by Henry Smith, president of the provisional government, and Sam Houston, commander of the army.

Less than a month later, a Mexican army under General Cos was forming around the garrison at San Antonio. Outside the town a motley group of Texans was also gathering. They rushed the Mexicans before dawn on December 5, dug into the town's outskirts, for five days fought their way in from house to house, finally dislodged the Mexicans who retreated to the fortified mission buildings at the Alamo. A few days later the Mexicans surrendered, were ordered to retreat posthaste toward the Rio Grande.

[290]

Many a Texan thought the war was over. But Stephen Austin did not think so. He knew Santa Anna. Soon after he heard the news from San Antonio, Austin was on his way to the United States. Men and money would be needed. There was going to be hell to pay in Texas.

★ I ★

"NEARABOUTS to five thousand acre of land they give you to settle there. That's why I'm going." Leaning over the railing of the boat, the man spat into the Mississippi, then with his forefinger quickly cleaned the long moustache drooping around the sides of his mouth.

"I'm mighty glad to hear you're going. But from what they're saying now, you may have to fight for them five thousand acres. That's my main reason for going—to get into a fight. I just got licked out of one fight, and it's been worrying me so I been feeling like a dog with running fits. Maybe striking out into new country and having to depend on my rifle again for a living instead of on my tongue, maybe it'll cure me up."

"Say, friend," asked the long-moustached man, "what was your name? You're from Tennessee, all right, ain't you?"

"The name's Davy Crockett."

"Well, darn my soul! Let me shake your hand. Mine's Tuck Crutchfield. Say, I know your boy, John, school-teaching over in the seminary."

"You must be from Paris?"

"Sure, I'm from Paris. Last year Sam Houston was there, telling all about Texas, how much good land they had down there, how they needed good men. Well, about that time my folks got cheated out of their land over by Paris, and then we had a bad crop on rented land this year. I been thinking about it a long time, and now I've made up my mind to get to Texas or bust."

They leaned over the railing, watching the water swirling around the mud-caked sides of the steamboat. Brown leaves, sifting down from the trees along the banks, showered into the waves.

"My boy, Willie, wanted to come mighty bad," said David, "but somebody had to stay home to run things. There're five boys with me though, from around my neighborhood."

"Yeah, I was talking to a feller from the Obion country while ago; Henry his name is."

"That's Abram Henry; he's the only married one except me. We been knowing each other a long time. Abram says his reason for going is because he don't know where Texas is, just heard about it, and he wants to find out where the damn place is."

Crutchfield edged closer to David. "Would you be a-minding if I joined up with you fellers?"

"Be mighty glad to have you," replied David.

He and Crutchfield got out their rifles in the afternoon, taking pot shots at objects floating in the river. "Mighty fine rifle you got there, Colonel Crockett."

"This is my Betsy. Made especially for me in Philadelphia."

Crutchfield examined the barrel, felt its smooth surface with his fingers. "She's some rifle."

"I wouldn't go to Texas without her."

The journey was the most tedious he had ever made, the old steamboat twisting and turning back on its course down the snakelike Mississippi. To pass the time, he tried playing Abram's fiddle, and found it surprisingly easy. Every night they danced, stomping and beating on the rotten boards of the boat deck. Occasionally at stops along the way other men, Texas bound, would join them.

They reached Little Rock on a chill November day, climbing up to the sprawling town, high on the river bank. "Kind of reminds me of Nashville, ten years ago, before they built

[293]

it up," said David. They walked along a muddy street parallel-ing the river, turned a corner, and found themselves on the edge of a noisy crowd.

" What's going on here? " asked Crutchfield.

" Might be most anything. Don't smell like politics though." They pushed through to where they could see a small plat-form against a wall, where two puppets were dancing madly about, slapping each other over the head, while screaming voices accompanied the action behind the scenes.

" It's a Punch and Judy show; I saw one once in Wash-ington." Between dialogues, a fiddle squeaked unseen behind the paper scenery. Abram Henry, who had pushed ahead of David, turned around, grinning. " Say, that's good fiddling." Judy was pounding Punch over the head with a broomstick, when suddenly the side scenery piece collapsed. On a chair behind it, fiddling furiously, was a white-haired old man, with a shiny bald spot in the middle of his skull. His face reddened, his toothless mouth grimaced in comic embarrassment, his bow was suspended in mid-air.

" Preacher Boone! " cried Abram. " Old Preacher Boone! "

The musician's bright blue eyes blinked at the crowd. The puppets hung grotesquely on their strings while the operator hurried out to set up the scenery.

" Let's hear some fiddling," shouted Tuck Crutchfield, " from old Preacher Boone! "

" You know that feller? " asked David.

" No, but Abram does."

" Sure, I know him," said Abram. " He used to live down below me on the river. Preached around some. He'd come over to my house to fiddle on the sly, afraid his congregation wouldn't like it if he fiddled at public places."

The spry old man had pushed his way out to Abram, wav-ing his fiddle over his head. " What you doing way out here in Arkansas, Abram? "

[294]

"We're on our way to Texas, with Davy Crockett here."

David shook hands with Preacher Boone. The puppet show-man meanwhile was passing his beaver hat through the crowd, seeking a collection; but the name of Davy Crockett was being whispered from mouth to mouth, and everybody had suddenly lost interest in Punch and Judy.

A man in a heavy fur coat broke through the tightening ring, and pulled at David's sleeve. "Excuse me, Colonel Crockett, but we just learned you were among us. I'm Mayor James Pitcher." Two men behind the mayor, breathing heavily in the crush, reached out to shake hands also. "This is John Boyle and this is Dan'l Ringo, two of the city officials. We got a regular city government here now. What you think of Little Rock?"

"It's a ring-tooting town," said David. "Folks sure are friendly here."

"Well now, you've not been here long enough to enjoy real Little Rock hospitality. We want you to be the guest of the city at the Jeffries Hotel long as you can stay in town."

"Thank you, gents, thank you, but I've got six Tennessee boys here with me; we're heading for Texas, you know, and unless you could put all seven of us up, I reckon I'll stay with the boys."

Mayor Pitcher scratched his head, then smiled. "I suppose we can find room for all you boys in the Jeffries."

"You folks are mighty considerate, more'n we deserve."

"Now, you won't mind making a little speech at a dinner tonight, will you, Colonel?"

David frowned. "A speech? No, sir, it's no go. If I've got to make a speech I'm backing out of your invitation right now. I'm through with making speeches or attending dinners."

"Our hospitality still holds," replied the mayor, "even if you don't open your mouth to speak or to eat."

As soon as they could escape the crowd, David and his six

[295]

companions went with their hosts to the hotel where they were soon comfortably lodged. The hotel keeper, a rotund smiling man who looked more like a butcher than a landlord, was delighted with his guests, even refusing payment for drinks. Tuck Crutchfield and David downed a couple of stinging corn liquors and then went out to see the town.

When they returned, the hotel keeper approached David with a worried expression upon his broad face. "Mayor Pitcher was telling me you wouldn't come to supper tonight and make us a speech. Why, Colonel Crockett, hundreds of Little Rock folks are coming here tonight to hear you."

" But I ain't got a thing to say, sir, not a thing. And I figure I oughtn't to come to the dinner if I don't make a speech."

The man shook his head sorrowfully, and waddled away. But in a few minutes he was back again, beckoning with a chubby finger for David to follow him behind the counter. He leaned over, whispering, " Colonel, would you just oblige me by stepping out here into the back yard a minute? "

David followed him out to a smokehouse. The man flung open the door. Hanging from the beams were two fat bears, several haunches of venison, a plump turkey and several other smaller fowl.

" Well, Colonel, what do you think of my larder? "

" Fine," said David.

"Now, will you come to our dinner? "

David laughed, nodding. " My head says no, my stomach says yes."

" Let's go drink on it," said the landlord, slapping him on the shoulder gleefully.

Before dark, the crowd began gathering for the dinner, pushing through the doors into the long dining room. Tables had to be set up in the lobby and in the hallway to make room for the numerous guests.

A fife and a drum at one end of the dining hall set up a

[296]

brisk tune together. Tuck Crutchfield and Abram Henry hurried over to watch the musicians. They were playing *See the Conquering Hero Comes* when David walked down to the head table with the mayor and the landlord, and David felt more important than he ever had on his trip to the cities in the East.

The tables were heaped with food. Everyone ate noisily for several minutes, then toasts were drunk in the fiery Arkansas corn liquor that seemed to be the standard beverage. After every toast, the drum and fife boomed and squealed in salute. "By God," the landlord said to David, "that drum sounds like an old horse with stomach heaves and the fife like a stuck pig. Why don't you get up now, Colonel, and do your talking and shut the damn things up?"

David nodded. The corn liquor was warming his insides.

"Our distinguished guest, Colonel Crockett." Roars of applause sounded through the dining hall, out into the hallway, into the lobby. Outside, people were leaning in the windows, eager to hear what he had to say.

"If this is the way you Little Rock folks treat a rundown politician, I'd sure like to see what you do for a real live, kicking politician. Now, I been up and down the nation, and I seen some first rate men here and there, but never, I'll swear it, never did I see such a breed of half-horse, half-alligator men as live here. Nowhere on the face of the universal earth could there be such folks as are here in Arkansas.

"Now, for you all who don't know it, I'm through with politics, and I can say what I damn please. I don't mind saying I was feeling mighty low in my mind afore I got to Arkansas, I was so low I didn't put much stock in my fellow-man. But one or two days in Arkansas, and already I'm a new man. If I hadn't set my mind to go to Texas, by gum if I wouldn't stop right here in Little Rock the rest of my days, and try to pay you folks back for the good you've done me."

[297]

David was up shortly after dawn the next morning, and as soon as he could pull on his clammy leather breeches, he jerked the bedcovers off his six companions. " Get your tails in the air, boys, we're riding out of Little Rock soon as we can eat."

During the supper of the previous evening, a man named Bushrod had introduced himself as a friend of Sam Houston, offering David's party the use of horses as far as the town of Fulton on Red River.

" The quicker you men can get to Texas, the better it'll be," Bushrod said. " I've been here in Little Rock six months trying to persuade men to go down and help the Texans. There's going to be a revolution down there, and it's coming soon."

Bushrod was waiting in front of the hotel, with seven horses tied up at the watering trough. " Come in and take a bite with us," said David. " Even after all that eating last night, I'm hungry as a bitch wolf."

They finished breakfast hastily, then hurried out to the horses, tying on their scant baggage. The air was frosty. David pulled his fur cap tight over his head, swung up on a horse, and reached down to shake hands with Bushrod.

" One last favor to ask you," said Bushrod. " Here's a letter to a man you'll find at Fulton. Name's Ed Johnson. He'll take care of sending the horses back."

" Be glad to carry it." David looked around, counting his companions. " Now where in hell," he cried, " is Abram Henry? "

Everybody looked blank. Tuck Crutchfield blinked his sleep-swollen eyes. " He was here a minute ago, Davy."

They could hear horses' hoofs beating on the street behind

the hotel, then five horsemen swerved around the corner. Abram was in the lead, the tail of his coonskin cap flying in the wind.

" Ho, Davy. Can we take four more fellers? "

" Hell, yes. Well, if one of you ain't Preacher Boone! "

Boone pulled his horse to a stop alongside David's. " You mind an old codger like me going along? "

" Can you shoot? "

" Good as I can fiddle."

" That's good enough for me. We need a preacher in the party anyhow."

" Well, I ain't much of a preacher. I got such a weakness for fiddling and good corn liquor."

"Shucks, Preacher Boone, if fiddling and drinking was sinful, Hell would be too full to hold the sinners. Let's go, boys! "

The small crowd that had gathered in front of the hotel was cheering when the horsemen galloped away down the street and turned southwards in the blue-smoke haze of morning.

Water was rising in the Saline bottoms, the muddy trail slowing their progress. The Ouachita was almost out of its banks; David had to whip his horse, forcing it into the chocolate-brown stream. Preacher Boone's courageous little mare took the lead, and the old man turned halfway around in the saddle, beckoning the others to follow, showing his toothless pink gums in a half-smile, half-grimace. " I recollect one time I got caught in a creek flood in a sulky," he cried, " and there I was with the water getting higher and higher, and my old mule refusing to budge. You know what I did, boys, I just got out my old fiddle and played *Over the Water to Charley* loud as I could, and 'twa'n't no time a-tall till some folks hearing the music come to offer help."

When they were all across, David ordered a halt. They built a fire of pine knots and dried their clothes.

"Did you get your fiddle wet?" David asked the preacher.

"Nossirree, I kept it up out of the water."

"I'm right glad you're along, Preacher Boone," said Abram. "Now we got two fiddle players in the party."

"By God, we got three fiddle players," said David. "I'm learning so fast I'll beat you both first thing you know. Let me have your fiddle, Preacher Boone, maybe I can play *Crockett's March* for you." But he couldn't remember the tune; it seemed as far away and dark and unreal as the evening in Washington when he had heard it for the first time.

Through forests of red-leaved oaks and yellow-leaved hickory and pecan trees showering nuts, they rode across sandy lands and then hill lands with scrub pines green against the gray November sky. Again they were in bottom country on a sticky black gumbo trail beneath sycamores and cypress, and they came to the town of Fulton, a row of log shacks near the Red River.

The tavern was the largest building in the town, the entrance room floorless, the hard-packed earth covered with dirty bearskins.

"I'm looking for a man named Ed Johnson," David said to the tavern keeper.

The man pulled a corncob pipe out of his mouth, and spat against the wall. "More'n likely you'll find Ed 'round to the back in the blacksmith shop."

In the blacksmith shop, a young boy of about twenty was busily shoeing a horse. "Say, boy, is Ed Johnson around anyplace?"

The young man set the horse's leg down gently and stood up. "That's my name."

David scratched his chin. "Sure it ain't your pa's name too, son?"

Johnson's handsome tanned face crinkled in a slow-spreading smile. "No, sir, I'm the only Ed Johnson in these parts."

[300]

David extended his hand. "Sure wasn't expecting to see so young a lad. We got some horses to go back to Little Rock."

"Bushrod sent you then?"

"Yeah, I'm Davy Crockett."

"Davy Crockett from Tennessee? I've heard some talk of you. Didn't know you was heading for Texas though."

"There's eleven of us, counting myself. When does the next boat go down the river?"

"Tomorrow. I'll likely be going with you."

"That's good, we'll need somebody knows the country. Can you come out and meet my boys—but, say, wait a minute, I got a letter here for you, Bushrod sent it."

David unlaced one of the pockets of his leather hunting shirt, and pulled out a thick travel-stained envelope. Johnson took it, glanced sharply at David, then broke the seal. He read slowly, moving his lips, then folded the message, and thrust it back in the envelope. "I guess I won't be on that boat after all, Mr. Crockett. Got something else to do now."

They walked out of the blacksmith shop around to the front of the tavern. Ed Johnson shook hands cordially with all the members of David's party, but his thoughts seemed to be elsewhere.

That night, David was sleeping on a prickly pine-straw mattress with Abram Henry. He rolled over and over, trying to go to sleep.

"Whyn't you be still and go to sleep?" mumbled Abram.

"By God, I wonder what was in that letter I brought to Ed Johnson. That boy sure is worried about something."

Next morning after breakfast, Johnson signaled to David to follow him out behind the tavern. The boy was dressed in tight leather leggings and buckskin pants and coat. "Colonel Crockett, I got to ask you to do me a favor. You're going down on the boat today, and I know I can trust you."

[301]

David nodded.

"You see them boxes stacked up on the landing? Well, they're full of guns and lead and powder. Somebody's got to watch after 'em till they get to Natchitoches, and somebody's got to watch 'em there, till I can get there."

"Well, son, I guess I can keep my eyes on 'em till we get to Natchitoches. But if I got to sit there on 'em for a month waiting for you to come claim 'em, it's no go. We're in a hurry to get to Texas."

"But I'll be in Natchitoches in less'n a week. Can't you wait that long? They're going to need that stuff bad in Texas."

David reached out his hand. "For sure, I'll do it. But how you going to make it so quick? There won't be another boat for two weeks."

Johnson smiled. "I'll get there. Good-bye." He turned and started down toward the river. David watched him until he reached the bank, where a man in a rowboat paddled him across to the wilderness on the opposite side.

"That boy, Ed Johnson, is sure a mysterious feller," David was saying to Abram as they walked along the side railing of the small steamboat that had just left the Fulton dock.

"Yep," said Abram, "I guess so." He was watching the dark red flow of the river. "This river was sure named right. Gets redder every mile we go."

"It's a red river, all right. I wonder what could've been in that letter made the boy run off that-a-way."

"What I can't figure," said Abram, "is why we got to go way down south into the state of Louisiana in order to go west into Texas."

"They say it's quicker traveling. If we struck out west now we'd run into swamps and thickets. It's funny, though, that's the way Johnson was heading."

The boat, striking a snag, swung them hard against the rail.

"Like riding a new colt." Abram was looking up ahead. "Say, what's going on up to the front end?"

A crowd was gathered around a man seated on one of the boxes David had promised to guard. He and Abram walked closer. Tuck Crutchfield was already there.

"Gambling man," said Tuck. "He sure is tricky. Plays with thimbles."

A man wearing a tall white wide-brimmed hat cocked on one side of a head of curly black hair was moving three thimbles back and forth on top of the rough box. Somebody handed him a small coin; he covered it with a thimble, moving the other two deftly with his slender fingers. "Name the thimble, sir," he said, looking up at the man.

"The middle one." Smiling wearily, the gambler lifted the thimble; the coin had disappeared. The crowd laughed.

David moved closer, dropping a coin down on the box, and the gambler repeated the performance. "The one on the left," said David, sure that the coin was there. But when the gambler lifted the thimble, no coin. Grinning, David dropped another coin. "The middle thimble," said he, when the man finished his business. The gambler's fingers reached out, but David's hand beat him to the thimble. He lifted it and the coin was there.

David's face was within six inches of the gambler's; the man's black eyes were emotionless. "You've won the bet," he said, fishing a coin from his pocket, handing it to David. "Let's go half a dollar this bout."

"Let's take the half dollar and buy a drink," replied David.

The gambler uncrossed his long legs. "What's the difference? You buy me a drink with the money, or put it under my thimble. It's my gain either way."

They walked into the tiny boat saloon, some of the bystanders following after them. David dropped a half dollar on the bar, and the barkeep set up a big-bellied brown bottle,

[303]

pouring out two glasses. " Now that I've bought you a drink, how about your name, stranger? "

The gambler was wiping his lips with a handkerchief. " My name? I've had so many, I could offer half a dozen. On this Godforsaken river they call me Thimblerig. Call me Jones or Thimblerig, what's the difference? " He pushed his white hat back on his head, watching David with lacklustre eyes.

" There sure are some mysterious people in these parts," said David. " Thimblerig is all right for a name, though, I guess." He poured out another pair of drinks.

" And what's your name? " asked Thimblerig.

" I thought you knew."

" Why? "

" Well—almost everybody seems to—I'm Davy Crockett."

The gambler's expression did not change. " Where you from? "

" Tennessee."

" Lots of Tennesseans going west these days. What'd you do for a living? "

David swallowed his drink; his lips twisted in a grin. " I was a politician."

" Politician," laughed Thimblerig. " Politician or gambler? What's the difference? "

That night David found sleep impossible. Every time his eyes closed, the little boat jarred against the bank or crashed into a log snag, shaking him awake. He finally got up and walked out on the narrow deck. A man was sitting on the heap of boxes up front, the boxes of guns and ammunition bound for Texas. He remained motionless even when David approached within a few feet of him, and stood facing him silently, his thumbs hooked in his belt.

" Not worried about these boxes, are you, Mr. Crockett? " It was the gambler.

"What business is it of yours, the boxes?" replied David angrily.

"None at all," said Thimblerig. "I merely wish to reassure you that nothing will happen to them. I've made this run a dozen times this year, and the boxes always arrive safely in Natchitoches."

"You mean there've been other boxes going down?"

"Certainly. My good friend, Ed Johnson, usually accompanies them, but I see that he's entrusted them to you this trip."

"You keep a sharp eye out and know about everything that's going on, don't you, Thimblerig?"

"I'm a smart man, Mr. Crockett, too smart for my own good. If I hadn't been so damn smart, maybe I'd still be gambling on the Mississippi instead of on this red swamp creek."

"You ever been out to Texas?"

"Texas? Why go out to Texas? Texas, Arkansas, Louisiana? What's the difference?"

"You might pitch in and help out Texas, save it from the Mexicans."

"Save Texas? Save the country? Some country somewhere is always on the brink of ruin, Mr. Crockett. People are always out to save the country. What good is it, saving a country? Save it for what?"

David took out his plug of tobacco, and bit hard into it. "Thimblerig, you're a queer varmint. If I felt the way you do, I'd crawl off somewhere and die."

"Perhaps I shall, Mr. Crockett, perhaps I shall. Die today, die tomorrow. What's the difference?"

They found the river town of Natchitoches filled with a strange assortment of human beings, buckskinned travelers, well-dressed cotton planters, adventurous wanderers—all gathered in the rickety shacks that served as boarding houses and hotels. Everybody seemed to be waiting for something. Very few men were heading west for Texas.

David and his party had to share one long room in a pine-log house built high on stakes near the river. Thimblerig helped them find the place. " There're so many people in Natchitoches right now, it's well-nigh impossible to find shelter." He also helped them carry the boxes over from the boat; they stacked them in one end of the room, and then made pallets on the floor with blankets from their packs.

Thinking that Thimblerig was anxious to be off, David held out his hand to bid him good-bye. The gambler smiled queerly, pushing his white hat back on his head. " Would you mind, sir, if I lodged with you for a few days? "

"Well, it's right rough lodging for a gentleman," said David.

" I won't complain," said Thimblerig, and he unrolled his pack and spread a long black cloak on the floor beside David's blanket.

In the evening they went up to the largest inn; David and Tuck matched pennies with the gambler for the drinks. They heard a dozen rumors from Texas. Mexican armies were being formed all over the country to put down the Texans. There had been a battle at Gonzales settlement. Sam Houston was organizing a big army to drive out all the Mexicans.

For a week they stayed in Natchitoches, waiting impatiently for Ed Johnson to arrive and claim the boxes. " By God," complained David, " the boy could at least of told us where he was going. It's December now, and I wanted to get set down someplace in Texas before winter."

Johnson appeared at dusk one day, with two teamsters and their wagons to take the boxes. The boy's face was scratched, his clothing was ripped in shreds. " We sure do thank you, Colonel Crockett. And I hope I may be able to pay you back sort of, for this favor. You see, I'm going out in Texas myself tomorrow morning. My folks and my sweetheart live out there. We could all travel together and you could celebrate Christmas by resting up at our place."

Later in the evening, when they were alone, David talked again with Ed Johnson. "Boy, you're scratched up like a hound dog that's been through a thorn thicket."

"I been doing *some* traveling." The boy grinned. "That letter you brought me, I had to get it through to Sam Houston."

"Sam Houston! You seen Sam Houston?"

"No, he's too far out. But I got it to a Comanche, and I'll bet it's in Sam Houston's pocket right now."

"Sam Houston is rising fast in Texas," said David. "I used to know him back in Tennessee."

"Yeah, and you ought to know the man who sent that letter to Sam Houston. I guess it won't do no harm to say who it was."

"Who?"

"President Andy Jackson."

"Andy Jackson—well, I'll be a ——" David slapped his thigh, and let out a yelp. "So Old Andy is putting a finger in Texas, too? And me toting his messages for him—well, I'll be a son of a bow-legged bull!"

⋆ 3 ⋆

Their departure from Natchitoches was delayed another day because David and Ed Johnson were unable to round up enough horses to carry the men. Finally, through one of Johnson's many friends, they secured enough mounts, and at dawn the following day made ready to leave.

Thimblerig stood by, his face morose, flipping a coin from

one hand to the other, his long cloak clasped tightly around his shoulders.

" Cheer up," David shouted at him. " This ain't a funeral party."

Thimblerig shrugged. " I'm in a slough of despond, Colonel, in a slough of miry despond up to my very chin."

" Then hold your head up, before the slough reaches your mouth."

" What's the use? " The gambler pulled a slender roll of tobacco out of his pocket, bit off the end, chewing it nervously. " You don't know how it feels to know you can never live like an honest man again. I'm a gambler. All right. A crooked gambler, I'm that. The world won't let me be otherwise. When I die, they'll say: He was just a crooked gambler."

" It's not the world makes you what you are."

" *You* can say that. But *I* know it's not so."

David swung up on his horse. " Well, if you can't live like an honest man, you might die like one."

" But I can't even die like an honest man."

" The folks in Texas are making ready to fight, die if they have to, for their freedom. Maybe if you'd come join up with 'em, fight with 'em, you might find your own freedom."

Thimblerig's dull eyes opened wide for a moment. " Could I swing up behind you on that horse, and ride with you till I can find a mount? "

" Climb up," said David. Thimblerig did so immediately.

Ed Johnson was riding up and down the line of men. " How many in our party, Colonel? "

" Twelve."

" What about him? " asked Johnson, pointing to the gambler.

" Well, he does make thirteen."

" Unlucky," said Thimblerig, starting to drop off.

" Stay on, by God," cried David, spurring his horse. He

[308]

took the lead, along with young Johnson, and the horsemen raced off toward the west, following the moss-draped old Spanish trail. A damp December wind cut into their faces.

After leaving the Red River bottoms, they passed through thick pine forests, under tall straight trunks covered with heavy brown bark scales. They crossed the Sabine River, and a few days before Christmas were on the outskirts of Nacogdoches, at the farmhouse of Ed Johnson's family.

David's eye caught the buffalo head mounted over the entrance door. " That's what I want to do for Christmas, hunt buffalo."

" They're a long way from here," said Ed. " Out on the plains. You might see some west of the Brazos if you go that far out. What I aim to do for Christmas is just eat and pay court to my gal Kate."

David laughed. " I reckon I'll have to get me a Comanche squaw and eat beans and hominy."

" You're staying right here, you and all the boys. Can't promise you any Comanche squaws, but man, the Johnson womenfolks sure can cook."

On Christmas Eve they rode into Nacogdoches to buy some liquor and learn the latest news. The town lay in a hollow, low forested bluffs surrounding it, a small river skirting the edges. As they turned into the long main street they could see little knots of men gathered in front of the stores and saloons.

" Something's in the wind," said Ed, " else everybody would be inside drinking their skins full."

Something was in the wind. A messenger from Washington-on-the-Brazos had arrived a few hours earlier with the news that a small army of Texans had captured San Antonio de Bexar from the Mexican garrison, and had ordered the Mexican troops to leave Texas.

" It's all over now, boys," said a jovial saloonkeeper. " The Mexicans are licked before they got started. Texas is our country now. All we got to do is set up a government and elect Steve Austin President."

Ed Johnson downed his glass in one gulp, swung around and faced David. "That's what he thinks," he said slowly. "I'll bet there'll be a Mexican army back on San Antonio before spring."

"How far off is this San Antonio?" asked David.

"A good three hundred miles, maybe more."

David turned to his companions, Abram Henry, Tuck Crutchfield, Thimblerig, and the others. "You hear that, boys? San Antonio, that's where we're heading for, soon after Christmas."

When they finished drinking, Johnson asked David if he would like to meet some of the leaders of the town. "I sure would."

They left the others in the saloon, and turned up a side street to a stone-front cottage. Johnson knocked on the door; an old man opened it. He was pleased to meet David and, after a short conversation, asked him to wait until he could bring other men in to talk.

Ed Johnson used the opportunity to excuse himself. "I've got to see my gal Kate. When you finish talking, Davy, come down to the other end of the road, to the big log house. I'll be there with Kate."

The Nacogdoches leaders seemed to be divided as to the meaning of the victory at San Antonio; some believed that the revolution was over, others thought their troubles had just begun. "Whatever happens, Colonel Crockett, you can depend on it we're mighty glad to have a man of your talents in our midst. If the Mexican government attempted to enforce the decrees levied against us, life would become unbearable. We'd have to fight."

It was late when he left the stone-front house, and walked down the narrow road to the log house at the end. His hosts had passed around several bottles of Christmas liquors; his step was none too steady. He could hear music somewhere, a voice singing:

> " I'd like to have a little farm,
>   And leave such scenes as these,
>   Where I could live, without a care,
>   Completely at my ease.
>   I'd like to have a pleasant house
>   Upon my little farm,
>   Airy and cool in summer time,
>   In winter close and warm."

He suddenly realized the voice was Ed Johnson's. Crossing the front yard, he stumbled up on the porch. The music suddenly stopped, a door opened, and a candle fluttered in his face.

" It's Colonel Crockett, all right," shouted Ed. " Colonel, this is my Kate." A round-faced, brown-eyed girl smiled at him; her teeth were white in the candlelight.

" She's sure purty," said David.

While he waited out on the road for Ed to kiss her good night, he was thinking of other Christmas times, dark in the past, Polly, and the birth of Little Polly, and he felt so homesick he wanted to put his hands over his face and cry for a minute, but this was Texas, life was new all over again, and a man does not shed tears just because he's had a drink too many and gets to thinking of things.

During the midst of the Christmas festivities at the Johnson farmhouse, an Indian appeared one evening at the back door; he and Ed walked out to the barn, and a few minutes later the boy came back into the house, looking excited. But he said nothing, and the merriment went on as before.

Later in the evening he had an opportunity to talk alone with David. " That redskin was one of Sam Houston's friends. Houston is out rounding up all the tribes to take sides with

[311]

us, because his guess is the same as mine, that the Mexicans will be coming back. And the place they'll most likely strike first is San Antonio. You said that's where you were heading. Could you use another man? "

" Boy, if I could take my pick of any man in Texas to go with us to San Antonio, it would be you. When you want to start? "

" That's just it. I got to wait here till the next shipment of guns comes through. Can you wait till the end of the week? "

" We'll wait."

And so at the turn of the year, the party of thirteen men left Nacogdoches, a small crowd in front of a saloon firing pistols into the air to cheer them on their way. As they made the last turn at the end of the street, a small brown-eyed girl ran out after them, waving a kiss to Ed Johnson.

" She's sure a purty gal, Ed," said David. " If I had a gal that purty I'd think a long time about riding three hundred miles away from her."

" Hell," said Ed, " I got it to do."

" The fact of the matter is," spoke up the gambler, who was riding between them on a recently acquired white horse, " the fact of the matter is, the lad is doing this for her. All men who set out on daring missions, if this be a daring mission, do so because of a woman somewhere."

Ed looked at Thimblerig, coloring slightly.

David grunted. " What about me? The only woman I ever loved is dead."

" Dead or alive, it doesn't matter," declared Thimblerig. " You're still doing it for her."

" Hell," said David. " Didn't you ever hear of a man risking his life because his belly was empty, or a man facing death to do something because he knew damn well that something he was about to do was the right thing to do? "

[312]

"All balderdash," cried the gambler. "It's always a woman."

"You just lived too long in Mississippi," said David. "That's all's wrong with you."

"He's full of sh——" Ed added.

David turned on his horse, grinning at Thimblerig's saturnine face. "You been acting mighty damn cocky since you got into Texas, wearing that white Vicksburg hat set back on your head like a king."

"We'll have to cut him down a notch." Ed reached out suddenly and kicked Thimblerig's horse with his spur. The horse's sudden start threw the gambler almost out of his saddle; his prized hat sailed back into the muck beside the road. He had to turn and dismount to retrieve it, while David and Ed raced on ahead, laughing loudly.

Later the three were riding together again, but Thimblerig made no mention of the prank that had left one side of his white hat stained with mud. As if nothing had happened he began to talk casually of Natchez.

"That was some town before law and order came along and cleaned out the brothels. The strumpets used to run up and down the streets singing dirty songs, and if the men wouldn't stop to listen they'd sail after 'em. One day I saw a pack of women tear a man's clothes clean off him, and then scratch all the skin off his back and front. Growing up in that town, I couldn't've been much more than what I am."

David interrupted. "Don't go feeling sorry for yourself now, Thimblerig, just because Ed played a trick on you."

"Hell, no, I didn't mean no harm," said Ed. "You're a fine feller, Thimblerig. Why, look at me, I ain't so much either. You know what I used to do for a living till I got to working with Sam Houston? I used to hunt bees, yessir, hunt bees, trail 'em down in the woods and rob their hives, a dozen or so in a day."

[313]

"What did you do with all that honey?" asked Tuck Crutchfield, who had pulled his horse in beside him. "You can only eat so much honey."

"Wasn't the honey I was after. It was the wax. I sold it to the Mexicans. They used to pay a-plenty for it too. They use it in their churches, burning candles long as a man's arm."

"It was an honest living," said Thimblerig.

"Maybe the bees didn't think it was," replied Ed.

The weather was turning cold and sharp on the day they crossed the Trinity River and started plodding through a wilderness of canes that reminded David of some of the brakes he had seen in west Tennessee when he had first settled there. As they climbed into upland country again, the wind increased in velocity, and even the thick stands of loblolly pines offered little protection. Though it was still daylight, a long log house beside the road, with blue smoke flowing from its clay chimney, was too welcome a sight to pass.

Ed, riding in front, jumped off his horse and hurried up to the door to ask if the party might stay overnight.

"Look at that Ed," said Tuck, "always running in first to get in good with the womenfolks so's he can stand around and chew the fat while we have to take care of the horses."

Already, Ed was talking to somebody in the doorway; he turned and signaled that it was all right to stop. They all dismounted, began removing saddles and bags, and started rubbing down their horses. David's teeth were chattering from the cold.

"Guess we better put blankets on these horses tonight," he said to Thimblerig. "It's going to be a hard freeze."

A Negro boy had walked up behind them. "Mistah Johnson, he sent me out to take care of his horse fo' him."

"He did, did he?" replied Thimblerig quickly, then lowering his voice asked: "How did Mr. Johnson look? Is he turning pale?"

"Suh?"

"I say, is he turning pale? He didn't jump at you, did he?"

The Negro boy stared at the gambler, astounded. "No suh, he didn't jump at me, no suh. He was a little bit pale, though."

"Well, I'm warning you, boy, don't go any closer to Mr. Johnson than you have to. He might hurt you."

"Yes, suh. Is sump'n wrong with Mistah Johnson?"

Thimblerig stepped closer to the Negro. "That's what we're waiting to see. Mr. Johnson was just bitten by a mad dog."

David coughed, to cover a laugh, and flung an old blanket over his horse. The Negro had stepped around behind Ed's horse, which was shaking itself, impatiently waiting to be unsaddled.

"Now don't be afraid, boy," Thimblerig was saying, "Mr. Johnson hasn't bitten anybody yet."

At that moment, Ed came striding down from the house, stamping his feet to start the blood running. "Hey, boy," he shouted at the Negro, "I thought you told me you'd unsaddle my horse."

The boy stood staring at Johnson, his eyes turning in fright.

"Take off that saddle," Ed yelled.

The boy jumped, then ran wildly for the back door of the log house.

"Well, I'll be damned," said Ed. "Is he crazy?"

"Kind of touched, I reckon," said David, as he and Thimblerig started for the warm fireplace, leaving Ed to unsaddle his horse in the cold.

A man and his wife, their two daughters and one son lived in the pine-log house. The man and the son stood near the fireplace talking in friendly fashion with their guests, but a few minutes after David and Thimblerig entered, they saw the two girls run excitedly from the kitchen and peer out the door at Ed, who was still down by the road with his horse. Thimble-rig winked at David.

When Ed returned, the girls stood in the kitchen door staring at him; he looked up once or twice, smiling at them, whereupon they would retreat hastily.

"He thinks he's made a killing with two bashful females," whispered the gambler. David's mouth was twisting in a suppressed grin.

At the dinner table, the girls stayed as far distant from Ed as possible, pushing the food fearfully across the table to him. As soon as the dishes were cleared away and the men had returned to the blazing fireplace, Thimblerig and David stepped casually into the kitchen.

"Oh, sir," whispered one of the girls to the gambler, "is it true that the young man with you has been mad dog bit?"

Thimblerig nodded sadly. "But there is no certainty, Miss, that he will go mad. Whatever we do, we mustn't speak to him about it. It may pass."

"But you will"—said the mother in alarm—"you will guard him during the night?"

"Certainly, madam. My friend, Colonel Crockett, and I will sleep by the door with our pistols cocked."

Next morning as they were preparing to leave, Ed took it upon himself as usual to pay for the lodging. After all the horses were saddled and ready to go, he walked up to the front door. But the two girls who were standing there turned and ran inside, slamming the door behind them. Ed scratched his head in perplexity, then banged on the door. The girls' mother opened it slightly. "I want to pay for our lodging," he cried.

"Young man," screamed the woman, "if you will only leave the house at once, you are all welcome to your lodging."

As Ed turned away, his mouth half open in wonderment, the man of the house who had been informed of Thimblerig's

joke walked up to him and accepted the money without saying a word.

"What's wrong with your womenfolks?" Ed demanded.
"I'm not going to bite 'em."

"No, but they think you are," drawled Thimblerig. Sitting
on his horse, the gambler looked solemnly down at Ed, and
began turning the soiled brim of his white hat slowly in his
fingers.

Next day they crossed a wide stretch of open rolling plain;
the sharp wind was dying down, but clouds were thickening in
the wintry sky. By the time they reached Washington-on-the-
Brazos, a mixture of sleet and rain was falling.

"This'll probably last a week," said Ed. "Let's hole up in
the town till it fairs off again."

ANTONIO LOPEZ DE SANTA ANNA *was a crafty, charming,
bloodthirsty Mexican. His jaw was hard and cruel, his lips
thick, his skin sallow, but he had noble blood in his veins, and
eighteen years after he was born in Jalapa he was an officer
in a Vera Cruz regiment.*

*"Since my earliest years I found myself inclined to the
glorious career of arms, feeling a true vocation for it," said he.*

*During the years of his meteoric rise in the army he was
charged at various times with treason, robbery, seduction and
rape, but he made high marks in his studies, learned faster
than most how to kill scientifically, and by 1821 was commander of a district.*

*Before he was thirty he helped other generals win revolu-
tions, had begun laying plans to start a revolution of his own.
In 1829, he was the hero of all Mexico after he had demolished
Spain's army sent over to recapture the lost colony.*

*To gain more power he joined forces with Mexico's young
liberals who were struggling to set up a democratic govern-*

[317]

ment; he offered his army in support, urged representative government for all Mexican states, including Texas. For two years Antonio Lopez de Santa Anna rose higher and higher; even the suspicious Texans took a liking to the dramatic man of action. For a time his most loyal follower in Texas was none other than William Barrett Travis, later commander of the Alamo.

But under cover, the shifty Santa Anna was playing faction against faction; when he saw that reaction against liberalism was rising fast in Mexico, he set about lining up the leaders of the anti-democratic forces.

In 1834, backed by the spiritual prestige of the Church, the wealth of the conservative landholders, and the power of the army, he suddenly dissolved the Mexican Congress, personally locking the doors of the legislative halls.

A few weeks later, Stephen Austin was in one of Santa Anna's dungeons, and the Texans were beginning to rage. The more they raged, the harsher became Santa Anna's decrees. Fearing the loss of their liberty and their lands, the Texans took up arms in revolt.

"If the Americans do not beware, I shall march through their own country and plant the Mexican flag in Washington." Santa Anna was bluffing when he said that, but he knew he had to put down the Texas revolt immediately if his dictatorship was to stand. To his own people he began preaching the destiny of Mexican blood, unloosing a flood of propaganda about terroristic acts committed by the "execrable Texans" against innocent Mexicans. He quickly organized a Legion of Honor, dressed them in brilliant uniforms, decorated them with silver and gold crosses, then mustered a tough army of 6,000, and set out across the barren plains for Texas. Through bitter wind-driven snows he urged his army on, the dying falling by the way. Under burning suns, in blinding rains they marched. It was a heroic feat, inspired by a man of remarkable powers.

He called himself the Napoleon of the West.

And though he may not have been the military genius he

thought he was, Santa Anna was ahead of his time. He used the guise of liberalism to gain his ends, he knew the power of propaganda, he professed to believe in the destiny of his race, he posed as the Protector of the Church, he knew all the tricks of the theater, he concentrated his political enemies in dungeons, he despised democracy as a government for weaklings.
He was a full century ahead of his time.

★ 4 ★

Late in January, David Crockett and his twelve companions left Washington-on-the-Brazos, following leisurely down the course of the river to San Felipe de Austin, then turning straight west, crossed the Colorado and moved on to Gonzales, where they heard vague rumors of a Mexican army marching northward. The chairman of the local Safety Committee believed the rumors false, and informed them that most of the Texans in the San Antonio garrison had gone south to San Patricio, and might even march on into Mexico to Matamoros to check any attempted invasion by General Santa Anna.

At first, David and Ed Johnson talked of following after the army that was heading for Mexico, but they had traveled so far through a winter-bound country sparse of vegetation that their horses were showing signs of weariness.

"I guess we'd better go on to San Antonio," said David, "and see what's going to happen before we start off wild-goose chasing."

They were advised to stop at the house of Madam Candelaria in San Antonio. "She's a Mex," said the safety committeeman at Gonzales, "but she's a revolutionist. Hates the Mexican army because they killed her husband. Steve Austin and Sam Houston always stay at her house when they're down there, and most of the officers at the garrison eat at her table."

[319]

They started west again, across country that spread out before them in vast distances. A false February spring had come to the land; the air was warm and dry, the great ultramarine curve of the sky flawless of cloud traces. Nearing San Antonio, they rode through chaparral and mesquite; then twisting over a rise of hills, they saw the town before them, a flat-roofed collection of yellow gray adobe houses around the garrison and the plaza. Just across the river was the wall of the Mission del Alamo.

Along the streets of the town they saw many Mexicans in dirty, bright-colored clothes; finally one who understood English directed them to Madam Candelaria's house, a rambling adobe with a patio in the middle.

Madam Candelaria welcomed David in broken English. " We have expect you, Señor Crockett."

" Ma'm? " David looked closely at the brown-faced woman standing in the entranceway.

" Señor Bowie, he is here in my house, a sick man, very sick man. He receive message from north that you bring men this way."

" That a fact? And Jim Bowie's sick? Why, he's in command of the garrison, ain't he? "

" Si, he was in command."

David stood in the doorway, his fur cap in his hand. " Could I see him? "

She bowed, her stiff red skirt crackling as she turned for him to follow. " Come on, Ed," said David. " Let's go in and see him." Turning toward the others who still sat waiting on their horses, he cried: " Be back in a minute, boys, we're going in to see Jim Bowie."

Bowie was sitting up in a cot, a great towering man, with a heavy stubble of blue-black beard on his face, his powerful shoulders sunk in the pillows. He was coughing when David and Ed entered.

"This caballero," said Madam Candelaria, "is Señor Crockett."

"Hello, Davy Crockett." Bowie's voice was husky; his wide friendly mouth opened in a weak smile. David shook his hand; the grip was still firm.

"Mighty glad to know you, Jim Bowie. This boy with me is Ed Johnson, one of Sam Houston's boys."

"Seems to me I've seen you before, Ed. Over Nacogdoches way."

Ed grinned. "That's right. You was in that scrap we had over there with the Mexican garrison sometime back."

"Sure was. I knowed I'd seen you." Bowie started coughing again, almost choking before he could stop. "Got it bad in my chest. Fell off a horse last month and hurt my side. Gets worse. I just turned my command over to Bill Travis yesterday, he come riding in the day before, and I figured he ought to take charge long's I'm laid up. He'll sure be glad to see you two."

"We got eleven others with us."

Bowie's feverish eyes blinked. "Sounds good. We only got about a hundred men here now, most the rest went gallivanting off toward Mexico. Bunch of damn fools."

When they left Bowie, they found Madam Candelaria waiting outside the room. "Señor Crockett, I have place for you and your friend to stay, but not enough places for others. They will stay in *barracas*, no?"

"I guess they'll have to, madam, and thank you right much for fixing a place for Ed and me."

They rode their horses on through the streets to the plaza, and up to the garrison where a small group of Texans were waving their hats, cheering. "Hiya-ah-ah! Davy Crockett!" somebody yelled. From a low window a tall young man had dropped down to the ground and was walking across the plaza. He was less than thirty, this young man; he wore a close-

[321]

fitting military coat, with a high collar decorated with a single star; his face was thin, his forehead high and round with a tuft of reddish hair waved back. His eyes set close together looked out upon the world as if he were always amused at what he saw. He walked straight up to David's horse, his tall boots clinking on the smooth stones, and saluted him. "Colonel William B. Travis, sir, at your service."

David slid off the horse and thrust out his hand. Men were running out of the garrison, surrounding the horsemen.

"David Crockett, sir, at *your* service."

The crowd began cheering.

Travis said softly: "They'll expect a speech; some of them are Tennessee men, and know your reputation."

"Ah ——" David waved his hand deprecatingly.

"A speech, a speech," somebody shouted.

"Just a few words," said Travis, smiling. "I offer you a command here. You can make a speech of acceptance."

"Here's a box for you," a soldier said, pushing one forward.

David stepped upon the box, grinning, shaking his head. "Seems like I can't go no place, even to the wilds of Texas, 'thout making a speech." He threw his head back. "Fellow citizens ——" They broke into cheers again. "Fellow citizens, we've come out to your Texas country to offer our help, if you need it. All we hope is that you'll think of each one of us as just one of yourselves. Colonel Travis here is offering me a command. Well, all I want to be is just a high Private like the rest of you. We're with you from now on in the cause of liberty!' "

"Hurrah for Private Crockett!" a man shouted, as David and Travis started walking toward the garrison.

Arrangements were soon made for quartering the new arrivals. Travis was pleased to learn that David and Ed were staying at Madam Candelaria's, as he had a room there also, adjoining Jim Bowie's.

[322]

"Jim is right bad off," said Travis, "and he's worrying too much about the expedition that went south. We haven't heard news from them for over a week."

"You think a Mexican army will try to come back here?"

"They're bound to. Maybe soon, maybe not till summer. If they should come now, with the garrison almost empty, we'd be in some trouble, believe me."

Late in the evening, Travis walked with David around the town. The sky was still clear as it had been for several days, and pale stars were visible in the early twilight. They walked down to the San Antonio River, facing the deserted Alamo mission; they stepped out on a narrow bridge that led across toward it. "If we should be attacked," said Travis, "we'd have to give up the garrison and move to the Alamo. Even there, we'd be so short of men —— Here's the way things are, Colonel Crockett, there're plenty of men in Texas willing to fight for freedom, plenty of men. But they're all scattered out. Before Bowie or I got here, that Scotsman, Grant, talked the San Antonio boys into heading for Mexico City. He took the best men and most of the supplies. He's land conquering crazy, Grant is. Then there's a good bunch of boys down at Goliad under Colonel Fannin. And Sam Houston is back north someplace trying to gather another army together. There are four armies, four small armies ready to fight for Texas, but each one too weak in itself. If we were all together now ——"

David shook his head. "Sounds like Congress to me, just like Andy Jackson and the Congress."

As they walked back into the town, they saw fires burning in the middle of the plaza, bright bonfires flickering shadows against the mud walls of the buildings.

"What are they for, the fires?" asked David.

Travis chuckled, looking at David. "Oh, some of my boys thought we ought to celebrate your arrival."

[323]

At Madam Candelaria's a long table of food was waiting for them. Jim Bowie, propped up by pillows, sat at the head. Behind him, a big woodfire was crackling in the fireplace.

Bowie introduced David to his physician, Dr. John Sutherland, a black-bearded man who shook his head as if to say there was nothing to be done about such a mountain of a patient as Jim Bowie. There was also a Lieutenant Dickinson who had offered his services to the garrison; he had been in the United States army before moving his family to Texas.

The dinner was scarcely begun before Madam Candelaria interrupted Colonel Travis by tapping him on the shoulder, then whispering in his ear. Travis excused himself and went out of the room. David was sampling the strange-flavored liquor served by the hostess when Travis came back, his forehead wrinkled in a frown.

Jim Bowie was eating slowly; he watched Travis' face anxiously. " News? "

" Bad news," said Travis.

" From where? "

" Captain Juan Seguin brought it."

" Seguin, eh? What'd he say? "

" Says his cousin just got into town with a report that General Santa Anna and a big army were crossing the Rio Grande a week ago."

" Just crazy Mex talk, maybe."

" Maybe. But I told Seguin to go bring the boy here to my room. We'll hear what he's got to say."

Bowie, Dickinson, and David were with Travis in his room when the Mexicans arrived. Seguin, a slender olive-skinned man, entered first, the boy following him. " Señors, my cousin, Blaz Herrera. He, too, is a revolutionist against the government of Santa Anna, and has no reason to tell untruths."

Travis spoke first: " Just what did you see, Herrera? "

The boy crumpled his straw hat in one hand, gesticulating

with the other. " A great army, Señors, many men, crossing the Rio Grande."

" How many men? " asked Bowie.

Herrera opened his hands five times. " This many hundred, I think."

Travis whistled shrilly through his teeth. " Impossible! "

Herrera shrugged. " The horsemen come first. Maybe one, two thousand."

" Just when was this? "

" Four, five days ago."

Bowie was coughing again, his face turning purplish with fever. " How did you happen to be there, on the Rio Grande? And why did you come here so quick? "

Juan Seguin spoke: " I sent him there, Señors, myself. There has been much fear among Mexicans here. Many revolutionists here, afraid of Santa Anna."

They talked for some time, the six men; Bowie finally became so exhausted from his coughing that he crept away to bed. Then Travis dismissed the two Mexicans, thanking them for their information. " I still don't know whether to believe the boy or not. He might have seen a hundred Mexicans on a scout, and magnified them to five thousand. If such a large army was coming up from Mexico, Fannin's scouts or some of the boys to the south ought to be riding in here to tell us about it."

The next day was Sunday, and at dawn a cold wet norther swept suddenly across the town, the wind whistling around the corners of the buildings, sheets of rain beating against the adobe walls, streaking them with ugly stains. Madam Candelaria kept blazing fires going in the house all day.

The rain fell harder during the night, and Monday morning the streets were cut with little gulleys; the San Antonio River was flowing wildly over the edges of its banks, but the blow was over, and the sun was out warm again in the fleckless blue sky.

David walked down to the garrison to see his boys. He expected them to be excited about the rumors of the approaching Mexican army. Instead Tuck Crutchfield and Thimblerig were debating with Preacher Boone about the moral aspects of Mexican fandangos. "They're starting one this evening," said Tuck. "Preacher Boone here says fandangos are nothing but drinking and whoring parties. Thimblerig and me claim they're just plain fiddling parties like we have to home, 'cept a little different because they're Mexican."

Preacher Boone shook a forefinger under Tuck's nose. "You won't catch me messing around with them sinful Mexicans."

The fandango was in full force by dark, shouts and songs and music coming from a dozen houses across the plaza from the garrison.

After dining together at Madam Candelaria's, David and Travis saddled their horses and went for a ride south and west of the town, climbing to the top of a slope about a mile and a half away. Here they could see for some distance in all directions. In the starlight the chaparral and mesquite bushes were dark patches against the earth.

"I guess it was just another Mex fairy tale," said Travis.

They rode back into town slowly, their horses slipping and stumbling on the muddy trail. Guitar music and laughter rang up and down the streets of the town. "Let's turn in this place," said Travis, "and see how the fandango is going."

It was a low-roofed building with an elaborate stairway curving up out of a room filled with men and women. Dense smoke from the long candles swirled in the air.

"There's a couple of my boys," said David. Tuck Crutchfield and Thimblerig, with two Mexican girls, were sitting on a bench across the room. Thimblerig had one arm around his girl, and he was explaining his gambling tricks to her with the other. Tuck's girl was in his lap; she was trying to keep him from biting her ear.

Travis tossed a coin to a fat Indian woman sitting in a corner, and told her in Spanish to bring him a bottle of pulque. For a long time they sat drinking in the warm room, watching the merriment. "This pulque stuff has even got Arkansas corn liquor beat," said David. "Makes you wild. Look at those Mexicans dancing over there."

"It's strong stuff," Travis agreed. "They know how to use it in the Mexican army too. It makes them fight like crazy bobcats."

Through the smoke haze, David saw Tuck Crutchfield swinging his girl up to his shoulder; she was sitting there, kicking him with her heels, pulling his hair, but Tuck was carrying her up the stairway, and she stopped screaming when they disappeared through a door.

Travis had become moody and silent; after a while he asked David if he would ride with him around the town again. "I can't get the thing out of my mind, and we don't have a single scout out on the plains."

Sleepy as he was, David agreed to go; they went outside to their horses and started east on the Gonzales road, then turned back and rode up the same slope where they had been earlier in the night. On the way up a shadowy figure darted out of the mesquite. Travis shouted a command to halt; there was a sound of running feet, then silence. "Damned queer," said Travis. But up on the top of the slope, all was quiet as before.

As they turned back slowly toward the town the sky was growing pink in the east; it was dawn when they rode into the outskirts. The music and the laughter had ended; the fandango was over.

But there were Mexicans in the streets. They passed two

adobes in succession where household goods were being loaded into carts.

Abruptly Travis stopped his horse. " Colonel Crockett, I been thinking that something was wrong. Now I know it. In the first place, the morning after a fandango you'd ordinarily never see a Mexican awake until the sun was well up. In the second place, look down that side street to your left. Every Mexican down there is moving out."

Men and women with bundles on their shoulders were scurrying across the plaza; another cart rolled by, piled high with bedding.

" Say, boy," Travis shouted to the driver. " Where you going? "

The boy looked frightened, then made a sign as if to say he did not understand English.

Travis' jaw tightened, his eyes met David's. " What do you think? " he asked quietly.

" They must know something we don't know," replied David.

" We'll soon find out what it is. You go wake up the garrison. I'll ride down to Juan Seguin's place. He'll know what's up, if anybody does."

⋆ 5 ⋆

By the time Travis returned to the garrison with Juan Seguin, David had all the men out of their bunks; a sleepy-eyed lot they were too, from dancing and drinking at the fandango most of the night.

Travis ordered them to get their rifles and assemble on the civil plaza immediately. As soon as they formed ranks, he faced them on his horse. " Men," he cried, " I think there is no longer any doubt that a Mexican army is somewhere in the neighborhood. How many there are, or how far away they are, we don't know. But you only have to look around you at the townspeople moving out of here with their goods to guess what's coming. Your guess is as good as mine. First, I want about eight scouts, good horsemen. You, Doc Sutherland, and Porter and Hensley, you all have horses. Doc, you pick five other men with horses, and ride out on all trails. If any of you see anything that looks like an army, whip your horses to a lather coming back into town. Get going. Now you others, fill your powder horns full and form squads to stand guard on the streets leading out of town. Stop any wagon or anybody on foot trying to leave. Bring them back here to the garrison for questioning."

In a few minutes, a dozen frightened Mexican citizens were in the garrison, where Travis shouted questions at them. All of them claimed they knew nothing of any invasion; to a man they replied that they were moving out into the countryside to begin their spring plowing.

But shortly after nine o'clock a horseman, one of the scouts, was galloping madly across the plaza. He was off his horse before it stopped running. "Colonel Travis," he shouted through the open window, "there's a troop of Mexican cavalry in Leon!"

Travis climbed out of the window, David at his side. "Coming this way?"

"They're close to the village, looked like they was getting ready to start. I'd say they'd spent the night there."

Travis looked at David; his eyes still held the half-humorous quality that always seemed to lurk in them. "May or may not be an advance guard. Anyway we'd better act fast. Colonel Crockett, get one of your boys up the tower of that church across the plaza, tell him to ring the bell if he sees troops moving. Then come on down to Jim Bowie's room; we're going to hold a council of war." He turned and called to

Lieutenant Dickinson, and they started down the street toward Madam Candelaria's house.

David saw Abram Henry out on the plaza; he walked over toward him. "Well, Abram, looks like we rode into something when we came here."

"More exciting than politicking, ain't it?"

"Colonel Travis asked me to send a man up on the church tower. You still got a good eye, haven't you?"

Abram nodded, and started for the church.

"Pull that bell rope hard now, if you see anything a-tall," David called after him.

The council of war was brief. Acting on Jim Bowie's suggestion, Travis ordered immediate evacuation of the garrison to the Alamo mission. He also informed the Mexican citizens that anybody could now leave the city; any who wished to do so were invited to join the Texans in the Alamo.

Swirling waters from the recent rains still raced down the bed of the San Antonio River. The narrow bridge was too flimsy for transporting the heavy cannon and other supplies, but above the town was a wide ford which could be crossed with some difficulty.

Travis and Dickinson proceeded immediately to the Alamo, leaving David to command the garrison until all supplies and men were moved. Near noontime, a wagon crossed the plaza. In it were Madam Candelaria, her Negro servant, and Jim Bowie, who was sitting behind them in a big chair. David rode his horse alongside, following down the street and across the ford. "Keep your feet dry, Jim," he shouted to Bowie, then turned back to the plaza.

He had scarcely reached the garrison when the church bell began clanging. Cupping his hands, he shouted to the few men left in the building: "Hurry up, boys, they're coming!" For another minute the bell rang loudly, then he saw Abram Henry running across the plaza toward him. "Goddammit,

Davy," shouted the freckle-faced Abram, "they's a hundred million of them Mexicans coming across the plain!"

"All right, all right, get going for that Alamo. Grab onto that supply wagon."

David trotted his horse up and down, up and down. The plaza was almost deserted now, but up the side streets there were still plenty of Mexican townspeople thrusting their heads out of windows like so many tree squirrels. The last supply wagon was pulling out of the garrison.

From the west he heard drumming hoofs; in a moment a horseman riding full speed was on the plaza. It was Doc Sutherland, one of the scouts. The man's black beard was matted with red mud, his right trouser leg was ripped open at the knee.

"Over a thousand men out there," Sutherland gasped. "I was within a few yards of them. They saw me, waved their swords at me, but didn't fire. They're on good mounts, and well armed, some cannon. In new uniforms, everything all polished up. They look like they mean business."

"What happened to you?" David reached out and touched Sutherland's bloody knee.

"My horse slipped, in the mud."

"Well, the men are all cleared out to the Alamo now. Let's get over there and give your report to Travis."

They turned their horses down the street, galloping. Crossing the ford they climbed up toward the Alamo, meeting two horsemen coming down. David had seen them around the garrison, but had not learned their names.

One of them spoke to Sutherland. "Say, Doc, you're not going up to that Alamo, are you?"

"Sure we are. Aren't you coming back?"

"No sirree, there's not enough men up there to hold the place. A good Mexican army could take it in half an hour. You all better come go with us to Gonzales."

"No, thanks," replied Sutherland. "I've got a report to make to Colonel Travis."

The man laughed. "We'll wait for you a piece down the road. You all both better leave out of here while you can."

David and Sutherland urged their horses across a narrow brook, then turned up toward the low south wall and the entrance gate where two cannon had already been set up. All along the outside of the wall was a dry ditch. To the right of the gate a high stockade stretched across to the side of the church.

"Look," cried Sutherland, "on top of the church!"

"A flag."

The red, white, and green flag with its two stars flapped slowly in the noonday breeze.

Inside the walls, everything was in chaos. But they found Travis calmly seated at a table in one of the old mission cells; he was writing and did not look up until he had finished and signed his name.

Sutherland immediately gave his report of the approaching army. Travis did not appear to be surprised. "Over a thousand," he said, "and we've only about one hundred and fifty." He turned to David. "Are you and your men staying with us?"

"Give us a position to defend. We'll stay."

"The south wall is yours, the stockade," Travis replied shortly. "Now, Doc, how is that knee of yours, can you stand a ride to Gonzales?"

"All I need is a fresh horse."

"You'll find one in the pen out back of the barracks. I want you to take this message to the Gonzales Safety Committee, tell them we'll need every man they can send. Keep your eyes open, there may be some Mex cavalry north of the river. Good luck."

Folding the message into his shirt pocket, Sutherland limped

[332]

out of the room; in a few moments they heard his horse galloping out through the gate. Travis stood up, pulling at the tuft of hair on his forehead. " Maybe I shouldn't have sent Sutherland. Doc Pollard's been feeling puny, and we may need two doctors before we're done here." He stretched his long wiry arms. " Now I got to pick a man to ride to Goliad. That'll be a dangerous ride. Juan Seguin told me a while ago he had information that General Santa Anna himself was directing the army; if that's so, there'll be Mex reinforcements scattered all along the way between here and Goliad. I need a man who knows the country. Who would you say, Colonel Crockett? "

" Only one of my men knows this country, that's young Ed Johnson."

" Ed Johnson? Could you send him in here? "

" Sure, I'll go round up my men now." David started out the door.

" Wait a minute." Travis walked around the table, and caught David's arm. " Maybe you ought to ask your men if they want to stay. They could get away to the northeast now. We may be able to hold out until help comes, but we've no food supplies except a few bushels of corn and about twenty cows we drove in off the road."

David grinned. " I'm about twicet as old as you, Bill Travis, and I been in lot tighter places than this. My boys will stay."

He stepped out into the long mission plaza, and walked around the grounds, getting the lay of the land. The mission was a rectangle, surrounded by thick adobe walls. Down the middle was a row of monks' cells converted into barracks, and behind them were the cattle and horse pens. Along the west wall was a row of sheds, and in the two northwest rooms Travis and Bowie had set up headquarters. Diagonally across from them in the southeast corner was the church, built in the form of a cross, the tallest structure on the grounds. The

[333]

stockade ran along its south side west to the entrance gate, and it was this sector which had been assigned to David and his twelve men.

Just inside the gate, the supplies and cannon had been piled together, and he found Jim Bowie, still in his chair, directing the distribution. David told him that Travis had assigned the stockade to him.

"Good," said Bowie. "If things go bad, that corner and the church will be our best position. Take them fourteen small cannon, and stick 'em all over the walls. We got plenty ammunition for them small ones; not so much is left for the big ones."

In a few minutes, David found all his men, and ordered them to gather in front of the church. He sent Ed Johnson to see Travis, then began directing the setting up of the cannon.

With Tuck Crutchfield and two others, David climbed to the top of the high church wall. They were beginning to raise the first cannon with ropes when they heard shouts coming across the river from the town.

"Hey," cried Tuck, spitting out his chew of tobacco. "Look across there, Davy."

Down the slope west of San Antonio, filed an apparently endless line of cavalry, the men in bright blues and scarlets, their sabers and rifles glinting in the sunlight. Rolling along beside them were the gun carriages.

Inside the Alamo, men were climbing up on the walls to see, and a sudden silence fell over the place as they watched this enemy come nearer and nearer, twisting and turning into the town where the shouts of the Mexican citizens joined those of the soldiers.

David turned his head and looked along the church wall at his men. All of them were there except Ed Johnson. "Boys," he said quietly, "if you leave now, you could get back to

Gonzales safe enough. Anybody want to go?" Nobody said a word. Tuck Crutchfield wiped the tobacco juice off his curly moustache, and bit a fresh chew from his twist. Abram Henry was scratching his long freckled nose. Preacher Boone was shading his old eyes to see better. Thimblerig was flapping a piece of lead from one hand to the other, his face empty of expression.

In a few minutes they saw a lone horseman coming slowly down the road to the ford, a white flag flying over his head. Immediately, Travis, who was standing at the entrance gate, sent out two men to meet the Mexican. The horses met; then the Texans turned and came riding back full speed. David dropped off the wall, and started over toward the gate, his men following him.

While all the men gathered near, Travis unfolded the written message sent by the Mexicans. The writing was in Spanish; he moved his lips silently, leaned over to Jim Bowie, pointing at a word, then he stood up straight, and translated aloud: "Surrender arms and retire under oath not to take them up again against Mexico. Colonel Don Juan Almonte."

The men could hear each other breathe; there was no other sound. "All right," said Travis sternly. "You heard it. What's your answer?"

"Tell 'em to go to hell," said Jim Bowie.

"Fire off that cannon, Hensley. Let that be an answer."

The men had their hats off, waving them, cheering until the cannon boomed; there was the crash of a shell striking just across the river into the brush, and then the echo rolling back from the town.

A few minutes later Mexican cavalry were riding in parade formation up and down the front street, flying blood-red flags. But most of the men inside the walls were too busy setting up cannon and storing ammunition to give much attention to the display.

[335]

"In case you don't know," said Travis, who had walked back with David and Ed Johnson to the church, "those red flags mean no quarter."

"Nobody aims to surrender anyhow," replied David. "What about Ed? You going to send him to Goliad?"

"Soon as it turns dark. He wouldn't have a chance getting through to the south by daylight."

As soon as David and his men finished setting up their cannon, they moved over to the north and west walls to help the others throw up earth mounds, a task made necessary because of the absence of loopholes in the thick mission walls. Only in the stockade had holes been cut; along the other walls the defenders would have to stand on the mounds and fire over the top. By dusk, they had several embankments up, and David hurried over to Travis' headquarters to see Ed Johnson off.

Ed had picked the best horse from the corral back of the barracks, and was so excited he could hardly wait for the twilight to deepen. Travis repeated his instructions several times. "If we can get Fannin's men and guns over here, we got a good chance to lick those rascals, so don't you take any chances getting through."

Darkness was almost complete except for a glow in the western sky. Stars were beginning to flicker overhead. They watched Ed ride slowly along the outside of the south wall straight east along the river, and then he was lost in the night.

Ten minutes later, the sounds of a horse coming from the direction in which Ed had gone brought David and Travis back to the gate.

"Halloa," the horseman called softly.

"That you, Ed?" David answered.

"I'm James Bonham."

"James Bonham," said Travis. "I know him. Open the gate."

[336]

Bonham let out a long sigh of relief before he climbed off his horse. " Things sure have happened around here since I left last week. I was way down the river when I heard your cannon go off this afternoon, and figured something was happening. Soon as I started riding I kept running into marching Mexicans. They're thick as flies on a dead horse. I met Ed Johnson back there, and he told me where you boys were. I just now rode through a camp of Mex women, camp followers."

" So they've already brought up their women? They must aim to stay in Texas a long time."

Bonham laughed. " I've heard Santa Anna treats his soldiers right. The men loafing around had plenty chances to pick me off. I rode right through their women's camp before I knew where I was. But I guess they figured they'd take me after I got in here. They're acting mighty cocky."

David suddenly realized that his head was nodding forward all the time Bonham was talking. He was sleepy as a bear in January; he hadn't been stretched out for a rest for two days now.

But Travis was speaking again: " Colonel Crockett, could you take your men outside and tear down those shacks on the southeast corner? We'll need the wood for cooking, and tonight may be our last chance to get them."

While they were knocking down the old buildings, a small force of Mexicans opened fire on them from the river bank, but the shots went wild. They carried the dry wood back inside the walls as quickly as possible; shortly afterwards a larger body of the enemy crept closer, hiding in the brush along the ditches outside. There was intermittent firing all through the night, and David's eyes were red and swollen before the dawn broke and the Mexican snipers finally retreated.

★ 6 ★

Breakfast was prepared by Madam Candelaria and the wife of Lieutenant Dickinson, the only women in the mission. " You boys had better eat these johnny-cakes slowly," warned Mrs. Dickinson. " We've used our last pound of meal."

They had set up a temporary kitchen in that part of the church which was without a roof; powder and lead were stored under an adjoining shed. Nearby the pallets of David's " Tennesseans " were laid out, though as yet they had scarcely made use of them.

David felt much better after breakfast. He borrowed a chew of tobacco from Tuck Crutchfield, and proceeded to climb up to the top of the church. As he swung his leg over the parapet, a rifle cracked and a slug whistled over his head; he ducked hastily back to the ground.

" Guess I'll use the loopholes from now on. I'm afraid the cannon we put up there won't do us much good without some barricades." He grinned at Preacher Boone, who had got out his scarred fiddle and was sitting in the sunshine, plucking at the strings.

Through a loophole, he could see the enemy on the river bank, less than four hundred yards away, busily erecting batteries, drawing up cannon, and piling rocks and bags of sand in strategic positions.

The morning passed quietly, with only an occasional spat of a rifle as the watchful men inside the walls took advantage of any Mexican who carelessly exposed himself to their deadly marksmanship.

But in the afternoon, the Mexican cannon along the river opened a fierce bombardment against the west wall. The balls thudded against the thick adobe, throwing up a fine yellow dust.

Travis ordered the six cannon along that side to reply, and for several seconds echoes and re-echoes rumbled over the smoke-filled grounds. Then there was a period of quiet that was nerve-wracking. Late in the afternoon the Mexicans fired spasmodically, causing little damage.

Against orders, Thimblerig climbed to the top of the church, and was firing away at a detachment of snipers in a nearby ditch, when David ordered him down. Before he could obey, he was hit; blood was flowing from his shirt when he stumbled to the earth, David at his side.

"You damn fool, what was you doing up there?"

"I been wasting too much lead on the rascals. I figured if I got up high enough they couldn't duck down on me."

Ripping his shirt open, David found the wound, the bullet still embedded in the soft flesh. "Just a glancing hit, otherwise you'd be a dead man, Thimblerig." In a few seconds he had the bullet out with his knife. "Here, take it and make a watch charm."

"Lead's too scarce around here for making watch charms. I'll fire it back at 'em."

Mrs. Dickinson had brought a gourdful of water and started washing the wound with strong lye soap. The gambler's jaw tightened from pain, but he said nothing.

At dusk while the Mexicans were quiet, the hunter's horn, which Travis was using as a bugle, sounded hoarsely, and those men who were not on guard at assigned posts went to the plaza in front of the commander's headquarters.

On the hard-packed earth near the shed, Jim Bowie sat in his big chair, his face pale against the darkening sky. Colonel Travis, standing beside him, held a long sheet of paper in his hand. "I wanted you men to hear this," he said. "It's another message I'm sending off to Goliad, in case Doc Sutherland didn't get through." He unfolded the paper. "To the people

[339]

of Texas and all Americans in the world. Fellow citizens and compatriots, I am besieged by a thousand or more Mexicans. I have sustained a continual bombardment for twenty-four hours and have not lost a man. The enemy has demanded a surrender at discretion, otherwise, the garrison are to be put to the sword if the fort is taken. I have answered the demand with a cannon shot and our flag still waves proudly from the walls. I shall never surrender or retreat. I call upon you in the name of liberty, of patriotism, and everything dear to the American character, to come to our aid with all despatch. The enemy is receiving re-inforcements daily and will no doubt increase to three or four thousand in four or five days. If this call is neglected, I am determined to sustain myself as long as possible and die like a soldier who never forgets what is due to his own honor and that of his country. Victory or death!"

Shouts resounded within the walls. Jim Bowie was nodding his great shaggy head. "These are my words," said Travis. "Victory or death. Do all agree?"

There was no dissent. "Victory or death," David whispered to himself as he turned back to the stockade. He had a queer cold feeling in his stomach.

Jim Bonham had volunteered to take the letter through to Gonzales. He rode out into the darkness on the big dun-colored horse on which he had entered the Alamo the evening before.

After a supper of boiled beef, David called his men for a short council in front of the church. "We all got to have more sleep tonight. Most of us been on our feet for three days. So I'm dividing you up into two watches, six to a watch, and we'll take six-hour turns day and night from now on. But if the Mexicans come too close, everybody will have to take positions."

Travis passed by a few minutes afterwards for a hasty glance at the inside of the church. " Colonel Crockett," he said quietly when no one was in earshot, "things are looking black. Juan Seguin made his way through the lines today and came back with the news that two or three thousand Mexicans under Santa Anna himself are coming to join Almonte. We may have three or four days' respite until the Mexican armies are consolidated, but then hell will pop. We'd need a full thousand men to hold the north and west walls. We may have to give way and fall back to this corner and the church. And it ought to be better fortified than it is."

" We could sandbag it," suggested David.

" That's what it'll take. Better start on that job first thing in the morning. I think there's plenty of canvas up in one of the west sheds." He turned abruptly and walked away in the darkness.

At dawn, the enemy began bombarding the west wall again. At the same time they started moving more cannon to the north, and a large detachment of cavalry crossed the river and established a camp on the hills to the east, blocking the road to Gonzales.

" Boys," said David, as they worked away at filling the hastily improvised bags with earth scraped from the plaza, " they're trying to surround us. But if we can pile up enough sandbags they'll never be able to blow us out of here."

Toward evening they were resting a few minutes from the strenuous labor of digging and stacking, but Abram Henry, on guard at the stockade, interrupted their brief leisure by announcing that some Mexicans were dragging a cannon out of a ditch a few yards away. Every man ran to a loophole, ready to fire.

But the Mexicans were concealed by a low hillock over which the cannon barrel pointed. David grabbed up his Philadelphia rifle and called to Tuck Crutchfield to follow him; they scaled the church wall to the parapet where Thimblerig had received his wound. Crouching low, they both fired simultaneously, then swung behind the wall, clinging with their fingers. They had to drop their rifles below for reloading; then armed once more they rose and picked off two more Mexicans. Before nightfall, the cannon was surrounded by a dead crew. After dark, David and four of his men crept out through the gate and rolled the gun inside, their first spoils of war.

Some time during the night, Juan Seguin left for Goliad to urge Colonel Fannin to hasten his march. Travis was taking no chances on Ed Johnson's possible failure to reach the garrison; he figured that Seguin, being a Mexican, would have a better chance to escape the vigilant Santa Anna.

" I'll bet Ed makes it though," David said. " He'll be riding back in here first thing you know."

In the morning he went around to see Jim Bowie; the old fighter was flat on his back in the shed next to Travis' office, his eyes sunk in his pale face. He was too weak to talk. Madam Candelaria, who watched after him every spare moment, brought him some corn gruel, but he couldn't keep it on his stomach.

During the day the cannonading continued with little damage against the low west wall; all was quiet along the south side. When darkness fell, smoky clouds obscured the stars, and the Tennesseans sat along the stockade listening for any suspicious sounds from outside.

" Has anybody," asked Abram, " noticed them pecan trees over to the east? Plenty nuts down there, I'll bet you. I'm getting kind of tired of boiled corn and roasted corn and fried corn."

" Me, too," said Tuck. " Let's go out and get them pecans. I'm tired setting around chewing corn, waiting for them Mexicans to do something."

[342]

David had already sensed their restlessness; a forage outside was what they needed, some action. And it was dark enough tonight to take chances. " All right, half of us will go; we'll give the whippoorwill signal every once in a while so you boys will know where we are."

He took Abram and Tuck and two others, and led the way down into the muddy ditch just outside the stockade. Some yards to the east they ran into a noise-crackling nest of dried brush, and all ducked down for a minute to listen. But nothing happened. At the edge of a small creek they found several pecan trees; they stuffed their pockets quickly, gathering the nuts from the ground.

He sat down beside Tuck for a moment in the sand beside the creek where the water gurgled quietly.

" I'd sure like to be back home right now," whispered Tuck. " It'd be about time to start plowing."

" Yeah. The ground smells good too, don't it, when you first plow it up in the spring. But I reckon we'll have us big farms around here soon as we clear out these Mexicans."

" We could get away right now if we kept heading east," said Tuck. " Be back in Tennessee in a month or two."

" You want to go, Tuck? "

David could hear him scratching his long moustache. " Hell, no. Santy Anny can't chase me away."

They were starting back toward the mission when a snapping twig far to the left brought them to a sudden halt. Abram Henry raised his rifle and fired into a clump of shrubs before David could stop him.

" Crazy fool! Now, we'll all have to run."

Rifles cracked out in the darkness as they dropped down into the ditch.

" Let's give it back to 'em," cried Tuck.

They emptied their rifles into the shrubs, and then stooping low, ran for the mission gate. David whistled a whippoorwill

[343]

call as they passed the stockade, and Preacher Boone met them at the gate, his vein-corded hands trembling violently. " Everybody safe? " he asked anxiously. David counted heads quickly. " Not a scratch. Here, have some pecans, Preacher Boone."

After serving his watch during the first part of the night, he dropped off to a sound sleep at midnight on his hard pallet, but it was still dark when Abram woke him. " Davy, something's up out there. It's too damn dark to see what. We been taking luck shots, but they won't go away." Rubbing his sleep-filled eyes, David walked to the first loophole. In the cloud-blanketed darkness he could see nothing, but there were sounds of metal knocking against wood, and low voices.

" We'll fix up a torch, and fling it over the stockade far as we can. Maybe then we can see what's what."

When the torch of dry wood and old cloths was lighted and flung over the barrier, they could see plainly, for an instant, a large group of the enemy, building a crude bridge over the second ditch. The sudden flare of light took them completely by surprise; they stood stock still while a half dozen charges of lead were blown into their midst. For an hour David and his men continued to pour bullets in that direction.

The sun rose over a half completed bridge and a dozen bodies heaped near the same hummock where still lay the others who had died beside the cannon.

Somebody said it was Saturday, as if the day of the week mattered. Before noon of that day, the Mexican mortars raised their range and bombs were bursting inside the Alamo, narrowly missing a dozen Texans before they learned the trick of walking close to the walls instead of in the open plaza. The Mexicans also dammed the stream which flowed through the grounds, cutting off the water supply, but Travis remedied that by assigning a crew to dig a well.

In the afternoon cannon balls were falling inside the churchyard, a few feet from the stockade, but no one was injured.

[344]

"Reminds me of Congress," David said to Mrs. Dickinson who was boiling corn behind the row of sandbags. "A lot of loud noise but it don't amount to much."

Saturday night rain fell, raw and drizzling, but Sunday morning was cloudless and still, the sun warm. There was an unpleasant odor near the stockade, the smell of decaying flesh. Buzzards were wheeling in the blue sky.

"We ought to go out there and throw some dirt over them dead Mexicans," David said to Thimblerig.

"And get shot for our pains? One ball in my chest is enough for me, thank you."

During the day they watched the enemy move another line of cannon a hundred yards nearer, but there was nothing they could do to stop them.

That night, two frightened settlers reached the mission, and were admitted to Travis' headquarters. One of them had lost his wife and child in a flooded stream while trying to escape Santa Anna's army. They told incoherent stories of terror-stricken Texans, fleeing toward the north.

Monday the temperature dropped, but the sun's rays were warm, and the circling buzzards were flying lower over the ditches outside. In the evening they were making quick landings on the ground, flying away when a cannon exploded a charge. Thimblerig was watching them through a loophole, fascinated by their skill at gliding, when David walked up, holding his nose. "By God, we're going to throw some dirt over those dead men out there tonight."

Thimblerig nodded; he was playing with a long knife.

"That's a Bowie knife, ain't it? Looks like the one Jim Bowie carries."

"That's what they call it. I had it in my sack. Thought I might better get it out and have it handy. Can't ever tell when I may need it."

"You could tickle a feller's ribs a long time with that afore you'd make him laugh. I never could stand the idea of a sharp point of iron touching my insides." He scratched the stiff beard that had grown out on his face. " It don't bother me much now though. It's funny, how a man can get used to things so quick. Take those dead men out there now. A few days ago, if I'd met one on the road I'd've passed the time of day with him, maybe we'd of had a drink of pulque together. Now they're dead and stinking to heaven, and I guess my finger on a trigger put more than one of 'em where he is. Get to thinking about things like that and a man couldn't stand it. The Mexicans are right brave fellers, but I'll bet they don't know why they're doing what they're doing. And maybe we don't either. But we got to do the things we think we got to do."

⋆ 7 ⋆

When it is early spring in southern Texas, the first few moments before the sun breaks over the horizon a light as gray as a mole's skin covers the earth, softening the harsh colors and lines of the plains. In this light, natural and man-made objects are dark and mysterious, all sounds are unearthly, moving things become blurs on the landscape.

It was at this time of the gray light that a volley of shots rang in the hills to the east of the Alamo. A few minutes later a line of horsemen began splashing across the stream below the church.

Abram Henry, in charge of the second watch, awakened David and the others; they took up their positions immediately at the stockade, rifles ready. The horsemen had disappeared in the brush, but the sounds of horseshoes clinking against rocks indicated that they were still heading up the ditch. In a moment, the first horseman was in full view, hunched forward on his mount, a fur cap squeezed over his ears, a brown beard curling down his chest. One of the Tennesseans fired, striking the second rider in the foot, bringing his horse to the earth.

" Hold your fire! " cried David. " They're Texans! "

The line of horsemen was turning back. The wounded animal lay on its side, thrashing its legs and whinnying. Its rider was limping hastily to cover.

David had shinnied up to the top of the stockade. " Where you from? " he shouted.

The bearded man stood up in his stirrups. " Cap'n J. W. Smith and thirty-seven men reporting from Gonzales."

" Hi-yi-ahh! " yelled Abram, and the others joined in.

" Better ride up to the gate fast as you can, or the Mexicans over by the river will be gunning you any minute."

" Hope they don't shoot as straight as the feller that hit me," retorted the wounded man, who was swinging up behind Captain Smith.

As a result of the commotion, the entire garrison was at the gate when the thirty-eight volunteers rode in, several men running forward to embrace them.

David and Travis walked with Captain Smith back to headquarters, the latter thrusting his fingers in his ears when the Mexicans opened a sudden bombardment against the west wall.

" Keep close to the wall in case they lift the shot over," Travis warned him. " Otherwise they don't do much damage."

Captain Smith informed them that Doc Sutherland had arrived in Gonzales four days earlier, and was still there, organizing another group of men. " Sutherland's leg is so swelled up he can't walk, but he's riding all over the country rounding up volunteers."

" Did you have much trouble getting through? "

" Last night we met up with a company of Mex cavalry,

[347]

but we gave 'em such a chase they never knew which way we went."

" What about Sam Houston? " asked David. " Any news from him? "

" Houston is over at Washington-on-the-Brazos. Convention is meeting there, and from what I hear, they aim to make Houston commander-in-chief of all the Texas armies."

" They better act fast," said Travis. " We can't hold out many more days here."

The cannonading ceased abruptly. Smith looked at both the others as if waiting for something.

" Sounds funny, all right, the quietness," said David. " We're so used to that boom-boom all day and half the night, we don't notice it till they stop."

" I could take some drinking liquor," said Smith, running his fingers through his beard. " You boys got anything? "

" Not a drop," said David.

Smith laughed, his teeth showing through his whiskers. " That's what I thought." He reached out his spurred boot and dragged his saddlebags near, reached down and pulled out a brown jug. " I brought along some bitters for you."

" Jim Bowie could sure use a taste of that," said Travis. " Let's step in his room."

Bowie was lying on his side, facing the door, when they entered. He was too weak to rise up and shake Smith's hand. They had to pour his drink into a gourd, and David held his head up while he drank. " Sure tastes good," he whispered weakly.

" If Sutherland got through," Travis was saying, "maybe Ed Johnson and Seguin reached Fannin at Goliad."

" Sure hope Ed did," said David, smacking his lips over the bitters. " I took a mighty liking to that boy. He's got a purty little girl waiting for him back in Nacogdoches, too. Be a shame ——"

[348]

"Nobody's waiting for me." Jim Bowie, stimulated by the drink, raised his head. "My wife and kid died of fever. Not a soul ——"

"And my wife ——" Travis did not finish. He took another long swallow from the jug.

"Well," said Smith, "there'd be more'n one woman around these parts be missing me." He laughed heartily.

Travis was staring out the door. "Maybe we're damn fools staying on here fighting for freedom. What is freedom, anyhow?"

"Freedom?" David lifted the heavy jug. "We used to argue about freedom a lot in Congress. I knowed a rich landholding man, said he believed in freedom because it gave him the right to do as he pleased. He skinned many a poor feller off his farm too, to add to his holdings, but he claimed he had the freedom to do it under the Constitution, and that everybody else had the freedom to do as he was doing. I don't tie to that idea. You can't have freedom unless men are free to—well, free to work and live along together so as every man has all he needs to have."

"At least," said Travis, "we don't want the freedom Santa Anna would give us, freedom to live under his military."

"If we could lick Santa Anna right here now, before he gets past San Antonio," Smith drawled, "there wouldn't be no danger of that kind of freedom."

Travis turned toward him. "That's it, exactly. Localize the fight here, otherwise Santa Anna's armies will march across Texas, laying waste all the farms and towns, and women and children will die along with the men. If enough volunteers would only join us here, we could hold them off until we were strong enough to attack and chase them back across the Rio Grande."

"My first wife, Polly, once told me," said David, "that it wasn't the men who did the fighting that suffered the most,

[349]

but the women and kids staying behind. This time the women and kids can't stay behind. If we lose the Alamo, Santa Anna will take this war right into their dooryards."

In the mission plaza they could hear excited shouts, and from far away in the direction of the town, a muffled sound of cheering. Quickly, they ran outside and climbed up on one of the earthen ramparts where a group of men around a cannon were looking across the river, shading their eyes against the brilliant morning sunlight.

"What are they doing over there now?" asked Travis.

"Listen," a man said.

They could hear the cries quite plainly now, a chant repeated over and over: "Santa Anna! Santa Anna! Santa Anna!"

And they could see a double line of horsemen in bright uniforms filing down the slope behind the town, the bodyguard army of the dictator of all Mexico.

The following day, Captain Smith volunteered to ride directly to Washington-on-the-Brazos to ask Sam Houston to organize an army and march to the aid of the Alamo.

"I'll tell you what we'll do," said Travis. "We'll fire our big eighteen-pounder three times every day, morning, noon, and night. You may be able to hear that as far away as the Brazos. By that, you'll know we're still holding the fort. And tell every volunteer to bring ten days' rations."

Smith went out the gate at dusk. Less than an hour later, James Bonham arrived, after seven days of riding around the triangle from the Alamo to Gonzales to Washington-on-the-Brazos and back. He was so exhausted he could hardly talk, but he brought a written message from Sam Houston.

After he read the note, Travis crumpled it up and threw it on the ground, and started cursing. "Blow up the Alamo, he says, and come back to the Brazos. Can't he see that if we

[350]

give an inch to these pirates now, we'll turn them loose on all of Texas?' "

David said nothing. He knew Sam Houston's reputation. Once Houston had made up his mind, he'd never change it.

" Damn their wavering souls! Our only hope now is from Fannin at Goliad."

James Bonham lay on Travis' bunk, breathing heavily.

Outside the bombardment continued steadily. The batteries to the north had broken great cracks in the walls across from Travis' headquarters, and the men were piling up sandbags for reinforcement. After a while, David went back to the stockade, standing his watch until midnight, and then tried to sleep, but each time that his eyes closed, a fresh cannonade brought him abruptly back to consciousness.

He heard a horse's hoofs tramping in the churchyard, then excited voices. He raised up from his pallet, rubbing his eyes wearily. Then he recognized Ed Johnson's voice. In a second, he was out in the yard.

It was chilly, and the men had a small brush fire burning. In the light he could see Ed, bareheaded, his hair knotted and twisted around his ears and forehead, his buckskins covered with powdery dust.

" Ed! You made it! "

" Sure did; purty near killed a horse doing it though."

" What about Colonel Fannin? Is he bringing his army up to join us? "

Ed shook his head slowly. " Soon as I told the Colonel the news he started making ready to come. Every man at Goliad, about three hundred of 'em, was yelling to come, but they got no horses, only oxen to drag the cannon wagons, and trying to cross the flooded river they all broke down. They got nothing to eat either. When they saw a bunch of Mex cavalry, they got scared, sitting out there on the plain without provisions or much ammunition, and they turned back to Goliad. I

[351]

figured I belonged here with you boys, so I put my horse's tail in the air, and here I am."

"Boy, when you tell Colonel Travis that, it'll break his heart. We just got news tonight from Sam Houston that nobody is coming from the north, either."

"Sounds bad. There's so damned many Mexicans camped around this place, you could shut your eyes and touch one."

Tuck Crutchfield, chewing his tobacco, moved closer. He rubbed his long moustache with his finger. " Maybe we better clear out of here while we can."

In the reflection of the flames, rising and falling from the fire, David could see the faces of his companions. For the first time he sensed a feeling of fear among them. Only Thimblerig's face was impassive.

"Travis and Bowie will never leave here," said David.

"Hell, no," cried Abram, stepping across the fire, turning his white, freckle-splotched face into the light. " Hell, no, they want to die!" Abram's voice was shrill. " Bowie's eating his heart out because his wife and kid died, and Travis don't care for hell because his wife ran away from him. I know. They want to die. But I don't. I got a wife back in Tennessee ——"

"Shut up!" David caught his arm. " You'll feel better in the morning."

"Abram is right," said Tuck. "Bowie and Travis would as soon die as not. But not me. I like to eat and sleep and have a woman once in a while."

"You're all just getting scared," David said coldly. Motioning for Ed to follow him, he turned and walked toward Travis' headquarters, keeping close to the wall, for cannon charges were exploding in the plaza, splashing streaks of fire in the darkness.

Early the next morning, the hunting horn sounded in front

[352]

of Travis' shed, and the men assembled, lining up against the sandbagged north wall. Jim Bowie was not sitting in his chair this time; he lay on his cot, with the Mexican woman, Madam Candelaria, kneeling at his side, mopping his forehead with a damp cloth.

Colonel Travis' face was gaunt, his hollow eyes had lost their gleam of humor, but he held himself up straight as he faced his men.

He said only a few words, his voice clear and firm. " You all know the truth as well as I. There's no hope of any immediate help from anywhere. But if we surrender now, Santa Anna will line us up and shoot us down like so many cattle. If we cut our way out, we may save our lives but we desert everything we believe in. Though we save our lives, at the same time we may lose the freedom of the Texans forever. And life without freedom would not be worth living." He stepped back a few feet, digging a long deep line in the hard earth with the heel of his boot. " I for one am staying here. Every man who believes as I do, cross this line! "

A dozen men stepped across immediately, then others followed, twenty, forty, eighty, a hundred, then everybody except three men. One stood there trembling, then sobbing, caught his cap in his hand and ran like a crazed animal across the plaza to the entrance, where he did not wait for the gate to be opened, but climbed over the log framework and dropped out of sight. There was a volley of fire from the river, and the Mexican cannons to the west began thundering again.

The second man was Tuck Crutchfield. He stood facing the crowd defiantly, watching the other man run out of the mission, then began chewing his moustache savagely. " Oh, goddammit," he cried, and stepped across.

The third man was Jim Bowie. He had raised himself halfway out of the cot. " Boys," he was whispering huskily, " boys, won't any of you help me across that line? "

[353]

David and Thimblerig stepped forward, picked up the cot, and set it across the line. Madam Candelaria followed. There were no cheers, no sound but the persistent thundering of cannon charges against the crumbling walls.

★ 8 ★

All day Friday they watched enemy troops moving out of the town across the river to the heights north of the mission. From the belfry of the San Antonio church, a blood-red flag was whipping in the cold wind, and the standard bearers of the Mexican cavalry units were carrying similar banners. Leading the long lines of moving infantry, was a loud band, playing fast march tunes.

Along the river, the cannon had been moved forward until they were in easy rifle range, but the gunners had grown cautious, offering the Texans few opportunities to pick them off.

Apparently, Santa Anna was concentrating his forces on the north; tents had been staked behind the heavy mortars. In the afternoon these big guns opened the heaviest bombardment of the siege. Placed as they were above the mission, the charges ripped holes in the plaza, and fragments of shells flew against the inside of the south wall, forcing the guards at the entrance gate to retire. Three men were wounded, none seriously.

After dark, the defenders dug a trench and threw up an earthen barricade just inside the gate. David's men helped in the work, and when it was done they returned to the stockade, where a large fire was burning. It was so cold they had to sit close to the fire, or keep moving up and down.

Preacher Boone had brought out his fiddle, and he and Abram took turns playing it. Mrs. Dickinson, with her young

[354]

daughter in her lap, sat close by, listening. David took the fiddle once and tried to play *Bonny Barbara Allan,* but when he saw tears forming in Mrs. Dickinson's eyes, he stopped, handed the fiddle to Preacher Boone and walked away.

At dawn Saturday the enemy greeted the defenders with a cannonade from both north and west. The Alamo gunners answered the charge, and for some minutes black smoke billowed over the mission, clinging to the earth.

"Looks like rain is coming the way that stinking smoke hangs to the ground," David said to Lieutenant Dickinson. They were eating parched corn and drinking watery soup cooked with dried beef bones. Dickinson looked up through the open roof of the church. "Sky is a bit scaly."

Except for occasional spurts of cannon fire, the enemy was quiet during the forenoon, and the Texans, following orders issued by Travis, set about digging in for a long siege. Holes were cut in the solid walls of the monks' cells so that the men might use them for defense positions if the Mexicans should penetrate the crumbling north wall and take possession of the plaza. More sandbags were piled around the church, and Lieutenant Dickinson took charge of the fourteen small cannon which still lay unused on the top walls of the building. Fence poles were torn loose from the animal pens and built into a scaffolding in the northeast corner of the church. They lifted several bags of sand to the top, stacking them around to form a solid rampart; then the small cannon were placed in a ring, their barrels pointing in all directions.

"If they should take the plaza, we could still give them a withering fire from up here," declared Dickinson, when the work was completed.

David had climbed up the scaffolding beside the lieutenant. This was now the highest point within the mission, and the whole countryside spread out before them.

For the first time he could see the extent of the enemy

[355]

lines; day by day they had drawn the noose closer and closer until it was now obvious that escape would be next to impossible. On the east was the cavalry camp, the horse corrals brown and black dots on the edge of the hill. To the west were the long batteries of cannon that had been edging forward day by day. To the north was the great encampment of infantry, their white tents protected by heavy siege guns. And to the south, in the irregular ditches and gulleys were hundreds of Mexicans armed with small cannon.

" We could knock over a bunch of those fellers in the ditches right now," said David.

" We could, but maybe we'd better save our shot for a needier moment."

For a while they watched the nearby Mexicans; all seemed to be unusually busy, hammering and chopping with axes.

"What would you say they were doing?" asked the lieutenant.

" I was just trying to make out, looks like they're making ——"

" Ladders! " cried Dickinson.

" Ladders is what they're making all right; why, they got a big pile stacked over there! "

They looked at one another. David saw Dickinson's fists clench tight as the lieutenant peered over the edge of the scaffolding down into the nave of the church where his wife was washing clothes. " If they ever get those ladders against our walls ——"

David was measuring the distance from the stockade to the natural trench where the Mexicans were working; he stared at the two little mounds of dead men out there, their bellies swollen and bloated, their brown faces turning black under the sky. He turned, and climbed slowly down the scaffolding, and went to tell Colonel Travis of what he had seen. Travis replied with a bitter laugh: " I've just come in here from watching Mexicans building ladders in the north camp for the last two hours."

Not wishing to talk, David went outside again, and walked around the north and west walls, listening to conversations, looking at the faces of the men. A heavy weariness had fallen over the Alamo. Suspense was drawing the men's nerves tighter and tighter, but the news of the ladders seemed only to have heightened their determination to fight more bitterly than ever.

As night fell, the clouds thickened, pressing down to the earth, mingling with the streams of acrid powder-smoke from the constant cannon fire. The thin moon disappeared; one by one the stars were wiped out. Then the wind began to blow.

At ten o'clock enemy firing which had been heavy on all sides stopped suddenly as if by prearranged signal.

The silence was so intense that the drive of blood from one's heart through the ear passages was as the throbbing of a great drum.

★ 9 ★

A fine cold mist was falling when David's watch ended at midnight. Though he was so weary that he could hardly hold himself erect, 'he knew he could not sleep. He walked over to Travis' headquarters through the black gloom of the mist, stumbling in the holes cut by cannon fire.

Travis' shed was dark, but he could hear him coughing in his cot, so he went inside. " This is Crockett," he said softly. " You awake? " Travis lit the stub of a candle on his table, and sat up in the bed. " I just now lay down. Told the boys on guard to be sure to call me if they hear anything suspicious out there. But it's so quiet I can't sleep."

" Wonder why they stopped firing? "

"I figure it's one of two things, either they shut it off to protect their own men who're moving up close to our walls, or they're doing it to worry us."

"I think your first guess is the right one." David sat down on a stool facing Travis. The commander's reddish hair was rumpled, his face showed marks of the straw pillow. "Well," said he, "it's too dark to see what they're doing, and if they are doing anything they're making no noise at it. We can't fire our cannon at something we can't see or hear."

They sat and talked for a long while, David wishing for a chew of tobacco. Finally, Travis' head sagged back against the pillow, his eyes closed, and the candle smoked itself out. David was half asleep, half awake, dreaming about his family and the farmhouse back on the Obion, wondering if the boys were getting the plowing done. He could see crows all over the fields, cawing raucously, flying down to eat up the corn as fast as the boys dropped it. One crow, larger than the others, as large as a buzzard, cawed in a shrill voice, screaming like a bugle call, and all the crows started flapping their wings, flapping them with a strange noise, like the sound of horses' hoofs. And then he was awake suddenly on the stool, facing Travis who was awake too, stupid with sleep, and they both ran out on the plaza in the dark gray light, rifles in their hands, listening to the drumming of horses' hoofs, and the beating rhythm of a thousand men's feet running on the hard earth.

In the gray shadows everything that happened was as mechanical and absurd as a dream, but he followed Travis up to the sandbags, where a gunner was tightening the lock-strings on his cannon. Then the big gun roared like thunder, bringing him wide awake, and he saw Travis stop to pick up a bag of rusty nails they were using for shot in the twelve-pounders and throw it up to the gunner.

Travis caught his arm, pointing to the rampart on the

[358]

northeast corner. " Pick off the cavalry and the cannon bearers first! " he screamed, and then smoke and mist was swirling all over the sky, and Travis was running toward the west wall.

David hurried up to the rampart. James Bonham was standing there, reloading his rifle; his cheeks had round white spots in the centers where his tightened jaws drew the skin tight over the bones. David looked over the top of the wall and saw the enemy, four columns of them, vague gray shapes in the early light, two bearing straight down on the north wall, another on the west, the fourth veering to the east. He fired at a horseman dragging a cannon; the horse fell, whinnying shrilly, and the cannon rolled over, turning upside down against the animal and its rider.

Already four or five ladders had been placed against the north wall, but the Mexicans were blown back by cannon fire; black lumps of dead men lay still or crawled grotesquely on the earth. He picked off a dragoon, and then, while he was reloading, turned to speak to Bonham, but Bonham had slumped forward on the rampart, blood spurting out of his mouth. He started to turn him over, but suddenly realized there was no time for it. A ladder was thrust up a yard from his face; he kicked it back with his foot, and then fired straight down at the man who had placed it there.

Slowly the Mexican columns, their first ranks blasted away by the Texans' deadly accuracy, drew back out of range. David shook his head, cold beads of sweat dropped off his nose. Somebody put a gourdful of water into his hand. It was Madam Candelaria. He drank, and she passed on to the next man. He turned James Bonham over on his back; he was dead, his frilled hunting shirt sticky with blood.

The sun was up, ringed with violet mist.

Ed Johnson appeared suddenly out of the smoke. " We beat 'em back, didn't we? " he cried jubilantly.

" Did they try to mount the stockade, too? "

" A few, but they never crossed the ditch with a single ladder. I was asleep, but Abram roused all of us soon as the attack started. We were wondering what had happened to you. The Mexicans got a ladder up against the east wall of the church but Lieutenant Dickinson talked to 'em with his little cannons, and they high-tailed it back to the brush in a hurry."

The sun's rays touched the tip of the wall; deep black shadows lay inside the mission.

He and Ed ran down to the center of the north wall where men were frantically stacking sandbags in a breach opened by one of the Mexican cannon that had been brought up in the attack.

A few seconds later, the sound of bugles blared again, far off in the enemy camp, and the band began to play, the drums beating angrily.

" Here they come again! " yelled a gunner.

" Listen to that band," cried Ed. " They're playing the *Deguello!* " He stepped up to the wall beside David, rifle ready.

" The *Deguello?* "

" Means they'll cut our throats this time."

" In hell," said David. " Say, maybe you better get back to the stockade. They might try again there. Tell the others I'm staying here where the fighting is the hottest."

Ed ran off across the shell-pitted plaza, while David gripped his rifle barrel and fired at the first cavalryman. This time all four columns were concentrated against the north wall, the foot soldiers running at double speed with horsemen driving hard behind them. Again the front ranks were leveled by the Texans' well-timed fire, but the momentum of the others propelled them over the fallen bodies, and a dozen ladders touched the low wall. David fired straight down, reloading,

[360]

firing again and again. Their ranks depleted, the Mexicans fell back once more behind their cannons.

Choking in the burning smoke, he turned around, trying to find a spot of clean air, but his smarting eyes widened when he looked toward the church. Several Mexicans had mounted the wide wall a few feet from Lieutenant Dickinson's redoubt, and were stabbing their way forward with bayonets. The sun was shining bright now, and he could see Dickinson quite plainly, waving desperately to the men below to come to the assistance of the two Texans between him and the Mexicans on the wall.

David leaped down from the rampart and started running for the churchyard.

The men at the stockade were so occupied with firing through the loopholes they had forgotten Dickinson and his gunners up on the redoubt. As soon as David reached the churchyard, he shot one of the Mexicans off the wall, then shouted to his men: " The church wall! The church wall! "

They all swung around, running to the door of the church, firing at the remaining Mexicans, who tumbled off the wall, one of them screaming headfirst into the unroofed chancel of the church.

Dickinson grinned down at them, waving. " While they're quiet, could you fellows bring up some of those cannisters of nails? We're running low on shot."

They carried up the remainder of the nails, some broken bits of metal and a keg of powder. David took time to refill his powder horn, then shinnied up the scaffolding for a look at the enemy.

As soon as he reached the top, he could see that Dickinson had made good use of his cannon; about twenty-five of the attackers lay dead or wounded below the east wall. Turning toward the north he saw the line of the enemy's mobile cannon drawn up only a few yards from the wall. A long column of infantry was deploying toward the west. Rifles cracked up and down the north wall, but Travis was holding his cannon fire, waiting for the Mexicans to try another assault.

Then suddenly the enemy cannon began exploding, one, two, three, four, one after another, one, two, three, four. And they were blasting their charges, not against the north wall, but over the wall and into the row of wooden sheds along the west.

David could see Texans knocked into bits, falling off the western ramparts. A fire blazed up in one of the sheds, and smoke from the flames and the cannon covered everything for a minute. When it cleared, the Mexican soldiers on the west were climbing over, swinging axes and crowbars, demolishing the row of sheds. Seizing one of the Texans' cannon on that side, the invaders turned it about, and began firing into the men trying to defend the north wall.

At the same time Mexicans began leaping over the low north wall. Caught between two fires, the Texans ran madly across the plaza, taking cover in the monks' cells that stood along the center line of the mission.

Dickinson began quietly inspecting his circle of cannons; his two assistants had reloaded all of them. " Soon as our men are clear from the plaza, I'll open fire."

David peered into the smoke-covered square. "Wonder where Travis is?" he said aloud. Two or three wounded Texans stumbled into the churchyard, and Mrs. Dickinson led them into the church. Madam Candelaria had already joined her there; she was busily stripping up pieces of cloth for bandages.

Dickinson opened fire into the plaza, but with little apparent damage, for the invaders in their bright blue and scarlet uniforms were streaming over both north and west walls, like two endless lines of sheep jumping fences. A narrow breach had been cut into the north wall, and a company of dragoons filed into the plaza, the officers flashing their shiny swords. In a few moments the captured Alamo cannon were reversed, and began blasting holes into the thin walls of the monks' cells. Each fusillade from the Texans was weaker than the one which preceded it. After the cannonading, squads of Mexicans began charging each cell, silencing the deadly rifle fire.

David slid down from the scaffolding, ran through the church, and out into the yard. His men at the stockade were in trouble; the Mexicans outside had crossed the ditch and set up some of their ladders. Instead of shooting through the loopholes, the defenders had drawn back and were firing at the Mexicans as they appeared at the top of the ladders.

"Colonel Crockett!"

He turned to see who had called. It was Travis, limping across the courtyard, his face black, his hair singed from powder burns.

"Draw your men back behind the sandbags in front of the church. The enemy will be on the churchyard gate in another minute. We'll make a stand in the church!"

David ran along the line of men, slapping each one on the shoulder. Ed, Tuck, Preacher, Abram, Thimblerig, seven others. "Behind the sandbags, boys, or you'll get shot in the back!"

There were two lines of sandbags, one a few feet from the churchyard gate, another just in front of the church door. Quickly they took positions behind the front row of bags, still picking off the Mexicans trying to vault the stockade. Already a dozen Texans were retreating through the churchyard entrance, firing at the enemy in the plaza. David shouted to them to take cover with his men.

No Mexican as yet had come over the stockade. Wary of the defenders' fire, no more brown faces were appearing at the tops of the ladders there. And the Mexicans in the plaza were still too busy digging into new positions to attempt a rush into the churchyard.

The men were breathing hard, their bodies smelling of sweat and burned powder. David took time for a glance up at Dickinson's redoubt. Travis was up there, crouched on his long legs, firing into the plaza, his tuft of blackened hair hanging over his forehead.

Inside the church, the wounded men were groaning.

The suspense of waiting was telling on his nerves. He could see his hands tremble, and he gripped his fingers hard into one of the sandbags to steady them. He wondered what had happened to poor old Jim Bowie, lying helpless in his cot. Only about thirty men left now to hold the church. Thirty against four thousand! If they had to hold the Alamo all alone, fighting all alone, they didn't have a chance. They didn't have a chance this side of hell.

A Mexican ran into the churchyard; ten rifles riddled him with lead. "Nine charges wasted!" cried Thimblerig scornfully. A dozen other enemy soldiers had darted hastily back out of range. David glanced up at the redoubt. Dickinson and Travis, their backs turned now, were firing their cannon at the Mexicans on the east side who had attacked again, throwing ladders against the high wall.

He turned his eyes back quickly to the churchyard entrance. A moment later he heard a woman screaming behind him, and he whirled. Lying on the church floor was a contorted body; the head was half torn away by a cannon ball; the long legs jerked convulsively, then stiffened.

Up in the redoubt, Lieutenant Dickinson, leaning over the edge, was covering his face with his blackened hands.

The man on the floor was Travis.

Ed Johnson had seen what had happened. The boy's face turned white; he vomited, and his legs gave way; he sagged against the rampart. David slapped him back to consciousness with his open hand. Ed wiped his mouth on his sleeve.

Abram was yelling: "Hi-yi-ahh!" and David looked up to see Mexicans storming into the churchyard, first through the gate, then over the stockade. Twenty or more fell, but twenty more took their places, and while the Texans were reloading, they swarmed over the sandbags. David fired point-blank at a swarthy man who was stabbing wildly with his bayonet. The soldier fell, but his bayonet had caught Preacher Boone in the chest, and the old man fell backwards, screaming, "Sinful heathens!" But his scream ended with a rattle as blood poured up into his throat.

David caught him under the arms and tried to drag him back behind the second row of sandbags, but his foot slipped on something; it was a man's head, and when he stumbled forward he saw the face. He could not believe it was Abram Henry, the eyes wide open staring at nothing, the freckles splotched all over the color-drained face.

A swinging gun butt smashed his ear, and he fought back blindly, the pain throbbing through his brain as he staggered behind the second barricade, his hands and face sticky with blood and powder. He rubbed his face against a sandbag to clear the sweat from his eyes. Dead Mexicans were heaped grotesquely over the top of the first barricade.

For a moment there was a lull. They had lost five men, including Abram and Preacher Boone; most of the others were cut or bruised.

Tuck Crutchfield was cursing at the top of his voice. When he saw David glance at him, he cried out: "Goddammit, Davy Crockett, if I hadn't listened to you, I wouldn't be here!"

"Shut up," said Thimblerig. "You had your choice of staying or leaving."

David's head was spinning with pain. "We ain't lost this

fight yet, Tuck, and I'll bet you wouldn't quit if you had the chance."

Tuck licked his curling moustache with his tongue. " Honest, you think we got a chance, Davy? " The question was a plea, in the tone of a child seeking reassurance.

David squeezed his roaring head with both hands. " Hell, yes, we got a chance, Tuck. The fellers out there trying to smoke us out of here, they're fighting for just one little stinking man, but we're fighting for a thing all of us ——"

" Look out! " screamed Thimblerig. He knocked David aside, and then plunged over the top of the barricade. One of the Mexicans, apparently lifeless, unseen by all except the gambler, had raised his gun up from the ground, firing at David.

With his sharp Bowie knife, Thimblerig stabbed the man in the throat, but the wound he had received when he pushed David aside left him too weak to rise again. He lay with one arm across the dead Mexican's chest, his white hat crumpled in the dust beside him.

Speechless, David started to leap over the barricade after the gambler, but the enemy was storming the churchyard entrance again, dragging in a cannon. While the defenders raked them with rifle fire, the Mexicans blasted a cannon charge that tore sandbags loose, showering dirt into David's face.

A second blast followed the first, crashing into the barricade. Black smoke boiled over and swirled into the church door behind them. Officers, waving their swords, charged the barricade, then retreated hastily. The cannon roared again, shaking the earth.

Back, back, back, they retreated toward the church entrance, clubbing blindly into the smoke curtain with their rifle butts, hoping to bring down any enemy in reach. Confused, David turned completely around, and saw Tuck Crutchfield far over in the sheltered corner where the powder was stored, leaning over a powder keg, trying to explode it with his flintlock. David choked in the smoke, and then he saw Tuck fall forward, grabbing at his wrist; it was shattered and Tuck had his mouth over the wound, sucking at the blood. He dropped flat on the floor, rolling over and over, squeezing the wounded wrist in his crotch.

Smoke flowed in great billows over the churchyard, and then the sun shone through for a second and David could see straight ahead the two barricades shattered by cannon fire and behind them a hundred Mexicans, shiny bayonets fixed, moving slowly forward.

He was standing now in the door of the church, and he looked up quickly at the redoubt, but the cannon were silent; Dickinson and his gunners were no longer there.

Inside the church he could hear the wounded men groaning, and one of the women praying. At his side was Ed Johnson, a long gash on his arm, holding a broken gun stock high over his head.

But there was nobody else, nobody else.

He heard Tuck Crutchfield cursing, and then a great blast of fire flashed over the corner where the powder was stored. The earth trembled, a section of the church wall cracked, and bits of adobe fell at his feet.

But the shining bayonets were coming over the barricade now, stabbing, slashing, and a man must fight, a man must . . .